PROLOGUE

Northwest Brittany
August 1944

At 29,000 feet he began the long, slow curve southeast, back from the seaward boundaries where the English Channel became the North Atlantic. Above him, the night-time black sky was studded with glimpses of stars. To the east, the sunshine cleared the horizon, laying a golden haze across a cloud bank like a duvet over Northwest France, stretching into the Channel by several miles. He'd been flying for over two hours, having taken off from the depths of the English countryside whilst the sky was pitch dark. Flying west by compass bearings, time and map, until the Bristol Channel, then south-south-west, climbing steadily after take-off. Levelling at 25,000 feet, his toes grew cold as the air thinned and held no warmth. He'd said a little prayer when luck and bearings appeared to be working. The sky cleared for nearly thirty minutes and far below, right where it was meant to be, the vague outlines set against the surrounding sea, the silvery surf and sand all picked out by moonlight were the Scilly Isles. Flicking his radio dial across, he picked up the sounds bounced in his direction sent by the FRB (Final Responder Beacon) at Peninnis Head. Which was set up on the islands to aid returning aircrew from making the wrong turn and heading into the wide, unforgiving Atlantic

1

Ocean.

The letters PRU etched into the blue-painted, stream-lined Mark IX Spitfire showed his mission to be Photographic Reconnaissance. For this mission, he knew everything he needed to know. Curve out around the tip of Brittany and make for the Brest approach, whereupon he was to start his 'recon run' up the full length of the estuary. Pass over the French city of Brest. Turn. Run back down the southern side of a pre-designated corridor. Head out to sea. Turn for home. The D-Day landings had taken place in June, a short time before. Allied Forces were breaking out in all directions, consolidating their bridgehead and forming their own Fortress Europe. What would be helpful would be securing a good-sized port or harbour somewhere in Brittany or Normandy, where they could bring in ships for the resupply of troops, machinery and other supplies to keep the war machine moving.

The Americans had faced fierce German defence at Cherbourg on the Cotentin Peninsular. The Germans had rendered most of the harbour unusable, whilst inflicting heavy losses on American troops. When they attempted to acquire the port of Saint-Malo, they'd met similar resistance there. The plan now was to skip these close yet obvious ports and try for Brest. Before the Allied forces got there though, they needed to know what defences were around, not only the city, but the approaches via the sea and for that they needed photo-recon.

Flight Officer Peter Urbawicz felt confident of success when he set off. The Rolls Royce Merlin 61 engine sucking eagerly at fuel held in the drop tank. He had to reach his location, make two runs, stay out of trouble and return home.

With luck, he'd be back in time for drinks at the 'Barleycorn' in the village. He'd felt confident until he'd seen the cloud layer covering the landscape below. It was a long journey to have made, only to return home without shooting any film whatsoever. Operations Control had been convinced that the cloud base over the Breton landscape would clear well before he arrived at his destination. It had not. Urbawicz overflew the coordinates once, realising visibility from that height was non-existent. But if he went lower, he could see if the cloud was hugging the ground like a sea mist, or whether there was a gap between cloud and land he could squeeze through; if so, he'd resort to 'dicing'.

'Dicing', normally an operation used to photograph buildings and even troop movements, involved low-level flights at great speed using an obliquely-mounted camera. His plane was equipped for such an eventuality. Urbawicz turned towards the ocean, then losing altitude turned back toward land. By now the sun was brightening the cloud layer. He was able to see outcrops of headlands and the break between, where the estuary cut its way inland towards his target. He set himself up for the 'photo run', positioning the plane to skim the undersurface of the cloud. His first run would be easy. Hurtling between the opposing headlands at 300 miles an hour, with just 180 feet beneath his wings. Any lower, the cameras wouldn't pick up detail. Any higher, he'd be back into cloud. He went the full length of the estuary and overflew the docks and city walls of Brest before any flak appeared. They weren't expecting anyone from that direction. Their enemy, coming overland from Normandy, was by all accounts still days away.

Inland, away from the ack-ack at Brest, he pulled back into the clouds to lose engine noise amongst the fluff, hoping to make the enemy think he'd gone. Then he curved south and dropped out of the cloud for his second run, west along the southern side of the estuary. He hit the throttle hard, the air-speed indicator marked 295 miles an hour. All hell broke loose. Puffs from exploding shells appeared around him, fired from both sides of the estuary; he felt the plane rock, judder, as explosions ripped through the morning sky. It was all he could do to keep the plane level and give the cameras a chance of capturing what was going on below.

F/O Urbawicz was almost at the seaward end of the estuary when the anti-aircraft battery on the cliff top, above the village of Roscanvel on the southern peninsula, began pumping shells into the sky, creating a curtain of fire that Urbawicz had no option but to fly through. At nearly 300 miles an hour, he had little time to respond to the danger ahead. He pulled back on the stick, trying to climb above the curtain of explosives being laid across his path, but the starbursts in the sky continued to rise ahead of him until eventually, they both met in a crescendo of noise and smoke. Shrapnel ripped the side of his cockpit. He felt pain; chunks of hot metal tore into his left knee. One chunk went clean through and on exit, took his left thumb clean off, which was lucky, as it stopped it from hitting the joystick. Smoke filled the cockpit, so he hit the release to lose the canopy and duct the smoke away. Seconds later, the engine became a juddering wreck as oil, fuel and debris fell away before his eyes. The Merlin began losing its rhythm, its heartbeat. In his favour, the stick was still responsive. He levelled out above the maelstrom of shellfire and began to bank the plane to the south, keeping the stream of oil and smoke from engulfing the open canopy. He had quick choices to make. He knew he wasn't going to be in the pub tonight, regaling fellow pilots with tales of derring-do. One other option was to attempt to jump and hope his chute hadn't been damaged by shrapnel that had spattered through his cockpit. If the chute did open, he meant to float down to land somewhere at sea, eager to be picked up before he drowned. Or he could attempt to make landfall, belly her in on some gorse-covered headland and there await capture. His banking curve suddenly fluttered into virtual silence after the roar of the previous five minutes. The engine finally died and the prop came to rest. He took stock of his situation. He was losing blood from his leg and left hand. He could feel something trickling down the side of his face, but couldn't tell if it was blood or oil.

Urbawicz lifted himself up enough to see through a clear section of screen and realised his questions had been answered for him. His curve to the south had levelled just off the coast and the plane had decided to make for the headland on the southern side of the estuary. His only worry was losing height too fast and burying himself into the cliff face. Once the engine failed, the controls became almost unusable. He applied as much force as he could on the stick and felt relief, as the nose came up a fraction, enough to make it over the brow of the headland. The wind rushed past his open canopy. There was little he could do to control where he'd touch down. He skimmed the tops of gorse and scrub across the headland. He heard then felt them, snagging the underside of the plane. There was an open area of rough grassland ahead and as the last vestiges of tree life grabbed the fuselage, the belly of the Spit' touched base. It bounced and touched again. Then, right in front of him was a gun emplacement, the barrels facing the other way. Men were climbing out of the dugout, trying to get out of the way. The last bounce across scrubby grass was enough to clear the boundary sandbags as the underbelly tore apart across the metalwork of the battery, ripping open the Spitfire's fuel tank and dumping the contents over everything and everybody. Sparks from metal-to-metal contact ignited first the vapour, then with a 'woof', the fuel itself.

Urbawicz was clear of the fireball that engulfed the emplacement and its crew. Both he and the plane went careering across yet another area of grassland. Eventually, the plane lost forward momentum and the under-skin snagged on metal posts and wire, bringing it to a sudden halt, allowing it to rise up, then stand on its nose before settling back down gently onto scrub and bracken. Urbawicz knew he had to get out and get out fast. But his energy was gone, adrenaline depleted. He wasn't even sure he could remember how to get out; getting in now seemed a lifetime ago. He managed to release the harness. Using his right hand, he gripped the edge of the cockpit and hauled himself up onto his seat, but there he stayed. His left leg wouldn't work. Somewhere behind him, he heard screams, panic and pain accompanied by explosions. He was losing consciousness, struggling to coordinate his movements and see any point in doing anything other than sleep. Then he felt somebody grabbing his arms, attempting to drag him from the cockpit. He saw a face, a young face, blonde hair, blue eyes. He heard a voice. He had no idea what the face was saying.

Then the world went dark.

CHAPTER ONE

Detective Inspector David Lancaster and Detective Sergeant Marie Vidêt were enjoying a meal in a French restaurant on the waterfront in Plymouth, Devon, when Lancaster's mobile buzzed. His initial thoughts were, *ignore it. It's Friday evening.* The buzzing had to be work related. Eventually, thirst quenched by chilled Chablis and a thirst for knowledge overrode his desire for a quiet meal with a colleague. Lancaster looked at the screen.

"It's Craven," he said. "I'd better take it."

DS Vidêt smiled and took the opportunity to get in amongst the shells of her 'Moules Mariniere' in search of any that may have got away, well aware that their boss, Detective Chief Inspector Craven, was under the impression that 'work' constituted a 24-7 role for anybody in his team.

"'Evening, sir," Lancaster said. "What can I do for you?"

"You can stop pretending you're pleased I've called," Craven replied. "I'm presuming you're out on the town, celebrating putting the case to bed. And so you should be, 'Bomber'. By the way, don't forget to give 'Frenchie' some extra time off."

"Oh, I intend to make sure she gets a little extra time in bed, sir," Lancaster said, smiling across the table at Vidêt. Craven was the only person in the station who used Lancaster's nickname of 'Bomber'. Most detectives in the office were too young to know that his surname, Lancaster, was a long-range bomber during the Second World War. Craven thought it amusing to give his detectives nicknames, so 'Bomber' became chosen for Lancaster.

"I need to ruin your Saturday. I need you in my office for 8:00 tomorrow morning. Clean shirt and smelling nice, understood?"

"Understood, sir. May I ask why?" Lancaster knew 'clean shirt' meant meeting someone important.

"You may indeed, 'Bomber'. See you at 8:00 then." With that he was gone.

"Well, that's a bugger," Lancaster said. "The boss wants me in his office first thing in the morning."

"Do you want me to come?"

"Better not; I don't even know what he wants me for yet."

"What was that about extra time in bed?" she asked, with raised eyebrows.

"Well, I thought we might start using up some of that extra time tonight," he replied, raising his glass to meet hers across the table.

Vidêt and Lancaster, her boss, had been in a relationship for several months. It was a secret affair. A subordinate detective and her senior boss sleeping together was frowned upon within the department, but it was a mutual understanding between the two of them, that for the moment they'd rather keep quiet than risk the possible consequence of being split up within the office.

Lancaster arrived at Craven's office at 7:55 exactly. He liked to be punctual. His boss spent much of his working time down at 'the coal face' as he liked to call it. But when there wasn't a major case underway, he could be found residing in a reasonably-sized, well-furnished, top-floor office, complete with potted plant; the ultimate sign of status. Lancaster heard the rumble of conversation behind the closed door. At exactly 8:00, he knocked briskly.

"In," was all he got.

Lancaster stepped into the bright office. He'd been in this room before and was always slightly envious. Whereas his window looked directly out onto the hideous façade of the city shopping mall, DCI Craven had a corner office looking down the road, taking in the ruins of the 18th-century Charles Cross Church. It was bombed almost out of existence by the German Luftwaffe in the Second World War. The remains were secured; a permanent memorial to the lives lost during the raids. Lancaster had always preferred looking at the ancient, bombed edifice over the modern shopping precinct any day.

He closed the door behind him, turning to face his boss's desk. It was then that he realised who the other person in the room was. Lady Pamela Stottard. Lady Stottard was an active local magistrate who recently came second in the running to be Devon & Cornwall Police & Crime Commissioner. She had powerful and influential friends. Lancaster had crossed paths with this lady during their previous case. A case involving Lady Stottard's late husband, Sir Philip Stottard, and the murder of one of his lovers. It had been a murder in which the family was completely exonerated of any direct dealings. When they'd last parted company; Lancaster had the feeling he'd pushed the boundaries of their acquaintance too far, and thought there could be trouble ahead.

Lancaster kept his stance official as befitted a call to a top-floor meeting: feet apart at the stand-at-ease position, hands clasped behind his back, nestled into the curve of his spine. He made no acknowledgement of Lady Stottard's presence.

"At ease, Lancaster," his boss said with a smile, aware of how awkward his subordinate was feeling in her company. "Take a seat," Craven said, waving in the direction of the only other chair available. "I presume you remember Lady Stottard?"

"Indeed I do, sir," Lancaster replied, nodding courteously to her. "Good morning, Lady Stottard," was all he could say. He sat back, waiting for whatever complaint was about to come his way and hoping he had an answer for it.

Craven opened the conversation. "Lancaster, Lady Stottard has been highly complementary about your and DS Vidêt's work on the murder of Abdul Mehemet. She is, of course, very grateful to us for managing to close the case yet keeping their family name out of the papers. I have, of course, stated that at no time did any of us have any thoughts that the family had any involvement with the tragic end to the young lad's life but obviously questions, some of which were of a very personal nature, had needed to be asked."

This comment had Lancaster smiling inwardly. Craven had gone out of his way to give Lancaster and Vidêt all the space they needed, in the hopes they found a link between the murder of Abdul and the Stottards, primarily Sir Philip, who for some reason unknown to Lancaster, his boss appeared to loathe. Craven had been convinced that Lady Stottard's husband had been using the boy as a 'mule' to smuggle drugs, and may even be part of a larger drugs cartel.

DCI Craven continued, "Lady Stottard has asked us to use the same expertise to investigate what she believes to be another unsolved crime."

Lady Stottard interrupted, "Not just unsolved, Chief Inspector, uninvestigated."

Craven smiled and continued, "As Lady Stottard points out, she feels this particular crime was never investigated with the rigour or seriousness she'd have liked by the force in charge at the time. Now I've looked into this and I have to agree there are questions that were never asked. Many aspects appear short-changed and undocumented. Basically, the file's too thin for my liking, with not enough detail. No meat. A conclusion was made early in the case and then nothing else was investigated. My gut feeling is that somebody decided to call the death accidental. That made life easier, less fuss. Would you agree with that hypothesis, Lady Stottard?"

"It's one possibility, Chief Inspector," Lady Stottard replied. "There is also the possibility that somebody on the island, somebody in a position of power, was involved in the crime and had it swept under the carpet to avoid being implicated."

"Well, yes," Craven agreed. "There is, of course, always that possibility."

Lancaster raised a hand, not too high; he didn't want to

appear as if asking permission to speak, but just alerting them that he was going to anyway.

"If I may, Lady Stottard," he asked, looking straight at her for the first time and getting a smile in return. "You said 'someone on the island.' May I ask which island you're referring to?"

"I refer to the Island of Jersey, Detective Inspector. My family home prior to my marriage and home to my parents since just after the war. The crime I'd like investigating is the death of my father, Peter Urbawicz."

"If I may just continue," Craven said. "It's my opinion that there's a shortfall of investigation in the file I've managed to obtain. The States of Jersey Police may well have missed something here. But following the debacle of 2008 with the 'Haute de la Garenne' investigation, when the UK sent in some of our boys to investigate suspected child murders with nothing new being found, what I don't want to do, is go down there telling them we think they've got something wrong again. We'd not be well received. What I've managed to get sanctioned from on high, and based on your previous work, is for you and your sergeant to go over there incognito. Sniff out the lie of the land. Be discreet. Ask questions. Find out what the locals are thinking. If you find any grounds for reopening the case, then we can make it official. Lady Stottard will fill you in with as much information as you may need, is that OK, Lady Stottard?"

"Very much so, Chief Inspector." Then, turning to Lancaster. "Would you come and see me tomorrow at the lodge? Say 10:00. For coffee? I presume you don't mind working on a Sunday?"

Lancaster looked to his boss, who'd be picking up the tab for the overtime and got a minute nod of the head.

"That'll be fine, Lady Stottard," Lancaster replied. "I'll bring Detective Sergeant Vidêt. She might just as well be in on this right from the start."

The following morning, having updated Vidêt the previous evening, the pair drove across the South Hams border and turned into the gateway for Boldean House. The main manor house having been converted into expensive retirement accommodation, Lady Stottard now lived in the old gatehouse just inside the imposing gateway. Vidêt turned into the parking bay beside the lodge. The two detectives walked to the front door, which was opened as they reached it by the Lady herself.

"Bang on time, detectives, well done. Do come in. Coffee as promised is on its way."

The detectives followed her into the large lounge, then through patio doors to the terrace at the rear of the house. As they arrived, so did the coffee, by virtue of delivery by the maid. Two minutes later she was gone, back into the bowels of the house, leaving the three of them alone to sit and view the garden, the breeze stirring the branches and leaves of the mature trees surrounding them.

"Now let's get straight down to business," Lady Pamela said, sipping from her cup. "To start with, I wanted to say how impressed I was with the way you both handled the Abdul thing. I know there were times when we saw each other's rough edges. There were questions that at the time I felt unnecessary, but later, realised you needed to ask. I was also grateful that at no time did you appear to relish the situation vis-à-vis my husband and I. Indeed, you managed to complete the entire case without the family name coming into the public eye, though that may change if and when the case ever gets into the courts, but then that's beyond your or, in fact, my control. Time alone will tell how that turns out."

"Well, at the moment we know the Crown Prosecution Service is still uncertain what to do with Mr Baylis," Lancaster replied. "There's no doubt he carried out the murder just as he told it, but it's now been confirmed he's suffering from a form of dementia. At present, he's on virtual house arrest with his son and family, so you're right, at the moment none of us have any control of where this is going to go."

"Quite," Lady Pamela replied. "Detective Chief Inspector Craven's filled me in on the way you two pieced the whole story together and your incognito visit to France to find out about young Abdul's previous life. He's told me enough to make me realise that you two are the ones to pick this thing apart. I've no doubt you'll find discrepancies in the original investigation. My father was not a man who had accidents. He was not unsteady on his feet and the location of his apparent accident was a place he'd fished from so many times before, that I find it highly unlikely that one day he'd forget where he was and promptly fall to his death. My mother thought the same, but for some reason was never willing to pursue the issue."

"Lady Pamela," Lancaster said. "Can you tell us exactly what you know about your parents, their life on Jersey and your father's death? DS Vidêt will record it for us, if you don't mind. We need to get a complete timeline starting right from the beginning if we're going to make any sense of this."

Lady Pamela went on to tell them what she knew.

Her mother was originally Brigitte Danielo from Brittany. When this story began, she was a mature, strong-willed seventeen-year-old. When she'd first met Pamela's father, Peter Urbawicz, he was a Polish Spitfire pilot. He was shot down over the Brest Estuary in the August of 1944, a few months after the D-Day Landings. He'd been flying a mission over the estuary prior to the American siege of Brest, in September of '44. Her parents had told her the romantic way they'd met. Peter's Spitfire crash landed on the plateau above their village, Roscanvel, where Brigitte's grandparents had a farm. Brigitte's father was headmaster of a school in nearby Crozon, and whilst they stayed in town, she'd been sent to the farm for safe-keeping for the duration of the occupation. There was a long-held family belief that Brigitte's father, Pamela's grandfather, was actively involved with the resistance movement but never spoke of it to anyone after the war, so they never really knew for sure.

Brigitte had heard the Spitfire as it passed along the estuary and had run up the hill to see if it had crashed. When she'd reached the top, the plane and its smoke trail had disappeared from view. She was about to retrace her steps to the farm, when she saw the plane reappear. It was coming in from off the coast and gliding, with the propeller no longer turning. Then followed the horrible ripping and tearing noises of a crash, followed by a tremendous roar of flame as the fuel from the plane exploded right across the gun emplacement. Pamela's mother told her how the sound of the terrified screams of the engulfed German soldiers had stayed with her for many years.

She could do nothing for the burning Germans, but she saw the pilot attempting to extricate himself from his plane, which had bounced clear of the flames, skidded across rough grass and come to a standstill, its nose imbedded in the gorse bushes. She'd automatically rushed to help, and between the pilot and herself, managed to drag him up, out of the shattered cockpit and down onto the grass. It was as she was helping him crawl away from the wreckage that she was aware of a glowing yellow and red, ghost-like ripple of movement rushing across the open grassland towards them, as the fire the plane had left in its wake, tracked and followed the remnants of the fuel trail along the drag lines of the plane, like a bloodhound on the scent. No sooner had Brigitte and the injured Peter crawled through the skin-shredding gorse bushes and into clear space on the other side than, with a gentle 'woof', the hound dog arrived and bit into the wreckage. Tongues of flame licked up, in and over the fuselage, eager to devour the cause of all this pain.

As Brigitte and Peter crawled and stumbled their way down the cattle track, her grandparents arrived, took one look at the situation and went straight into rescue mode. Realising more troops would be on their way, they needed to get Peter out of sight. Their hope was that nobody had seen them escape and that by the time anyone inspected the burnt-out remains of the fighter, there'd be so little left, they wouldn't notice the loss of the pilot's body. Brigitte's grandparents got Peter to the farm and into the hayloft. Here her grandfather had already built a false wooden wall at one end of the loft. In front of this wall was a loose stack of hay bales and behind the wall itself, more bales to act as sound-proofing. It was within this hidden, semi-silent room, lit by one thin, glass-filled skylight in the roof, that her grandfather kept the chickens; a valuable commodity in the latter months of war, as food had become scarce. He also kept Calvados, jars of pickled vegetables and additional food supplies they'd acquired, along with the chickens.

Initially, Peter lay on a platform made of hay bales, much to the amusement of the chickens who immediately hopped on top to investigate this person laid within their space. Peter had to constantly flap them away. After two days, with German troops going up and down the track taking the dead and wounded away and replacing the guns and ammunition, her grandfather realised they didn't appear to be searching for anyone else, so he made Peter more comfortable. He constructed a separate room, using chicken wire to create another wall, giving Peter separation between the feathered flatmates and himself. It was narrow, but big enough for him to lie on a wider platform made of four hay bales, covered with a feather duvet. At night, Peter and the chickens slept well; the latter content with human company. Her grandmother and Brigitte made a start on cleaning Peter's wounds. Whatever had ripped into Peter's knee had travelled right through and out the other side. On closer inspection, the women realised the metal had gone through the upper part of the leg just above the knee and, fortunately, it hadn't caught a main vein or artery but had torn and shredded a lot of flesh on the way through, making the wound look a lot worse than it actually was.

Brigitte's grandmother cleaned and stitched the worst with

a needle and thread. There was a chance of infection, though treating the wound using Calvados, it was highly unlikely any bacteria would survive. There was nothing more they could do; outside, the area was so busy with troop movements there was no way of getting him off the farm. He'd have to stay where he was and take his chances. It was during this period of internment that Brigitte and Peter fell in love. In actual fact, for the seventeen-year-old Brigitte it had happened as she'd helped the man exit his plane. For Peter, it had been waking up most mornings to find this beautiful blonde-haired girl, sitting beside his makeshift bed with her head resting on the blankets, fast asleep. Next to her, the bloody bowl of water and dirty bandages which said she'd changed his dressings yet again as he'd slept.

When they spoke, he'd spoken in French and English. Knowing a lot of both but fluent in neither, they managed to make themselves understood; this helped build a bond. He was well-educated, but for the war would have been in university. She was the daughter of an ex-teacher and a head teacher and also well-educated. 'Knowledge means a good life' her parents had said and they worked tirelessly to ensure she understood all that was around her, even during the occupation. She could speak German, French, Breton and some English. She was a survivor; given those skills by her parents. Several days after Peter had been hidden, word reached them from Crozon that American troops had arrived and the siege and battle for Brest had begun. A battle that would be longer and bloodier than the besieging troops had truly bargained for. Movement along any part of the Crozon peninsula was now a dangerous pastime. Planes came over regularly to support the Allied troop movements and ensure no German troops across the peninsula were coming to attack the Allies from the rear. All roads leading off the Crozon peninsula were now blocked, either by the resistance or the Allied forces.

Brigitte's grandfather decided they needed to move, but he needed to go ahead and pave the way. The next night he cycled the dangerous journey to Crozon to seek out his son, the headmaster. The following night, Grandfather returned with Brigette's father and a friend from the town with a two-wheeled handcart. After a worrying day in the chicken loft, and as darkness fell once more, they made their move. They got Peter onto the cart, wrapping a scarf around his mouth for all their sakes. They all knew the journey was to be rough, bouncy and dangerous. They reached Crozon before dawn and were hidden in yet another loft space, this time within the school. There they stayed. The Allies now held the east side of the Térénez Bridge across the River Aulne and no one, but no one, would be allowed to pass. It was safer for them all to stay-put and keep their heads down.

For several days, Allied planes were everywhere, strafing German positions and vehicle movements or bombing the centre of Brest across the water. The following week on the 19th of September, there was silence across the land. Those Germans who'd survived laid down their arms and surrendered. Later, American and British tanks rolled onto the peninsula to accept the full surrender of those based there, under orders of the German commander in Brest who told them it was time to call it a day. The following week, German troops were led away toward the east, Allied troops filling the void, including the town of Crozon. Brigitte's father spoke with an American major and told him of their injured pilot. The major made a visit to the school where all the family were now gathered. They explained that Peter couldn't walk because of his leg injury; the major could see how bad the wound was. They were asked if they'd continue looking after him until such time as help could be arranged. For the moment, one injured pilot was the least of the Allies' worries. Paul had said they were happy to look after him. With that, the major left.

Lancaster and Vidêt had listened to this story of blood, sweat, bullets and bravery for almost an hour, and although Lancaster found the story fascinating, moving even, he wondered just where they fitted into this tale.

"Can I ask how your mother and father came to be living on Jersey?" Lancaster asked, hoping to move the story on, closer to the task in hand.

"Well, Inspector," Lady Stottard said, looking slightly surprised, having been lost in a Second World War historical romance for the past hour. She'd always loved the story of her parents meeting and their love affair together. "There were difficult days between the allied take-over of Northern France before they ended up in the Channel Islands, but I'll keep it brief."

Peter's leg was not improving in its mobility. The family had an uncle who was a doctor in the town of St Brieuc on the north Breton coast. He worked at the hospital, attending civilian and German injuries, so hopefully, he was awarded some protection during the conflict. The decision was made.

Peter, Brigitte and her father would use the last of the hidden fuel to fill up her father's van and make the journey across Brittany to the coast. They drove into the remains of St Brieuc the following morning. Uncle Jean-Claude was not only alive but still at his place within the hospital. They hastily told their story, and Jean-Claude had Peter taken straight into a ward. This part of the story was now almost complete. Brigitte and her father stayed with Jean-Claude for several weeks. Jean-Claude made the decision to open the wound back up and see what was stopping him from being able to bend the knee. He discovered a piece of shrapnel partly imbedded within the bone above the kneecap in the lower part of the femur, stopping the hinge mechanism with the patella from having any movement. At the same time, a body of infection had developed within the joint itself which needed draining. Here, Brigitte came into her own, again acting as a volunteer nurse. She stayed with Peter, changing dressings and bathing the wound to aid his recovery.

Brigitte's father made the decision to return to Crozon, but agreed Brigitte could stay under the protection of Jean-Claude. Weeks went by and the war moved on. It was November. The Allies were almost at the Rhine. In Saint Brieuc, Peter had recurring bouts of infection, sapping his energy and reducing his mental state to almost depression. By the December of '44, they'd procured regular supplies of antibiotics. The road to medical recovery was being won. Mental recovery was a different matter. The one thing Peter knew for certain was that he wasn't going back to war. He'd no intention of putting a uniform on and would never fly into battle for anyone ever again. In this, both Jean-Claude and Brigitte supported him.

By January, Peter was virtually free of infection. In February, Jean-Claude removed Peter from the sterile confines of the hospital ward to a room at his own home in the town. The idea being that natural surroundings, regular meals and a log fire would revive his spirits. Over the next few months this appeared to work. His mood lightened.

In May, the war was finally over, though the official signing of the document didn't happen until September. There was jubilation throughout France, not least in Saint Brieuc. Relief that the war was finally over was tempered by the fact that Peter had realised he didn't want to go to England to be demobbed, nor repatriated to Poland. He wanted to start a new life, anywhere other than where he'd come from. Brigitte relayed all this to her uncle and her parents in Crozon. She took this opportunity to tell them that she and Peter were in love and wished to be married. By now Brigitte was 18 years old and mature for her years. She was a young woman who knew her mind and Peter was what she wanted. Her parents weren't surprised; they'd seen this blossoming right from the start. They drove up from Crozon, and the pair were married the following week. The past years had shown them all that time in life was of the essence and to be grabbed with both hands when the moment arrived.

"Here, detectives," Lady Stottard said, "was where the Channel Island connection began."

Having talked over the position Peter was in and all having been through the same war—the terrors, blood and death around them—they sympathised with Peter's chain of thought. It was time for him to step out of the war and begin again. Jean-Claude had family, Marie, who lived on the Channel Islands. Her husband, Clement, was a bank manager there. Contact had been made when the news had reached them that the islands had been liberated the previous month, so they knew they'd survived the occupation. Jean-Claude contacted them again, asking if they could help set the couple up, to which they agreed. So, the following week, the pair left the mainland and set off for Jersey to begin a new life.

"Did nobody ever attempt to find your father?" Lancaster asked.

"Not that I know of, Inspector. My parents never really talked about it, apart from those early years. They were determined I should know where they came from, but apart from that, nothing was deemed important. I imagine that either the Airforce believed he'd died in action, having never had my uncle's information handed on, or they just thought that being Polish, at the end of the war, he'd gone home. After all, it wasn't as if he put in for any kind of pension; he just started a new life on Jersey. Like so many displaced persons after the war, he had new papers drawn up at a local office and that was that. He became Peter Urbawicz, a Polish refugee, who worked in the bank. I suspect they just wrote him off and forgot all about him. You have to remember, Inspector, thousands of servicemen of all nationalities disappeared during the war, deemed 'missing in action'. One lone 'Pole' wouldn't make any difference."

"And once they were set up on the island," Lancaster asked, "they lived openly under your father's Polish name, Urbawicz?"

"Well, yes, obviously. It was my surname until I married

Philip, before he even became Sir Philip. They never hid the fact he was Polish. Never hid the fact he'd been a Spitfire pilot, but they never made a big thing about it. A lot of people did the same after the war. Those that could forget about it, did."

"Did your father recover from his injuries?" Lancaster asked.

"Well, yes and no. He got the strength back into his leg and got the knee functioning better, but I always knew him with a limp from the left leg. It was just something he always had. Sometimes he'd walk with a stick but most times not. He just limped."

There was a moment of silence, which, after a full hour and thirty minutes of story time, felt like a lifetime. Lancaster spoke again.

"I've read the file on your father's death in 2008. The police report implies your father lost his footing whilst fishing off rocks and fell to his death. Bearing in mind you say your father walked with a limp, sometimes needed to use a stick and was over eighty years old, what makes you think that that was not the case?"

Again, silence. Lady Stottard looked at Lancaster as if trying to work out what was in his mind before she replied,

"Inspector, that's the whole point. My father always walked with a limp. From 1944 to the day of his death, he walked with a limp. He knew how to balance with a limp. He danced with a limp and could walk with a limp. He fished off those same rocks several times a week, either with rod and line or using pots on ropes, but always... With a limp. Why-oh-why, pray tell, would he suddenly forget he had a limp... And lose his balance doing something he did every week? He was a strong man, Inspector. He'd developed a strong upper body to counteract his injured leg; he did everything from the shoulders. Being eighty had nothing to do with it."

Again, a moment's silence. Lancaster took all that had been said into his head, processing it for later.

"Do you have any theories as to why your father would have been murdered?"

"After the war, Great Uncle Clement took my father under his wing. Apparently, Pa was good with figures and worked well in the bank; he was just glad to have something new to fill his head with other than war. But as time healed Europe, the money started to come back. Investors, those who'd made money during the war, were all looking for places to bank. Jersey, having its own constitution as such and running its own banking regulations, was ideally placed to fulfil that role of offshore banking. My father took the Jersey Bank into a new era, where it wasn't just about hanging on to Mrs Smith's bank account and diamond earrings. It was about the wealth of Europe looking for somewhere close to keep their cash, with very few questions asked, and don't make a face like that, Inspector, it's how things work, and people pay highly for that kind of service. Don't forget, during those early years people became very worried about the Russians, who showed very little sign of wanting to turn around and go home, so keeping your wealth in an offshore account close to home appeared to be a good idea."

"So you think his death may be connected to his banking interests?"

Lady Stottard laughed. "That's your job, Inspector. You're thorough in your investigations. All I ask of you and Sergeant Vidêt is that you do for my father what you did for young Mehemet. You ask all the questions, look at all that's gone before and then come to a conclusion. If you think there's something not right here, tell me. I just want to know that somebody's treated my father with due respect and not missed anything, worse still, hidden anything."

"Sergeant Vidêt will be in contact later today for a full list of addresses and contacts on the island," Lancaster said.

"Pre-empted, Detective," she replied, producing a manila envelope from beside her chair with a smug smile. "You see, Inspector, we both like to be thorough. This is a complete history as I have told it. I could have just handed you this and spared you the hour of time gone by, but then... I like to tell the story. There are also dates, addresses and people who may be able to help and can keep quiet about your presence. There are also maps showing where my father fished and a couple of other little points. Now unless there is anything else, you have my private mobile. Contact me if you need anything, but I must get on, things to do, after all, it is a Sunday, Inspector."

CHAPTER TWO

Lancaster and Vidêt were in their office, complete with coffee, reviewing the information in hand. They'd copied the details from Pamela's folder and Craven's file and were reading through them, throwing comments and ideas into the pot as they went.

"Ok, first thoughts?" Lancaster asked.

"Having read the original investigation, if you can call it that, I think somebody decided Peter Urbawicz was a doddery old guy who fell off a cliff and died. Maybe they were right. But right or wrong, it would appear there was little in the way of enquiry at the time."

"My thoughts exactly. I get the feeling they were in a hurry to put it to bed. Mind you, at the time, their force only amounted to just over two hundred officers and about a hundred civilian staff and they were in the early stages of an enquiry at the old children's home of Haut de la Garenne, investigating historic stories of child abuse. At the time, they hadn't even started the excavations that turned up what they thought were human remains. Even so, I'd suspect the historic enquiry would've involved a lot of the staff that were capable, so getting a call to say an old guy with a limp had fallen off a cliff and died would've been something that was just going to get in the way of a proper enquiry at Garenne. They probably sent a couple of junior officers; they came up with the obvious answer. Yep, he fell off a cliff."

"It says in the file," Vidêt noted, "that Lady Stottard and her mother, Brigitte, made comments to the police that they thought it was unlikely that Peter had just fallen to his death. They appear to have ignored them and signed the case off."

"The post-mortem report says he died 'as a result of a fall, leaving the body impaled on a metal spike, jutting from a concrete base'. His actual death was caused by 'massive blood loss'. It's easy to see why the whole thing appeared to be black and white."

"So is the plan of campaign to travel to Jersey," Vidêt said, "and interview those that have already been involved, plus have a sniff about?"

"What I'd like, if Lady Stottard's up for it," Lancaster replied, "is to get her there at the same time; we then go as her guests as our cover. It'll also mean we have an on-tap local historian who can help make introductions and point us in the right directions. If we come to the decision that she's right, then she'll be there to action the upgrade to a full enquiry."

"What do you see as the timescale here?"

"Well, it'll depend on how soon Lady Stottard's available. In the meantime, would you upload all this, or at least précis it, so we can take as much info as possible with us?"

"I can have that by close of play today."

"To be honest, Marie, we've been here before. The death occurred nearly twenty years ago. He wasn't cremated, so he still waits for a conclusion. The only pace put on this is by Lady Stottard. It's Sunday and time for a late lunch. Let's call it a day and start afresh in the morning, say 7:30 back here, in the meantime, how about we go and eat?"

The following morning, they regrouped. Fresh coffee in hand.

"OK," Lancaster started. "How about you make a start on uploading the info. After 8:00, I intend to put a call through to Lady Stottard and request her company in Jersey; see what she says."

Vidêt set about her tasks. Lancaster sat back and began reading. *Without a doubt, the dangerous love story that formed Peter and Brigitte's start in life together was romantic, but it all happened such a long time ago,* he thought. *If there was a wartime connection to the death, why wait over seventy years before doing anything?* Lady Stottard might have hit the nail on the head when she talked about the modernisation within the offshore banking industry. Not only did the wealthy all have advisors suggesting places such as the Channel Islands as a tax evasive loophole, but the criminal fraternity was also using these same systems to 'stash the cash' and operate a laundry service. Providing clean funds in exchange for dirty money. Or so the stories went. Lancaster felt that if there was any doubt with regards to the death of Peter Urbawicz, then this was where the cause could lie.

At 8:00 on the button, Lancaster put in a call to Lady Stottard's mobile. She answered after three rings.

"Good morning, Inspector. You've caught me putting my face on; it takes a while these days. What can I do for you?"

"Lady Stottard," Lancaster began, before being pulled up short by her.

"Look, Inspector. If we're going to work together, please just call me Pamela. We haven't got time to keep going through the formalities every time we speak. You and your sergeant just call me Pamela, is that clear?"

"Very well, Pamela," he replied, then put in his request for her to share their visit across to Jersey. It made sense to arrive incognito by all means but at least as her guests. That way, if she was showing them around the island and introducing them to interested parties, it would be much more convincing. She'd also be on hand to answer any questions that came to light. Much to his surprise, she was keen to oblige, promising to call back later that morning once she'd had a chance to reschedule magisterial duties and get cover if possible.

By mid-morning, Lancaster had re-read all the information they had, such as it was. He'd come to the same conclusion. There was a shortfall in investigative detail. Beyond that, there was no evidence of malpractice as such, and no evidence visible that would point to anything being swept under the carpet. But the whole case was too neatly sewn up. Something didn't smell right. It would need a visit, a shake-up, to find out what was causing the smell.

A short time later, Vidêt arrived with a memory stick filled with everything they'd need to support the investigation, which she loaded onto Lancaster's pad. At 11:55, Lady Stottard phoned. Her case load had been postponed or transferred to another magistrate. Pamela was ready to move and could fly tomorrow or Wednesday if the detectives were ready to go. Lancaster said he'd speak to Craven and get back to her. Lady Stottard said to leave it to her. She'd ring back. She was back within ten minutes. She'd spoken with Craven. They had permission to fly at their convenience. Again, Lancaster said he'd phone her back. Two minutes later, Craven was on

31

the phone telling him it was a go. By lunchtime Vidêt had the three of them booked on a flight out of Exeter Airport for the following lunchtime, dropping into Jersey just after 2:00. The flight was less than an hour long. The work could begin properly then. Lancaster put in a call to Pamela. They agreed to meet at check-in the next day. It was time to go home, water the plants and pack for an uncertain length of time.

DI Lancaster sat on his balcony with a glass of wine, making one of his lists. He needed a methodical, itemised system in place before he started on any case. His dyspraxia demanded this approach. He'd been diagnosed with this brain-to-motor disability many years ago; it was something he'd learned to live with. He'd developed a series of avoidance techniques. It gave less problems for day-to-day living. One of those techniques was lists. He'd found if he was under any kind of 'face-to-face' stress, or was put on the spot in any way, it had the habit of leaving him flustered, momentarily unable to function. Over the years he'd found that if he knew what his plan was, then led with it from the off, he had a greater chance of forging his own way. It didn't mean he couldn't adapt or change direction at any stage, even take on board other people's input. It just meant that if he started with a plan, he could follow it to a conclusion. If he reached that conclusion, then had to start again with a different plan, that was OK. It meant he'd chased down an avenue and found it lacking.

He was putting his second list into better order when Marie's text came in and raised a smile.

'Would it be a good idea if we left for the flight tomorrow from your place?'

This relationship between himself and his subordinate had

been evolving for the last six months, following one night of incredible passion in the south of France. Since then, Lancaster had found himself noticing what Marie was wearing, what colour her nail varnish was and what jewellery she chose. Being incognito whilst in France had meant it was the first time either of them had seen the other wearing casual clothing as opposed to functional wear for the workplace. It had come as a shock for Lancaster to be aware that, in fact, dressed in a short skirt, loose shirt, flip-flops and with bare tanned legs on display, his French sergeant was not only a very smart cookie, but extremely attractive, sensual and overtly sexy at the same time.

It appeared the feeling had been mutual, as after a moment of drama in a dark French street when muggers attempted to rob them and the detectives had fought them off and made a run for it, they'd ended the evening sharing a bed in an intimate and very enjoyable night of passion. They'd agreed it was something they'd both wanted. There'd be no regrets, no recriminations and no pressure. The relationship would be casual and mutually respectful of each other's situation. In Lancaster's case, he'd lost his wife and unborn child to a traffic accident nearly twenty years before. This had left him damaged. More damaged than his dyspraxia could cope with. He'd fought through bouts of depression and suffered an obvious sense of loneliness. He struggled to cope with social occasions, where everybody from 'their' past would put an arm around him and ask, 'How are you, David?' meaning, 'Have you got over it yet and when are you going to lighten up?' The answers to which were always, 'No' and 'I don't know'. But he was still human, still male, still young. The urge to 'be with someone' rose within him from time to time. He'd been accustomed to channelling this lust during drunken encounters, usually with various women around the station, which was not proving an ideal course of action.

In Vidêt's case, her reluctance for relationships stemmed from spending years being physically and verbally abused by an aggressive father back home in France. Watching her mother and elder brother suffer sustained attacks, day in, day out, had left her wary of men. Eventually Marie had escaped by becoming a French Police cadet, then transferring into the Police Nationale and becoming a detective constable. Then, following her rejection, with force, of the attentions of her boss when she was based in Brest, she became transferred to the Metropolitan Police in central London, posted theoretically as the French liaison for a drug-smuggling case both countries were working on. On completion of that, she managed to stay in the UK and transferred full-time into the Met. Marie then set about getting a transfer to Plymouth, Devon, where she joined the CID and immediately started working with DI Lancaster. A position she greatly enjoyed.

Both detectives could be classified as 'different'. For Lancaster, it was because of his dyspraxic way of working, coupled with a dislike of social events and gatherings, an obvious distaste for any kind of sport and an out-and-out refusal to engage in anything that looked like a 'team event'. This didn't endear him to other detectives working in CID, though most of them had a begrudging respect for his success rate. This was fine by Lancaster. As luck would have it, his immediate superior, Detective Chief Inspector Craven, for some reason, tolerated his oddness and virtually cultivated it.

He tended to put 'weird' cases his way. Lancaster kicked up a fuss when first told he was getting a sergeant. He felt he worked better alone. But after a frosty start, he grew to appreciate Vidêt's candid opinions, her commitment to each job and her dedication to fulfilling any task that Lancaster gave her. He also liked the fact that she had no qualms about throwing her own ideas into the pot whenever she felt like it. At times, Lancaster thought she could also be dyspraxic, but he'd never say it. But without a doubt, she was, like him, an outsider.

Lancaster texted back: 'Sounds like sensible logistics'.

Following an enjoyable, stimulating night, they headed off to Exeter Airport to meet Lady Stottard. They arrived in time to see two giant suitcases being loaded onto the conveyor, whilst her Ladyship engaged in debate with counter staff regarding what she regarded as 'hand luggage'. The three of them then passed through control and headed for coffee to await departure.

"We've managed to get rooms at the Court Hotel," Vidêt said. "Do you know it, Lady Stottard?"

"That's two mistakes in one sentence, Sergeant," she replied. "Number one, please just call me Pamela. We don't have time to keep spelling out Lady this and Lady that, so it's Pamela from now on, agreed?"

"My apologies, Pamela. You said two mistakes, what's the other one?"

"Booking a room on Jersey. My mother's in a nursing home. I intend to stay at the family home. It has five bedrooms and I can't remember how many bathrooms. What's the point of having me there to show you around, if you two are not sharing the house? I mean, one doesn't want to pry and I'm no prude, you can share a room or have separate ones; it makes no difference to me whatsoever. But it would be a damn waste of space for you both to be off in some hotel."

Lancaster noticed Marie had coloured up. Her cheeks flushed and she wasn't quite sure what to say. He filled the void.

"I think that would be a splendid idea, Pamela. May we book two rooms please?"

"Consider it done." She got on her mobile and had the housekeeper make up extra beds.

The flight, as promised, was quick if a touch boring. Flying to the Channel Islands was almost continuously over the English Channel; all he could see was blue sea and the occasional ship. By 2:30, they'd picked up two hire cars and were driving out of the airport en route to the Stottard/Danielo home. The journey didn't take long. They'd soon driven through Le Portelet and turned into a short, private drive between imposing gate pillars, parking at the front of a large residence built in the French, almost Breton style. The building was constructed of natural stone, two storeys high with a low-pitched roof. All the windows as far as Lancaster could see, were shuttered, although all the shutters were open.

Following her Ladyship inside, they found themselves in a warm, well-furnished home. Despite the fact that her mother had been in the residential home almost since her father's death over sixteen years ago, the house was well maintained, clean and well blessed with vases of cut flowers. The reason for this became clear when a middle-aged lady with red hair came through from what appeared to be the kitchen, arms open wide, hug at the ready, she wrapped her arms around Pamela.

"Oh, Pamela, why have you been away for so long? We have not seen you since Easter! You are very naughty leaving us for such a time."

The hugs were reciprocated by Pamela. This was obviously a long-established relationship.

"Josette, it's been too long, forgive me? The house looks splendid; thank you for the flowers, they are all gorgeous."

"Oh, *pas des problème, mon chéri*," she replied. She then turned and looked at Lancaster and Vidêt waiting for an introduction.

"Josette, let me introduce you," Pamela said. "These are my friends from Devon, David Lancaster and Marie Vidêt; we've all come for a little holiday. I intend to show them around for a few days. Have you made up the extra rooms?"

"But of course. Let me show you the way, then I will make a pot of tea for us all."

They went upstairs. The detectives were shown into their respective rooms, side by side, with connecting doors to a shared bathroom. The rooms were at the rear of the house. Both their rooms and Pamela's room further along the corridor shared a wrap-around balcony that stretched the full length of the back of the house. Wide and overhung by the roofline, it had a collection of wicker tables and chairs outside each balcony door. The view was of a grassy headland, separated from the neatly cut rear lawn by a post-and-rail fence. After the headland, the blue sea could be glimpsed, topped here and there by the white tips of waves rolling across from France.

They unpacked and then went downstairs to find the promised tea. Pamela and Josette were in conversation when the pair joined them. Josette poured tea, then departed, leaving them to talk. Pamela led them onto a terrace, sheltered and covered by the overhang of the balcony above. There were large urns around the terrace, filled with clumps of agapanthus in flower. The nodding blue heads, each the size of a large hand, looking gloriously tropical in this setting.

"Right, Inspector, what's your plan of campaign?" Pamela asked.

"Well, the first thing we need to do is to get you to call us David and Marie if we're two friends from Devon."

"*Touché*, David. And after that?"

"If it's not too distressing, I'd like to see where your father actually died."

"Your reason being?" Pamela questioned.

"With respect, Pamela, the reason being is that in real life I'm actually a detective and when on a case, part of my task is to understand and get a complete picture of what happened and when. Then I work out for myself what the timeline is. Who was around? Who was involved? Who could've been involved but don't appear in the file and why they were left out of the original enquiry. Although I've read and re-read everything about this case to-date, I won't take any of that as gospel. It's my job to work it all out for myself with Marie's help, then see if we come to the same conclusions. If I just read and follow what's gone before, we'll have achieved nothing, nothing at all. At the moment, the obvious place to start is the beginning of what we've come to investigate: the death of your father. Where that happened, would to me, appear to be the starting point."

"*Touché encore*," Pamela said. "Forgive me. I've lived with my father's death as a miscarriage of justice for so long I'm wary of letting anybody else in. I forget it was I who asked for you and Marie in the first place. Trust me, this will get easier, but for the moment it seems strange having you as part of this story."

"It's not a problem, Pamela, it's strange to us too. But as you say, it'll get easier as the days go by."

"That being the case, finish your tea, both of you, and grab a jacket. We may as well get it over and done with straight away."

The three donned footwear and jackets from garments in the cloakroom. Exiting the garden by a side gate took them onto a grass pathway running alongside the garden boundary, leading up and over the headland towards the sea. As they crested the brow, the breeze got up. It wasn't cold, it was still September, but it had the smell and salty taste of the sea upon it, blended with the sweetness of rain in the offing. They stood for a moment taking in the scenery, the headland was almost an island within an island. Lancaster could see the sea to his right, in front, and then away to the left, the built-up area, harbour and sandy beach that was St Helier, the main town on Jersey.

"It's beautiful, isn't it?" Pamela said. "Never fails to take my breath away."

Pamela led them across rabbit bitten, grassy slopes and over a small car park, the landscape dotted with concrete slabs and platforms once used to position the gun batteries the Germans established during their occupation. This was the only part of the UK to suffer German footfall, other than the feet of German POW's. Pamela continued around the headland in the direction of the view to St Helier, then took them both by surprise by taking a sudden turn towards the cliff edge, whereupon she momentarily disappeared from view. It wasn't until they caught up with her that they saw she'd taken a narrow, twisting, switch-back path that wound its way down the edge of the cliff, culminating on a narrow stony beach, a tidal expanse of rocky 'shillet' and occasional sand, forming a small cove at the base of a horseshoe bay. She led them along the little beach, boots slipping on discarded seaweed cast up by the last storm, then up, over the outcrop of rocks that formed the eastern side of the cove until Pamela stopped at the end of the short cliff.

Lancaster and Vidêt joined her and found her staring over the rocks towards the surging waves that swirled gently around the point, then pulled back again, gathering their energy, rushing back for another assault against the rockface.

"I presume this was where it happened?" Lancaster said, looking down at the rocks some ten feet down.

"Do you see that worn chunk of concrete wedged between the rocks down there?" Pamela replied.

Lancaster and Vidêt could see the piece she was referring to.

"Well, that chunk of concrete has a metal stanchion protruding from it. Until recent storms, the metalwork pointed upwards, but since a big storm some years ago, it's completely turned around. Now the spike faces downward. Ironic really. If the storms had come sooner there would've been no spike for my father to land on."

"What was your father doing at the time of his death?" Lancaster asked the obvious question, bearing in mind the precarious nature of their climb down to the beach followed by the climb up onto the rocks where they now stood and the fact that the victim had a gammy leg.

Pamela knew what he was thinking and replied, "He was doing something he did regularly as I've said before. He used to come up here, depending on the season, two or three times a week. He'd use rod and line, sometimes a roll of line and half a dozen hooks. He'd cast out from here and see what he could get. But on the day of his death, he was here with a handmade lobster pot. He'd made it years before out of split hazel and woven willow; he was very proud of that pot. If the swell wasn't too great, he'd put bait in and drop it down into that gulley between the outcrops of rocks. He'd tie it off for an hour or more whilst he fished with the line, then he'd pull it in and hope for a crab or two, sometimes he'd leave it overnight. Then he'd load up whatever else he'd caught into a waterproof backpack and head for home."

"I know you've said your father wouldn't have just lost his balance, Pamela," Lancaster said, bravely going where he was determined to go. "But isn't it just possible that that's exactly what happened here?"

Pamela looked at him for a moment before replying, "Follow me, both of you," she said quietly, turning to retrace her steps back down over the rocks until she landed back on the beach. "Now both of you take off your left boots." They both did as they were asked. Pamela then passed both of them a small, flat stone. "Now pop this inside your boots and put them back on again." Again, they both did as they were asked; it was uncomfortable, but bearable. "Now follow me," Pamela said, climbing back up to her father's fishing spot. Lancaster and Vidêt followed. They realised straight away what Pamela was attempting to prove, and it worked. The stones in their boots forced them to limp. It forced them to take each left step with caution so as not to place their foot exactly on the stone in their boot, but climb they did, carefully and slowly. Lancaster thought, *if I did this several days a week, I'd know the right places to put my foot without giving myself pain.*

Where they regained the fishing position atop the rocks, Pamela walked across to the rocky face of the cliff to their rear, away from the seaward side, tucked her hand into a cleft in the rock face and pulled out a discus-shaped, smooth rock with a hole through the centre.

"This was the weight my father used to take the pot down to the bottom. Rather than have to carry this back and forth along with the pot and his backpack, he'd untie the stone, wedge it back inside the slot in the cliff, then sling the pot over his shoulder using the pull rope as a harness. On the day he died, they said he'd fallen whilst throwing the pot out to sea and lost his balance during the act of throwing. But the pot was found not in the gulley but out past the rocks. Nothing lives there; there's too much of a swell. My father always dropped the pot into the gulley; that's where the crabs hide to avoid being pulled out to sea. Although the rope was tied off around this little rocky pinnacle, which is where my father would have tied it, he'd never have thrown it out so far and he would certainly never have thrown it without putting the weight in. It would move too much with the swell. I think whoever murdered my father caught him as he was getting set up. Dad had tied the rope to the pinnacle but before he had time to put the weight in, somebody killed him, then threw the pot in to make it look like he'd fallen when he threw it. My father was murdered, David, I'm sure of it." With that, she turned and climbed back down to the beach.

Lancaster and Vidêt followed, slowly, due to the stones in their boots. When they reached the beach, they regrouped. With their backs against the warmth of the rock face, they removed the hindrance to their walking. Lancaster needed space to think so walked to the water's edge and stood with his hands in his jacket pockets looking out across the sea.

"Is he always like this?" Pamela asked Vidêt.

Vidêt turned to look at her. It was rare for her to be included in conversation when on a case. It never bothered her. Her role was to listen, observe and record. She was Lancaster's live link. A hard-drive to all sources of information, numbers and addresses he may need during any investigation. At the end of the day, she was capable of replaying all the day's events, interview notes and conversations, so her boss could add whichever parts he wanted to the extra-large whiteboard he preferred to use. But that didn't mean she wasn't capable of making her own comments.

"Yes, he is, I'm afraid," she replied. "It's something you get used to. I should not be saying this... But his brain is wired differently than most. Once you understand that, it gets easier to put up with him."

"How long have you two been together?"

"I've been working with him since 2017. Ever since I moved down here from London. DCI Craven interviewed me before I came down full-time, and the moment I arrived he put the two of us together. To be honest, David was a bit off when I first started. I don't think he liked the idea of sharing his office with anyone else."

"I actually meant how long have you two been an item?"

Vidêt looked shocked. She now realised just how dangerous

it was to have conversations with clients. She must learn not to relax. But at the same time, she wasn't aware of letting anything slip with regard to their relationship.

"We are not an item, Lady Stottard," Vidêt said with a straight face. "What made you think that?"

Pamela chuckled, not a full-on laugh but a chuckle. Linking her arm through Vidêt's, she leant in towards her ear.

"Because I'm older than you, my dear. I've seen more relationships than you've seen hot dinners. But let's say no more about it, shall we? Let's go and see what the maestro's thinking."

Lancaster heard the crunch of feet and turned as they approached. He was surprised to see the two looking so friendly. He wasn't sure he liked this at all.

"Can I ask, Pamela, it doesn't say in the file, but who actually found your father's body?"

"Me," she replied, colour draining from her face. Vidêt laid a hand on top of hers in silent support. "Pa was late home for dinner, which was unusual. I mean, it wasn't unheard of or anything, but that night was my last before I was due to fly back to the mainland having been out here for a couple of weeks. I said I'd go and see what he was up to. I didn't pass him on the way here and couldn't see him on top of his rocks; my first thought was that he might be having problems getting the pot back up. It wouldn't have been the first time. Anyway, I climbed up and there he was, face down on the rocks below. The tide had changed, the waves were washing against his face... So, I climbed down..."

"Stop just there a moment, Pamela," Lancaster said. "I'm sorry if this brings it all back but this is very important. Imagine yourself back on those rocks. Close your eyes. Imagine that night. Now look around you. Can you see anything on the rocks that shouldn't be there, anything out of the ordinary?"

"It's funny you should say that; I can tell you exactly what was out of place. There was a chocolate bar wrapper. It was held against the knot on the rope, just by the breeze. I picked it up and looked at it just before I looked down and saw him there, his arms spread out in front of him. I stuffed it into my jacket pocket when I saw Pa, then I climbed down..."

"Stop again, Pamela. Sorry, but why was the wrapper unusual? Couldn't your father have just dropped it?"

"My father never ate chocolate. He never touched the stuff; he'd never liked the bitter aftertaste. He never ate chocolate from when I was a child to the very end." On saying those words, 'the very end', tears started to roll down her cheeks.

"Pamela, I know this is hard but stay with me on this. Don't lose sight of the picture in your mind of those rocks; apart from the wrapper, is there anything else out of place?"

Pamela stood quite still holding Vidêt's hand, keeping her eyes closed fast, but not tight enough to stop the trickle of tears running down her face and taking her mascara with them.

"No," she said. "No. Apart from the wrapper, there's nothing out of place."

"Why did you pick up the wrapper?"

"It was litter! Rubbish on my father's rocks. He hated litter; he wouldn't have allowed it to stay. He'd have picked it up and brought it home."

"Just one more look around, Pamela. Can you see any blood on the rocks? Around the pinnacle or near the rope?"

Pamela stood with her eyes closed. "No, I just see the rocks.

I'm sure if there'd been blood, I'd have noticed it when I picked up the wrapper, but no, I can't see any at all."

"OK. What did you do next?"

"I climbed down until I reached him. I knew he was dead. He was face down in the water. He never moved apart from the gentle swaying of his arms with the swell. I could see blood everywhere in the water... It had changed colour all around him... It swirled and moved with the waves."

"Wait," Lancaster stopped her again. "You say there was lots of blood in the water?"

"Yes. The water around him was deep red, like an oil slick with the swell. I had to get into the water and try and turn him over, but I couldn't move him. I tried to get a better foothold but then I slipped and fell right into the gulley. It was horrible. I was swimming in Daddy's blood. I panicked and started flapping about, then the swell just lifted me back up onto the rock next to Dad. I got an arm under him to try to turn him over and that was when I felt the spike. I realised he was impaled on it. That's why I couldn't turn him. I had to leave him... I didn't want to... I wanted to stay with him so he wasn't alone... But then I got up and ran. I ran all the way back to the house and phoned the police. I had to tell my mother. I waited outside until I saw the lights of the police car and the man from the coastguard. By then it was getting dark, but we all went up to the cove and I showed them where my father was. Then the policeman told me to go home and leave them to it."

"We're nearly done, Pamela, just one last thing. Keep your eyes closed. Go back a bit further to before you found your father. When you were heading across the headland towards the cove, did you see anybody? See anything else at all? Not necessarily out of the ordinary, just anything at all during your walk to the headland?"

Pamela was standing stock still holding Vidêt's hand. Lancaster could see the look of concentration on her face, matched by Vidêt's, who was willing her to think of something, holding her hand tightly, letting her know she wasn't alone in her darkness.

"No. Nothing at all. I didn't see anybody else, well, apart from the hire car in the car park."

"What hire car?" Lancaster asked quietly, not wanting to sound excited.

"There was a small, red Ford in the headland car park. A Fiesta. It had a sticker on the driver's door," she said, opening her eyes. "It was a 'Your-Hire', the firm at the airport where we got our cars from. Do you think it's important?"

"Well, for a start, it wasn't mentioned in the file from Jersey Police."

"Well, that's my fault," Pamela said. "I never told them. It never occurred to me."

"No, Pamela, it's not your fault. Any decent investigating officer should have asked that question at the time. It wasn't your job to put forward information in case it may be relevant. It's their job to find it out. I'm also sure there was no mention of the blood in the report either."

"Again," Pamela added, "it wasn't something I was asked about. When we got back to my father, the tide was almost fully in. He was completely submerged and it was almost dark. I don't remember if there was any blood around then; I would imagine the sea would have washed it all away, is it relevant?"

"It could be, Pamela. When you arrived, there was lots of

blood. You say it was deep red, you specifically said, 'It was deep red like a slick'. That tells me your father had only just died. The water hadn't had time to wash it away or dilute it, and if it happened just before you arrived and you saw no one, and no other car but the hire car, then there's a very good chance the car belonged to our murderer. You were lucky; whoever it was must have been watching. There could have been two murders that night."

"So you do believe my father was murdered?"

"I think the evidence points in that direction. Already, we have a list of items that should have been originally investigated: the wrapper, the weight stone, the location of the pot and more importantly, the hire car. It would've been easy to go to the hire company when it happened, ask for their list of hirers for that day and cross that person off if not relevant. Now... Years later! It could be much harder to find a client list. But it's still worth a try."

"Do you think it's time for us to contact DCI Craven?" Pamela suggested. "Is it time to relaunch the enquiry?"

"Definitely not. We need a lot more facts at our disposal and a complete timeline of whatever points were missed. We also need a dossier of issues before we put it to DCI Craven. He won't want to cause another Haute de la Garenne incident without good cause."

"But this is a good cause," Pamela said indignantly.

"Pamela, please, you must trust me. After all, it was you who asked for us. Yes, it's obviously a good cause, but if we jump too soon, we risk having it closed down before we can get the evidence we need. Then it'll all disappear when we come back to look at it, to avoid embarrassment. Take your time and get all the pieces in place before we flag it up. Forgive me, but your father's been dead for nearly twenty years, you've waited this long for a decent investigation. Don't do what they did and rush it."

Pamela looked at him. He was, of course, completely right, and she knew it.

"You are what you are, and you're right. I asked for you for exactly this reason. OK, I shall shut up and wait. You are meticulous in your actions. I applaud you for it, but now I need tea... Maybe even gin."

By the time another pot of tea had been made, Vidêt had looked up their invoice from Your-Hire. Their outlet at the airport still provided a large fleet of cars. Lancaster took himself off with his iPad and started filling in his pro-forma whiteboard. He'd never used this before. Vidêt had set it up. It obviously wasn't as good as a huge white space covering one wall of the office, adorned with photos, dates and 'stick-it' notes, but then, he was a philistine; this was supposedly progress. Not his words; Vidêt's. He smiled at the thought of her insubordination. *Of course she was right.* Lancaster started his timeline:

Peter Urbawicz.
Born 18th June 1926
Moved Jersey June 1945
Died 20th August 2008

Between those items there'd be other relevant dates and incidents, which would stretch the timeline as necessary. He noted things Pamela had said that flagged up warning bells not mentioned in the original file, bullet-pointing key items in order.

- Your-Hire.
- Chocolate wrapper.
- Weight.
- Blood.
- Arms.

Lancaster was disappointed looking at the bullet points. He hated sloppiness. He hated system sloppiness; it gave all police departments a bad name. All became tarred with the same brush. Were these mistakes sloppiness or deliberate avoidance? Only time would tell. Whatever the reason, these points could have held crucial information directly after death, which could have given a definitive answer to the question raised: was it an accident or murder?

Vidêt joined him. "Pamela's gone for a nap. I think going over it all was traumatic for her. She will be back later. So, what are your thoughts?"

"At the moment, Marie, if I'm honest, I can't put my hand on heart and say, 'There's a case to be answered'. I can say a proper enquiry wasn't carried out at the time of death, and if nothing else, we owe Peter Urbawicz and Pamela that much."

"Do we have a plan of campaign?"

"I want to talk with his banking colleagues first. I want to know if there was anybody Peter was dealing with who might want him out of the way. Secondly, I plan to use Pamela's long-term hire history with Your-Hire and persuade them to look back into their books by twelve years if they can. See if we can find who hired that red Ford. At some stage, I want to find out who did the post-mortem on Peter. I need to leave that until the very last moment really, in case they decide to alert the police. I want to get as much as possible into our file before they find out we're here."

"I presume there isn't a name attached to the autopsy or you would have said; that's strange, isn't it?"

"Not necessarily, it's just attributed to 'Jersey Coroner's Office'. It could be down to a duty coroner if there was nothing suspicious with the death. It's not like it is on the UK mainland, where departments are interchangeable and they call on a specialist pathologist to carry out an autopsy, someone with a particular specialism. Here they have quite a small department. I know they should treat every death as a special case, but bear in mind it came in at night. They would've been told it was a tragic accident; man fallen off cliff, impaled on spike. If that's what they saw when they looked at the body, then I couldn't see any reason for them to investigate further. Not only that but at Haut de la Garenne, they were starting to accumulate stories of historic child abuse, so having an old guy who fell off a cliff come in through the doors and it kind of shrinks in comparison. So coroner's report comes out as, 'Man fell from cliff, landed on spike, death by loss of blood', end of."

"How are you getting on with the iPad whiteboard?"

"It'll do," he said begrudgingly, but with a smile. "No, honest, thanks for putting it together; I'll get used to it. I may even use it a lot, but don't get any bright ideas; my wall in the office stays."

Vidêt went into the lounge and returned with her pad. She flipped it open and keyed in her password. The file page materialised.

"Right, let's see if this file share works," she said, typing in the next password. "Well, I'm in so that's a start. May I ask, sir, with your bullet points, I get all of them but the last one. 'Arms'?"

"I tell you what, let's take a leaf out of Pamela's book and do a reconstruction." Lancaster led Vidêt into the lounge. He removed the base cushions from the sofas. Then gathered as many cushions as he could find. Having moved the coffee table from the centre of the room, he placed the base cushions side by side on the floor and then piled the scatter cushions in the middle.

"Right, stand with your toes touching the base cushions, then fall forward onto the pile."

Vidêt looked at Lancaster and smiled. "You do realise Pamela could walk in at any minute?"

"Stop it," he replied, wagging a finger at her. "Just do as I ask... Please."

Vidêt stood, then fell forward. By the time her face touched the cushions, she knew why 'Arms' were a bullet point on the list. Her subconscious clicked in the moment she'd started to fall forward. Instinct made her bring her arms to the front so her hands could protect her from the fall. A fall that was nothing more than a soft landing onto some cushions. She was sure that if she'd seen a metal spike heading for her, she would have responded more vigorously. If that was the case, why were Peter's hands and arms spread out in front of him?

"OK, I understand now. There's another thing, but you may have already thought of this. If I'd been impaled on a spike, my hands would have been 'scrabbling' to release me from it, the same as when somebody is being strangled, we often find not only their own skin and DNA under their own nails but also the perpetrator's."

"Exactly," Lancaster replied. "And that's another reason to find the original pathologist. We need to find out if there was damage to the fingers or hands. I can only imagine the panic of being impaled on that spike, your face half in the water, but I'm damn sure I'd have been in major panic mode. I'd have been scratching and attacking that spike with every last breath I had. My nails and fingertips would have been ragged before I died. Remember Abdul Mehemet? When his body was found, he had inhaled waterweed as he died. Sucked in with his last breath. I'd have thought if you were flailing about impaled on a spike, your face under the water, you're more likely to die from drowning before loss of blood, don't you? Now, let's get these cushions back before anyone gets the wrong idea."

"Who says it's the wrong idea?" Vidêt said coyly, adopting an overtly seductive pose laid across the cushions, which Lancaster couldn't help thinking that even wearing a sloppy sweatshirt and the bottoms of her jeans still tucked into a pair of 'wellie-boot socks', still didn't look that unattractive.

"Marie, behave," Lancaster said with a smile. "Come on."

They had the furniture back in place in minutes. No sooner had they sat down to get their breath back, in walked Josette.

"More tea?" she asked.

That evening, after a wonderful meal prepared by Josette,

the three of them moved to the lounge to plan the next day's events. Lancaster laid out his wish list: his desire to speak to any of Peter's banking companions. Pamela agreed, she'd find contacts for Peter's old friends who'd be discreet about their enquiries. They also came up with a convincing story with regards to getting information out of Your-Hire. Pamela planned to explain that her mother, now in a home (true) and suffering from dementia (not true), was now remembering details of her husband's death. At the time of his death, they'd been greatly impressed with the support they'd had from a stranger, a holidaymaker at the scene, driving a red Your-Hire, Ford Fiesta. They'd love to get in touch to give their thanks, even after so much time had passed. Pamela didn't meet the person at the time, and now her mother couldn't even remember if the person was a male or female. But she'd become distressed about it and was determined to say thank you before she left this world.

Lancaster sat amazed. Pamela had rattled off this plan as if it were completely true.

He also knew that Craven must have a confidant in the Jersey police to have obtained the brown file on the case. He was planning on putting in a call in the morning to see if he could use that contact to get him the name of the pathologist who did the original autopsy. If he couldn't, it would have to wait until they finally went big with the case, if they went big. It would be down to Craven to make the decision as to whether there was a case to be answered. Lancaster thought, *having Pamela with us might carry more weight with Craven than any evidence dredged up.* So, with a plan of campaign set for the morning, they decided to call it a night and make a fresh start the next day.

The following morning, they moved into their pre-planned roles. Pamela had drawn up a short list of people working within the banking system who'd worked with her father and more importantly, could be trusted to help and keep quiet, then started telephoning them to make arrangements to meet. Vidêt was tasked with noting down everything that had happened the previous day and everything Pamela had said; something that should have been done at the time of Peter's death, but obviously, had not. Lancaster took himself off to the terrace again to telephone Craven, to give him the update and find out about his contact on the island and see if he could be of any help.

The number rang several times before DCI Craven picked up.

"'Morning, Bomber," the voice on the other end said. "And how are you and the lovely Lady Stottard getting on over there? Well, I hope."

"I think we're doing OK, sir. We've been busy and have a full day ahead, planned and up and running already."

"So let's cut to the chase then, my old son," Craven asked. "Accident or murder?"

"Bit unfair, sir, we did only arrive yesterday lunchtime."

"You forget, Bomber, I know you, I know the way your mind works, well, actually I don't. It's a bloody mystery to me, but I do know you look around a room and get a handle on things straight away. So, you've had a chance to look around that room and I can smell your gut instinct over the phone, so come on, is the Lady potty or has she got a point?"

"Between you and me, sir, I think she may have a case to be answered. There are huge gaps in the original enquiry, in fact, there doesn't appear to have been an original enquiry. Everyone made up their minds that Peter Urbawicz was an old man with a gammy leg who fell off a cliff and died. End of enquiry."

"Bugger," came the response from Craven. "I had a horrible idea you'd say that. So what sort of grounds are we talking of then?"

"Well, there's good evidence to point to the fact that Peter wasn't alone on the rock when he died. There's also good evidence to say he was dead before he was pushed off the rock."

"And of course, none of this was in the original file?"

"Exactly. I don't know yet if that was deliberate or just slap-dash work, but there were several questions that should've been asked of Pamela at the time but weren't, plus a possible witness or murderer at the location in a hire car, that was never even recorded and therefore never followed up."

"So it's Pamela now, is it?"

"It's all part of our cover, sir," Lancaster replied. Annoyed at having to explain simple facts to his senior officer. "We're here as friends of Lady Stottard, so we're using Christian names whilst here."

"I was joking, Bomber. Don't be so bloody touchy. Anyway, what do you want to do now then?"

"Well, it's too soon to flag it up, but we've several irons in the fire today to beat out. I wondered if you could pull any favours and get me the name of the original pathologist who did the autopsy. There are several clues to Peter's death that

I want to check out which have absolutely no mention in the file. The death is just registered as accidental, by order of the island coroner."

"Could be tricky, my son. Leave it with me; I'll give you a tinkle later this arvo. Right, must go, catch you later, you and... Pamela... Be sure to have a nice day."

Lancaster liked his boss, but some days he really pissed him off. Today was one of those. As he put his phone down, Pamela joined him with yet more coffee.

"Your first interview is on its way," she said excitedly, setting out cups and pouring from the pot. "Maurice Devaux. He was a junior partner in the bank in the seventies, Les Banque des Isles. He'd be only too pleased to come over for a chat. To be honest, he'd be even more pleased if he could hop into my bed, but I'll see him in a box before that happens. Anyway, he'll be arriving in about an hour, if that's OK?"

An hour later, true to his word, Maurice Devaux arrived. A well-dressed gentleman. Late sixties at a guess. Wearing an immaculate pin-striped, three-piece suit that looked out of place at 10 in the morning; he was obviously out to please someone. His full head of slicked-back, silver hair was neatly cut and groomed. He carried a black leather briefcase with gold trims and a lock. He looked every bit... A banker. Pamela made the introductions, much to Lancaster's surprise, introducing Lancaster and Vidêt as 'Private Detectives', which brought a quizzical look from Lancaster and a small shake of the head from Pamela in reply. Maurice had already been briefed on her belief that her father had been murdered, and the two detectives were going over all the original enquiry.

"Can I ask, Mr. Devaux?" Lancaster started. "If you could tell us exactly how long you worked with Peter?"

"Well, I started working with Peter in the 1970s. I must've been in my twenties then. I actually went to work with my father, Max Devaux. He and Clement Begue founded the bank in the 1930s. I presume you already know that Clement was married to Marie, Brigitte's aunt, so banking was in their family. Well, both families really."

Devaux went on to tell them he'd started as a junior clerk. In the 1970s there was still a family-orientated banking industry. Banks looked after accounts of families who'd banked with them for years. Certain island families banked with Les Banque des Isles, others banked elsewhere and never the twain should meet. He'd liked working with Peter, who was older than him but had a great sense of humour. A confident, intelligent man. Peter had seen the potential for expansion, offering personal, tailor-made services for certain customers. Wealthy customers who knew the bank's confidentiality was second to none and that investments would be safe in their hands. During the 1960s and '70s, there were considerable tax savings that could be accessed by banking on Jersey. Like the Isle of Man, they had different systems in place than the UK mainland. It became recognised as a place where the rich, moneyed clientele from around the world began to 'stash their cash'. In a world pre-internet, people in Europe who wanted to find a safe place to bank, looked close to home so they could visit their money from time to time and make sure it was all still there.

This 'wealth-creation assistance' came at a cost. The clients paid considerably high premiums and charges for this no-questions-asked private bank vault surrounded by water, yet easily accessed. The staff at Les Banque des Isles would tailor-make accounts for an individual customer. Peter had a way of making everyone feel welcome and valued. The bank recognised this and paid for him to spend a couple of years under the wing of a family friend in London during the late '70s and early '80s. During this time, he frequented various banking houses and gentlemen's clubs throughout the city, getting to know people and clients. He'd be quite ruthless. Searching out people he considered would make good customers and held no qualms about poaching them and sending them to Jersey to open accounts there. In fact, that was how a younger, pre-knighthood Philip Stottard came to the island and managed to meet a younger Pamela Urbawicz.

"Do you think this cavalier attitude to fellow bankers and their clients could have made Peter any enemies?"

"Oh, almost certainly. I should imagine they simply hated him. I'm not certain any of them were of a mind to kill the poor chap though, I mean, it's just not the banking way. Enforcing bankruptcy or encouraging the Banking Standards Committee to investigate ethical standards would be more their style."

"Obviously we wouldn't want you to betray customer confidentiality here, Maurice," Lancaster said, ever hopeful of just that. "But there must have been some shady money coming into the bank. Money even you guys would've thought was of, shall we say, doubtful origin! Can you think of any transactions that may have caused Peter problems?"

Maurice sat and looked at Lancaster, then at Vidêt, before looking to Pamela for some support. It was not forthcoming.

"Pamela, you know the island banking world," he said in a slightly helpless voice. "I'll be black-balled and abandoned if it gets out I've told tales out of school."

"Maurice my dear," Pamela replied. "I'm convinced, in fact, we're convinced, that my father, your friend, was murdered. So, if you think you know something that may help lead us to who did it and why, and you fail to tell us now, getting black-balled will be the least of your worries, I can assure you."

Maurice gave an audible sigh. He'd known all along he'd be required to put something on the table; he just wanted people to know he'd resisted. For a moment anyway. He unlocked his briefcase and pulled out a folder of photocopied papers. He slid them across the table as if he was a spy. Lancaster picked it up and opened it.

"What am I looking at here, Maurice?"

"In the late 1970s," he replied quietly, in case anyone was listening. "One of the clients Peter sent across from the UK was an Irish gentleman. I use that term in its loosest sense. From the moment he entered the office, he frightened me. There was an ominous niceness about him, a smile I didn't trust. I was very surprised that Peter had wanted anything to do with him. He claimed to have a construction company based in Northern Ireland with projects north and south of the border as well as in the UK. Well, that should have raised alarm bells with Peter straight away. My father treated him to dinner at a restaurant in Saint Helier. A couple of days later I was asked by my father to do some sniffing around. Companies House, construction magazines, etc. I found that the company did exist. They filed tax returns and had contracts all over the place, but to be honest, the sort of money he was talking about banking and wanting traded amounted to more than I thought a firm of its size should be trading." At this point, he looked around the room to make sure nobody else was listening. "My feelings were that it was dirty money... I believed it was IRA."

"Did you mention your fears to your father?"

"Well, of course, I did. My father said that as long as we'd done our homework, the account was ours. But I never liked it. From that moment on, whenever I saw paperwork concerning dealings with them, I took copies as a safeguard. I always thought that one day the chickens would come home to roost. I wanted to ensure I had some protection."

"Does the bank still do work for them?"

"That's the bit that concerns me. During the 1980s, a ship called the Eksund was intercepted carrying a significant number of arms bound for Northern Ireland, all believed sponsored by Colonel Gaddafi in Libya. Well, a year prior to that, I'd copied a payment transfer to a shipping company apparently based in Holland for the hire of a ship called the Elkhound, supposedly picking up Italian marble from the Mediterranean for delivery to Northern Ireland. As far as I was concerned, when I heard the name of the arms ship, the similarity was too close for comfort. I raised my concerns with Peter and my father and they both took it very seriously. Of course, we had no direct evidence that one and the other were the same ships and, to be honest, we didn't want to know for certain, that was up to other parties. But it appears my father and Peter had both developed concerns about trading for the company over a couple of years and decided it was time to close down the account and freeze the assets until the company provided another bank address to transfer their money and portfolio to. It was decided that Peter, having been the one who first engaged the fellow, should be the one to inform him of this."

"And how did that go down?"

"According to Peter, the man was not best pleased. In reality he had very little say in the matter. He was hardly going to raise an issue with the banking ombudsman, was he? It appears he didn't want to make a fuss, but if I had to put my money on somebody who had a grudge, it would have to be him."

"When was the account closed?"

"You'll have to check the file, but I'd say during the late 1980s."

"You haven't given us any names, Maurice," Lancaster remarked, flicking through the folder. "I presume they're in the folder?"

"What folder? What names?" Maurice said, getting up to leave. "It was lovely to meet you all, but I must go. Busy day and all that. I'll be in touch, Pamela."

Pamela showed him out. On her return, Lancaster was waiting with a question.

"Why private detectives, Pamela?"

"The banking fraternity doesn't like police involvement in anything relating to the bank. There's an age-old dislike of them on the island. Some of which stems from the war years when they were forced to open up their files and vaults for the Germans. Luckily, quite a lot of people had already seen the writing on the wall before the occupation took place, so they managed to carry their wealth back to the mainland, but there's still a stigma attached to officialdom over here. But private detectives are a regular occurrence. People wanting to track their relatives' wealth. Detectives employed by a partner before they decide to divorce; you know, the sort of thing. So, is this a possibility or not?"

"I need to go through it, see if I agree with their suspicions. The doubtful bit's why they would leave it for nigh-on twenty years before acting out revenge. If it does, in fact, involve the IRA, that doesn't make sense; they tended to rule by fear. That only really worked if the person who'd aggrieved them was punished straight away as a sign to others. But it's a start and something that has to be looked at before dismissal."

"I feel the need for more coffee."

Lancaster went through the file a page at a time. The company in question was Devlin Ground Works & Construction. Headquarters in Belfast. Most of the transactions and signed documents, were signed off by the MD, Sean Devlin. Within the file, there were copies of cash transfers and currency exchanges along with cash payments for two yachts. Admittedly, this was with quite a time-lapse between them so they could be perfectly legitimate acquisitions. Alongside these were any number of transactions made by the bank for payment on heavy plant machinery. Bulldozers, large trucks and large-scale, bulk purchases of construction materials, all of which looked perfectly legitimate. Other than the fact that the company was based in Belfast and the MD was Irish, Lancaster couldn't see why Maurice had jumped to the conclusion that it had to involve the IRA, but he realised he wouldn't have come to that decision lightly, so homework had to be done. He passed it to Vidêt with instructions to go over it all with a 'fine-tooth comb'.

Pamela had an appointment with the manager at Your-Hire that afternoon. She'd been using the company for years, not just for herself but for friends whenever they came to the island. Peter had also pointed bank clients to them, so the manager had been intrigued when Pamela telephoned to make an appointment specifically with him. Pamela had also persuaded another of the bank's old employees, who worked at the same time as her father, to come over for lunch and a chat at 12 noon. When Lancaster told his boss, Craven, that the day was going to be busy, he wasn't far from the truth, so when his mobile rang and the screen said 'Craven' he was keen to speak to him whilst he had a gap in his day.

"Morning, sir." Lancaster kept it short.

"Bomber, hope you're keeping busy over there?"

"Been busy so far, sir. I'll have a full update for you either this evening or first thing in the morning, whichever suits?"

"Make it the morning. I like a bit of news over my breakfast. In the meantime, I've news for you with regards to the autopsy; it turns out they were all a bit busy at that time. The local police at the scene had come to the conclusion it was plainly an accidental death and reported it as such to the coroner's department, with no autopsy deemed necessary."

"Isn't that a bit odd, sir?"

"Not really. I wouldn't read conspiracy into it. Under Jersey law, bearing in mind they don't have access to just pull in staff from next door, etc., unless the police or a medical practitioner dealing with the deceased, considers there to be anything unusual about a death, then the coroner is notified and he signs off a death certificate. They don't need an autopsy at all."

There was a moment's silence as Lancaster processed this information. He had a horrible thought in his head but it was too early to put it out there. But Craven heard it ticking.

"Bomber, you're thinking," Craven said, a nervous edge to his voice. "You know I always worry when you start to think. What is it?"

"It's too early to say, sir."

"No, it isn't. You know I don't like surprises, Bomber, forewarn me. What are you thinking?"

Lancaster thought a moment longer but knew he'd have to tell his boss. He'd worked under Craven for a few years now; they'd fostered some kind of professional relationship, built on trust. Lancaster still didn't know why Craven gave him so much leeway in his working practices, but he knew Craven would always watch his back. He also knew Craven had his eye on the bigger picture and always gave good advice, even if he, Lancaster, didn't like it. He'd have to sound him out on his idea now, especially as it may take some planning and 'string pulling' if they were going to get it to happen.

"Bomber... Still waiting."

"I need to finish the interviews that we've planned," Lancaster said. Feeling that if he laid down some reasoning before dropping the bombshell, it might make it easier to swallow. "Then I need to run my thoughts past Lady Stottard, because without her say-so it won't happen. But so far, we have definite proof of a lack of work carried out during the original investigation. We've reasonable grounds to believe this wasn't in fact an accident. We have a possible witness or murderer who was never even investigated and we may possibly have a pissed-off IRA link from Peter's banking past. As I said, today's too soon to put this in motion but as you wanted to be forewarned... I may want to exhume Peter Urbawicz's body and get Rover out here to perform an autopsy."

Lancaster had worked with the Plymouth-based pathologist before. It had been Rover's meticulous forensic work that had brought so much detail into Lancaster's previous case, the death of Abdul Mehemet. This time it was Craven's turn to be silent. Lancaster left him to think. He knew it was a big ask and may still prove to be unnecessary, but at least now the 'big man' knew what he was thinking.

"Speak to me in the morning, Bomber. Finish whatever you have to do today. Take stock of the information you accrue and come back to me at 8:30 in the morning with an update. Think long and hard about whether it's necessary and we'll speak again in the morning."

In the silence that followed the click of the finished call, Lancaster sat and worried. *I may have played that card too soon.* In truth, he still didn't have any really strong evidence of foul play, but as was so often the case, he had a feeling in the pit of his stomach that something wasn't right. He was becoming convinced there was a crime to be investigated. But there was more to do today and things may yet change; galvanise the case further.

CHAPTER THREE

Christopher Warren arrived just before 12 p.m. Executing a precise three-point turn and parking his BMW as if ready to leave at a moment's notice. Pamela greeted him and made introductions. Again, Lancaster and Vidêt were private detectives employed by her. Mr Warren hadn't been made aware of the reason for his invite, other than Pamela had somebody she wished him to meet and something to discuss, in private. Over the course of lunch, crab and prawn salad followed by a selection of cheeses and crusty bread, accompanied by chilled Normandy cider, he was made aware of the premise for the meeting. Pamela told him she believed her father had been murdered and that Lancaster and Vidêt were searching for evidence to support her claim prior to informing the police.

It was noticeable to Lancaster that Warren looked decidedly shocked at Pamela's suggestion of murder. "Are you serious, Pamela?" his only comment.

"Very much so, Christopher," she replied. "I can't give anything away at present, but we've already discovered several flaws in the original enquiry that lead us to believe it couldn't have been an accident, as well as at least two possible suspects so far."

Lancaster watched for his response.

"My god," he said, putting his knife down, abandoning the goat's cheese he was about to smear across his bread. "Are you really certain of this?" he said looking at Lancaster. Lancaster nodded. Mysteriously. Just to compound Warren's fears.

"I'd always wondered if this would happen," Warren continued. "Why do you think I retired so early, Pamela? I became increasingly concerned about some of the deals we were getting involved in during the '90s and into the new millennium. There were people we did business with that we shouldn't have touched with a barge pole. It was a consequence of the expansion of the internet. It became harder and harder to draw clients into Jersey banks with their carrier bags and suitcases full of cash when they could use the internet. Give themselves a greater separation from the loot, banking it via an intermediary across the world in the Caribbean or Singapore. We'd always struggled to compete with the big boys. That's when we started to close our eyes to who our customers were. We asked less questions."

"Can I ask please, Mr Warren?" Lancaster said. "Just exactly what your role was at the bank?"

"I was a Currency Exchange Fund Manager."

"And in simple English, that was what exactly?"

"Simple terms, Mr Lancaster. My task was to follow rates of exchange of currencies around the world and use a client's money to buy foreign currency. Then retrade for a different currency if I thought that currency was about to go down in value. Obviously, all with the client's approval. Many of our clients wanted their monies to accrue a greater rate of interest than just the actual interest rate. They didn't just want their money sitting in a bank, they wanted it to be used to make more money. Sometimes trading shares on the open market, then again, sometimes using currency markets. That was what the bank paid me for. Obviously, the bank made money out of every pound they increased the account holders by; my salary came out of that."

"Not wanting to appear a complete idiot, but I'm presuming there's serious money to be made doing this or nobody would do it?"

"Well, obviously there's always a risk in any financial gambling, but that was my job. The clients knew the risks and had to accept it when they signed their account contracts. Not wanting to sound smug, but I seldom made a loss. You had to watch the political situations in the countries whose currencies you were dealing in. Factors like a country's inflation rates, maybe public debt, even if there was due to be an election. All these factors could lead to a fluctuation in currency values. The trick was to read all this and buy and sell accordingly. My god, I get excited just talking about it. Every day was like playing blackjack but knowing at least three of the cards in the dealer's hand before the game started. Always a buzz. The joy of it was, it wasn't your money."

"Did you ever ask where the money came from?" Vidêt asked.

"None of my business," Warren replied. "That was the job of the bank. They were supposed to be checking the ethics and assets of their clients. Seriously, it just wasn't my job."

"You said earlier you had concerns with regards to some client's funds; what did you mean by that if you say it was none of your business?"

Warren sat for a moment and took a sip of his cider before continuing, "There were times when the amounts of cash a client wanted me to trade seemed foolhardy in the extreme. It was my job to tell them this and I did, but the client was quite carefree with the sums involved. They had no interest in my advice; they just wanted me to trade."

"Why did that cause you concern?"

"Have you ever bought a scratch card, Mr Lancaster?" Warren asked.

"Of course."

"Why didn't you buy twenty?"

Lancaster thought for a moment. "Aah... I see what you mean. Because I know how much money I have and I know I can't afford it."

"But if it wasn't your money...?"

"So your theory was that the casual air with which your client showed this cash, was a sign that they were playing with somebody else's money?"

"Exactly. It's not for me to say, of course, but one of the things we were supposed to be keeping an eye out for was foolhardiness with finances. It could show a gambling addiction or possibly money accrued by illegal means. I mentioned this up the ladder to my employers, but according to them, I should do as I'd been asked. Then sometime later, I was told by Peter and Mr Devaux to pull the plug and cease trading with that client's money. Cash all trade in and return the funds to the central account. I was never told why, but I did as asked. Well, the client was obviously watching the account action, saw the close of trade and he was on the phone within minutes. I can tell you he was not best pleased, in fact, he was exceedingly rude, one could say, quite threatening. He insisted I maintained trading. I had to tell him I was only an employee of the bank... His answer was that if I didn't do as he asked, I wouldn't be working anywhere... I told him he should speak to Mr Devaux or even Clement as it was out of my control. I can tell you... He was the first customer who ever frightened me."

"Can you tell us who he was?"

Warren thought for a moment before speaking. "His name was Jean Batise. He ran a very profitable boat business, well, super yachts really. He was like a used car salesman and broker. He traded yachts all over the world."

Lancaster looked across at Vidêt who had the same shocked expression on her face as he.

"Do you have any paperwork to verify what you've told us, Mr Warren?"

"Good god, no. The last thing I wanted was a paper trail leading to me. If you're after evidence I suggest you ask the bank; they'll have it all on file. After that, you should be able to come to your own conclusions, but I want nothing more to do with any of this. I wish you well in your quest for truth, Pamela, but I'm retired and hope to remain that way for some years to come."

Christopher Warren departed, leaving a drift of gravel against the front of the house, a pair of furrows across the driveway and a receding cloud of dust in the air. Lancaster wasn't sure if this was bad driving, bravado, fear or a bit of all three; either way, his departure was a statement.

Vidêt was sitting in the lounge, the hint of a smile curling the corners of her mouth. Lancaster on the other hand looked worried. He saw nothing to smile about.

"So... Jean Batise," he said. "I could've done without that name cropping up again."

"You know him?" asked Pamela.

"Sadly, we do," Lancaster replied, looking to his sergeant to tell the story.

"When I was working in Brest," she began. "I was part of an investigation into a drug smuggling gang, importing cocaine from the Caribbean across the Atlantic, using fast yacht races to hide their crime. Although small amounts, each parcel was worth a considerable amount of money. Spread across a fleet of yachts it amounted to a tidy haul. They didn't target all boats in a fleet, just a selection. The drugs were attached to the undersides of hulls, inside tubular masts, sometimes moulded onto the keel. They had a collection of coerced customs officials, race organisers and even local police involved. It didn't matter which of the finishing ports the race ended up in, there would be somebody who'd turn a blind eye to someone slipping in over the side, cutting away the offending load, letting it drop to the bottom of a marina until the coast was clear or waiting until the yacht was moved to a less observed space, then stripping it of its cargo by local chandlers. Of course, this plan only worked for a while. We were never sure how long it had been going on when we got to hear of it. The fact that they'd spread the secret amongst too wide a group of people was eventually their downfall. At some stage, somebody decided they weren't getting a fair deal and they let the police know.

By the time we'd picked up enough evidence to make a case, we realised drugs were also being shipped across the Channel into small ports along the English coast. Falmouth, Plymouth, Dartmouth and so on, places where, by the time the local customs man had arrived to check papers, the load had been dropped and was awaiting pick-up."

"It was that UK connection that led to Marie being co-opted into the British side of the investigation," Lancaster added. "It became a cross-channel liaison between France and the UK. I became aware of it because of the Plymouth connection. Although it fell into the hands of the Drug Squad, there were characters involved locally that happened to be part of a completely different enquiry I was running, involving shifting stolen property, so both teams joined forces to observe and exchange information."

"Did you get your man?" Pamela asked.

"We got quite a few of our men. But the whole police operation leaked like a sieve. The police had the same problems as the criminals. We had so many different departments involved on both sides of the Channel, customs, coastguard, local police, DEA, the Metropolitan Police and regional drugs squads, that somewhere down the line word got out that we were on to them, and they started to disappear off the radar as fast as we found them. One of the key players who dropped out of sight early on was Jean-Luc Batise."

"When was this?"

"Well, we got involved in 2013 in France," Vidêt added. "But we were sure it had been going on for years before we found out about it. We reckoned probably about 2010. There were so many people involved it must have taken several years to build up such a network. I came to London in 2015. Most of the arrests took place during 2016. We knew about Batise, but he'd been long gone by the time we were ready to bust him."

"But that's too late for any involvement in my father's death."

"Not if what Christopher's told us proves to be right," Lancaster said. "The operation Marie was involved in was huge and that takes money. Everybody needed paying or it doesn't work. The ringleaders must have built cash reserves to put it all into place; it's my hunch they started this smuggling empire years before, built up their business maybe legitimately buying and selling yachts. At the same time moving in all the right circles, looking for the weakest links in chandlery stores, customs police and port officials. They may have spent more time building the network than bringing in the gear, so for them to have been banking and trading in foreign currency, raising capital sounds about right to me. If we can find out when this account was active, we may find it fits with our timeline exactly. They had an account working for them during the early 2000s and had the account closed down in 2005. Get their own back in 2008. It might even be that your father found something that encouraged him to have the account closed, and they wanted to silence him. It's all speculation at the moment and I need time to get my head around it before we do anything, but it could certainly be a contender."

Pamela had to leave for her appointment at Your-Hire. Lancaster suggested Marie accompany her. His reasoning was two-fold. Firstly, Marie would pick up the conversation first-hand and be able to record it. Secondly, it would give him the house to himself to be able to set out his timescale and get his head around all the information that had come in that day. Then he could make better sense of priorities and actions to be taken. The pair went off just before 2 p.m. for the journey to the airport.

Lancaster settled in a chair on the terrace and opened up the 'whiteboard' application. He kept Peter's timeline across the top of the page.

Peter Urbawicz
Born 18th June 1926
Moved Jersey June 1945
Died 20th August 2008

It was worth knowing where somebody's life began. In Peter's case, if truth be told, if he hadn't died in 2008, he'd probably be dead now anyway of natural causes. But that wasn't the point. Now he wanted a new list.

People of good Reason

They'd need checking out on the mainland and pursuing with the bank before they took them further.

- MD, Sean Devlin. Devlin Ground Works & Construction (Poss. IRA) – *Account activated during the late 1970s. Closed 1987. (Eksund) (Elkhound)*
- Jean-Luc Batise Yacht trader (Ocean Yachts) –

*(Known Drug Trafficker) (Operation Ferry) Banking
under Ocean Yachts during early 2000s to 2005*

Both of these gave cause for concern. Not because they
could've been involved in Peter's death, that was a given,
but because both these individuals were flagged up in bigger
pictures. In Devlin's case, he wouldn't find out anything
without crossing swords with Counter Intelligence. These
days you couldn't mention the word IRA without someone
from on high telling you to step back. There were deep politics
involved here. As for Batise, he was still on the Interpol 'Most
Wanted' list. Even if Lancaster could prove involvement, there
was little chance he'd find the man. If he did, Batise would be
pulled from under his nose by everyone who wanted a piece of
him. *This is going to be trickier than I'd hoped,* he thought. *We
need a new list.*

Questions for Craven
Whereabouts: Sean Devlin
Intel: Jean-Luc Batise

If he could find these people's whereabouts, he could at
least give Pamela reasons for why they'd not be brought to
justice. Should he decide one or other of them was guilty, and
on this, Lancaster still felt the jury was out, there'd be much
more leg work to be done. There was still time to find out more
about this period and more names may go into the hat, but
between now and tomorrow morning, Lancaster had to decide
if there was enough 'reasonable doubt' to warrant exhumation

and autopsy. Then the cat would be out of the bag. It would have to go official. If that happened, it was unlikely they'd let a humble Detective Inspector run the show. It would almost certainly involve the arrival of DCI Craven, and he hated flying.

Lancaster noticed Marie had added more detail to the file in an add-on folder. He double- clicked. Vidêt had researched Devlin Ground Works and Construction. She'd cross-referenced many of the expensive items in the invoices Maurice Devaux had given them, checking them off against old machinery catalogues of the time. It appeared these catalogues were now collector's items for machinery buffs. *Weird.* This showed huge differences between what was being paid for those goods and what they were actually worth. Initially, Lancaster couldn't work out why they'd be doing this, until he got to the bottom of the list and realised that the bulk of this heavy-duty plant, tracked diggers, JCBs, tarmac machines and dumper trucks, were all destroyed in a warehouse fire on a trading estate on the outskirts of Liverpool in 1979. Vidêt had also flagged up a lorry load of construction materials, purchased at considerable expense and sadly destroyed when the articulated lorry they were being transported in caught fire; its cargo going up in smoke. In both instances, the insurance company paid out to the invoice cost, as all the items were brand new. They also paid out to cover loss of trade whilst replacements were found. In all, it amounted to nearly two million pounds. Lancaster thought it could be an instance of dirty money used for purchase; clean money coming back into the coffers via insurance payments. He had no evidence, but it was decidedly fishy either way.

Vidêt had also found information with regards to the ship, the 'Elkhound'. It was registered in Greece, leased to an Italian shipping agency and supposedly shipping marble from central Italy to the UK for Devlin. Although she'd managed to find payment for the cargo, she'd not found any record of a shipping manifest or any record of the 'Elkhound' setting sail from any Italian port. She'd also noted that the purchase order for goods and the date of sale were supposed to be April 1987. Following this, she'd noted, 'MV Eksund' also registered in Greece. Also leased to an Italian shipping agent. Detained at sea November 1987. Although Vidêt had listed and dated all references and signatures of Sean Devlin throughout the file, putting them in date order, all signs of him stopped in 1987, after the account closure by Peter Urbawicz.

He also noted they'd both now added the heading:

Jean-Luc Batise

But as with Lancaster's heading, there was no more to add.

Lancaster sat looking out over the garden. He could hear the sea in the distance and smell and taste the salty breeze that creaked the trees. It was indeed a lovely spot. He tucked the pad under the cushion of the chair and went for a stroll around the garden. It was neat but simple. At the far end of the lawn was a group of huge Monterey pines. Their wide, elephantine trunks leaning into the prevailing winds as if to say, 'Come, do your worst'. Below the coniferous copse, a carpet of pine needles deadened the footsteps as he passed over it.

He was leaning on the paddock fence when he was brought

back down to earth by a text coming in on his phone.

'Get Josette to put the kettle on. Good news. Home in 10 mins. Pamela.'

What now! he thought, retracing his steps to the house. He couldn't bring himself to call Josette just to put a kettle on, so by the time Pamela entered the kitchen, he had the cups out, tea in the pot and was pouring when the pair strolled in.

"What, no Josette?" Pamela asked.

"Pamela, please, I'm quite capable of making a pot of tea for three," he replied.

Pamela laughed. "Oh David, what are you like? You can take the policeman out of Plymouth but you cannot take Plymouth out of the man."

Lancaster didn't take offence. He continued to pour, then lifted the milk jug.

"Milk, your Ladyship?"

They took their tea onto the terrace. Pamela put down her cup.

"So... Go on, ask us how we got on?"

Lancaster wasn't certain he liked this new 'we' but remembered it had been his own stupid idea in the first place to put the pair together; he'd just have to roll with it.

"Go on then," he said. "What happened?"

"Well," Pamela started. Then went on excitedly to tell Lancaster how they'd put their story to the owner of the hire car company, Mr Basil Fortune. They'd told him her mother, Brigitte (whom fortunately Basil knew), was now in Mont Pleasant Nursing Home and Marie, who was nursing her, ("I know, brilliant wasn't it," Pamela said) was keen to find some stimulation for Mrs Danielo; give her something to focus on. One of the things that had troubled her for years was that she wished to thank the person who gave her so much comfort the day her husband Peter died. Sadly, her dementia was such that only little things stood out. She distinctly remembered the person had a Your-Hire Ford Fiesta. She remembered it was bright red. Pamela could obviously give Basil the date of her father's death, the 20th of August 2008 and that she herself had been driving one of their Ford Granada's, a blue one. She'd had it on hire since the 1st of August 2008. It should be relatively easy to track anybody who hired a red Fiesta around that time. Mr Fortune was only too keen to help. He'd dispatched a lady to the records room. When they left, she was going through all the paper files, the ones that they used to print out and fold up into a tray with perforations down either side. Back then, though they had a computer system, it wasn't very sophisticated and they'd had system failures that led to information being lost, so they'd always kept a paper back-up. They were hoping to hear back from them later that day.

Lancaster was impressed. If Basil came through with names, it shouldn't prove difficult to whittle them down to a likely suspect or two. Lancaster felt it was too soon to broach the subject of exhumation and autopsy. There was no way of knowing how she'd take it and at the moment, he felt they were all getting along just fine, he didn't want to rock the boat until it was really necessary. Whilst Pamela popped out of the room, Lancaster took the opportunity to congratulate Marie on the information she'd provided with regards to the Devlin Company and its banking interests.

"It's a good piece of work," he said. "I wouldn't mind betting that if we dug a bit deeper, we'd find the insurance company was based in Northern Ireland as well. I'd be grateful if you'd upload the details of the conversations we've had today: the interviews with Maurice and Chris Warren and your chat with Mr Fortune. I need to get Pamela to find somebody from the bank, still in position, so we can get access to the dealings with Batise. This banking community won't take kindly to strangers bumbling around their filing systems, but if Pamela waves the family name about, we may stand a chance of finding what monies Jean-Luc was trading in. Also, where did the money go after they closed the account? They must have had a transfer account, a new bank to pass the money on to. It'd be interesting to find that out."

Marie disappeared to her room to work. She thought that over the course of two days, the three of them had achieved more than the Jersey Police had done all those years ago, but then, neither she nor Lancaster were investigating old stories at a children's home. She knew what it was like to be under pressure during an investigation. Like a cider press, the screw was turned from above; everything pressed tighter with every turn. It would've been easy to ignore the case of an old man falling off a cliff while fishing. Marie also realised what would be going through Lancaster's mind, that although the evidence was compelling and characters had emerged who could be involved, it was still only circumstantial. Also, both characters had too much to lose to go committing murder on what, in fact, was quite a small island. Then again, she and Lancaster knew that both these men were very dangerous. If crossed, as they thought they'd been, they'd have had to have done something rather than lose face. So murder would not be out of the question. Either way, sometime in the near future, her boss was going to have to decide if this was a case of murder or not.

Downstairs, Pamela returned to an empty terrace and abandoned tea cups on the table. A brief movement at the end of the garden alerted her to Lancaster underneath the pine trees. She found him leaning on the top rail of the garden fence, arms folded, staring out towards the headland.

"Am I disturbing you?"

Lancaster turned to meet her gaze. "No, not really. I was miles away."

"Thinking about the case?"

"I suppose I should say yes, but in truth, no. No, I wasn't. I was thinking about the house my wife and I owned on the coast near Plymouth. We loved that salty smell you get when you're this close to the waves. We used to smell it indoors even with the windows shut, well, we thought we could, that was all that mattered really."

"DCI Craven did tell me of your loss. How long ago did she die, if it's not too painful to talk about?"

"2009. The year after your father. And no, it's not too painful to talk about."

"But the salty sea air brings back fond memories?" she asked.

"Yes... After her death, I needed to sell the house and walk away; she was in every room. I couldn't open a door without thinking she was going to be there. I had to let it go, well, let her go really. It may sound silly, but I couldn't help feeling that she couldn't leave that house unless I was gone as well. To this day I'm not sure if I should have stayed or not."

"We're all different of course," she replied. "But it's been my experience in life that when bad things happen it's always best to move away from the scene and start again afresh. You'll remember the good bits, but it gives time for the scars to heal and start new memories, hopefully good ones."

"You're probably right but being here has made me realise I need to sell my flat sometime soon. Get back to the sea rather than just the harbour side."

Pamela Stottard thought Lancaster would probably not appreciate any comments with regard to Marie. She felt, however that his desire to start again in a new home was part of putting as much distance between his past, his deceased wife, and the future. And a life with his sergeant. Just then her mobile buzzed.

Basil Fortune.

"We've been very lucky, Lady Stottard," Basil said enthusiastically. "Mary's found the paperwork for 2008. As luck would have it, we only got the Fiestas in April of that year. I won't bore you with details but vehicle registrations changed in March of that year so when we ordered new cars, they weren't delivered onto the island until the end of March. Even better, we chose a selection of vehicles in different colours. We only had four red Fiestas. One was leased for the year by 'Island Cottages' and had their logo added under ours. That left three cars and we have all the hirers during the year up to and including the end of August 2008."

"That's just brilliant, Basil, thank you so much. Do you want me to pop down?"

"Not at all, Lady Stottard, they're being scanned as we speak and e-mailed to you in the next fifteen minutes."

"That's so kind," she said with some conviction. "I'll pop down with a bottle of something later in the week."

"It's my pleasure, Lady Stottard, please give my fondest regards to your mother."

Pamela and Lancaster returned to the house. Pamela went straight to her study. Five minutes later, she was back downstairs with three copies of the list. Lancaster called for Vidêt to join them and Pamela handed out the list. The red Fiestas were listed by their registration numbers. Between the 1st of April and the 1st of September 2008, the three red Fords had been rented out eight times in total. Lancaster thought, *that doesn't sound like a lot for a car hire firm,* but on closer inspection, realised one of the hirers was, in fact, an insurance company. They'd contract-hired a red Fiesta from the 15th of April through until September. It was still on hire after the 1st. One down, two to go. They'd have to contact Staverton Insurance and find out why they'd had it. Vidêt made a note to follow that up.

That left two cars and seven hires. One was hired twice to Hill Top Floristry in Saint Helier. Their hire dates were early in the year. Then once to a Mr Levon Shawbuck, listed on the hire form as 'American Citizen' (Tourist), Pennsylvania, USA. On hire for three weeks as a block, starting on the 4th of August, ending on the 24th of August. The same registered vehicle was also rented one more time during the time period to a German tourist, Paul Steiner, from Berlin. His hire was for a week during early June.

The final red car was rented by Island Airways for a four-month period starting on the 10th of April, extending until the end of July. Then twice by, at a guess, the same Mr Paul Steiner, a German tourist from Berlin. Once at the end of July for a week, then again for another week from the 18th of August until the 24th of August. It looked like Steiner was in Jersey for business rather than pleasure. *Visiting three times in one year seems more like business than anything else*, Lancaster thought. Lancaster came up with a work schedule straight away. Pamela was to phone Basil and ask if they were certain that these were the only hires for the red Fiestas they had. He couldn't help thinking they'd not been on hire much over the space of five months. Vidêt was to contact the insurance company, Staverton's, and enquire about the five-month hire. Following that, she was to start searching for Mr Levon Shawbuck. Lancaster would research Paul Steiner of Berlin.

He began by trying 'Telefonbuch'. It was easier than he thought. Throughout Germany, there were one hundred and twenty 'Steiner P's listed. He decided to stick to what he knew. His P. Steiner was living in Berlin in 2008. So, using the search engine for 'Telefonbuch', he managed to track back into the archive and found 2008. During this period there were only fifteen P. Steiner's registered in the city. Lancaster cut and pasted these 15, dropping them into an MSWord document for safekeeping. He then checked the German equivalent of 'Yellow Pages', 'Gelbe Seiten Deutschland', in case it turned out to be a company name. He checked through their Berlin numbers. This produced another list of Steiner's. Five of them. By pasting this information into the same file and then cross-referencing details, he realised all the new names matched the ones he already had, but for one. He took this one and added it to the first list. Now he had sixteen P. Steiner's. All he needed to do now was find out how many of these were Paul as opposed to a Philip, a Peter or a Peppi. It would have been easier if they had more detail from the hire car spreadsheet, but details were limited. Somehow, he was just going to have to make do.

Lancaster noted down numbers and addresses from the 16 in the phone books and added them to his file for safekeeping. He wasn't sure how to follow this up. He couldn't just ring them and say, 'Were you the Paul Steiner who visited Jersey in 2008?'. If one of them had anything to do with Peter's death he was hardly going to say yes. If he telephoned all 16 and they all said, 'No, they didn't visit'... Then he was back to square one. Apart from that, he'd have alerted them to the fact that somebody was asking questions. He was going to have to think about this; his train of thought was interrupted by Vidêt.

"Guess what Mr Levon Shawbuck, American tourist from Pennsylvania, USA, does when he's not on holiday in Jersey?"

"Is he a cowboy?" Lancaster asked with a smile.

"Almost... He owns a gun shop."

"Well, well, well," Lancaster replied. "Is that a coincidence, DS Vidêt, considering the Northern Ireland connection and the cash of arms discovered on the Eksund?"

"You know what we say about coincidence, DI Lancaster. I quote: 'When investigating a murder, there is no such thing as a coincidence until it has been disproven'."

"My concern with our IRA man though, is the length of time between Peter closing down his account in December of 1987 and the murder in August of 2008. Twenty-odd years is a very long time to hold a grudge before taking any action. If Shawbuck is connected, the same question applies. I mean, maybe he helped broker the deal in Libya, although highly unlikely. The reason Gadhafi was so keen to help fund an Irish insurrection and supply a boat full of arms was that he hated the British and the Americans. It was the Americans with the support of the UK who'd just bombed his country, and if the stories were correct, they'd managed to miss killing Gadhafi but killed one of his daughters, so Mr Shawbuck would've been walking into the Lion's den. No, I don't think he was involved in the Eksund deal, but he may well have been involved in others. America was a hotbed of IRA sympathisers. Maybe he hadn't been paid for a shipment because Peter had closed the account. But we come back to the same question, why did he take over twenty years to do anything about it?"

"Do you think that puts them out of the picture?" As she asked, she knew what the answer was going to be.

"Not in the slightest. We have them as 'possible' until we prove them not to be. Just remember the Abdul Mehemet case. We kept having new people drop into the frame. Each time we worked through the process, we discounted them one by one. And before you say anything, I know we ended up with a complete outsider coming into the picture right at the last minute and he never appeared in the enquiry until then. But if we hadn't crossed everyone else off the list, we'd never have come across him in the first place. So, our system works as long as we're adaptable and don't discount anyone until we've no other option."

"What about this Paul Steiner? Have we found him yet?"

Lancaster laughed. "Better than that, Marie, I've found sixteen of them. Well, I've found sixteen P. Steiner's in Berlin. Unfortunately, being incognito, it's hard to find out who's a Paul and who's a Peter. If we went official, I'd get access to Interpol or German police and they'd do a quick search for us, but at the moment I've sixteen people. At some stage, we can research further and narrow it down."

"Can I ask, why do you not just contact Interpol online? They won't know you're in Jersey, and they will e-mail you the information you're after."

"I've thought about that, but it's too risky. If they speak to anyone else at any stage, Steiner may go to ground. If they backtrack his passport, it may well show his trips to the island, then they may contact somebody here, blah-blah-blah. No, I don't need the info yet, it'll keep a little longer."

"What are your thoughts now after being here for two days? With respect, I know what you're like, you normally get a gut feeling about a case, evidence or not. So, what are you thinking?"

Lancaster sat looking at the screen of his pad thinking. She was right, he did normally get a gut feel for a case and this one had proved no different. There was no doubt that Pamela's enactment of her father's fishing routine gave him serious cause for concern in the original decision of accidental death. As a policeman, he felt sorry for the original investigators though. They were up against it at the time; undermanned, with the Haute de la Garenne enquiry gaining momentum and media attention. Peter Urbwicz's death would've been so easy to write off as an accident.

"I have to say, Marie. My gut feeling is that there's enough going on here to warrant an investigation. I'm not positive it wasn't an accident, but as I said, there are all the points we've listed so far, along with the fact that we now know Peter upset people along the way and those people were not nice people. Yes, we have a problem with timescales, but I still think there's plenty here for us to worry about. I need to talk to Pamela about a clincher. I'm not sure she's going to be happy about it."

"What is it?" Vidêt asked.

Just then Pamela walked into the lounge looking pleased with herself. Lancaster felt she was actually enjoying the role of investigator.

"I've spoken to Basil," she said, a conspiratorial smirk on her face. "According to an embarrassed Basil, who originally chose the vehicles for the fleet, the reason the red Fiestas don't appear to have been on hire very much is that, apparently, people on the whole don't like red cars... I know, I was surprised as well. Apparently, they like silver, white or grey cars first, then they may go for black. Well, you learn something new every day, don't you? So those rental dates are correct. Basil traded them on the following year. Oh, more news, he says Mary's found the card index for that year. Apparently, when taking down details from the client, they used to fill in a hirer card. It was a leftover from before the computerised system improved. So, when they uploaded onto the computer, they only filled in the basics, things like the client's address, driving licence number, etc. are all written on cards. Anyway, she wanted to know if they were of any use to you at all."

Lancaster and Vidêt looked at each other and smiled. Maybe now they can track down their P. Steiner without Interpol or the German police. Lancaster told Pamela that getting the cards would be a lovely idea. Now he'd short-listed them, he knew the ones he wanted them to scan and send ASAP. Pamela went to her study to get Basil to scan and send the cards. Vidêt asked Lancaster what the 'clincher' was. He explained his thoughts on the need for an exhumation. She agreed it would be needed to see if evidence had been missed but, like Lancaster, wasn't sure how Pamela would react to the idea. Vidêt told Lancaster she'd managed to contact Staverton Insurance Brokers in Norwich. After some protracted conversation and the eventual use of her warrant card, they agreed to search their archive to find the reasons for the long Jersey car hire. She'd made arrangements to phone them back in ten minutes.

The next interruption was Josette arriving with yet another tray full of cups, teapots and milk jugs.

"Her Ladyship's asked for tea for you all."

Pamela re-joined them, handing over the printouts of names to Lancaster, but forbidding him to look at them until after a cup of tea, so Vidêt poured.

"I have to say, David," she began. "I've found the last couple of days completely invigorating. I know I probably shouldn't have, bearing in mind the subject matter, but I actually feel I'm doing something rather than just being bitter. It's been a long time just festering, not knowing how to go about the process of getting anyone to take this seriously. To be honest, I don't think I'd have had any joy getting anyone on the island to take an interest at all."

"That's why we do the job, Pamela. We wouldn't do it if we didn't enjoy the process. I don't know about Marie, but I've always enjoyed piecing things together. Doing research, chasing down characters, searching for clues on the ground or in files. There are always stories that unfold as you hunt and things that don't necessarily have a direct influence on the outcome of a case but do tell how a story unfolded. Sometimes they help you understand why something occurred in the first place."

"It's the same for me," Marie continued. "From the very beginning, I wanted to know the story surrounding an incident. Remember the Abdul Mehemet case? Well, if we had not gone to his hometown to find out about his life, we would never have worked out how he came to be where he ended up. It was obviously not my idea though, it was David's. He had the idea, knew it needed to be done to finish the case and he was right."

Pamela smiled. She was positive about the connection between the two detectives even if they denied it. So be it. They must be allowed their secrets. She felt envious if truth be told; young love for her felt such a long time ago.

"So," Pamela asked. "Where do we go from here? Do you see a picture forming yet?"

Lancaster put his cup down. Tomorrow morning, he was going to have to call Craven with a plan of action to take this case forward or go home; the latter didn't appear to be an option. He had to broach the subject with Pamela at some stage; this was as good a time as any, while they all felt positive. He needed to build a picture that made it appear inevitable; like it was, in fact, the only course of action.

"To my mind, there's a picture forming. To start with, the points you raised on the cliff top are relevant and give me serious cause for concern. Secondly, this red Fiesta. It was never investigated. If this person wasn't the murderer, and it's a long shot at the moment, but if they weren't, they most certainly could have been a witness to something. Thirdly, nobody ever looked into Peter's banking connections. In two days, we've found at least two dangerous individuals that your father upset, big-time. This could all be circumstantial. They could both be completely separate from the incident. But the point is, you cannot just say, 'This was an accident' without looking into these points. There's another issue that worries me more than anything."

"What is it?" Pamela asked.

"After your father's body was recovered, no autopsy was carried out."

"What do you mean no autopsy?" Pamela replied, surprised. "There must have been. How could they have come to the decision it was death by accident?"

"It turns out that in Jersey, they differ from the mainland. If the police or medical practitioner on the scene at the time of death informs the coroner's officer that a death was caused by natural causes or an accident, then an autopsy isn't deemed necessary. It's just not carried out."

Lancaster stopped there and let that sink in. He knew

that as a practising magistrate, Pamela would understand the significance of this information. It meant that the result stated for her father's death was not proven; was supposition only. Perfectly legal and above board, but not proven. To anyone else this may not matter, but to Pamela...

Lancaster could almost hear her brain ticking over as the information was dissected and sorted to a natural conclusion.

"So, in your opinion," she asked quietly. "Is it too late?"

Lancaster knew what she meant but needed her to spell it out. "Is what too late?" he asked.

"David," she said quietly, looking straight at him. "Don't make the mistake of taking me for a fool. You're well aware of what I mean and you're in danger of harming this little three-way friendship by making me spell it out. Is it too late for an autopsy to find anything of value, if I grant you permission to exhume my father's body?"

"The simple answer is no. If there's anything to find then no, it's not too late. I can't say for certain that we'll find anything. But one thing I know for sure is that an autopsy should have been carried out during the original enquiry. In the Mehemet case, the body had been buried for over twenty years, yet we found out where he was born, his age when he died, what season of the year he was killed and how many years his body had been interred, so anything is possible."

Pamela sat for another moment thinking. Becoming resigned to the inevitable.

"What in particular would you expect to find that would have a bearing on the result or help to prove this case?"

"Honestly? I don't know at this moment in time, Pamela.

But if it isn't too upsetting for you, one thing I'd like to investigate is, and honestly, there's no kind way to put this, but if I was alive and had fallen onto a spike, I would fight till my last breath to get free of it. That would mean damage to my fingernails, even the fingers. I'd have rust embedded under any nails that weren't broken. Not only that but in my panic, I'd have sucked in copious amounts of seawater into my stomach and lungs. My death would more than likely be as a result of drowning, the inhalation of sea water rather than blood loss."

Lancaster watched as the penny dropped and sudden realisation hit. "You're thinking that if none of that's present, then maybe my father was already dead before he went off the cliff."

"Exactly. But you need to be aware, Pamela, that we'll also be looking for anything else that may account for your father's death. For example, he may have had a heart attack as he was setting up his pot and just fallen over the edge. The only way we'll find out is by a belated autopsy, and the only way we do that on Jersey is with a relative's full permission."

Pamela sat a moment before saying, "Well, you certainly have my permission, but will you hold off alerting the island authorities until I speak to my mother? She's always believed Father's death had had a proper investigation. But this island has a small community; I wouldn't want her to hear this from anybody else but me. But will the island coroner grant a request and will the local pathologist be any good?"

Lancaster explained the island coroner would have to follow the family's request if it was supported by new evidence. He intended to put a detailed file together, giving a good reason for reopening the case and conducting a new enquiry. As for the pathologist, he told her his plan to fly out their pathologist from Plymouth, Benjamin Landy. Then they'd have somebody not only good at the job but trusted and unlikely to be intimidated by another authority attempting to lean on him for a conclusion in their favour. The call to Craven was set for first thing in the morning. Pamela was all for ringing him there and then and getting the process underway. Lancaster managed to persuade her that wasn't a good idea. To start with, it was late. Craven would find it hard to get anything moving at his end before offices closed. Secondly, Lancaster wanted time to write a full report to e-mail his boss to ensure there was enough weight behind the request for him to get on board. The more reason he could give, the easier it would be to encourage Craven to come in, all guns blazing.

Vidêt re-joined them, following her return call to the insurance brokers, Staverton's. It appeared all was in order as far as they were concerned. The long hire was verified by them as brokers, due to the need to replace a car insured by them and driven by one of their clients. It had been badly damaged by an articulated lorry inside the Portsmouth to Jersey ferry. Staverton initially provided a hire car whilst the client was on the island, starting from the 15th of April. The client needed to return to the UK at the end of April. Sadly, the claim was hard to finalise; the lorry involved off-loaded its cargo on the island and then departed on another ferry bound for the French mainland. As Staverton's had struck such a good deal with Your-Hire, when their client wished to return to England, they continued the hire right up until the matter was finally concluded at the end of September of the same year.

That suited Lancaster; it meant he could take that car off his database. If they'd returned to the UK at the end of April, they were out of the picture. That meant that for the period they wanted, there were only two people who could have hired a red Fiesta and been parked up on the point that night. Levon Shawbuck, a gun shop-owning American, and Mr Paul Steiner, an unknown German 'tourist' who appeared to have liked being on Jersey so much; he visited three times in one year. Now all Lancaster had to do was find out who these two people were and what they were doing on the island at that time. It may turn out that both were genuine tourists, but until they were ruled out of the picture, they remained worthy of investigation.

Lancaster had almost forgotten the sheet of information that Pamela had received from Basil. He picked it up. Studied it then smiled. Now he had a Berlin address for Steiner, a phone number and a driving licence number. Lancaster cross-referenced this against his information from the Berlin phonebook. He now had one match. That was all he needed. Lancaster was now shackled by the very nature of their presence on the island; the fact that they were here incognito and not an official police representative. Once they opened this case up, he could gain access to all that Europe could offer in the way of police information, he would also get access to American intelligence. It would take but a matter of minutes to find out anything they needed to know about Mr Shawbuck, if there was anything to find. Lancaster checked his watch. The other thing he'd wanted to get done today was to contact the bank and see if there was a way to find out about both closed bank accounts. His time check showed it was too late to speak to anyone; it would have to wait until morning. *Tomorrow is going to be a busy day, but could prove interesting.*

Over dinner, Lancaster outlined how the following day was going to go. The first call of the day would be Craven. Before he turned in for the night, he'd finalise his dossier in readiness for the morning. He asked Pamela if she still had influence with senior partners at the bank.

"What do you need?" she asked.

"I need to find out what happened to the accounts Peter closed. I know the bank may struggle to work with me, but I wondered if you might be able to pull some strings?"

"I still have influence. I'm a major shareholder and Father's name still carries considerable weight; I don't think there'll be a problem."

It had been a long day and a late dinner. The detectives retired to Lancaster's room to finish the dossier. Lady Stottard settled in the lounge and began making some late phone calls. For her, calling during office hours was meant only for official business; this was personal. As she made contact with a few key members of the board, she was open with regard to where developments had taken them and where she believed it would end up. She found a lot of support. Before she turned in that night, she had a promise she'd be granted full access and full assistance finding the information regarding those two accounts.

†

The following morning Lancaster settled into a chair in the dining room. In front of him was a complete dossier of what they'd managed to accumulate so far; even he was impressed. He put in the call just after 7 a.m. hoping to catch Craven before he left for the office. Craven answered on the second ring.

"Morning, Bomber, I hope you've given a lot of thought to what you're about to tell me, my son. I wouldn't want us jumping in with both feet without just cause and all that."

"Morning, sir. Without wanting to sound rude, shall we cut the chit-chat and get straight to business?"

"Best had, Bomber, best had. Away you go, I can eat toast," Craven said, crunching on a crust for effect.

"I've no doubt, sir, there are grounds for reopening the Urbawicz case. So far, we've several unexplained, unexplored issues at the original scene of death. All of these should've been investigated at the time but were ignored. I won't bother explaining them now; I'll e-mail a complete dossier after this call. We also have an uninvestigated car at the scene. We've looked into this particular car hire. It appeared to have either been hired by a known American gun dealer or a German gentleman we've traced to Berlin. So far we've taken no further action for fear of frightening them off until we're ready. It's also come to light that Peter Urbawicz had made enemies of two separate individuals that we should investigate. One a known IRA man, the other a name I think you'll be familiar with: Jean-Luc Batise." Lancaster was aware of the sound of crunching toast coming to a standstill but carried on regardless.

"There are also aspects of the way the body was found after death that should have raised alarm bells, but somebody had removed the clangers, so to speak. I've sought permission from Lady Stottard for an exhumation of her father's body and she's given it. I have it now in writing. It'll form the final page of the report I'll e-mail, but she intends to telephone you to concur. We've more work to be done here. We've a meeting planned at the bank where Peter was senior partner, to investigate the two accounts that were held there in the names of the two individuals I mentioned previously. It may be these accounts are already known to UK officials, but if not, it could lead to the trail of two sizable chunks of money. One, destined for the IRA. The other, well that was Batise; I don't have to speculate what that money was intended for. I should stress though that at this moment in time, none of this definitely proves murder. But you asked us to come over here to see if the original investigation was sound. The answer is a definite no. At the end of the day, sir, it's your shout, but when you read the file, I think you'll agree with our findings."

There was silence on the other end of the line. As was often the case with calls to his boss, Lancaster knew he was still there, brain ticking, cogs whirring. Craven would reply when good and ready. Pamela walked into the room and went to speak, but Lancaster put his finger to his lips in a request for silence and, a moment later, Craven replied.

"You know I have to clear this on high, so what do you want from me right now, Bomber?"

"Several things really, sir. I'll put them as an attachment with the e-mail I send but basically, I need you if possible, to get hold of whoever can release Rover from general duty at Derriford Hospital and get the ball rolling. I'll call him and forewarn him. I also request you keep the lid on this until I give you the nod. Lady Stottard wants to warn her mother before the shit hits the fan. And if you could, sir, would you speak to Counter Terrorism and find out what you can about an Irishman called Sean Devlin? Again, details are in the file. Finally, could you find out what's the latest from Interpol on any suspected whereabouts of Batise?"

"You sound as if you're presuming I'll be going ahead with all this?"

"No disrespect meant, sir... But to be honest... You taught me most of what I know and when you look at the file, I know you'll reach the same conclusion. So, unless some other political reason comes up that would call a halt to another enquiry, I won't be packing for home any time soon... Sir." He added respectfully.

"E-mail me within the next five minutes, Bomber. And ask Lady Stottard to call me as soon as. We'll speak later, don't bugger off to the beach." With that, he abruptly disconnected.

Lancaster relayed Craven's request to Pamela and she left the room for her study to make the call. Lancaster wasn't planning on 'buggering off to the beach' but was more than ready for breakfast and a cup of tea, but first, he had to send Craven the dossier.

Thirty minutes later, they were gathered around the kitchen table drinking tea and ladling copious dollops of plum jam across the torn insides of fresh croissants. Lancaster's e-mail had been acknowledged by his boss. Pamela had had a long conversation with Craven and had pre-empted his belief that the request to reopen the enquiry would have to be taken higher. Earlier that morning, prior to Lancaster making his call to 'the boss', she'd called the High Sheriff of Devon at his private address and relayed the chain of events that had taken place over the previous two days. She'd also relayed the fact that Lancaster would be speaking to DCI Craven with a view to reopening the enquiry. It was only a matter of time before Craven took the request to his superiors. A nudge from higher up the food chain might help move the thing on a pace. The High Sheriff, an old family friend, was only too pleased to oblige. Pamela felt that by the time Craven had read the report and confirmed justification for a new enquiry, he'd be receiving permission before he even asked for it. Pamela had told Craven all this in her call to help him come to the right decision, should he need any help.

Lancaster laughed. How the wiles of the high and mighty work. A phone call here, an e-mail there, a drink in the right club could pull so many strings and change the course of somebody's future. Pamela heard the scoffing laugh and knew what it was directed at.

"Do you have a problem with my actions, David?"

"No. No, of course not, Pamela,." he said, not wanting to upset her or be disrespectful. But he couldn't let it go. His dyspraxia needed to shake this bone. "I just wonder why DS Vidêt and I are here. All you had to do was take your concerns to the High Sheriff and DCI Craven and they'd have reopened it for you. You didn't need us here at all."

Pamela sat quietly, a look of hurt on her face. Lancaster felt sorry he was the cause of this. But it was too late now. The dyspraxic within him, his inability to know when to shut up, had been stirred. It had been said.

"You do yourself and Marie a great disservice, David. Yes, I could have brought pressure to bear in high places, have the verdict of accidental death overturned and a new enquiry launched. But who would have carried that out? It would have stayed here on the island; the verdict would have stayed. If this case was to be taken seriously it had to be looked at by somebody trustworthy, somebody who'd not be swayed by the 'high and mighty' or by pressure of authority. I watched the way you worked through the Abdul Mehemet case. It didn't matter to you that it involved a knight of the realm and his wife. You weren't put off by the effect that any proven involvement of my husband would have had on me or his sons. You worked your way into my ex-husband's flat in London, without a warrant I might add. You managed to access the home of Piers Ward and get him to tell you his life story. You stuck your nose into every crevice you could find and didn't give a damn if you had permission or not. I knew you two were the people who'd look at this case with a non-judgemental eye and come to your own conclusion. Was I wrong?"

"I apologise, Pamela. I was disrespectful. I shouldn't have said what I did. No, you're not wrong. Between the two of us, we're the right people to be looking at this. Marie, for her organisational skills and observance. Me, for my big mouth, which for most of the time has my foot wedged in it."

Marie and Pamela laughed; the moment of disharmony broken. All were aware that what Lancaster had said was fact.

His dyspraxic tendencies often meant he spoke out of turn. He could often say the wrong thing, in the wrong place, at the wrong time and often managed to do all three with gay abandon. Sometimes with absolutely no idea that he'd just done so. But that was his life; others had to get used to it.

Pamela had arranged a meeting at Les Banque des Isles with two of the major shareholders who were also senior managers. Before they left for that meeting, Lancaster was keen to contact Ben Landy, 'Rover' as everyone knew him. Lancaster scrolled through his contacts, found him and went straight for the 'call' button.

"Ben Landy, who's calling?" the voice said abruptly.

"Bloody hell, Rover, are you having a bad day?" Lancaster asked, surprised by the other man's abruptness. "Is my name no longer on your caller ID, mate? Have I been cast aside like an old sock? It's DI Lancaster."

"Bomber! Sorry, mate. I got a new phone," the man replied. "You know what it's like; doesn't matter how easy they claim it'll be, I got a new phone, retained the same number, swapped the sim and for some reason, lost half my contacts; you were obviously one of the ones to get scrapped. What can I do for you... Sir?"

Lancaster outlined the situation, explaining the need for secrecy, made him aware that Craven would be pulling strings behind the scenes as they spoke and that the case hadn't gone live but he was adamant it would before close of play that day. Rover started to ask questions with regards to the case but Lancaster put a block on that; he wanted him fresh of mind when he arrived, not having jumped to any conclusions. Rover said he'd start transferring items from his diary. As luck would have it, they'd recently taken on another consultant pathologist. Rover was confident the jobs on the board could be carried out by his second. Once he had the go-ahead he could be on the island within days. Lancaster told him to start packing, get his house in order and key his number back into the contacts list.

Pamela drove them to the bank. It was cunningly non-descript, looked decidedly private and blended expertly into the street. The construction was a normal office building with all the upper floor windows tinted. No fancy stonework, no ornate door, no sign saying 'Bank'. The only sign of any sort was a small brass plaque, the name engraved in simple text, 'Les Banque des Isles'. Access through the door was by intercom. Directly above the intercom, raised two feet above the buzzer, Lancaster could see a camera. Pamela stepped up to the buzzer, made the call, was instantly recognised and buzzed in. A young woman appeared through a door at the rear of the vestibule. She greeted Pamela with a double kiss and a simple hug.

"*Bonjour*, Pamela," she said. "Good to see you, is your mother well?"

"So-so, Madeline, at least she is still happy and smiling," Pamela replied. "Are they ready for us upstairs?"

"Of course, come on up." She led them up a red-carpeted stairway lined with photos and portraits. Madeline trotted up ahead of them in her high heels, covering ground like a mountain goat. At the top floor, they were shown through another door, into a large, panelled room, down the centre of which sat a huge, oval, equally ornate, deeply polished table. At the top end of this, two elderly, well-suited gentlemen both stood as the newcomers entered.

"Pamela, so good to see you," one said, coming around the table to greet her with great affection. "How is Brigitte?"

"Good morning, Max," Pamela replied, giving the older man a return hug and brief kiss on his cheek. "Mother's doing well, thank you; she said to say thank you for the flowers on her birthday; they were lovely. And *bonjour*, Paul, *comment vas-tu aujourd'hui*?" Paul was obviously unsteady on his feet and stayed beside his chair, one hand braced on top of an elaborate silver-topped cane. Pamela rounded the table and gave him a hug also, helping him to sit back down again in his leather, high-backed chair.

"I'm made young again in your presence, my dear," he replied. "It's so good to see you; you must come and see us more often. We miss you."

Pamela made formal introductions. This time there was no illusion of secrecy. Both detectives were introduced for what they were, incognito police from the mainland acting on Pamela's behalf to relaunch the investigation into her father's death.

"Max told me of this last night on the telephone," Paul said. "You are serious about this, Pamela? You actually believe Peter was murdered?"

"Yes, I'm serious, Paul. I said at the time it happened that I couldn't believe it was an accident, but no one would listen. Everybody patted me on the head and said 'there, there', as if I was some demented schoolchild. But I've always believed the verdict was wrong."

"Detective Lancaster, what are your views on this scenario?"

Max Devaux asked.

"I've sent a detailed analysis of the case to my superiors in Plymouth," Lancaster replied. "In it I've recommended reopening the case. I'm not at liberty at the moment to divulge any further information than that but suffice to say, we've found enough inconsistencies in the original enquiry and enough missed evidence to make us all think the case needs a proper investigation to prove either way. As we speak, wheels are in motion in the UK to make a formal application to the senior coroner on Jersey to exhume Peter's body and bring over our own pathologist to carry out a fresh post-mortem."

"What bearing does this post-mortem have on the investigation of our files? What do we have to do with it?" Paul Bedot asked haughtily. "You must know our client confidentiality is sacrosanct; it's what makes us a safe place to bank."

Lancaster bit his tongue. Being a safe place to bank was probably what had got their partner murdered. And God only knows what other criminals were stashing ill-gotten gains in this 'safe bank'. But he needed them on-side, so said nothing of what was going through his mind. Vidêt could see the look of frustration on Lancaster's face and stepped in before he could possibly speak his mind.

"It's our belief, Mr Bedot, that two of your former clients," Vidêt cut in calmly but politely. "A Mr Devlin and a Mr Jean-Luc Batise both had accounts closed down by Peter due to doubts about their legitimacy. One of these, Jean-Luc Batise, is known to us and is in fact on an Interpol wanted list. The other, Sean Devlin, is being looked into at this very moment with regard to his possible connections with the IRA. Both of these men would be dangerous individuals to annoy and if murder is proven, they would come straight to the top of our list as suspects." She looked to Lancaster as an apology for the interruption and received a smile in return.

"Pamela said you wanted details about these clients," Max Devaux said. "Do you have anybody else with accounts that you'd like to see?"

"Well, now you mention it," Lancaster replied. "I'd be interested to know if you've any dealings or accounts in the name of Paul Steiner, a German gentleman from Berlin, and a Mr Levon Shawbuck, an American from Pennsylvania. Both of these appear in our files for one reason or another at about the same time as Peter's death. I'd be intrigued to find out if they had any connection with either the bank or Peter himself. It's a long shot but it's still worth a try."

Max pressed the intercom. Madeline entered carrying two folders. She handed these to Max who glanced at the wording on the cover, then slid them across the table in Lancaster's direction. He asked Madeline to search for anything on the two other men Lancaster had enquired about, print it out and bring it up as soon as possible. Lancaster asked if they could take the paperwork back to Pamela's and study it fully. This made Paul Bedot visibly twitch.

"I don't think that's a good idea, Detective Lancaster," the man said. "We have a reputation to uphold here. We can't be seen to hand out client's information as easily as that; this isn't Facebook. This whole process is a very private affair and must stay so."

"For God's sake, Paul," Max said loudly. "Please... Shut up... To my knowledge, these two clients are no longer that, clients. We closed their accounts years ago and told them not to darken our doors again. In fact, technically, they broke the contract of secrecy with us, so do not have a legitimate say in the matter. It was a long time ago but I'm sure both of them were bringing the bank into disrepute when we asked them to remove their assets, so let the detectives take the files. I'm sure Pamela will vouch for their safe return." He looked to her for confirmation. "It's occurred to me, Pamela," Max continued. "That the upper echelons of bank management were just as guilty of originally taking these clients on. So sadly, if it's proven either of these people were guilty of being involved in the death of Peter, then we carry some of the burden of blame. That saddens me greatly. I had a great fondness for your father as you know; I won't be happy until I know either way if his death was accidental or if one of our clients had any involvement."

Lancaster briefly opened the first of the folders and had a quick glance at its contents. They included two screen grabs from the doorway CCTV. One of which was a clear, detailed photo of a man in a hooded, waterproof jacket. Hood up. Face looking straight at the camera, one arm outstretched. A single digit of his right hand extended accusingly. He looked at the picture for a second before realising that the camera must be hidden as part of the outside intercom key-pad. He'd seen the other, discreet but obvious camera, set in the wall above the intercom. So of course, would everybody else. Those who wished to avoid its observation need only look down or straight ahead to remain unrecorded on film. But cunningly, anyone who wished access had to press the buzzer and were therefore recorded for posterity.

Lancaster flicked to the cover note. Devlin. (Sean). Devlin Groundworks & Construction. He quickly looked at the other folder. On the front, it said, Batise. (Jean). Ocean Yachts. Lancaster flicked the cover open. There was a similar photograph of Jean-Luc Batise staring at the camera, finger extended. Eyes shielded by dark glasses. He looked at the picture for a moment before passing the open dossier to Vidêt. She picked it up and looked at it. Lancaster watched her reaction. As with him, she flicked the cover shut to double-check the name, then flicked it open to look at the photo. She glanced at Lancaster who shook his head, enough to tell her to say nothing. Vidêt closed the file and handed it back.

"Why do you have pictures of your clients?" Lancaster posed the question openly to both men.

"Please, Inspector," Max Devaux said. "We run a private banking service. We need to be aware of who enters our building, but in case of any problems with clients, it's convenient to know when they arrive and when they depart. It is also very handy to have a record of who our clients actually are. It will also be a convenient source of photographic evidence should the police have need of it," he said with a slight smile.

Lancaster closed the folder, resting his hand upon them both, laying claim to their presence. He was about to stand and make ready to leave when a double knock on the door was followed by the entrance of Madeline, holding yet another folder.

"Sorry to disturb, but I thought you might need this," she said, handing the file to Max. "We've absolutely nothing on file or hard drive referring to Mr Steiner, but we've done business with Mr Shawbuck. We opened an account for him in 1988. It's still active and accessed by him. I've downloaded all the details, though for some reason there appears to be a problem with stored information on the hard drive. Somebody's put a password access-only attachment on it, so chunks of info are at present not available to us. The tech guys think somebody 'cocked up' when uploading data, but they're working on it. The rest I've printed out, including dates, accumulated finances and a current balance."

Lancaster's heart skipped a beat. That gave him four 'persons of interest' to investigate. It was time to go home and study this new information and search for relevance where possible. They said their thanks and goodbyes and left, with promises from Madeline that as soon as the tech department had broken the password and got access to the 'lost' detail regarding the Shawbuck account, they'd forward it. Lancaster was like a kid going home from a trip to the toyshop. He couldn't wait to get back and open the presents. Pamela went through the prolonged hugs and kisses expected in a semi-French social environment and they headed for home.

CHAPTER FOUR

During the drive back to the house Lancaster received a call from Craven. He picked up and said they were driving; he'd call back. Once they'd pulled into the parking area, Lancaster returned the call.

"Bomber, not down on the beach with the bucket and spade then?"

Lancaster was never sure why they had to go through this jovial, jokey phase before getting to the 'nitty-gritty' of whatever needed to be said.

"Just returned from an interesting meeting at Les Banque des Isles," he replied, cutting through the nonsense. "We've just got back to the house to read through files and extract whatever's of interest. What have you managed to find out for us, sir?"

"First and foremost, Sean Devlin. Step away from the 'oche', my old mate. He's not a person of interest as far as you're concerned."

There was silence on Lancaster's end of the line, which Craven had been expecting and made space for before reiterating the point.

"He's to be left well alone, is that understood?"

"Am I allowed to ask why, sir?" Lancaster asked. Having a

reasonable idea of what the answer was going to be.

"Of course, you're allowed to ask, but obviously I won't be telling you. Suffice to say, Bomber, just do as I ask and back away from him, pretend you haven't ever heard of him. Just concentrate on everybody else you've come across."

"And if we eliminate everyone else and the only one left is Devlin?"

"Then the verdict could turn out to be murder by 'persons unknown'. That's if it turns out to be murder. You still have to prove that."

"With all due respect, sir..." Lancaster started.

"With all due respect noted, Bomber, you've been told. Now leave it."

"But I have a right to know if this is just an order from on high or something else, sir. I'm going to have to tell Lady Stottard something."

"To be honest, you don't have to tell her bugger all."

"Can I quote you on that, sir?"

"Don't be a 'twat', Bomber. Look, all I will say is this. You asked me to speak to Counter Terrorism about your man Devlin. I did. Now leave it."

"That's all I needed to know, sir. I just needed to know what department the clamp-down was coming from. Now I know."

"Bomber... Bloody let it go... Leave it, and that's an order," Craven said in desperation.

"Of course, sir. What's the news on Batise?"

"Absolutely nothing," Craven replied. Glad to have moved on from Devlin, but not confident Lancaster was planning to obey his instructions. "Interpol have him popping up two years ago in the Cayman Islands but even that was brief and uncertain. He appeared last year in Paris and was followed for two days before giving them the slip. Since then, nothing, so he could be anywhere by now."

"Did you manage to pick up any 'intel' on Paul Steiner?"

"An interesting find, Bomber," Craven said. "From what we picked up from... Wait for it, the *Bundespolizei*! That's the German Federal Police to you and me. They're not keen on your man Steiner. Not from any criminal activity or anything, but apparently, before the wall came down, your man was from East Berlin. He was in the Stasi, the secret police. By all accounts they were bastards. I mean it wasn't just the West and spies who didn't like them, everybody hated them. It's as if they got a bonus for being a bastard. The more people they stitched up the better. Once the communists lost the plot and the wall came down, he managed to get a job in the new German police force as a CID officer but it didn't last; he brought too much Stasi to the role. Didn't take too well being told to stop beating people up. He ended up being given early retirement with a state pension and told to piss off out of it. He still lives in the same house in East Berlin he was given by the state when he joined the Stasi."

"Any ideas as to what his business was on Jersey?"

"Nothing on the radar; that's your job, pretend you're a detective. My guess would be he stitched up so many people during his time he managed to stash funds. Once the wall came down, he probably needed somewhere to invest his retirement fund, chose Jersey for the same reasons other people did, the 'no questions asked' business. He's probably taken it out of the country in small amounts. Although he might not have banked it with your bank; it's not the only one on the island, so get digging."

"What about Shawbuck?"

"Well, according to the FBI, who were a bit sniffy about us asking, he is what he is. A gun-shop owner from Philadelphia, Pennsylvania, USA. He's small scale, does steady business. Local supportive member of his church, runs a gun club in his spare time. They'd nothing much to report. He was married but his wife died of cancer ten years ago and he's been on his own ever since. FBI have him leaving the country quite often but they don't have a problem with it. He went to gun fairs, conventions and various places on holiday. They were a bit surprised about Jersey as a destination, mainly because they had no idea where it was. When I told them it was actually part of the UK, they were even more confused. Either way they didn't have him visiting the place, so he must have decided to visit as part of his trips to the UK, so that might need looking into."

Lancaster was scribbling notes as fast as he could. He'd piece it all together when he had a chance. He couldn't believe how much information they'd acquired during the last couple of days. It was going to take some sifting, sort the 'wheat from the chaff', but then that's what they were paid to do, it was the clever part. Craven went on to say that things were moving on the mainland. Rover would be released from hospital duties later that day and he'd join them once they'd got him a flight. As for the actual investigation, the whole enquiry was to be put to the Foreign Office later that day with a view to reopening the case.

"Just out of interest, sir, why the Foreign Office?"

"You need to Google it, my son. The relationship between the Channel Islands and the UK is a weird one. Your phone bill wouldn't cover the time to tell you how it works, needless to say, although the islands are what's known as British Crown Dependencies, the UK doesn't actually make the rules there. They have their own. Their own mini parliament. They can pick and choose what bits of British legislation they adopt and which to leave out. What's in our favour here is that Lady Stottard is a distinguished British figure and it's her father who died, and it's she and her mother who want the case reopened. She has dual recognition; her passport's registered as an islander but she is classed as a full British citizen. According to the Foreign Office, with regard to a UK government request to the Department of the Islands Coroner Office, as long as her mother supports her request for an exhumation and a new autopsy, along with a re-examination of the facts of the original case, there shouldn't be a problem. You have to be ready for the local police to be a bit grumpy, mind, they won't be happy with us sticking our nose in."

"To be honest, sir, although we'll need them when the exhumation takes place, I can't imagine they've got anything in their files that would add to our investigation. Hopefully, I can stay well clear of them for a while other than a courtesy call."

"Well, you just go gently, mate," Craven said. "We don't want to piss 'em off any more than we need to."

"I've a feeling, sir, that when they get wind of what we want to do, they'll be all over us like a rash. I'm hoping the Stottard name might carry some weight."

"I wouldn't hold your breath, Bomber. On a serious note, watch yourselves out there. It's not so far away as your trip to France but from what I recall, the locals on the island can be sneaky; they pull together and close ranks."

"I presume you'll give us the heads-up when it goes to the coroner's office?"

"You'll know as soon as I do, mate. Gotta go." Abrupt as usual, he rang off.

Lancaster sat in the car thinking through all that had been said, scribbling into his notebook. He was confident the case should be looked at again, but he knew he needed all his books in order, suspects identified and on file if they decided murder was on the cards. There mustn't be any delay in running up a list of 'Persons of Interest' if they expected assistance from the locals. If they found a weakness in his research, they'd be on him like a ton of bricks. Lancaster closed his notebook and followed the ladies into the house.

After lunch he gave Vidêt his notebook to copy up the notes in smarter order onto the iPad. He asked Pamela if she could use her influence to persuade either Max Devaux or Paul to contact other banks on the island and see if anybody else was providing an account for Steiner. There had to be good reason for him making several trips to the island during that year; banking would seem to be the most obvious. He also delegated Pamela to chat with Basil at Your-Hire and see if Steiner or Shawbuck had used them to hire a car since the 1st of September 2008. It had occurred to Lancaster that they'd set dates for the year of Peter's death but not looked after that time period. It would be interesting to find out if hirers in the time frame had stopped once the death had occurred or continued visiting the island on a regular basis. This might mean they were less obviously going to be involved in Peter's death. For his own part, Lancaster needed to blow some confusion from his brain. He needed a walk onto the headland in the hopes of pulling all this information back into perspective. He grabbed a coat and headed out into the breezy day.

His walk up the path and across the car park on the bluff certainly cleared the cobwebs. The breeze cut over the rabbit-trimmed grass that formed the tops of the semi-vertical cliff face. The air was filled with the scent of the sea and the cry of sea birds. To the left of the headland, where the path dropped away to 'Peter's Beach', Lancaster found an incline where he could sit and dangle his legs. Once settled into position his thoughts started to float to the surface. There was a lot to sift through and categorise. The problem was he found anger cast a fog across his train of thought; he tried to avoid it but didn't always succeed. At this moment in time, the thing that bugged him most was his inability to follow up leads on Sean Devlin. For various reasons, he hated the IRA. He hated the politics that hung around them like a flag, a flag of truce he didn't trust. 'The Troubles' were supposedly over, and there was a misnomer if ever he'd heard one: 'The Troubles'. Thousands of people were murdered in cold blood. Men, women, children and soldiers shot, blown up or disappeared. That was a 'War' not a 'Trouble'. But since it had been declared as over, there were murderers and bombers who'd acquired immunity from prosecution. It was part of the 'Peace Agreement', and Lancaster hated it. He hated anyone who got away with breaking the laws of humanity. He had a strong feeling Devlin fitted into this category. He knew in his heart-of-hearts that if he thought for one moment that Devlin was implicated in Peter's murder, he wouldn't be able to let it go. He wouldn't be 'stepping away'. He started to put the whiteboard up in his mind. The list of possible suspects had grown more than he thought it would when this whole thing began.

He now had Steiner. He wasn't sure how he fitted into the picture. Yes, the hire car timeline matched but he had no apparent connection with the islands and no apparent connection with Peter either. The thought crossing Lancaster's mind was that, knowing this man's employment history, could he be a professional hitman brought in because he was unknown to everybody? Was he employed either by Devlin or Batise, both of whom must have been pissed off at Peter for closing down their accounts.

And Shawbuck. Likewise, no direct link with either the islands or Peter. Could he be the killer? Employed by Devlin or Batise? He certainly had the right profile. Quiet gun shop owner from a quiet corner of a city. No record of criminal activity. Not on the FBI's radar. (Why did he not find that a surprise?) The fact he had an account on the island gave him cause for concern. *Why would an American gun shop owner come to the UK to bank cash? Aah... unless, of course, the cash was surplus to declared income. A pension stash maybe?*

Then there was Devlin. Lancaster's mind was tainted by the order to leave him alone. As far as Lancaster was concerned, this was the guy to put into the frame if the evidence appeared.

His biggest problem with this man was the gap between having his account closed and the death of Peter, nearly ten years between. *But if Devlin was in prison, that could explain not only the time difference but another reason for feeling the need to have Peter killed.*

Finally, Batise. Now this was interesting. It fitted much easier into the timeline. They knew he was a top-grade bad man; there were dead bodies all over Europe attributed to him. *He got his illegal cash account closed, then hired a hitman to come and make the point to everyone in the criminal world that you do not piss this man off.* But as both he and Vidêt now knew, they had a major problem with this man, but Lancaster would have to talk with her about that. He took one last look at the screaming seagulls, zipped his jacket and headed for the house and the inevitable pot of tea. He'd just started down the grass footpath beside the garden when Pamela walked up to meet him.

"I was just coming to find you, how was the sea air?" she said as she approached.

"Invigorating."

"I've managed to get Max to make enquiries amongst the banking fraternity with regards to Mr Steiner; he plans to ask around on the basis of suspected criminality of a client, that normally gets results if there are any. It's in everybody's interest to share information in the long run. He hopes to get back to us in the morning. I've also had a chat with Basil. He'll go through the books and see if Steiner or Shawbuck made return trips after September of '08. More importantly, there's a pot of tea made and ready for pouring."

Lancaster laughed. "So they're all on the case, Pamela. A veritable nest of detectives. If we don't turn something up soon, then there can't be anything to find."

"But you and I know full well, DI Lancaster, there's plenty to find and we'll find it soon."

Pamela linked her arm through his and the two of them headed for the kitchen and tea. Vidêt was sitting at the breakfast bar with Josette, both chatting in French. It was strange hearing Marie speak her native language again after their trip to France earlier that year. Lancaster liked the lyrical sound as it rolled off her tongue. She spoke with a deeper voice when speaking French. There was something exotic about it; it made English sound cumbersome. Josette poured two more cups then bid '*Au revoir*' and made a discreet exit. Lancaster felt uneasy about Josette's subservient role being so blatantly obvious but 'her house, her rules'.

"So where are we with everything?" Pamela asked. "What did DCI Craven have to say if I'm allowed to know?"

Lancaster filled her in with regards to the imminent arrival of Rover, explaining how the man had gone from Ben Landy to being called Rover. He added that enquiries into Devlin were ongoing. That conversations with the FBI in America had found nothing untoward in Shawbuck's history, though they were surprised he'd visited the Channel Islands as the FBI had no idea where they were. He also told them of their man Steiner and his Stasi background, hence Lancaster's request to find out if he was banking somewhere on the island or if visits the year of Peter's death were a one-off. Next, he told her about the plan to contact the Foreign Office and get the ball rolling for an exhumation and autopsy. He explained how the process worked here on the islands. Something, if truth be told, he didn't understand himself, but Pamela appeared to be fully aware of.

She was concerned things were dragging. Lancaster reminded her it was only day three. Already they'd achieved more than had been discovered previously, and the island coroner would be hearing from the UK government representative sometime that day. It would gain momentum and could all go 'pear-shaped', they might wish for a return to this period when they controlled the pace. Pamela left for an afternoon nap, announcing that this evening she was taking them to her favourite restaurant, a table booked for 7:30 p.m. The dress code was smart casual, which was convenient, as neither Lancaster nor Vidêt had packed for anything more. Pamela's departure was fortuitous; both parties needed to discuss issues they felt unable to pass on to their host. First, Vidêt was bursting to pass on information she'd discovered during Lancaster's afternoon stroll.

"I have to tell you what I have spotted," she said, as soon as Pamela was out of earshot. "I called the bank and got Madeline to e-mail me screen grabs from the keypad CCTV to add to our file on Shawbuck. I thought we should have some idea of what he looked like while we waited for Craven to get something from the FBI. I have done some Photoshop work on the picture to make it clearer, they are not the best images but come up well with the police software I'm using. I put the pictures through the same set-up and got them to match in size and shading. Look what I've found, tell me what you see?"

She handed two A4 sized photos to Lancaster who held them up as a pair.

Lancaster couldn't make any instant connection. Until he noticed the little 'nick' taken out of the lower edge of the left earlobe in one photo. Then like the 'spot-the-difference' pairings from a quiz book, he realised both characters possessed the same feature. It was clear in one photo, but in the other, the face had longer, darker hair, met on either side of the face with a full beard and sideburns. If it hadn't been for the fact that in the second picture, the face was turned slightly to the right, in half profile, setting the left ear into silhouette, it wouldn't have been spotted. It was unlikely that two men, the same height and build, would have the same piece missing from their ear; it wasn't impossible, but was highly unlikely.

"Marie, I could kiss you," Lancaster said staring at the photos in front of him.

"Well, don't let me stop you," she said in reply.

"Behave. It was a figure of speech."

"Shame on you, bringing speech into it," she replied, with a smile.

"Seriously though, this is brilliant, I'd never have noticed that earlobe if you hadn't highlighted it. I wonder what caused it. Maybe a bullet."

"I think he's lost an earring," Vidêt offered, saddened that the proffered kiss would not materialise. "My brother looked like that after he started working on the trawlers. He came home with a gold hoop earring. My father ripped it out. When he cried, my father said, 'Now imagine you've just had a bar fight and burst into tears; I've done you a favour'. After it healed that's what it looked like."

"Right again, Marie, bloody brilliant," he replied. He turned the pictures over and read the names Marie had written on the backs. He knew who they were going to be when he picked them up; he'd seen one of them before in the file given to him in the bank. What he was looking at were pictures of Sean Devlin and Levon Shawbuck, or in fact... Just Sean Devlin... Complete with a chunk removed from his ear. Then later, wearing a disguise or at least having grown a beard and his hair, dying both black.

"So why did you not want to speak of Devlin when Pamela was here?"

"DCI Craven has forbidden it," he said looking at her for a reaction.

"What do you mean forbidden?" she said looking amazed.

"Apparently, he's spoken to Counter Terrorism. They've told us not to investigate, enquire or pursue the man in any shape or form whatsoever. In fact, we are to forget we've ever heard of the man."

"Is he a spy?" Vidêt asked. A touch dismayed.

"Better than that, Marie," Lancaster continued this time with a touch of the anger rising. "He's a bloody IRA terrorist. I suspect one of the scum-bags given immunity when our government signed the Northern Ireland Peace Accord back in 1998."

"I know of this agreement. But why does he get immunity if he is involved in Peter's murder? This is a new murder, not a terrorist attack; why should he be free from arrest?"

"Because the powers-that-be, say so, Marie," he replied

with a smirk on his face. "So that's all there is to it. We mustn't spend any more time on this man, agreed?"

"I cannot believe that you of all people," she said, with venom in her Gaelic accent, which shone through when angry. "I cannot believe you would let authority tell you what to do. *C'est incroyable... incroyable.*"

Lancaster's smile annoyed her even more.

"Why do you find this funny?" she asked barely holding back her anger.

"Let me stop this before it gets out of hand," he replied, holding up both hands. "My boss has been told by his boss to tell us, that's you and I, that we are not to investigate in any way the man known as Sean Devlin. So we will not," he said, holding his hands up yet again to stop Vidêt from interrupting. "But thanks to you and your brilliant photographic investigation... We can now investigate... Levon Shawbuck... As long as we tell no one of these photos' existence... At least for the moment."

Vidêt looked at him with a smile on her face. She liked this man. He had a sick sense of humour and trod his own strange path, despite what he was told to do, even if the path he was about to tread was 'in part' following the instructions of his boss, it would lead to trouble in the end, they both knew it. But for her part she also knew Lancaster would say he'd ordered her to follow this line of enquiry should it come to it.

"So, before we stop asking questions about Sean Devlin," she asked. "What do we actually know about the man?"

"Nothing. I say nothing when what I mean is, not a lot. We know he's suspected of being an arms dealer, possibly a banker for the IRA. Now, given the Counter Terror boys' order to leave him alone, I'm bloody certain it's true. We know he dropped off-screen the moment his bank account got frozen, which reminds me, we must find out what happened to that account, but anyway, he dropped off the radar in 1987. It would've been good to know where he went then but I don't think we'll get that information now. But at some stage, he reappears as Levon Shawbuck."

"In actual fact, he only drops off the radar for a couple of months," she replied. "According to paperwork from the bank, an account was opened for him in January 1988. The account was accessed remotely once during that month, all other details are then unavailable as shortly after that, somebody placed a limited access password activation code on all details, so we don't know if it was used regularly or not. From the paperwork, when it was opened it had a lump-sum deposit of £600,000. Just over half a million so not 'peanuts', and before you ask, I've cross-referenced with Devlin's account. A month or two before his account was frozen, he had just under half a mil' in there, so my guess would be that whoever he was working for when the account was stopped had another opened in the name of Shawbuck. Then transferred the Devlin account, via another handling account in the UK, an account I can't track as the account number, sort code, etc. do not appear to exist any longer. Then after the money settled for a month or so, they topped it up for his troubles, transferred the new amount to the Shawbuck account and promptly closed down the handling account, thereby making it almost impossible to trace a definite connection between the two. What I have done, is get Pamela to ask Max if the bank can contact HMRC in the

UK and see if they've any knowledge of the handling account. It's not an unusual request from a bank. They have to be on the alert for 'money-laundering' scams so it shouldn't flag up any worries when they get the request. They may ask why the question's come up after so many years, but Max will just say they're carrying out an audit and the account cropped up, again, not unusual."

"You've beaten me to it again, Marie, cross-referencing Devlin was to be my next request, so well done. Our next problem is Batise."

"Ah, which Batise did you mean?" Vidêt asked. "The one we have a photo of from the bank or the one you and I have seen on the Interpol Wanted page?"

"Exactly. What do we do about that? It would appear that either there are two Jean-Luc Batises or one of the pictures is wrong. What do you think's going on?"

"It's one of two things," she replied. "Either the person we know as Jean-Luc Batise is the real man and he's using a different man to operate the banking side of things or it's the other way round. He's using a frontman to do all the face-to-face drug business, which would make sense. That's where the danger lies. Then he, the real Jean Batise, manages the 'suited' stuff. Opening bank accounts and getting Chris Warren to work the currency exchange deals. That way dirty money was coming into the bank and being exchanged for... Well... Virtually any other currency he wanted. That way he always knew what cash was available at any given time. That would account for why Interpol couldn't find him. They're passing around a photo of someone who may even be dead by now,

126

whilst the real Batise is splashing the cash all over the world."

Lancaster agreed. It was by far the most logical chain of events and would account for why, during the original smuggling investigation, the main man cropped up in surveillance photos. He'd been easy to spot in a group. When this enquiry was done, it would be good to get the old files out and see if there was any sign of their new Batise in the background of old photos. It would be just like the man to crop up some time, just to watch from the side-lines.

The conversation was interrupted by the arrival of Pamela returning from her 'power nap', curtailed earlier than anticipated, slumber broken by a call from Max Devaux. He had news. Firstly, there didn't appear to be anybody on the island operating an account for Steiner. He was confident that if anybody had, they'd have come clean. Secondly, Max had made enquiries at HMRC with regard to the Devlin account and its handling account. Initially they were quite helpful, saying they'd look into it and get back to him, which they did quite quickly, to say they were unable to help in this instance and thank you for calling. Thirdly. The tech boys at the bank had been attempting to break the password access for the Shawbuck account when it froze and disappeared. Obviously, the account is still there but at the moment nobody could gain access. Lancaster and Vidêt feigned a lack of interest in this news but thanked Pamela very much for the update. Both of them were thinking the same thing. Devlin/Shawbuck was a protected man, but as yet, nobody had warned them off Shawbuck.

Pamela left them, reminding them they were eating out and

leaving the house at 7:00 p.m. She'd a taxi booked. Once she'd gone back upstairs, they passed their views to one another. They were now positive that the Devlin money had been removed from the original account, turned around, boosted and rebanked under the Shawbuck account. It was obviously payment for something, but what? They both agreed it was something that for today they should withhold from Pamela. Lancaster confessed to needing a quick bit of shut-eye prior to departure, so both detectives went upstairs to their separate rooms.

An hour and a half later, after a short sleep followed by a shower and shave, Lancaster put on a pair of chinos, topped it with a short-sleeved shirt, ran a comb through his hair, then taking a blazer with him, knocked on Vidêt's door and heard her call, "Come in". He stepped inside to find her sitting at her dressing table. She was in the process of installing a pair of beautiful, long, Celtic-motif earrings, twists and curls of silver wire and in the centre were a pair of pale blue, glazed roundels. The colour of the roundels perfectly matched the stunning, pale blue dress that she wore.

Lancaster realised that, as so often, they'd become embroiled in the minutiae of detail and characters revealed by their research, that their 'by agreement', casual relationship had lapsed into liaisons. He'd always been this way. The case became all-consuming, with little room left for anything else. Looking at Marie he couldn't understand how he'd possibly allowed that to happen. Vidêt looked back at him through the mirror.

"Stop it," she said, noticing that he wasn't looking at her

face. "That is very ungallant, sir," she continued with a smile. "I may have to report you for sexual harassment."

"I don't believe, Sergeant Vidêt, that I sexually harassed you at any time."

"I know... But there is still plenty of time," she said, with an exaggerated French accent, a pouting expression on her face. It was in unguarded moments like these, when not sifting through facts and evidence or checking through files, that Lancaster had time to appreciate just how incredibly good-looking this lady was. Short, cropped, jet-black hair enhanced by the simple blue dress she wore, setting off the long tanned, fine-muscled lines of her legs. When she stood up, he realised the dress hem was quite short. This just extended the length of her legs. She'd be turning heads in that restaurant tonight; he was sure of that. She crossed to where he was standing and rising on her toes, leant toward him closing her lips, glazed by a little lipstick, just a little. As Lancaster readied himself for a taste of her lips on his, she lightly side-stepped around him, removed a long-sleeved cardigan from the back of the bedroom door and bent briefly to grab a pair of high-heeled shoes off the floor before saying with a saucy smile,

"Shall we go, we don't want to be late?" Opening the door to let him go first.

Downstairs, Pamela was waiting.

"Well, my, my, don't you two scrub up well," she said as they entered the kitchen. "You make me feel veritably shabby."

Lancaster thought this very sweet, but also ridiculous when he saw how glamorous she looked. She threw a pashmina around her shoulders and headed out the front door, where the taxi was parked. Pamela insisted she and Vidêt jump in the back and Lancaster take the front passenger seat. In no time at all they were at the restaurant and Pamela made arrangements for a return journey later.

Friday night, the place was busy. The manager greeted Pamela like an old friend, Lancaster and Vidêt were introduced as friends from the UK. They were shown to a bay window table, through which they could see the harbour, with yachts and fishing boats bobbing on the incoming tide. Pamela asked if the two detectives liked seafood. They replied in the affirmative. She suggested a 'Seafood Tier', a picture of which was on the menu. It consisted of a tall, metal cake-stand, but instead of cakes, it held a collection of seafood. A lobster, crayfish, a large red crab, mussels, oysters and dishes filled with prawns. Vidêt had indulged in these seafood mountains back in Brittany and loved the idea; for Lancaster it was new. A culinary adventure and Pamela was paying. They went for it.

They settled on olives, home-baked bread and dips to keep them going whilst their 'Tier' was formed. The restaurant was busy, Lancaster could see every table was full; a good sign of the meal to come. He watched as two young men entered and looked around the room but were met by the manager who informed them with a very friendly smile, that he'd no further space and wished them well for a table the next night should they wish to book. A waiter arrived, uncorked their bottle, lit candles and then poured.

Pamela raised her glass and encouraged them to do likewise. After saying they should have a proper night off and not talk shop at all, she proposed a toast,

"To new-found friends," which they drank to willingly.

Lancaster had arrived on the island as an incognito police officer almost employed by Lady Stottard, with a standoffish suspicion of her reasons. But without a doubt, he'd grown to like her. Pamela was funny, warm and generous. She was a smart, clever lady, dedicated to finding out the truth about her father's death. He admired her for that. He genuinely believed that if he proved Peter's death was in fact an accident, she'd accept it. Not happily. But she would accept it. But his forever trusty friend 'gut-feeling' told him otherwise. There was a case to answer here, of that, he was sure.

On Lancaster's left sat Marie. She was thinking almost the same. When she'd arrived on the island, she'd come willingly as a sergeant to her boss and, if the truth be known, though she hated to admit it this early in their relationship, she'd at the moment, follow him almost anywhere. She'd also come as an unusual kind of employee to Lady Stottard, who appeared to have some kind of controlling factor on Lancaster's boss, DCI Craven. She had no idea what the controlling factor amounted to; she didn't want to know. She'd become embroiled in office politics in the past and didn't want to go there again anytime soon. She was aware her relationship with Pamela had blossomed. Pamela had shown no 'airs and graces'. She'd been funny, warm, quick-witted and smart; something Marie admired. She'd also felt the woman was vulnerable. Slightly lost, lonely and in need of a friend and confidant. She appeared to have lost faith and lost trust in her own kind. Lost the belief, if she'd ever believed it, that money was the cure for everything. It was so obviously not.

The 'Seafood Tier' arrived, preceded by a waiter who cloaked all three of them in large, full frontal, blue plastic, sleeved aprons, which had them in hysterics as they put them on. Like small children at a messy play session, but who'd then been kitted out with 'claw crushers' and crab-meat pickers, making them look like they were in a mad professor's operating theatre. Lancaster joked, all they needed now was for Rover to walk in, blue rubber gloves on, and the scene would be complete. The trio spent over an hour crushing, snapping and picking their way through the mountain of food, to the extent that a waiter had to come twice to empty the buckets of debris and discarded carapace that gathered beside the table. Another bottle of wine disappeared after the first, and they were well into their third before a final search of the mound before them proved they were, in fact, done. Their feast of seafood was over. As the waiters came to clear away what was left and help them out of their 'play-suits' as Lancaster called them, the rest of the clientele in the room gave them a round of applause.

Dessert arrived courtesy of the manager: three raspberry tartlets. Glazed and singed with flame. Accompanied by a light, flavoursome sorbet and a glass of dessert wine. This proved to be the finale. Not only of the meal but Lancaster's ability to drink anymore. He was aware his vision was starting to blur and also of all the other conversations going on throughout the room, other than the one he was apparently having with Pamela across the table. The evening came to a close when the manager came to advise them their taxi was waiting. Pamela settled the bill. Lancaster helped wrap Pamela in her pashmina and then held Marie's cardigan for her to slip her arms into. He opened the door for the ladies and once outside, instinctively reached for and received Marie's hand without thinking. They giggled and laughed their way back to the house, the taxi dropping them to the front door. As Lancaster was holding the door for Marie, they were momentarily illuminated by a car's headlights sweeping across the front of the house as another vehicle went past the top of the drive, continuing up the road in the direction of the point and the lonely car park. Lancaster smiled as he thought of the courting couple parking up on the bluff.

The three made their way into the house, all 'slightly tipsy' as Lancaster's mother would've said. Brandy night-caps were declined. After goodnight hugs and thanks for a lovely evening, they all retired to their rooms. Lancaster took the opportunity of being alone with Marie at the top of the semi-dark landing to turn Marie toward him. Stroking her hair away from her eyes, he gave her a long goodnight kiss, replied with vigour by his partner, who broke away and stepped through the door of her room with a little wave, closing the door quietly behind her.

Lancaster came out of his bathroom to find the main lights turned off and the bedside light turned on, illuminating Marie, half under the covers, propped up on one elbow, head resting on her hand, wearing a black, shiny, silk nightdress of some kind and a wide smile.

"You didn't seriously think you were going to go to sleep, did you?" she asked.

Lancaster didn't bother to reply. He climbed in beneath the covers, then leaned across her to turn off the light, feeling the shimmering silky material against his skin as he did so, then returned to kiss her fully on the lips as she wrapped a long leg around his. At some stage during the early hours, he was aware of her untangling herself from his body, picking up her discarded nightdress from the floor and going back to her own room via the connecting doors of the shared bathroom. Having crept in through the bedroom door earlier, she felt it might make just too much noise in the now dark, sleepy house to not be heard, so she had chosen the sneaky way back to her bed. There was, after all, still an element of modesty to be maintained whilst staying as a guest in someone else's house.

Lancaster rose early. He shaved, showered, dressed and headed downstairs to find Josette already in the kitchen baking fresh croissants. Josette was surprised by anybody's early rising, having heard them return the previous night. Lancaster told her he was off for a brisk walk up to the point and back, to clear his head for the day ahead and give him a good appetite for the croissants.

Lancaster walked at a brisk pace. Without his trainers, he didn't want to jog, but did intend to raise his blood pressure, build up his rate of breath and be aware he was pushing himself. He'd spent a lot of 'brain time' over the last few days and not enough 'body time'. Well, last night with Marie being the exception. His heart raced at the memory of it, so he pushed it from his mind and walked faster, swinging his arms in time to his strides to stimulate the muscles and pump the system. He crossed the cliff-top before heading toward the bluff and the car park, stopping briefly to look out across the sea, feeling the salt-laden sea air blast his face. He inhaled deeply. God, he loved that taste and feel, nature in the raw fullness of itself. He turned and made his way across the car park, turning at the sound of a car crunching across the gravel, being just slightly annoyed that this morning was no longer his alone. He cut down across the grass towards the cliffs above 'Peter's Cove'. When he reached the little twisted path that wormed its way down the cliff face to the cove, he stopped for a second, then made the decision that the climb down and back up would do him the power of good.

Once down on the beach, he took the time to sit on a rock at the base, watching the waves crash against the rocks where Peter had fished. It was high tide at the moment. If he chose to climb the protruding rock face to revisit the site of his death, he'd have to pick his moment, as every other wave washed the lower steps. He made the choice. Now was probably not a good time to climb up there; it was better to make his way back before the croissants disappeared. Lancaster climbed. When he crested the top, he was invigorated, his whole system buzzing, the fuzz in his brain and the ache behind the eyes had disappeared. He strode out forcefully towards the car park and home. As he crossed the bluff, he could see the car that had turned into the parking area earlier. Leaning against the side of the car were two young men wearing what looked like waxed jackets. They were wrapped against the breeze with its autumnal chill. A second later, Lancaster realised one of them was one of the two men who'd come into the restaurant the previous night and not been able to get a table. A second later than that realisation, the two men looked in his direction. He recognised both of them as being in the restaurant.

Lancaster immediately reverted to his old adage, 'There's no such thing as coincidence in a murder enquiry'. He pretended he'd not noticed them and kept watching them from the corner of his eye. He left the soft grass, started to cross the edge of the car park. He saw them rise from their leaning position and start to cut across the car park on a route that he knew would cross with his before he made it to the sanctuary of the grass path. Lancaster stealthily slipped his watch from his wrist and dropped it into his trouser pocket. He didn't want to lose that. He pulled the zipper of his jacket down and slid it off his body, folding it over his arm as if he was getting hot, which he was, tucking his fingers into the 'hanging' loop in the collar so he could swing it flail-like if he needed to fight; its brass buttons and large zip were a handy weapon or he could drop it if he needed to run.

The closing of their paths fast approaching, Lancaster was thinking fast. Were they muggers? Unlikely. They'd never have got up this early, and certainly wouldn't be driving a BMW. Were they local police who'd found out about their enquiry? Unlikely. They'd turn up at the house, quiz Pamela before seeking him out; there'd be an island protocol to adhere to. The only thing left was that they could be hitmen, here because of their enquiry. *This could be tough.* Time was running out. They'd soon converge. Lancaster needed time to think. He pulled his phone from his pocket and, still pretending he hadn't seen the men, he pretended to take a call. He talked on his phone, speaking loudly to be heard above the wind. He told the imaginary person that 'he was up on the bluff car park'. He then asked where the imaginary friend was, 'oh, you're on your way up to the car park, that's handy, I can meet you there,' he said to his 'friend'. He turned on his heels to make his way across the gravel once again, still chatting on his phone. It was as he was about to walk back past the car to meet his 'friend' that he realised that the car was still ticking over. A condensation cloud emitting from the exhaust. In a split-second, Lancaster knew what to do. He grabbed the door handle and it opened. He dropped the phone back into his pocket and threw the coat into the passenger seat as he heard the sound of running feet across the gravel and voices shouting in his direction.

He dropped into the driver's seat, slapped the gear stick into reverse, slammed his foot onto the throttle and swung the wheel right round, spitting stones and gravel in all directions as he pulled a half circle, straightened the wheel, slipped it into first just as one of the men grabbed at the door handle. Lancaster hit the throttle hard, ripping the door from the man's grasp. The last he saw of him in the door mirror was a body rolling away from the side of the car. As the dust cleared from the screen, he was aware the other man had chosen to head him off at the car park entrance and was making for the gap between the granite pillars. Lancaster realised the man had no chance of stopping a speeding BMW, and although he really didn't want to kill anybody, he was not about to stop now. As he sped over the last few feet of car park toward the entrance, he saw the man had stopped and was holding out both hands as if in surrender. But in one hand he'd unfurled a set of cards in a wallet... Warrant cards... And he was holding them for Lancaster to see.

Even from the screen of a speeding BMW, Lancaster

recognised the crown in the centre of the top card. He chose to ignore it and swept through the pillars of the car park entrance. Once outside the car park and onto the tarmac, he looked in the rear-view mirror and saw both men now standing, looking dejected, but both now held aloft warrant card folders in a final gesture of hope. Lancaster felt he'd won this round and made his point. He flicked the steering wheel with one hand, yanked the handbrake with the other and pulled a full 'one-eighty' before the car stopped, facing back toward the two men, neither of whom moved. They both stood holding out their cards. Lancaster decided to risk it. If they'd been there to kill him, they could have shot him and pushed him off the cliff. If they didn't want to make a noise, they could have dropped a rock on him as he sat on the beach in the cove. Lancaster was also intrigued. Having had time to breathe and take stock, he felt he had a pretty good idea who they were and what they wanted. He dropped the stick into first and drove back into the car park, parking virtually where he'd started. He grabbed his coat, opened the door, exiting the car as the pair were crossing the gravel, one of them giving a slow clap of applause.

"Well, I have to say, Detective Inspector Lancaster," the clapping man said as he approached. "Needless to say, we weren't expecting that. Bravo. The advanced driving course didn't show up in your file."

"Don't take the piss and don't come any closer until you unroll those cards again," Lancaster replied, not trusting either man's intentions. "Or we all go into 'fisty cuffs' mode and we don't want that either, do we?"

"Fair enough," the clapping man said. Pulling the card back

out of his jacket pocket, he threw it in Lancaster's direction. Lancaster surprisingly caught it, whilst still keeping his eye on both men. The card showed the man was Steven Ainscough. Counter Terrorism Department.

"I presume he's the same?" Lancaster asked of the other man, who'd now joined them as he threw the card back to the clapping man.

"For fuck's sake, Chris, give him your bloody badge," clapping man said.

'Chris' threw his card in Lancaster's direction. He caught it and studied it, as he suspected and didn't doubt, that Christopher Cross also worked for the same department.

"Your parents had a sense of humour and a poor choice in music?" Lancaster said throwing the card back. He'd once owned a Christopher Cross album many years ago but had traded it for something with more body and content. The other man didn't reply, he was busy dusting off gravel and dirt from his trousers where he'd rolled across the car park, which could probably account for his general unfriendliness.

"Seriously though, Inspector," Ainscough said. "That was all a bit nifty, was that a police driving course?"

"A misspent life in my Plymouth youth, now, can we get to the point. I plan a busy day and you two don't figure in it."

"Look, let's start again," Ainscough said. "We only wanted a chat. It was you who went all 'Fast & Furious' on us before we had a chance to show our cards. Can we just sit and have a chat?"

"We can have a chat, but I don't like the idea of sitting," Lancaster replied. "Have to be honest, I still don't trust you guys so let's just chat."

Ainscough laughed. "Fair enough. Well, what it boils down to is this. You were asked very nicely to back away from Sean Devlin and pretend you'd never heard of him, yet you still appear to be sticking your nose up his arse. You're sniffing around his bank account and asking silly questions."

"Bloody hell, do you people really talk like this? 'Asking silly questions!' I'm a bloody detective. It's what I'm supposed to do, and it could be your man's part of my enquiry."

"There you go again. 'Our man', as you put it, is no longer part of your enquiry. He's not involved in your investigation. He may be part of ours, but he is, and I repeat, no longer any part of yours. Is that understood?"

"Why?" Lancaster asked bluntly.

"What do you mean, why? Because the powers-that-be, want it that way. There are bigger things at stake here than Lady Stottard's dead dad."

"Not good enough. This man could be involved in a murder and I see no reason why anyone should be absolved from justice."

Ainscough laughed. "Have you any idea how many murders this man's actually been involved in? Shit, if only you knew. The one I'm most sure he's not involved in is the one Stottard wants opening. And unless you want to be responsible for the government deciding they don't want to grant a state licence and issue a request to reopen the case or perform another autopsy, then I suggest you bloody well back away. You can't win this one, Lancaster. Trust me on that."

Lancaster thought for a moment. He knew the man was

right. He so hated this kind of politics. The kind of politics that pisses around with justice. He hated it with a vengeance and it angered him immensely, but in his heart-of-hearts, he knew the man was right. There'd be nothing he could do other than jeopardise the whole investigation.

"So does he work for you then?" Lancaster pushed.

"You really aren't going to know for sure. Please, for your own career's sake and the sake of your investigation, which may well bear fruit if you proceed... But not if Devlin's any part of it. Just drop him out. Look on the bright side, with him out of the picture you can invest more time in looking at other candidates. To be honest, I'd quite like to see what you find."

"Well, we do have people of interest," Lancaster replied, thinking this conversation had almost run its course.

Ainscough laughed again. "That would be very wise, Detective Lancaster. Just keep looking elsewhere and we may not have to meet again."

"Can I ask one question?" Lancaster pushed. Seeing raised eyebrows from his adversary, he pushed on anyway. "Do you actually have any knowledge with regards to the death of Peter Urbawicz?"

"Bloody hell. Now I'm the one who's being interviewed," Ainscough replied laughing. "Honestly? As far as I know, we had no involvement and, as far as I know, we know of nobody that was involved. Now that's not to say if it was murder or an accidental death, but what I can honestly say is, it wasn't us, 'guvner'."

Lancaster decided it was time to leave before anyone mentioned Levon Shawbuck. So far, his name hadn't been mentioned, so he was still a viable line of enquiry. Lancaster pulled his coat back on and zipped up.

"Enjoy the rest of your holiday, gentlemen," Lancaster said and, putting his hands casually into his pockets, he walked away. Something told him they'd meet again; he just hoped it wouldn't be too soon. He needed to find out more about Shawbuck or Devlin, no, he must forget he ever heard of Devlin... So it was Shawbuck he wanted info' on before that door also closed.

He carried on walking towards the house; he felt he'd earned those croissants, even if they were cold. He couldn't fault the exercise regime he'd just been through. A fast walk, a cliff climb and finally, an adrenaline rush like he hadn't experienced for quite a while. He laughed to himself as he remembered the encounter. The phone rang in his pocket, he checked the screen. Craven. Bugger. He knew this was going to be about Devlin. He stopped and leaned against the fence out of the wind and tapped the answer tab.

"'Morning, sir," he said jovially.

"Bomber, heads-up," the man replied. "I've just had a shout from my man in the CTD. He reckons they've dispatched two operatives to the island to have a chat with you about Devlin. Apparently, you didn't hear what I told you; you've been sniffing around asking bloody questions. Now watch yourself. These people get 'pissy' if you dangle your toes in their pond and you're liable to get a slap. Now I'm not saying you don't bloody deserve one but I'd then have to respond and then it all gets messy, so do yourself a bloody favour; leave it. Do you understand? LEAVE IT!"

"I've just had a chat with them, sir, they appear to be nice chaps. I thought we all got along quite well and understood each other."

There was a brief interlude whilst Craven absorbed this information before he replied,

"Seriously, bomber. Are you OK?"

"Thanks for your concern, sir, but yep, I'm fine. Honestly. We all had a nice chat, they appraised me of the current situation with regards to the gentleman in question and I quite understand why they wish me to leave the man alone. And I will do."

"Bomber... Leave it," the other man said, not believing Lancaster for a moment. "Look, if they decide to get their knickers in a twist, you and Lady Stottard will end up right up shit-creek without a paddle. No new investigation. No new autopsy and the body stays in the ground, do you understand? They carry more weight than I could, even if I ate steak for a year. These people were hiding in cupboards when Guy Fawkes bought his box of matches, and it didn't end well for him. You don't mess with them, son, they're worse than the masons."

"Honest, sir, there will be no more research into Devlin. But can I ask one favour in return?"

Craven thought for only a second before replying, "Go on."

"Would you at least ask your man in the CTD, was this guy IRA or one of ours? I ask because there just might be a chance that Peter got in the way of some other person who wanted Devlin out of the way. It would help me walk away from this guy if I had a better idea of where he fitted into the bigger picture."

Again, silence whilst Craven pondered this request.

"Leave it with me." And he was gone.

Lancaster headed for the house. He had a hankering for half-a-dozen croissants and fresh coffee. It had been a busy morning, and it was still only 9:00

Lancaster walked into the kitchen to the sound of laughter. A large plate in the middle of the kitchen counter held a collection of gloriously buttery pastry flakes, and three lonely croissants. Marie and Pamela were still licking crumbs from their fingers.

"I tried to save more for you, Mr Lancaster," Josette said with a smile. "But the gannets arrived and they were hungry." She slid a clean plate and knife across the counter, and he grabbed all three croissants before they too disappeared.

Josette poured coffee for him whilst Lancaster ripped apart the pastry and ladled in the plum jam. The girls chatted as he devoured two in rapid succession, then set about the third. He was hungrier than he'd thought and wasn't certain three of the 'crescent moons' were actually going to cut it. He needn't have worried; as he finished the third one, Josette slipped two big toasted hunks of yesterday's baguette onto his plate. Once these had been consumed, Lancaster picked up his coffee cup and gave a nod to the others that they needed to move to the other room. He'd made the decision, not without some trepidation, that Pamela should be told about Devlin and the guys from the CTD. His reasoning was the fact that if anything untoward should happen, at least she'd know the full story. She could make her own choice if she wanted to pursue this line of enquiry herself or not. They took their coffee out to the terrace.

"I've information I need to share, Pamela," Lancaster started. "Marie knows some of this, but I felt it necessary to withhold it from you until I knew the score; for that, I apologise in advance. If you remember, the bank gave us names of clients your father may have upset; one was a man called Sean Devlin. To just give you the facts, we've been told in no uncertain manner that we're not to follow up or ask questions about him, his bank account or, in fact, anything at all to do with him." Lancaster could see Pamela bristling with rage, he held up a hand to silence her until he'd finished. "Marie and I have still, despite the warnings, been 'spuddling' around in the murky waters of this man's life, but this morning whilst I was out for my walk on the cliffs, I had a visit from two members of the Counter Terrorism Department. They've assured me that Devlin's not involved with Peter's death. They've also suggested that if we persist in making enquiries in his direction, moves could be made that would call a halt to our investigation altogether. There'd be no exhumation, no autopsy, the case would be classed as closed for good and Marie and I would be on the next plane home."

Pamela could hold back no longer. "But why would they want to exclude somebody from a possible murder enquiry? He surely cannot be important enough to them to be left off the list if there's a chance he was involved. It doesn't make sense."

"Sadly, Pamela, it's not for us to know."

"It might not be for you, David," she said, obviously annoyed. "But you forget that I have friends in slightly higher places..."

Lancaster stopped her in her tracks with a raised hand. "Please, Pamela. You wanted us, Marie and me. You said you knew we'd do the job, so please, trust me on this. If you ask anyone to intervene, it will close this case. I know enough about the spooks and Counter Terror boys to know they'll screw us over big-time if we piss them off. Nobody will win and that'll be the least of our worries. They're like the masons; they'll not let us forget that they asked nicely the first time."

"But doesn't it stick in your craw, David?"

"Pamela," Lancaster replied with a smile. "Of course it bloody does. I hate it. But you have to work the system. We now know about Devlin. We don't have to investigate him anymore; we've other people to cross off the list, other avenues to go down before this is all over. If I find the case reclassified as murder and we've ticked all the boxes, gone down every alleyway, checked off all suspects and the only one left is Devlin... Then he comes back out of the closet. It won't matter a damn to me who tells us to leave him in there, but by then we'll have our post-mortem. Your father can be laid to rest again with the full knowledge that we marked our man."

Pamela sat thinking about Lancaster's comments. She knew he was right; she didn't like it but there it was. She'd started this process; it had to go the full course.

"OK, we go with what you say," she agreed.

From the depths of the house, the phone was ringing. Josette appeared at the open doorway to inform Pamela she had a call in her office.

"Did you have a problem with the guys from CTD?" Vidêt asked once they were alone.

"I thought I might, but as it happened, I think I took them

146

by surprise. I don't think we've seen the last of them though."

"Are we still looking into Shawbuck?"

"I think we give him a rest for now. As I said, we know where he lives."

Marie took a call on her mobile; Basil from Your-Hire. He'd been trying to get hold of Lady Stottard but her line was busy, so he called her instead. He'd been digging in the records and found Mr Shawbuck had hired a car with them after the end of August 2008. Regularly it appears. Once or twice a year, always pre-booking his car in readiness for his arrival and always paying cash. The last time he was here was this year, in March. As for the German, Paul Steiner, they could find no trace other than those bookings up to the end of August 2008. Vidêt thanked him for all the time he'd put in and promised Lady Stottard would call him as soon as she got time.

"So it looks like Steiner finished what he came to do and never returned," Lancaster said. "Of course, we don't know for certain that he didn't hire a car elsewhere but why would you? Your-Hire has a prime location across the car park from the arrivals' door. That's why we used it. No, I think the man visited several times during that year, then never returned."

"Does that make him more likely to be our man or not?"

"To be honest, I don't really know. But until we know any different, it certainly doesn't rule him out, that's for sure."

Vidêt's phone went again, **Basil.** "Hello again, Basil."

"I forgot to tell you," Basil said in his jolly voice. "Lady Stottard's request for information and our subsequent searching encouraged us to have a complete tidy-up of our files. It was time we opened some cupboards and looked into the old card indexes. Next year our company's going to be forty years old and we've decided to contact some old customers as a bit of a publicity stunt. We also have a bit of barter trading with the Hotel Grandé just outside Saint Helier, we've had a little office there since 2000, and anyway, I'm waffling away, sorry. What I wanted to say was that Mary's been down to the office there and cleared out all the old files. She's turned into a bit of a detective. She had a thought, when I purchased the Fiestas, I also struck a very good deal on two red Vauxhall Astras. I know you wanted Fiesta, but I thought you should know that one of the Vauxhalls was in fact out on hire from the hotel office during the two weeks you were interested in. In fact, he returned the car on the 21st of August, a day earlier than the hire was intended for. I mean I don't know if it's of any interest to you or not. I just thought that, as Mary had turned up the information, I should at least pass it on. The chap in question was a Henri Tanguyé, over here from Brittany. If it turns out to be of any interest, I can get Mary to e-mail you the details?"

"I am sure Lady Stottard would be grateful, Basil. Please send the information to her e-mail and thank Mary from us."

Marie relayed the call to Lancaster. He agreed that it was worth checking the details once the e-mail arrived. They'd have to check with Pamela and see if there was any chance she mis-recognised what car it was parked in the car park. That was a thought Lancaster hadn't bargained for. *If Pamela got the car wrong, that could open a huge can of worms.* He needed to get this sorted out ASAP. His plan to find Pamela was put on hold though. Craven was ringing. Lancaster answered. Craven was in a hurry, on his way to a meeting and didn't want to arrive late. Apparently, it appeared there was going to be a hold-up on the exhumation; it was taking longer than the powers-that-be had anticipated. There were still T's to be crossed, I's to be dotted. As soon as Craven had the go-ahead, he'd give them a shout; he figured it would be in the next day or two. Lancaster asked the obvious whether this was a coincidence or a result of him asking about Devlin. Craven was convinced it had nothing to do with Lancaster's run-in with CTD and told him to get a grip. He then asked if Lancaster was on his own. Lancaster replied in the affirmative.

"That being the case, I have a few details about the man we're not going to talk about. I'll talk you'll listen, understood?"

Lancaster felt he didn't need to answer that question... So he didn't. Craven continued.

"The man in question was apparently a genuine businessman with a profitable construction company. Then he got leant on by the 'boys' from across the border, the 'Pope's men', 'nuff' said. Anyway, he decided if you can't beat 'em, join 'em, then after a few disasters with his company, and still, nobody knows if he caused them or the 'naughty boys' did, trying to keep him in line, he started saving his own retirement fund from the 'boys' money. He was apparently taught a bit of a lesson one night and given a second chance to do some work for them. That was when the CTD spooks got to him. They turned him to become a double but the rumour has it that he was actually doing the treble. He was screwing the 'boys' over, screwing the CTD and screwing the various organisations he was supposed to be a middleman with. He was apparently an armourer on the quiet, so was pushing the suppliers for the very best price, yet charging the 'boys' full 'whack' plus some, and then, also not telling the full story to the CTD, hence the bank account over there. Somewhere down the line, it all went tits-up for the bloke. The 'boys' found out he was diddling them. The CTD found out he was also diddling them, with the result being, he went under crown protection, gave our blokes loads of names and this helped bring pressure to bear during the Peace Agreement. Then our guys spirited the man away somewhere and they still pay him a pension. It's all right for some, innit."

"I understand he was also thought to be involved in the Gaddafi arms shipment," Lancaster pushed.

"Rumour, my son. Probably based on fact, but still just a rumour. The thing is, the 'boys' didn't think it was a coincidence that the Eksund got pulled. They put a lot of money into that shipment and all they got to show for it was some bad publicity. It's no coincidence he went under the bedcovers just after that happened, you get my drift?"

Lancaster was confident his boss had no idea about Devlin re-emerging as Shawbuck. That being the case, for the moment he didn't feel it was his job to tell him. If he himself could pretend he didn't know they were one-and-the-same, it gave him the chance to sniff around a little more, then apologise later if need be. Craven said he'd give him a shout as soon as he knew when the exhumation was paper-worked, then as usual, as Lancaster was thinking of other information he could do with, the man was gone. Lancaster knew the man would be on the other end of the line if needed, so closed his phone and pondered his next move.

CHAPTER FIVE

Pamela came onto the terrace looking pensive.

"I don't know if it's of interest, but I've had a conversation with Max at the bank. He'd put out a general staff memo for information on the characters we've been talking about. It turns out the American, Shawbuck, has indicated he'll be coming to the island the week after next. His account's been unfrozen, it appeared to clear itself last night, so whatever the blockage was, everything's now OK. The tech guys still aren't sure what happened; the old section of the accounts is still password activated but they've opted not to try and open it again. They suspect Shawbuck wants to know what's going on. Despite an exchange of e-mails with the man assuring him it's all 'A-OK', he plans to come in person on his way to a gun auction in Holland."

"That could be interesting," Lancaster replied. "We'll have to wait and see what we can find out before he gets here. I have a couple of irons in that fire at the moment. Did Max have anything else to say?"

"In fact, he did. Your two CTD chaps paid him a visit last night. They were apparently very polite and showed their warrant cards and a covering letter of authority. To cut to the chase, they told him in no uncertain terms that the bank was advised to no longer forward any information with regards to an old client of theirs, Mr. Sean Devlin, to any third party without informing them first. As far as the bank should be aware, Devlin's account was closed and should be ignored. They also wanted all paperwork and computer details destroyed. So I suspect you may have upset somebody, David."

"That's probably true, Pamela. It's something I do often. You should also be aware that there will be a slight delay with the delivery from the UK of the order for exhumation of your father's body."

"What," she replied angrily. "How dare they...?"

Lancaster held up a hand before she went right off the deep end.

"DCI Craven doesn't believe the two things are connected. But funny enough, I don't share his optimism. I'd bet my life on this being the powers-that-be showing us what they could do if they wanted to, but they wouldn't want to piss us off too much, pardon my French. They know enough about me to know what my reaction would be if that should happen, no, this is just a blip, a constructed hiccup to show they can pull strings. We'll get the go-ahead reasonably soon."

"I hope you're right, David, or I may start playing dirty as well and call in my own favours, and that would start a Whitehall war between departments. If need be, we can start a war between the Bailiwick and the mainland and nobody would want that either."

"The what?" Lancaster asked.

"The Bailiwick of Jersey. It's what makes us different from the rest of the UK. The Bailiwick of Guernsey and Jersey and the other 'off-islands' is a self-controlling entity. The islands are what they call 'British Crown Dependencies', so we take some guidance and rules from the mainland. We've been controlling our own destiny here since the Treaty of Paris and that was signed in 1259, but we still like to think of ourselves as British. That's why we have this situation with regard to the exhumation. Even if the UK government requests an exhumation and another autopsy, there's no guarantee that the island coroner or the relevant 'bailiff', who's like a sort of MP or Mayoral role, will agree. Each of the 'bailiwicks' like to have their say in such things. They may just say 'no' to a request. Though I honestly don't think they'll bother to get in a tizzy over one autopsy."

"So even if the request gets here tomorrow, there's nothing to say we'll be getting a digger bucket in the ground any time soon?"

"Well, no, not really. Anyway, I'll be visiting my mother this afternoon so I'll tell her there's going to be a delay with the autopsy; she's been waiting to hear what happens next. Oh by the way, I have an e-mail from Basil, apparently you wanted some details and Mary's sent them through. The man you were interested in, Henri Tanguyé, he's a Breton. His address was listed in '06 when he hired his car as Les Chardons Blue in Morgat, oh... That's interesting... Well I never... That's not far from where my grandparents lived at Crozon; what a coincidence."

Lancaster looked at Vidêt, she was looking back at him. She knew his mantra. 'There's no such thing as a coincidence until it's been proved otherwise'. But there was a 'red' fly in this ointment. Tanguyé had not been driving a Fiesta. Vidêt had thought of this earlier whilst Lancaster had been talking with Craven and had planned ahead.

"Pamela, may I show you something?" Vidêt asked. She turned her iPad in Pamela's direction. "Do you know which of these cars is which?"

"What do you mean?" Pamela asked. Looking at the split screen showing side-by-side images that Vidêt had photoshopped together. In both side-by-side pictures, the cars were positioned at a slight sideways angle so you couldn't see the logo on the bonnet or grill. Pamela stared at the photos for a moment. "Well, obviously they look similar and the colour is almost identical, isn't it?"

"One of them is a Ford and the other is a Vauxhall," Vidêt replied.

"Oh, are they? Well, they all look the same, don't they?" she said, with no hint of the gravity of her statement. She looked up from the screen and took her glasses off, aware instantly of the look of shock, possibly even fear in the eyes of both detectives.

"What?" she asked.

Lancaster kept his voice cool, calm and controlled. "It's just that we've specifically been searching for red Ford Fiestas, as that was what you said you'd seen the day of your father's death. Now you're saying it could have been an Astra instead."

"Oh, damn," she replied, suddenly looking very sad. "Is this going to be a problem? I'm quite sure that what I saw that day was a Fiesta. Well... Maybe. Oh damnation, why did you have to sow doubt, David?"

"Sadly, Pamela, because we're detectives, and we try to enquire based on fact. Not always, if truth be told, but we do try. Could I ask a huge favour? Give Basil a quick call and double-check how many red Astra's he actually had?"

"I'll go and get my phone," she said, heading for the door,

as an afterthought adding, "It's probably time for more coffee; I need one."

After she'd left, Vidêt looked at Lancaster.

"As Pamela said, do you think this is going to be a problem?"

"It'll depend on just how many bloody red Astra's Basil had. Just keep your fingers crossed that there weren't too many."

Pamela returned, smiling broadly, talking on her mobile. When she got a moment to get a word into the person on the other end of the call, she asked if they could possibly repeat what they'd just said to her friend, David. She handed the phone to Lancaster and mouthed, 'Basil', then stood with a smug look on her face. Basil confirmed that with regards to the Astras, he'd made another disastrous deal when he purchased them. Although he got them cheaply, sadly people didn't actually want to hire them. He only kept them for a year before trading them at auction. He was sorry to tell Lancaster that the one sole hire during the period they were interested in was the one to Henri Tanguyé. Lancaster thanked the man for his efforts, tapped the off and handed back the phone. He asked Vidêt to start an internet search to see if the name came up anywhere and was relieved to see Josette arrive carrying coffee. He felt he was also ready for one.

Pamela asked Josette to pour whilst she stepped into the garden to call her mother and confirm her visit. The day was turning out warm, the westerly breeze had dropped away. While Pamela strolled, chatting on her phone, Lancaster decided he should call Rover with an update. When Lancaster got through, Rover had already been alerted by Craven to the problems with paperwork. Rover was not best pleased. He had his case packed but was going to have to put the trip on hold for the moment.

Pamela, returning from her 'phone-stroll', sat to drink her coffee.

"Interesting chat with Ma," she said. "I'll find out more when I see her after lunch, but she remembers the Tanguyé family from the war years. Most were Breton separatists, some people said collaborators. She was surprised to hear there were any members of the family left; she thought they'd all emigrated or were shot during the war."

"It'll be interesting to hear what else she has to say," Lancaster replied. "It may turn out to be relevant, may not, but whatever, the man was here at a crucial moment in the case. There's a connection. It may only be that he was here on holiday, but it's still a connection to the date your father died. I find that interesting in itself."

Lunch came and went, shortly followed by Pamela, having left to visit her mother. Vidêt had carried out research in the meantime and was keen to pass the information on to Lancaster.

"I was born and raised in Brittany, yet I am always amazed at how much of my own history I didn't know."

She went on to tell Lancaster that during the Second World War throughout Brittany there were many factions, all fighting for different reasons on different political platforms. The Communist Resistance wanted freedom from French rule to set up their own autonomist regime, with communism as their political basis. There was the Bezen Perrot. A Breton nationalist group, numbering eighty people at the most. These formed a militia, who envisaged that siding with the Germans would eventually give them free rule for Brittany. The Germans must have loved the fact that these separate bodies were happy to kill each other, saving the fascists from having to get their hands dirty. The separatist groups assassinated each other's fighters and murdered family members of opposing leaders.

Then there were the 'Maquis'. Many of these were dedicated Breton Nationalists, who knew at the start of the occupation that German forces were too great to be beaten face-to-face. So they conducted clandestine operations. Vandalising signage and disrupting railways. Eventually, just before the D-Day landings took place, they were joined by members of the Free French forces, who had been trained in England and parachuted into Brittany. These were to form up north of Vanne in southern Brittany and create mayhem, drawing in German forces from the rest of Brittany and Normandy to tackle the problem. It was virtually a suicide mission; it went wrong right from the start. Whether through betrayal or bad luck, the Germans knew about them almost before they'd packed away their parachutes. A terrible firefight ensued with many on both sides left dead in the woods and fields. The Resistance and Free French forces were all but wiped out, and the village around which the battle raged was burned to the ground by the Germans, including the church with villagers inside. The survivors of this joint force were spirited away through enemy lines, to be lost and hidden amongst their own kind out in the countryside, there to lie low until the invasion forces had landed. But for a while, they'd done their job, they'd drawn enemy fire.

Despite her research, Vidêt found no mention of Tanguyé's family or which faction they were affiliated to. Vidêt looked at Lancaster. He had that look on his face. She'd seen it before, many times and had come to recognise that distant stare, a sign the man was planning, thinking. She knew he'd been listening to her information update, but there was something formulating in his head, cogs and wheels grinding as he put the pieces together. Suddenly all cogs became aligned and the man spoke.

"Right, whilst Pamela's out, let's take a stroll and get some fresh air." With that he was up out of his chair, heading for the cloakroom and the shoe collection.

They followed the usual route. Out the side gate, up the path towards the car park. Lancaster had thrown on a jacket, hands thrust into pockets. Vidêt tucked her arm through his and they strolled the path together, the afternoon sun still held autumnal warmth. They crested the rise and started across the car park. The sea breeze cleared the cliff tops and brought the temperature down, enough to make them feel glad of the extra layer.

Lancaster was certain that when he returned to Plymouth it was time to start looking for another place to live. These few days on Jersey had reinvigorated his love for all things coastal. When his wife died, the cottage by the sea they'd bought held too many memories and ghosts. He'd made the choice to sell and move nearer to his place of work, originally purchasing his flat near Stonehouse in Plymouth, with its view across the harbour and the docking area for the Brittany ferry. Firstly, because it contained everything he needed at the time. Secondly, he could afford it on his inspector's salary and he knew, buying early in the development process meant he'd make money on a resale. And there was still money left over from the cottage sale. Thirdly, he thought it would give him that closeness to the sea that he craved. But it hadn't. On his days off, if he was lucky and at the right time, he'd watch the arrival of the ferry. But to be honest, it wasn't the same as being near the sea. It would no longer do. It was time to start looking again.

They crossed to the concrete plinth where the German artillery used to point out to sea, waiting for the battle that never was and sat down on the lip, dangling their legs over the edge, taking in the view. The blue-green of the English Channel. The grey and white of the seagulls hanging on the wind, and the bright blue sky, studded with frothy white clouds passing like giant sheep. Vidêt snuggled in against Lancaster's side, using him as a windbreak, her arm still tucked into his, feeling the warmth of his body through their jackets. What had started in the south of France months ago as a lustful, rampant, but thoroughly enjoyable joining of bodies in the heat of a French night, had developed through an agreed arrangement on both sides. That both of them were normal, hot-blooded grown-ups, neither of whom had a partner but both were in need of casual, no-strings-attached, sex. This relationship had now, at least for her, turned into something more important. More meaningful. *It is still too early*, she thought, *to call it love*, but it was certainly further on than casual. It had taken this man to allow her to trust again. Men could be bastards and had been. From her father to her previous boss in the force in France, and others along the way. She'd been determined to stay clear of getting involved again. But then here she was, doing just that, but feeling comfortable about it. She trusted this man David Lancaster and if he let her down, she thought she'd probably kill him. Then herself.

"It's beautiful, isn't it?" she said quietly.

"Yes, it is... It's just a bloody shame we have to work to be here. But I've made up my mind. When I get back to Plymouth, I intend to sell my flat in Stonehouse and look for another place by the sea, where I can walk and smell the salt in the air."

Vidêt sat and thought for a moment before saying, "Would there be any room there for me?"

Lancaster continued staring out across the white-capped waves in the bay as if taking his time to think about the proposition. Then replied,

"I kind of hoped you wouldn't need a separate room. I hoped you'd share the whole place with me."

He turned towards her with a smile on his face which she quickly smothered with her lips, giving him a deep and powerful kiss. Just to clinch the deal.

"So, is that a yes then?" Lancaster asked when they came up for air.

"You stupid boy," she replied, in a parody of a television programme, he'd quote lines from.

"But before all that, Marie," he added. Bringing the subject back to the operation in hand. "We have a murder enquiry to sort out and I've been pondering an idea. I had a thought when we found this other character, the guy with the Astra, Henri Tanguyé, who originated from near Pamela's grandparents' home in Brittany. That can't be a coincidence, surely. So bearing in mind we're waiting for an exhumation decree, we know who most of the characters in the picture are, and to top that off, one of them, our Mr Shawbuck, is actually planning to visit the island the week after next. My thoughts are that we should go back to the beginning of this whole story. We've been fixated by Peter's banking enemies and having the luxury of finding he had some has made us concentrate on them. Well, we now know just about all we can find out about them, so my thoughts are that we should go across to Brittany and see where this all started. The same as we did when we investigated the death of Abdul Mehemet. It was information we acquired from his early life that led us to his future and his murderer."

"You think we should investigate this Henri Tanguyé?"

"Well, it certainly wouldn't hurt. I think we should keep it unofficial. Obviously, we'll tell Craven and Pamela, but I reckon we should sneak over there and look at the locations where this whole story started, then follow the trail back here to the island. That way we'll know if there's another story we're missing. The worst that can happen is we get a couple of days' break in Brittany and discover nothing, but at least we then know that nothing was missed along the way. What do you think? Are you up for returning to the land of your birth?"

As the pair headed back to the house, they spotted Pamela's car turning down the drive toward the house. All three of them arrived in the kitchen at the same time but from different directions. This hadn't taken Josette by surprise though; she'd spotted Lancaster and Vidêt coming back down the path and heard the car in the driveway. The kettle was on and the cups were on the worktop.

Pamela, Lancaster and Vidêt retired to the lounge. The sun still streaming through the patio windows.

"My mother had a lot to say about the Tanguyé family," Pamela said. "She almost ran out of breath telling me tales of their misdemeanours."

According to the various tales Brigitte spat out with considerable venom sitting in her armchair in the nursing home, the family Tanguyé was remembered right across the Crozon peninsula. Before the war, the family were held in some regard as heroes of the Breton separatist movement. They were all, on the whole, members of the Breton National Party. Its founders, Olier Mordrel and François Debeavais, took their inspiration from the Irish Nationalist Movement and campaigned heavily for Breton people to have greater self-rule, their language taught within the school system and greater control over their own destiny as an autonomous region. It was when war became imminent that the family, and their supporters, took a turn for the worse.

Shortly after the occupation, the Germans chose to ban any mention of a Breton Free State. Germany wanted control over one country; it wasn't in its interest to engage with individual regions with varying forms of politics. This 'betrayal' by the occupiers caused unrest throughout the nationalists. Some of the Tanguyé family opted to migrate to Ireland during 1940. Some younger members of the family, angry at the apathy of fellow Bretons, joined a group known as the Bezen Perrot, a German support militia used to break up gatherings of Breton separatists, flush out anti-German factions and, in the event of the allies invading, fight a rear-guard action on the Germans' behalf. But by far the worst offence, as far as Brigitte Danielo was concerned, was that several members of the family joined the Landerneau Kommando, a group of German and Breton members, formed by the Gestapo. These militia were engaged in fighting against the general French Resistance fighters. Something, later in life, they'd struggle to live down. At the end of the occupation, a lot of scores were settled amongst these groups.

"All of this is a fascinating insight into the Brittany of the 1940s, but I'm not sure it gives a connection to Peter or your mother," Lancaster said.

"Aaah," Pamela replied, a knowing smile on her face. "The interesting fact my mother dropped into the picture right at the end was that one of the Tanguyé boys went to school with her. A chap called Yves Tanguyé. Not only that but he was apparently 'sweet' on her."

"Aaaah indeed, Pamela, that could make a tenuous difference, it could bring the family name into the picture. On that note, Marie and I have had an idea."

Lancaster outlined his thoughts that going back to the place where this story began may give them some clue that otherwise they may have missed and, if nothing else, not only would it give them a complete picture of where the Peter and Brigette love story began, but it would get them off the island for a short while, away from the boys from CTD. He had a sneaky feeling they weren't done with them yet. It was only a matter of time before they found out about Shawbuck's account being tripped, they'd be sure to put two and two together and be back for another chat. Pamela thought it was a great idea. For some stupid reason, it hadn't even occurred to Lancaster that she'd want to come with them, but she did, even better, she'd drive and be their guide. Lancaster advised that he'd have to run the plan past Craven for approval. Pamela said he should tell Craven she'd pick up all expenses for the trip. That should keep him happy. It did. Lancaster closed his call to Craven with the voice of his boss still ringing in his ear.

"Don't piss about over there, Bomber, it's not a bloody holiday. Go over, scout about, follow up this French bloke, 'turnkey', and suss out anything of interest. Put a historical fact file together, stay no more than one night, then get back to Jersey. Rumour has it we should have the go-ahead for the exhumation soon. Behind the scenes, our 'Minister for Buggering about with Foreigners' has already been in touch with the Jersey Bailiff and the Island Coroners Department; they'll all be fine with it once they get the paperwork, so we can crack on. Understood...?"

Lancaster relayed the basics of Craven's approval to the others. Pamela said to leave the rest to her. She'd book the car onto the ferry and get a hotel at Crozon as soon as possible. She disappeared to her study, excited to be a working cog within the team.

"Are you OK going back to Brittany?" Lancaster asked Marie once Pamela had left the room. "It's not going to be too raw for you, is it?"

Marie was grateful for his thoughtfulness. "No, it's not a problem, as long as we don't go into Brest. There is a chance we may bump into somebody from the force; I don't want the aggravation that could cause."

Pamela was true to her word; she'd booked them onto a ferry for St Malo the next morning. She'd spoken with Basil at Your-Hire, extended the insurance for the car and got a travel document e-mailed across to allow them to take the car to France. To top it off, she'd booked them into a hotel at Crozon. It had a highly recommended restaurant which accounted for why, unlike many hotels that closed for the winter, this one opened all year round. Lancaster went to bed feeling slightly guilty; he was actually excited by the prospect of another visit to France. It was a country he'd never visited before this year, now he was off for a second time in twelve months.

Lancaster had turned out his bedside light when he heard the connecting bathroom door open, the one from Marie's room. Two seconds later, he smiled as his connecting door opened and a shadowy figure walked across the room to his bed, lifted the corner of the duvet and slid inside. Marie snuggled up against his body and wrapped one arm around him, Lancaster leaned his head forward and kissed her. She broke off the kiss and leaned her head back against the pillow.

"Are you serious about us sharing a house together?" she asked.

"I am," Lancaster replied, stroking her hair from her face. "But there's no pressure, Marie. If you don't want to, I can quite understand. You've probably had your fill of men, well, I mean... I didn't mean you'd had a lot of men... I just meant the ones you've had have pissed you off and if you just want to keep this relationship as a..."

Marie pinched his lips together so he couldn't speak, giggling as she did so. "Sometimes, Detective Inspector, you talk too much. Of course, I would love to share a place together, but you and I both know, we are an odd couple. We both have our mood swings. We both have our dark times, so we should have a place that has at least two bedrooms. Then we can be apart if we need to be. We know we'd be there for each other if either wanted support, but we also know that sometimes we need our own space to get our heads together. When there is another person in the equation, we would always feel the pressure to be on our best behaviour and that would not be fair on either of us. But if you are happy on those terms then..."

Lancaster reached across and pinched her lips together.

"Sometimes, Detective Sergeant Vidêt, you talk too much. Now snuggle down and go to sleep; we've an early start in the morning." He un-pinched her lips, kissed them gently, then pulled her head in close to his shoulder. Two minutes later they both realised there would be no early going to sleep for either of them.

Lancaster was tired and sleepy when Pamela drove to the ferry terminal. He dozed whilst they sat in the car waiting to board. As per usual, Pamela had pulled favours from a friend who worked at the terminal, so they hadn't had to park with the 'common tourist' on the ramp. A handy little gap had been left down one side of the queuing motorcade. Shortly after they'd arrived, a high-viz-wearing man tapped on the window waving them off down the side of the parked traffic, where they drove like royalty down the ramp onto the car deck. A short time later, they were sitting drinking the first coffee of the day, watching the grey piers of the harbour slip past on a grey autumnal morning.

Pamela had asked what they hoped to gain from this trip. Lancaster was honest that he was never sure until it appeared. He explained that he often got a gut feeling about something and had to go with the flow. It didn't always pay off, but going through the motions served a purpose, checking out that gut feeling and crossing it off. Every now and then that same feeling turned up some information, a new character that hadn't, until then, materialized in the investigation. As an example, Lancaster quoted their visit to the scene of her father's death. When the original enquiry took place, the local police covered every inch of the location. They'd produced photos of the site. Measured and marked the position of the body and the angle of the fall. Convinced the death was a tragic accident. Lancaster believed that any good detective would have done all that and more, then looked at it from another angle just to cross-reference to prove the original prognosis was correct. That being the case, that's when they would've asked the grieving daughter and mother what they thought and what they'd seen. At that time, the Your-Hire car would've come to light, the anchor stone would've been mentioned and, the pot being in the wrong location; all these things would've rung alarm bells. What he'd done wasn't 'rocket science' as they'd say, just good detective work that in this case hadn't been done previously.

Pamela had asked what had triggered this sudden 'gut instinct' to set off for France. He'd repeated his old cliché, his mantra, 'There's no such thing as a coincidence in a murder enquiry'. Having Henri Tanguyé cropping up just then was not a coincidence. Now he knew even more thanks to Marie's research and the history lesson from Brigette. The fact that the family name cropped up in the Danielo history and again at the approximate time of Peter's death may be a coincidence, but he doubted it. That being the case, the only option was to go back to the very start of this family's existence, find out what the two families had as a connection and how it had survived to the present day. If you just sat at home and rang the man, the effect wouldn't be so good as turning up on his doorstep and asking him 'why he was on Jersey when he was'.

Just over an hour later they docked in St Malo. Lancaster was happy for Pamela to be driving. He was confident driving abroad, but she'd volunteered. They were soon over the Rance River, heading west towards Morlaix, then Brest. An hour or so later they were dropping down through autumn-coloured woodland and scattered farmland, dotted with creamy brown cattle, following signs for Morlaix. Pamela said that as she was picking up the tab for this trip, it was time for lunch. Marie agreed and, Lancaster went along for the ride. According to Pamela, she knew a restaurant which would do a light lunch; they may just get there before the locals arrived for their customary two-hour meal.

Pamela drove alongside the inland harbour-side, its marina stocked with yachts, then turned into a parking space in the main street. They strolled up the town towards the monumental, brick-built viaduct, straddling virtually the entire centre of the town. She then turned up a side street and they entered a little restaurant that was so French it looked like it had been built for a movie. Pamela's idea of a 'light lunch' turned into three courses ordered from a fixed-price menu. A melted cheese-topped bowl of thick beef soup accompanied by chunks of crusty bread. This would have done Lancaster in any other company, but the ladies were on a mission. The next course was a perfectly cooked, venison steak, served with a simple salad. Alongside this, a bowl of double-cooked chips, not a trace of spare oil on them. Lancaster was finished and so glad he didn't have to drive after this feast. The saving grace for Lancaster was the arrival of a pot of coffee that jolted his senses back into life from the very first sip. He couldn't help but think, *if this is the way Marie ate before she left France, how the hell has she managed to keep such a lithe figure?*

Returning to the car; Lancaster was worse for wear. He felt completely, uncomfortably full. It was a struggle to walk. He hoped this wasn't the standard to be maintained for every meal during this trip. He was pleased to be the one sitting in the rear seat for the next part of the journey to Crozon. Marie and Pamela were chatting away in the front, having a pretend argument with the voice on the sat-nav. Lancaster's head was laid back in his seat and he was fast asleep. It wasn't until they were taking a long right-hand bend coming off the main road, onto the approach for the town of Le Faou, that his head banged gently against the window, he opened his eyes and realised he had been asleep for nearly an hour. They drove through the town, turning down another road signed the D791 Crozon.

Lancaster was struck by how stunning the scenery was. On his right-hand side were glimpses and views of the Brest estuary. The road was a tourist's dream. A combination of Lake District and obviously, France. The road climbed through dense, wooded hillside, remerging into full afternoon sunshine, and there in front of them, a spectacular, cable-hung suspension bridge took the road across the water. *How like the French,* thought Lancaster, *to make crossing a river into an art form.* It was like driving through a harp. The cables hung from tall, concrete-panelled pillars that stood at odd angles, stretching the wires to either side of the roadway. In turn, as if this was not art in itself, the road then curved in an arc, taking the tarmac in a half-moon, across the river to the other side.

The countryside changed once more just to confuse Lancaster. It now looked like the depths of Cornwall, scrubby wooded clumps and roadside trees, stunted by coastal gales, tops curved inward, leaning across the road as if desperately trying to escape the salt-laden winds of winter. They were soon entering the small town of Crozon. Pamela, guided by the sat-nav, turned down a side road, continuing until they could see the sea, then into the forecourt of a small hotel, Les Hotel Ocean. 'You are at your destination' the sat-nav said.

Checking in, Lancaster had a sudden shock when Pamela, having chatted away in French to the man on the desk, then turned around and handed him the key to 'their room'. Lancaster didn't want to cause a scene at the desk but with a quick bit of thinking, asked Marie if she could pop back out to the car and get his jacket off the back seat. Pamela handed her the car key. Leaving their bags by the desk, Pamela and Lancaster strolled into the lounge, which had a huge bay window looking out across the sandy beach and the sea. Lancaster had a look around to ensure they were alone before saying.

"Pamela, I don't want to appear ungrateful, but you've booked Marie and me into a double room. I don't mind paying the extra for another room but..."

"Don't be ridiculous, David," she replied. "I'm not a bloody prude. I know very well you and Marie would much rather share a room. I don't give a damn. For god's sake, just make the most of it."

"But it's something that's frowned upon in the department; If Craven were to find out..."

"Well, he won't be finding out from me. Look, David, I know you two have feelings for one another. We're not in Plymouth; I don't care. I've grown to like the pair of you, and if you can get some enjoyment from each other's company then please do. I look on with some envy being a long-term widow. Just enjoy life when you can; as my father found out, you never know when the end is due. Just bloody well enjoy life."

Lancaster thought for a moment, said, "Thank you", and

accepted the key.

They agreed to off-load luggage and regroup downstairs in ten minutes for a stroll along the promenade that skirted the beach. Once in their room, Lancaster mentioned his conversation with Pamela to Marie.

"You know my thoughts on our relationship, David. I just want it to continue. We can sort out Craven later, you do know it's not a law, this idea of a boss being in a relationship with a subordinate...? It's just something they don't like because it might cause difficulties later if we were to fall out. But that would be our problem, not theirs. You were talking about us sharing a place together, is that not so?"

"Yes, of course."

"Well, how do you intend to explain that to Craven? Will we head off in different cars at the end of the day, pretending we are going our separate ways? At some time, we are just going to have to do this if we want to be together, and to hell with what other people think or say, is that right?"

"Completely right, as usual. I don't know why I see things as a problem when you just see things as they are. But then that's me. Take it or leave it."

Marie leant towards him, grabbed the front of his shirt, pulled him towards her and kissed him. "Then I think I shall take it, Detective Lancaster," she said softly, finishing the kiss. "But maybe later, after our walk. Let's go find Pamela."

The three of them strolled along the seafront in sunshine. Pamela asked how Lancaster planned to handle the Tanguyé situation. His plan was simple. Go to the address they had from the car-hire company and ask the man outright, 'What was he doing on the Island of Jersey that week at the end of

August 2008? And why return the car on the 21st a day early?'
He hoped taking the direct route may trip the man up. If he
fumbled and lied, Lancaster would be able to tell, which would
move him up the cast of suspects. Lancaster was also keen, in a
macabre, historic way, to see the original crash site and retrace
the steps Pamela's parents had taken at the end of the war.
Although a brief visit to France, it was to be a busy one.

On returning to the hotel, they changed and settled into
the half-empty hotel restaurant for an evening meal, which was
adequate for their needs. But an early start, heavy lunch and
a long drive, followed by a walk in the sea air had worked its
magic, so tired, they retired to their rooms, with a plan to be
up early for breakfast, then straight out on the hunt. Marie and
Lancaster were asleep within seconds of curling up together.
But this, Lancaster thought as he drifted off, *is a sign of a good
relationship*. It wasn't a partnership just based on enjoyable sex.

After meeting up the next morning and whilst Pamela
and Marie were at the buffet bar, the manager came through,
ensuring everything was to their satisfaction. Pamela replied
it was. The manager asked if they were here for the boat sale.
Marie saw an opportunity and replied in French that they were
not aware of the sale.

The manager told her about the sale of yachts being held
that day at the marina in Morgat. It was held every couple of
years and drew a wide audience of buyers; many of the hotel
guests were here for the sale. Boats fetched considerable prices,
but there were bargains to be had. Marie told him they were
actually here to find somebody whose family had a historic
connection to Lady Pamela Stottard's original Breton family.

The manager, his attention now fully given, asked what

Pamela's family name was and Marie told him it was 'Danielo'. At which point, the face of the manager lit up.

"Not Danielo the schoolmaster?" he asked in English.

"In Crozon, yes, he was my grandfather," Pamela replied. "Did you know of him?"

"But of course. He taught my parents, and most of the families here in Crozon. He was a great teacher, so patient; his wife was always with him to help and they were much loved here in the town. Have you been to the cemetery? People put flowers on their graves even now. Of course, he was a very brave man, working with the resistance right through the war. He never spoke of it; very few people knew about it until after his death. Another local man wrote about it in his book, then people found out. You must be very proud. Oh, madam, allow me." He gave her a respectful kiss on both cheeks.

Pamela was stunned into silence, not by the impromptu kissing, but by the fact that she had no real evidence of his working for the resistance. She'd always known the rumour of it and the story of the part he'd played in the rescue of her father, but her parents and grandparents had never said a word. In fact, apart from coming back for her grandfather's funeral just before she was born and, as far as she knew, they'd never returned to Brittany. The rest of the family had often been out to Jersey, stayed for holidays and several times Pamela and her brother had been put on the ferry, met by her grandmother and taken for a summer holiday in Crozon, but her parents had never returned to the place where they'd first met. Marie stepped in quickly to fill the void left by Pamela's shocked silence.

"Lady Pamela has, in fact, come here to research some

family history," she said, giving Pamela time to recover. "We've come to find out about members of the Tanguyé family, in particular a man called Henri Tanguyé."

The warm smile of the manager was replaced by a darker, sterner look altogether.

"Sadly, there are some Tanguyé's here," the man replied quietly. "I do not wish to speak out of turn, madam," he continued. "But it is a family name still shunned on the peninsula. They were not nice people before the war and they were not nice during the war. I am sorry if they are friends of yours, madam," he said looking at Pamela, who'd now regained her usual composure. "But I say the truth."

"That's quite all right," Pamela replied. "They are not family friends, but they did appear at some stage in my family's history; I'm keen to fill in the detail. Would you join us for coffee and tell us what you know; it may help piece things together and could save us a lot more research?"

The manager, Christian Perec, agreed.

"What do you know of the Tanguyé family?" Marie asked, "Do you know of Henri? We believe he lives around here."

Christian told them that Henri ran the boatyard in Morgat, just around the bay. He was organising the boat sale. Henri, if truth be told, was the best of the bunch; he'd almost managed to redeem the family name. Henri's great-grandfather had been an important separatist before the war, heavily involved in the Breton movement. He was outspoken and aggressive in his campaigning, but he meant well for Brittany. Henri's grandfather though was different. He continued the campaign for freedom for Brittany, but he was an angry man. When the Germans looked like they were going to start the war, he and others went to Germany to plead their case for a free Breton nation. Once the Germans became an occupying force, they ignored the Separatist movement altogether. The Germans went further; they formed fighting units to go into the countryside and fight against the 'Maquis', the resistance.

One such force was the 'Landerneau Kommando'. Three of the Tanguyé family joined this group. It was a fact that this group killed many people thought to be anti-fascist or members of resistance groups. But locally the action that would never be forgiven was the giving up of resistance fighters trapped on the peninsula when the Allies laid siege to Brest. The Allies had cut off access to the rest of the southern Breton region. At some point, resistance fighters near Crozon, helping to keep the Germans pinned down, ran out of ammunition. They eventually surrendered to what they thought were German soldiers, whom they'd been in a firefight with for hours. They were wrong. It was a splinter group of the 'Kommando'. The captured fighters thought that as the fight for Brittany was nearly over, they may spend a few days held captive, but they were taken as trophies and presented to the German forces. The Germans had bigger fish to fry and told the 'Kommando' to deal with the prisoners, which they duly did. They lined them up in a local farm and shot them all.

It was as if it never occurred to the 'Kommando' that the war would end and there'd be a price to pay. Within months, that was what happened. Then the seekers for vengeance went looking for them. Some were assassinated by the 'maquis' and others were killed by communist resistance members. Some separatists fled the country. Some moved to Ireland and some sought old family and friends in the USA. But within a year of the end of the war in Northwest France, so was the separatist cause. It went dormant for years, shunned by the rest of France. According to Christian, a lot of the blame for that was laid at the Tanguyé family door.

Henri Tanguyé was a third-generation returnee. His grandfather, Yves, was one of the lucky ones, slipping away at war's end and ending up in Ireland, but not for long. He, his wife and their young son, Leon, ended up in America. After many years, Henri, the son of Leon, appeared, eventually purchasing a property in Morgat. Some years later he bought the boatyard. He kept his nose clean, paid his taxes and kept quiet about his family history. He became a local.

Marie thanked Christian for his help. Lancaster was left wondering where, if anywhere, this man fitted into their investigation. The history lesson had been graphic and interesting, but as for Henri, his link with their story was tenuous, to say the least. The man wasn't even alive when Peter was here. If anything, everything they'd just been told put the man further out of the frame, but he wasn't truly out of the picture until proved so. That would be the task for today.

They made the decision that the best way to find Henri and get his story out in the open was to go to the boatyard, find the man and ask him outright. The sale didn't start until 11.00 and as it was still only 09.00, there was plenty of time to catch the man before the 'punters' arrived. They drove around the bay, the marina visible from the road and a mass of masts protruding into the sky. The bay was protected from the force of the ocean by a huge, rocky sea wall. They turned into the boatyard and parked. There were a few prospective buyers milling around and clambering over yachts on display. Most of the sale items were standing on the parking lot on rigs or trailers, but one whole length of a floating pontoon was also included in the sale.

The trio made an effort to look as if they were eyeing up goods for sale. As suspected, within minutes a young lady approached them, offering a glossy brochure and asking if they were looking for anything in particular. Lancaster stepped in and took the lead. He felt Marie and Pamela's stroke of luck in finding Christian should spur him into greater action.

"May I ask?" he said in his best English accent. "Should we wish to make a purchase, do the goods listed all have supporting provenance and appropriate paperwork?"

"But of course," the young lady replied in perfect English. "Anything you place a bid for will, on completion of the sale, have all paperwork and customs tickets applied. May I show you anything in particular?"

"You've been most helpful," Lancaster said. "But Lady Stottard would rather just stroll and see if there's anything that takes her eye. We'll come and find you if we have any questions."

Lancaster hoped the 'Lady' title would ripple back to the yard owner; he was right. Lancaster kept his eye on the main yard whilst looking through the brochure, scribbling details in the margins when he noticed the same woman come out of the office accompanied by a man. The woman pointed them out. The man headed in their direction.

"Brace yourselves, ladies, the manager is on his way," he said. "Pamela, your job is to appear completely aloof. Pretend you're actually... A Lady. Let me do the talking for you. Marie, when you're ready, join in, in French, and make him realise we're bilingual purchasers. Let's get him onside before we mention Jersey."

They were gathered together writing details inside the catalogue when the man reached them.

"*Bonjour, Monsieur, Madames, puis-je vous aider?*" the man said, holding out his hand. Lancaster took it and shook it but Marie cut in straight away.

"*Bonjour monsieur, mais mon employeur*, Lady Stottard, *ne parle pas français, parlez vous Anglais?*" Marie rattled off.

"But of course," he replied. "Though it will not be as good as your French, *madame.*"

"I am Breton, *monsieur,*" she replied brusquely, brushing his comments aside. "Lady Stottard wishes to look through your sales area. If she finds anything that takes her interest, she will be certain to ask for assistance. Do you have a card?"

"Of course." The man handed across an embossed card, upon which the name was clear. 'Henri Tanguyé, *Vendeur et Chandler*, Morgat'.

"Thank you, *Monsieur* Tanguyé. My colleague may like a word with you. Excuse me," she said, walking away to join Pamela on the pontoon looking at a sleek blue yacht.

Lancaster apologised for his colleague's abruptness explaining that, as Lady Stottard's personal secretary, she was very protective of her Ladyship's privacy. Lancaster asked if deals could be done outside of the auctions and was assured that 'all things were possible'. Henri stated that from time to time, a buyer would pay particular interest in a boat and put in an advanced, blind bid, often above and beyond the guide price. They'd then leave a covering payment and a 'Letter of Intent' stating the final price they intended to pay.

If during the auction that price wasn't met, then the boat was considered a 'non-sale' to the general bidders. It would then go to the person who'd placed the 'Letter' but for the price they'd offered. Henri suggested that should Lady Stottard find any yacht of interest, he'd be more than willing to discuss a final price with her to save her having to go through the public auction, although it wouldn't be possible to do that for the blue racing yacht she was at the moment looking over. This one already had a 'Letter of Intent' signed for. It wouldn't do to allow somebody else to 'overbid' the letter.

Lancaster decided to 'play the game' out a little longer. If Henri thought they may spend money, he may be more conducive to an extended conversation at the hotel bar, where they could grill him for as much information as they could. Lancaster shook the man's hand and said he didn't want to take up more of the man's time as he was obviously going to have a very busy morning. He promised to find him if Lady Stottard found anything of interest but felt he should go and tell her the blue one wasn't for sale. They parted company with Lancaster heading onto the pontoon to meet with Marie and Pamela, who were pretending to be interested in the yacht.

As Lancaster got to the ramp onto the pontoon, he stepped aside to allow another gentleman to come up from the decking onto the ramp. The man mumbled a "*Merci*" as he passed and Lancaster suddenly felt sick. He grabbed onto the handrail and stood still for a moment getting his breath back. He knew he had to move his legs and get his feet moving, not draw attention to himself. He half stumbled off the ramp onto the pontoon and walked a few steps before leaning against one of the lighting stanchions. It had been a long time since this had happened to him; the first symptoms of a panic attack were caused in the past by incidents of sudden shock. It was as if that when subjected to an incident like that, his brain couldn't compute what he'd just experienced and temporarily froze. It was a side effect of his dyspraxia and would quickly pass, but nevertheless, he hated being incapacitated like this. It had been such a long time since this had happened that his tablets, his go-to prescribed drug for such an occasion, were no longer in his pocket where they should be, but back in his suitcase in the hotel. He started his breathing routine. Long, slow, deep breaths, whilst choosing something to stare at, in this case, the instructions for a fire extinguisher beside the post. He concentrated hard on understanding the French writing, counting in his head. One, breathe in. Two, breathe out. Three, breathe in...

Marie arrived looking worried. She'd spotted something was wrong from the other end of the pontoon. She was shocked to see his face as white as a sheet, droplets of sweat on his brow.

"My god, David," she said quietly. "What is it, should I get a doctor?"

He held onto her arm, not wanting to interrupt his breathing regime, knowing it was already bringing his heart rate back down, but also aware he had to say something before she started to panic.

"I'll be all right, Marie..." He said between breaths. "... It's just a symptom of my problem... My dyspraxia." He breathed again, slowly. "I had a sudden shock, took me completely by surprise... Triggered this..." He breathed again. "This reaction... It'll pass in a moment..." He breathed again. "Look... I need you to do me a favour... But you must be very, very careful...

And not get noticed." He looked casually to his left, up the ramp towards the boat-parking area and spotted what he was looking for. "Listen very carefully and please, Marie, do as I ask, OK?"

She nodded her acceptance but still looked worried.

"I want you to take this brochure from me," he said holding it out. "Turn slowly to your left... As if you are looking for a boat, OK?"

She did as she was told, thumbing through the booklet as she did so.

"See the guy wearing the pale blue Storm jacket? Bright yellow shoulder pads; nod if you can see him."

Marie nodded; she could see the man.

"I need you to walk up the ramp as if looking for a specific boat. Walk past the man and, when you can, turn, get a look at his face, then come straight back to me, but for all our sakes, do not let him see you looking at him. Understand?"

She looked at him, realising by the look on his face that this was very important. She nodded and walked away carrying the brochure as if searching. Lancaster watched, breathing slowly and deeply, but feeling better by the second. He was back into detective mode once again. Overriding his affliction, as he'd done time and time before. He'd been joined by Pamela, who'd strode up beside him whilst his mind was occupied. He had to pull rank and control this situation. Before she had a chance to say anything, he turned to her quickly.

"Pamela, trust me, please don't question this. I need you to wait for us by that scruffy red yacht; this is important, go now."

She understood the urgency in his voice and did as she was told without looking back. Lancaster raised his eyes back up the ramp and saw Marie walking casually back down toward him. The look on her face confirmed his suspicions. As she reached him, she gripped his arm.

"It's definitely him. Absolutely no doubt. What shall we do?"

"We start with you walking to the end of the pontoon and getting Pamela. Tell her we have a situation developing and we need to return to the car now."

Marie handed back the brochure and strolled off along the pontoon. Lancaster retrieved his mobile from his jacket pocket, scrolled quickly and pressed call, praying Craven wasn't in a conference somewhere. Two rings and the man answered.

"Bomber, how's it going?"

Lancaster cut in quickly before the man went into preamble banter.

"Sir, I have a situation, pin your ears back," he said. Knowing this insubordination would get his full attention. "I am at a boat yard in Morgat in Brittany. There is an auction of yachts about to begin and standing in the boat park looking at boats is... Jean-Luc Batise."

Lancaster could hear the intake of breath over the phone.

"Bloody hell, Bomber... Has he seen you?"

"He doesn't know me from Adam, sir. I wouldn't have recognised him if it wasn't for the fact that he's come up in our enquiry and I saw a photo of him. The problem is obvious. I'm out of jurisdiction, so I can't make an arrest. I don't have any contact numbers other than my normal ones with me, so I can't even contact Interpol..." He was stopped in the middle of his sentence by his boss.

"Bomber, shut the fuck up," Craven said, not angrily, but

just to make a point. "Keep him under observation from a distance. Do not engage. I'll make calls and call you back. I repeat, do not engage."

Lancaster could still see the man out of the corner of his eye. Blue jacket, chrome yellow shoulders; an easy target to spot. Pamela and Marie rejoined him.

"OK, this is what we're going to do," he said calmly. "We'll walk through the sales area until we get to the parking ramp. We feign a lack of interest and casually stroll back to the car. I'm pretty certain we can watch him from there, and I can wait for Craven to call me with a plan. In the meantime, don't look at him, don't even look in his direction, just leave that to me."

The three walked up the ramp to the boat park area. Stopping a couple of times, they turned pages in the brochure before they reached the ramp leading to the car park. Here they stopped again, had a pointing session as if noting boats down on the pontoon, then casually strolled to the car, unlocked it and climbed in. As they closed the doors, Lancaster's phone rang. He hit accept and put it on speaker.

"Sir."

"Do you still have visual?" the big man said.

"Affirmative."

"And it's a positive ID?"

"Affirmative."

"I've had a three-way conversation. Interpol are sending two agents as we speak but have passed it into the jurisdiction of Brest, Drugs Squad. They're sending people to make the arrest as there's still an outstanding European warrant for him. The Brest boys are on their way; they say arrival within the hour. Keep the man under observation. If he moves and you think you can tail him, do it and call me and, Bomber, be bloody careful, my son. No heroics. You're on foreign soil and I can't help you any more than this, understand?"

"Affirmative." Lancaster cut the man off. Batise was on the move, heading down the pontoon ramp with Henri. *Is this business or are the two men working together? Could that be the reason for them both being on Jersey at various times? Is the boatyard connection a coincidence?* He thought not; he'd have to tread carefully, out of jurisdiction, incognito and short on back-up.

"Look, once the man's on the pontoon, I can't see him from here," Lancaster announced. "I need to move closer, but Pamela, please, this is so important, you must stay here. These men we've seen are dangerous. I can't look after myself and you out there. Please just stay in the car, promise?"

Pamela nodded in agreement. "Is there anything I can do?" she asked.

"Yes. Just sit still in the driving seat and lock the doors. Keep the key in the ignition. If we have to move, we'll be back and need to move quickly. If you see us coming back, start the engine, climb to the passenger seat and let Marie take the wheel. Understood?"

He and Marie followed their man at a distance, using the brochure with them for cover. Every time they came around another boat, Lancaster expected Batise to have disappeared, but there he was, casually strolling amongst the collection. Now he was down on the pontoon, deep in conversation with Henri, standing beside the blue racing yacht. Lancaster had a thought, *Batise could still be in his old business, looking for a fast yacht for drug transportation. Maybe he placed the sealed bid on this one, wanted it and could afford to keep out other bidders. But is Tanguyé part of the team?* He had to presume the answer was yes.

Lancaster's phone rang. Craven. "Still in visual?"

"Affirmative."

"Cavalry within thirty minutes, hold the fort."

"Affirmative."

Lancaster was watching through the window of a boat with Marie peering half at the brochure, half through the window.

"On the move," she said. They watched as Batise walked to the end of the pontoon. If they'd not been concentrating, they'd have missed the next minute piece of action. Batise walked casually to the end of the jetty and appeared to be talking on his mobile, but what Lancaster and Marie noticed was the nod he received from a guy sitting in a rib-raider floating next to the pontoon. Batise flipped his phone shut and turned, but with a slight nod of his head as he walked past the man in the dinghy. *So, he has an accomplice,* Lancaster thought, making a note to keep his other eye on him.

"He's planning a quick getaway," he said to Vidêt. "I reckon he probably has a car in the car park. If he has, you can bet he has a driver sat waiting. That could amount to three of them against the two of us, are you up for it if we need to move?"

"Of course."

They strolled casually to another boat, leaned on the foredeck, browsing the brochure, looking over the top at their target. The auction started with a group of people standing around a small yacht parked on a trailer at the far end of the parking area. The action was fast and within five minutes, three boats were sold. The pair moved on to ensure they couldn't get tangled up in the auction if they had to move fast. Batise had also moved to the bottom of the ramp and was leaning on the railing, talking on his phone in animated conversation. Then in the background, above the sound of the auctioneer shouting in French at an undecipherable rate of vowels, came the unmistakable 'dee-daa, dee-daa, dee-daa, dee-daa, dee-daa, dee-daa, dee-daa...' of approaching police. Lancaster turned and looked around the bay to the beach at Crozon Plage. There, in convoy, 'blues and two's' in harmony, were three police cars. Announcing their arrival to all and sundry.

"*Merde*," was Vidêt's only comment. Lancaster whipped his head back just in time to see Batise walking fast back up the ramp. Behind him at the far end of the pontoon, the guy in the rubber raider started the engine, an initial plume of exhaust venting into the sky before he settled down on his seat. Back to the man in question; he was making his way across the car park between the boats. Lancaster and Vidêt moved at an angle across the park, keeping boats between them and the target for as long as possible before they were exposed in the open. Then to Lancaster's annoyance, because he'd expected it, a black BMW saloon swung out of a parking bay at the far end of the car park and accelerated towards Batise, who began running towards it. Lancaster made a split-second decision.

"Get our car, I'm going for him," he managed to say, before breaking into a sprint across the tarmac. He was pretty sure, given a short burst, he'd get to the man before he'd have time to meet the car. He'd have no time to make sure Vidêt was doing as he'd asked; he just kept running. All three of them, Lancaster, Batise and the BMW, arrived at the same space, at almost the same time. Batise had a slight lead. Lancaster pushed his body to clear the gap, but it was not to be; he couldn't outrun a BMW. At the last moment, the 'wheelman' yanked the handbrake and spun the back end of the car in a half circle, catching Lancaster's hip and flicking him to one side to land with a thump on the tarmac. The car was now between him and Batise. Underneath the car, he saw the man's feet disappearing in through the back door. As that happened, he heard the engine revving and saw the reversing lights come on. As the car flew backwards in a deliberate attempt to run him over, Lancaster locked elbows into his sides and rolled, hard and fast to the right, away from the line of sight of the door mirror, in the reflection of which he'd seen the driver's intention. The back wheel was so close to his head that he could smell the rubber. Then the reversing lights went off, the throttle was down and the car accelerated toward the car park entrance.

Lancaster took a breath and cursed. Etched in his mind he had the registration, but that was nowhere as good as having the man. He pushed into a crouching position, wondering if he could cut the car off before it exited the car park. Then he saw the silver VW Golf, the Your-Hire sticker on its door, accelerating across the corner of the car park on a collision course with the BMW. Lancaster was up and running. When the two cars hit, Batise and his driver could come out shooting. The VW slammed into the driver's door, with enough force to knock him clean off track. He careered to the right, straight into a boat trolley. The VW's wheels were still spinning and screeching on the tarmac as the car forced the BMW further into the trailer until the small yacht on top tipped sideways and half landed on the roof of the getaway car. Lancaster got to the VW and opened the door to find Pamela, held in place by the giant puffball created by the airbag. Vidêt was nowhere to be seen.

"Are you OK?" he said to Pamela, aware she was conscious, mobile and swearing. She was trying to get out of the seatbelt and exit the car.

She suddenly shouted, "David, quick!" Pointing through the screen. He turned and saw Batise squeezing between the collapsed yacht and the side of the car. He had to leave her and run. Batise climbed over the towbar of the trailer and started running back across the car park. Lancaster gave chase, dodging people running toward the crash. He could see his adversary clearly and, as he ran, Lancaster had time to take stock of himself. He was breathing easy, the pain of his roll across the tarmac was, for the moment, gone. He could no longer hear the tumult of French voices shouting. All he could hear was his own breathing and the sound of his feet on the tarmac. He knew where the man was headed. Batise was making for the rigid raider, ticking over at the pontoon. He was a clever man, but Lancaster knew he'd catch him. He just knew.

As he reached the ramp onto the pontoon, he was aware, from the corner of his eye, of another figure running across the other side of the car park. He had no time to identify the figure; his eye was on the prize and he was gaining, their feet pounded along the decking. As he ran, Lancaster slipped his jacket and let it fall. He needed to lose the weight if he was going to get the man. At the last minute, as Batise jumped from the pontoon onto the rigid, Lancaster jumped. He flew through the air just as the raider started to move and he landed on Batise, wrapped his arms around him and the pair flew right on over the opposite side and into the water.

The shock of the cold hit him straight away, but he swam regularly off Plymouth. He was used to that initial shock. You just powered through it. But the shock hit Batise, making him gasp for breath, taking in seawater as he did so. He began to cough, which made him suck in more. Both men came to the surface almost immediately. As they cleared the surface, Lancaster headbutted the man, splitting Batise's nose and turning the water red around him. The man gave up, but as Lancaster dragged him to the pontoon, the rigid made a turn and headed to the decking at the same time. As he throttled back to idle, he pulled a gun from inside his jacket and pointed it at Lancaster. At the same time, a powerful voice shouted out in French,

"*Police. Lâcher l'arme. Vite.*"

Lancaster and the man in the boat turned to see Vidêt down on one knee, hands in front in shooting pose and pointing the barrel of a gun in the man's direction. Boatman dropped the gun. It bounced on the rubber and slid sideways into the water. He placed his hands behind his head and closed his eyes, accepting defeat. At that moment all hell broke loose. Suddenly the pontoon filled with blue-overalled French police dressed in paramilitary riot wear, customary balaclava and helmets, armed with sub-machine guns, most worryingly, pointing at Vidêt. But some made it obvious they were aiming at the chest of the man in the boat, the bouncing disco of little red lights illuminating the target. Vidêt raised her hands and shouted,

"*Je suis policier. Je suis police.*"

At this point, she dropped what they'd all thought was a

gun, but turned out to be a length of copper pipe. It landed on the deck with a tinny clunk, at which point the getaway man in the boat started to laugh. Some of the police on the deck, infected by the same lull in action, joined in. They didn't find it funny enough though, not to force Vidêt face down on the pontoon and stick a pair of handcuffs on her wrists. They did the same to a dripping wet Lancaster as they helped haul him and Batise onto the deck. As they got to the ramp, a senior officer arrived, stopping them all in their tracks. He rattled off something in French, but by now Lancaster had gone into clamp-down; he'd no energy left to discuss or argue, especially in French. Vidêt took charge on his behalf and explained that they were here by chance and spotted Batise. They recognised him from the Interpol online poster.

The officer then said in English, "Why did you not wait for us?"

To which Lancaster replied, in English, "Because some bloody idiot warned them, by using the bloody sirens, and they were making their getaway. They would have been long gone before you arrived."

CHAPTER SIX

Lancaster sat on the tailgate of a police four-by-four thinking this morning hadn't gone as planned. He was wet, tired and annoyed. His minimal understanding and use of the French language had now receded into the back catalogue of his brain. Sitting next to him on the tailgate was Vidêt, both of them still in handcuffs. Lancaster couldn't understand what it was she was saying to the detective who appeared to be in charge, but he could certainly hear the venom in her voice as she gave the man a complete Breton tongue-lashing. It was then that Pamela, The Lady Stottard, breezed into play. She arrived in amongst the group of paramilitary-dressed, machinegun-toting, booted men and waved her open passport in their faces like a warrant card. Nobody had any time to get a good look at it, but they were all aware it was something official.

"Who's in charge here?" she said in a polite but very strong voice in English.

The chief detective turned and said he was in charge and asked who she was.

"I am Lady Pamela Stottard, Police and Crime Commissioner for Devon and Cornwall Constabulary, England, and you are?"

"*Inspecteur de Détective* Christophe Ferec. In English, we

are Drugs Squad, Brest."

"Well, Inspector, for some reason you have my colleagues here in handcuffs," she continued boldly. "You must have your reasons, but from where I stand, I cannot fathom why. The man sitting on the ground over there is Jean-Luc Batise. He has an outstanding arrest warrant held with Interpol. He is wanted throughout Europe and is now in your custody. We want no praise for his capture; it's all yours, likewise for both of his getaway drivers. The one they are extricating from the BMW and the stupid one from the rib, you're welcome to the three of them. You can claim all credit for a brilliant arrest and detention. But if my people had not spotted the main man here, you'd all still be sitting in your office drinking coffee. So, if my two off-duty officers are not uncuffed within the next two minutes, I will be getting on the phone with the Head of UK Drugs Enforcement and will pass on your name, Detective Ferec. Do I make myself understood?"

Detective Inspector Ferec was silent for a moment, as was everybody else. He then gave the order to uncuff the two of them.

Pamela handed Lancaster his jacket, from within which he could hear his phone ringing. He retrieved it from the pocket. Craven. He hit the button and put the phone to his ear.

"They'll be with you any minute, Bomber. Are you still in visual?"

Lancaster smiled and looked across at the wet, bedraggled, bleeding man sitting in a puddle.

"Yes, sir, still in visual. Will call you back." It was his turn to cut the man off.

"Inspector Ferec, if you check Batise's pocket you'll find his phone. Just before you arrived, he was calling somebody. It could be a very important contact and, if I may suggest, you may want to grab it before he gets the chance to lose it." Lancaster was coming back into himself now the cuffs were off, suddenly a detective again. He turned to Vidêt and gave her a smile. "Are you OK?"

"Fine," she smiled back. "Inspector Ferec, you may also want to have a word with the yard owner, Henri Tanguyé. Both he and Batise appeared to have a lot to say to each other this morning; he could well be involved. The boatyard could be a cover for their smuggling operations; he has used them in the past."

"And you are?" Ferec said.

"Detective Sergeant Vidêt, Devon and Cornwall CID."

"Detective Inspector Lancaster, Devon and Cornwall CID," Lancaster added. "Any idea what time the guys from Interpol arrive?"

"They are flying in from Paris, so by lunchtime."

"Then can I ask that if you have further questions, we'll be in the bar of Les Hotel Ocean. I need a drink and a change of clothes; do feel free to join me for a brandy, Inspector." With that, he slid off the tailgate, helped Vidêt down and the three of them began walking away. It was only then that they remembered that their car was embedded in the side of a BMW and was going nowhere. What would Basil say...?

"Would you like a lift?" Ferec said with a smile.

The three detectives sat in the bay window at the bar in the hotel. Lancaster had changed, but for the time being, he only had the one pair of shoes so he sat with bare feet, feeling the chill rise through the floor. They raised a glass of Calvados and clinked glasses.

"*À votre santé*," Ferec said. They drank the brandy down in one and sent for three more.

Ferec asked how they came to be in France just at the right time. Lancaster gave an explanation. They were investigating a crime on the Island of Jersey for the UK Police and had been given the name of somebody who may or may not be involved, Henri Tanguyé. They'd decided to come over, find the man, ask some off-the-record questions, found the man owned the boatyard, went to have a chat and, then purely by chance Lancaster had spotted Batise. It was all just chance. Pure luck. He'd telephoned his commanding officer in the UK and the rest just happened.

Ferec looked at them both for a second or two, as if he doubted what Lancaster had told him was the full story, then raised his second glass. "Here's to chance then." After that, he told them he'd have to return to Brest to oversee the interviews, but he'd be grateful if the three of them would stay around the hotel for the rest of the day. He was sure the guys from Interpol would want a word. They shook hands, said they'd meet again at some stage before they returned to the UK and he'd get the Interpol guys to take full statements later. They should earn their money. After all, 'It was we who made the arrest, not them'.

Lancaster laughed but didn't say anymore. Pamela returned from the lounge; she'd spoken with Basil on the phone and explained they'd had a 'prang' and the car wasn't drivable. After a moment of shock, he'd asked if they were all OK. He suggested they hire another car from Crozon and put the company in touch with him. He'd get a recovery sorted and deal with the insurance if she'd pop into the office on her return and fill in the details. Lancaster told her they'd need to stay around until Interpol arrived but asked Marie if she'd pop to the outdoor centre they'd passed and get him another pair of shoes, size 11. He was fed up with cold feet and wanted to put some socks on.

Marie left Pamela and Lancaster sitting looking out to sea. He asked what had happened at the boatyard. Pamela said that she'd been watching what was going on as best as she could, when she saw Batise walking across the car park, then saw Lancaster crossing behind a boat trailer. When she looked back, Batise was running and the BMW was driving towards them. She'd put two-and-two together, realised it was a getaway car, presumed Lancaster would come to her so started the car in readiness, then saw him giving chase to Batise. Realising there was no way he'd get back to her if Batise got to the BMW, she made the decision to move closer. As the trailers were in her way she had to reverse, then come around from the other side of the car park. She'd lost sight of them for a moment. The next thing she saw was Lancaster rolling across the floor and Batise jumping into the back seat. She made the split-second choice to stop them. 'It was all quite exciting really' she said. She'd put her foot down and decided to ram the other car before it had time to get any speed up. When she hit it, she hadn't allowed for the airbag going off. It took her completely by surprise, she got her shoe hooked over the throttle and the car kept forcing its way forward until she saw the boat fall over. Then the engine stalled.

Lancaster laughed. "So when I said stay in the car and don't do anything, you did at least get the part about staying in the car. But honestly, are you OK?"

"Yes, actually I'm fine, it was all very exhilarating. Great fun."

"And thank you for bossing around the French police, you were magnificent. Though I didn't know you were actually the Police and Crime Commissioner?"

"Well... I nearly was... There were only a few votes in it, maybe next time."

Outside, an unmarked Volvo pulled up, blue lights flashing in the grill, giving away the fact that it was a police car. A policeman sat behind the wheel and two people got out and walked toward the hotel. One was a tall guy, smartly dressed, the other, a woman in well-fitting jeans and a check shirt, jacket thrown over her shoulders.

Lancaster stood as they entered. "Interpol, I presume." He held out his hand. "Fancy a Calvados?"

The two Interpol officers questioned them thoroughly and got a full statement. Lancaster added that they may want to do research on the blue yacht that had Batis's deposit on it. If it had been sitting around the boatyard for a while it might just have a cargo of cocaine stashed on it awaiting collection, just like the old days. Lancaster also alerted them to the fact that back on Jersey he had a photo of another Batise who operated the bank account. His theory being that one of them was the real Batise, the other a 'patsy', a frontman, there to take the fall if it all went wrong. He also mentioned the phone Batise was using was now in the hands of the Brest police. Although Lancaster didn't want to cast doubt on their trustworthiness, they should check out the last call he was on. Lancaster couldn't tell if it was incoming or outgoing, but if it was the former, it might have been a tip-off from Brest saying the troops were on their way. If it was the latter, the Batise in custody may have been speaking to the other Batise about the yacht purchase; it was worth checking out. Lancaster also mentioned he might want a favour in return at some stage. He'd like the opportunity to question Batise about his possible involvement in a death on Jersey in 2008, but there was no hurry; he'd know where to find him. The two officers thanked them, said they may want to question them further and to let them know before they left for the UK. They agreed, parting company in good moods.

All-in-all, it had been a very productive day. He asked for one more favour from Marie. He sent her up to the room to put his best shoes on the radiator, then retrieve his phone which he'd left in his coat pocket on the bed. When Marie returned, she was wagging a finger at him.

"You're in trouble; three missed calls from you-know-who." She handed him the phone and the jacket. DCI Craven picked up immediately.

"Where the bloody hell have you been, Bomber? What's been happening? Have they got him?"

Lancaster explained that yes, they had indeed got him, along with two accomplices. After which he'd been unavoidably detained, in handcuffs at first, then questioned by the local police, followed by questioning by Interpol. He apologised for not returning his calls but and this was in fact the truth, he'd only just been given his jacket and phone back. Craven was furious at this news. How dare they place his officers in cuffs, he'd make a complaint to their superiors straight away. Lancaster asked him to let it go. The job was done, so they could get back to their own task of finding Peter's killer. To this end, Lancaster asked if there was any update on the exhumation. Apparently, the paperwork was done-and-dusted and work to exhume the body would begin in two days' time. Rover was due on Jersey before the exhumation to make sure nothing was missed as the body came out of the ground. Lancaster confirmed that they'd be finished in Brittany by tomorrow night, presuming the local police had finished with them. Craven assured him that as far as he was concerned, they already had. Craven asked finally if they were all OK. Lancaster just said yes, they were fine that there was just the little detail of finding another hire car as Lady Stottard had had a slight mishap with the one they arrived in. 'Bloody women drivers, Bomber, don't trust 'em, mate'. Again, he was gone. *Women drivers indeed, if only he knew.*

While Pamela talked with Christian about getting another car, Lancaster had a chance to speak with Marie.

"So, what happened when I sent you to find Pamela and the car?"

"Simple. I ran round the boat trailers trying to keep out of sight, came out the other end and the car had gone! It was heading off across the car park. I knew what she planned to do, so I set off again running towards it. I saw Pamela ram the BMW and by the time I got near, you were off after Batise. I saw him jump over that trailer, but you looked like you would get him, so I stopped to make sure Pamela was OK. The airbag had deflated by then, and she was getting out of the car. There were people arriving so I left her and ran after you. I got to the dock and saw you flying through the air, taking Batise with you. I thought that was that. Then the idiot in the rib came back. I could see a shoulder holster under his jacket. I looked for something to throw at him then spotted the toolbox and the bits of pipe. I was going to throw it at him, but by then you were by the decking, and I saw him level the gun. I just thought on my feet, as you would say, assumed the position and hoped he would have bad eyesight... It worked, didn't it?"

Lancaster leaned forward and kissed her on the lips. "It certainly did, and I thank you."

"You may want to improve on the thank you later... Sir..."

Whilst they waited for the new car to arrive, they grabbed sandwiches from the bar. With the arrival of sandwiches, a pot of coffee and bowl-like cups, Pamela had ordered another three shots of Calvados, they stood in little glasses beside the coffee, looking menacing. They'd wait until after the sandwiches. Lancaster liked the idea of the French sandwich: crusty, flaky, half loaves filled to the brim with ham, salad and mayonnaise. As soon as you touched them, bits of crusty shrapnel snapped and broke free, covering everything for miles around in assorted sections of your lunch. Lancaster thought, at this moment, they just hit the spot.

After a semi-silent interlude whilst all three ate, it was difficult to speak when fighting your way through half a baguette, they finished and Marie poured the coffee. Pamela passed around the Calvados and raised her glass to them.

"You two were brilliant today," she said. "I've never seen two people pull a plan together, call in resources and execute an arrest with such speed and togetherness; it was a joy to be a part of. Here's to teamwork and friendship."

They drank to that, but Lancaster pointed out that it had nearly gone 'tits up' when Batise made it to the BMW. If Pamela hadn't taken the action she chose to take, the end could've been Batise and his driver disappearing into the distance and, if Marie hadn't known how to handle a piece of pipe and look like she meant it, he could be dead by now.

"That's very true, David," Pamela said. "But deep down, you knew damn well that I wouldn't have just sat in that bloody car watching. That's why you chose to run after him. Sending Marie back towards the car was just your backup plan, keeping somebody in reserve. It was a damn good plan and it all worked splendidly."

Lancaster looked at her and then began to laugh, followed by Marie and then they were all laughing hysterically. Lancaster wasn't sure if the cause was Pamela's vision of how the day had gone, the alcohol in the system or the after-effects of a sudden, adrenaline-packed morning, either way, it was a release.

After the exertions of the morning, followed by three Calvas, an after-lunch nap was needed. Craven would never approve, but then he wasn't paying the bill for this part of the enquiry. They agreed to meet in the bar in an hour and a half to take stock and plan the next move. Lancaster and Vidêt had just started to doze when the room phone rang. It was Christian at reception and, as he put it, "The Tanguyé is here to see you. I have put him in the bar."

They decided to let Pamela rest and go and see what he wanted. The man sat in the bar with a small beer in front of him. Henri Tanguyé had lost the sparkle of the salesman he'd been that morning. He looked tired; the beer glass was still full. He stood as the two detectives entered the bar. Lancaster held out his hand in greeting, but Henri ignored it.

"Why did you come to my boatyard this morning? Why destroy my reputation and lose me thousands of euros? What did I do to deserve this? I have spent the last two hours being interrogated by police about my relationship with the men arrested. I am humiliated in the eyes of local people and I have taken years to be accepted here. Why me?"

Lancaster looked at the man. Henri was almost in tears. Lancaster did feel a little sorry for him. He explained that the arrest of Batise was a complete surprise to them as well. It had been a freak chance that they'd recognised him from a police photograph. Lancaster said he was sorry the police had questioned him about Batise, but to be honest, what else did he expect? A Europe-wide manhunt had been going on for years looking for this man and he turns up at a boat sale in Brittany. The police had to wonder if he'd been here all along.

"As I told the police, everything was in order," Henri said. "Batise paid a deposit via a bank draft over the internet. He e-mailed a 'Letter of Intent' offering a very competitive price, above what I had been hoping for. This morning was the first time we had ever met. He wanted to be assured no one had put in a higher bid and he wanted to look over the whole yacht to ensure there was no damage. He was very particular, checking below decks, lifting all the hatches."

"And you still say you'd never met the man before today?"

"Yes. But it was not the first time we had done business," Henri replied. "He purchased two other yachts over the last three years in the same manner. Bidding higher than was expected, always winning the bid. But I never met the man. Other people collected the yachts. I always got paid, it was good business. I don't understand why you would have told the police that I may be involved?"

"Who told you I suggested that?"

"One of the policemen on the way to the police station. He told me you were English police and it was you who had been looking for Batise. So all of that about you wanting to buy a boat for your Lady whatever was just a lie. It has caused me lots of trouble and lost me money."

Lancaster had listened to the man politely, now he'd had enough. He was a detective in the police force, admittedly in the wrong country, but it was still his job. He'd done nothing wrong this morning, and if truth be told, this man had made a lot of money out of his dealings with Batise and had never questioned it, even though he'd known there was something odd going on, now Lancaster had run out of sympathy. The day was not done yet, but it already felt as if it had been a long one.

"*Monsieur* Tanguyé, in August of 2008 you were on the Island of Jersey, why?" Lancaster asked, taking the wind straight out of the French man's sails.

"What? What do you mean, what was I doing?"

"Exactly that, *Monsieur* Tanguyé. It's not a difficult

question. I repeat, August, 2008, you were on Jersey. What were you doing there?"

"I am a yacht salesman, *monsieur*; what do you think I was doing? I sailed a thirty-footer there, single-handed from here for a customer. It was a legitimate sale. I still have the paperwork."

"You hired a car from Your-Hire?" Vidêt butted in quickly, giving the man no time to think.

"I sailed the damn yacht to Jersey. I moored at the marina at Saint Helier as requested. When I booked in with the harbour master, he told me he had a message from Mr Clevis, the buyer. He'd been delayed and would be with me in two days' time to complete the deal and pay me for delivery."

"What was the name of the yacht?" Vidêt asked.

"It was the 'Ocean Star'."

"Why the hire car?"

"I was not going to leave the island without my money. I booked into a hotel, then got a taxi to the airport to find out about flight times back to Brest. I came out of the airport, saw the Your-Hire office, thought I might just as well hire a car and look around the boatyards and marinas, see if I could do any business. I spent the next couple of days doing just that. Then Clevis turned up and paid for the boat, the delivery and my hotel. I took the car back to the airport and flew home. But what the hell has this got to do with the arrest of that man in my auction?"

Lancaster told him it had nothing to do with today's arrest but played secretive when asked more. It was part of a much bigger enquiry and he should think himself very lucky that all he got was questioning and some loss of income. The people they were dealing with normally committed murder. Lancaster suggested, rather than sit here complaining about what had happened, that he should be making money out of it. He should contact the papers and television and tell his side of the story, how Interpol had arrested a known criminal right in the middle of his boat auction, but it would be best if he didn't mention the fact that there had been two English detectives there as well. If news of this got out, he may just regret it. If handled well, his next auction should be packed out.

Henri Tanguyé hadn't thought about that. He realised he had indeed been thinking this back to front; there was definitely a way of making some advertising for his next auction from this bad morning.

"So who are you? Do you work for Interpol or something?"

Vidêt leaned forward in her seat and looked the man straight in the face. Then without breaking into a smile, said,

"You must forget you ever saw us. We cannot tell you who we work for, it's safer if you do not know. Make sure you never mention us again. Is that understood, Henri?"

Tanguyé looked a little worried. "I will not mention you again." With that, he stood, held out his hand and both detectives shook it solemnly. Both maintained very serious looks on their faces. The man left the bar, his undrunk small beer still on the tabletop.

Lancaster and Vidêt watched the man go. They were taking it in turns to drink the man's leftover beer when they were joined by Pamela. They explained their apparent jollity, telling her what had been said during their encounter with

Henri, that he'd now gone away happier than when he arrived. Pamela wanted to know whether he had any involvement in her father's death, but Lancaster assured her that the man couldn't have made that story up so quickly and not stumbled in its telling. Lancaster was convinced the guy had been telling the truth; it would be a simple task to contact the harbourmaster and check the story. They'd also check Mr Clevis, who had purchased the yacht and check the airport with regards to flights out to Brest during that week. Their gut feeling was the man had nothing to do with Peter's death. Coming here and speaking to Tanguyé had always been a bit of a punt, a gamble. It had now been checked out and could be cross-referenced. If nothing turned up, they'd cross him off their list.

Vidêt wasted no time. She googled the harbourmaster, Saint Helier, got an e-mail address and telephone number for them and put in a call. She used her status, DS Vidêt, Devon & Cornwall Police, to gain the other person's attention, then asked if they had a database or file system for people who moored at the marina. This was confirmed. She gave them the names, dates and details requiring corroboration and was told it may take a while, but they'd come back to her later. Vidêt pulled rank and told them it was a matter of urgency. The information was needed as part of an active enquiry and that 'later' was not good enough. The receiving end told her they'd be back within half an hour.

Meanwhile Lancaster had been on the phone to Jersey airport. He'd given the dates of the suspected flight and had it confirmed. Yes, there'd been flights from Jersey to Brest, every day at 2:30 p.m. for several years, including that one.

All-in-all it looked like Henri's story was going to check out. He wondered if it wasn't time to head back and prepare for the arrival of Rover and the exhumation. He suggested this to Pamela, but Pamela came up with her own suggestion.

"As we've come so far together in this enquiry, while we're so close, I'd like to drive to the cemetery and lay some flowers on my grandparent's grave, then if we leave here first thing tomorrow, we can drive up onto the peninsula and visit my great-grandparents farm where mother and father met. We can walk to the cliff tops where his Spitfire came down. It's a place I've never visited, I don't know why. There was just never the right time, now we're here it would be remiss of me not to use the opportunity, don't you think?"

"Of course," Lancaster replied. "I think I'd quite like to see where it all started as well."

They decided the visit to the cemetery would be made now, before the evening meal. Pamela found where the town florist was, then left a message in reception in case the Brest or Interpol detectives came looking for them. They drove to the florists in a car lent by Christian, picked up flowers and then continued to the cemetery. Touchingly, there were pots and bouquets in various stages of decomposition, mostly with ineligible cards, but it was obvious that people locally thought a lot of Paul and Pamela Danielo who now lay, side by side in death, as close as they were in life. Pamela laid her flowers and made a solemn promise. She would be back on a more regular basis. The three then returned to the hotel and prepared for the evening meal.

The next morning, during breakfast, Christian informed

them their new hire car was outside and there was paperwork to be done. Pamela went to conclude the deal whilst Lancaster and Vidêt finished eating.

"How do you think your visit to France has gone this time, Detective Inspector Lancaster?" Vidêt asked with a smile.

"Well, Detective Sergeant Vidêt, I think it was quite uneventful really, don't you?"

They laughed at the irony. They'd come here looking for one person and ended up finding somebody else, who'd remained hidden in full sight for the last four years. The worst of it was, they wouldn't gain any credit; it would all go to the Brest police and Interpol. But those were the breaks. Lancaster put through a call to Ferec and got permission to leave; he knew where they'd be if needed. Pamela returned, telling of the car they now had, an almost identical VW Golf. But the steering wheel was on the wrong side of the car. Pamela handed the keys to Marie; it looked like she was 'wheel-man' for the rest of the trip.

The drive to Roscanvel was another rural joy for Lancaster. The whole route reminded him of Cornwall. Small fields, some put down to crops, rows of some sort of brassica. Lancaster also saw a sadness in the landscape, fields overgrown with gorse and scrub, cloaked by 'old-mans-beard', the wild honeysuckle. Once through the little village of Roscanvel, they continued up small lanes, following the map Pamela's mother had given her. The road crested a rise onto desolate moorland, filled with twisted, windswept trees and yellow-flowered gorse. They almost went straight past the track to the old farm, if it hadn't been for the fact that according to her mother's notes, just past the lane there was a granite cross. It was this that alerted them to the fact they'd gone too far. Vidêt reversed to a trackway on the left. They parked the car, not wanting to risk the track, and walked down between scrub oak and evergreen hedges. It was Vidêt who first realised the farm was no more. To her right she spotted stonework amongst the trees. On closer inspection, they realised it was the remains of the old outbuildings and farmhouse.

The more they stumbled through the undergrowth, the more they uncovered, only the bare bones remained, a skeleton of former lives and loves. Like some kind of magician, Pamela pulled a handkerchief from her sleeve and wiped her eyes, quelling the tears that spilt. The realisation that she'd left it all too late. Returning not to hugs, kisses, greetings from old family members and invites to 'come on in' echoing around the yard. But to the sadness, of finding it had all fallen down, slowly returning to nature. They discovered another track out of the farmyard, up to the top of the hill, where the sheep and milking cattle had wandered loose amongst the bracken and gorse.

Once onto the headland, you could see why Pamela's parents had chosen to build their home on Jersey where they had. The views were almost identical. To the north, across the estuary, the opposing cliffs. Between them and those cliff tops, boats were going up or down this piece of water, plying trades or out for pleasure. To the west, they could see the white-capped waves of the North Atlantic. If it wasn't for trees on their right, to the east they'd be able to look at the full length of the estuary, glimpses of which were still visible and seen through gaps in the foliage.

They crossed the cropped grass, lawn-like area, walking towards the cliff top. Here they looked down to the sea below, gently sloshing the escarpment base. Seagulls, frightened by the figures' arrivals, dropped off the cliff face, gliding out across the water, screaming curses as they flew. The three of them stood looking out across the estuary, watching the gulls stoop and hang on the wind. The scenery was spectacular, but the day was moving on and they had travelling to do. They turned their backs on the cliff, walking back across the grass and thrift clumps toward the gap in the undergrowth, leading down to the farm, they came across overgrown concrete, and rusted, twisted remains of angle iron protruding from the edge of the gorse. They looked at each other as realisation hit. This must have been the location of the original gun emplacements, the emplacements Peter's plane crashed into when it made its final landing all those years ago. Thanks to the Germans' formulaic obsessiveness for detail, the concrete looked exactly the same as the emplacements on the clifftops on Jersey. Same colour, the same exposed chippings breaking the surface, same perfect right angles on the plinth.

They retraced their steps to the farm. Making a U-turn, Vidêt turned the car for St Malo and the afternoon ferry. The journey home was uneventful, other than a call from Craven informing Lancaster that things were moving at a pace; Rover was arriving at the airport that evening. The exhumation was due to take place the following morning. The island police now knew of Lancaster and Vidêt's presence and their involvement in the reopening of this case. Craven suggested they should all watch their backs; he wasn't expecting an easy ride. They should be polite and on high alert for 'skulduggery'.

They opted to skip lunch, to ensure an early arrival at the ferry, the earlier boat, which would give them ample time to get to the airport and meet Rover. Pamela had already told Lancaster to tell the man that there was room at the house for him and to not book a hotel. Given Craven's warning, it would probably make sense for them to all stick close together. Lancaster wasn't happy that they may be working against the wishes of the local police. He'd come across inter-departmental warfare before; he hated it. As far as he was concerned it was simple. The previous examination of Peter's death was a farce. So many textbook errors had been made, it could have actually been used as a training manual on how not to execute an enquiry. Looking with a fresh pair of eyes, the mistakes were plain to see. The local police should be grateful to them for pointing these mistakes out, but somehow, he knew they wouldn't be.

With Vidêt at the wheel, they managed to get the earlier ferry, getting back to the house in time to offload luggage and grab tea and biscuits, then Lancaster and Vidêt drove to the airport to meet Rover. The flight was on time, checkout was easy. Rover walked out of the door looking his usual, if slightly wacky, self. Benjamin Landy, Rover to almost all of his friends ('Landy... Land Rover... hence Rover'), was a stand-out sort of guy. Lancaster had worked cases before which required the expertise of a good pathologist. The last case they'd worked together was earlier that year.

Rover had been involved in a pathology examination

of an ancient bog body, found not surprisingly, in a bog on Dartmoor. It had been Rover who'd not only aged the body to have only been in the ground just over twenty years but also that it wasn't the peaty soil that had turned the body's skin a leathery brown. He pinned the man's place of origin as North Africa and worked out what time of year the body had gone into the ground and what the cause of death was, which turned the enquiry into a murder hunt.

Rover was a surfer. He had full-sleeved, tribal-style tattoos covering both arms down to his wrists and by all accounts, these also extended across his back. His hair was black, tied back in matted braids. As expected for a man who spent his spare time surfing the waves, his exposed skin was permanently tanned. In his left earlobe was a large hole, filled by an even larger, silver earplug with a hole through the middle. He wore black, multi-pocketed trousers, a black short-sleeved shirt, exposing his tattoo collection to the world, and across his shoulder, a huge backpack. He came out of the swing doors like some kind of Special Forces veteran; several people on their way in stepped aside to give him room.

"Yo, Bomber. How's it going?" the man said as soon as he saw them.

Lancaster shook the man's hand and took the kit bag from him, immediately regretting it. It weighed a ton. On the way across the car park, Lancaster gave him the advice from Craven to tread carefully because the locals may not take kindly to them stirring up old cases. As expected, Rover wasn't bothered. He planned to make phone calls as soon as he was settled, double-check times for the next day's exhumation and ensure that as agreed by their bosses on the mainland, an adequate pathology space would be provided for the autopsy. This was something Rover wanted to get done as soon as the body had been lifted, prior to further decomposition setting in once the cadaver was exposed to the air.

Rover had another request. He had the cemetery address for the exhumation and wanted to visit the site before the lifting occurred the following morning. Lancaster thought the timing was right. Pamela was home. It would be a sensitive move to do this while she wasn't around. Vidêt punched in the postcode for the Cimetière St Helier, Jersey. It was a simple route to follow, which found them turning off the road and through the grand, almost stately home-style gateway, parking just inside the entrance. They could go no further anyway. A familiar, blue and white ribbon stretched across the tree-lined avenue, preventing further access. In front of the tapeline, a lone constable with a clipboard was eyeing them avidly as they exited the car. At times like these, Rover's appearance could sometimes cause alarm and the look on the constable's face showed this was such an occasion. As they approached the officer, Rover whispered to his colleagues to have their warrant cards ready and leave this to him.

The constable pulled himself up to full, attentive height, attempting to look as official as he could. Rover smiled at him, pulling a sheet of paper from the pocket of his combats and handing it to the constable.

"Good evening, Officer," Rover said in a friendly fashion, an attempt to diffuse the moment of tension. "My name's Benjamin Landy. I'm the Forensic Pathologist sent out from Derriford Hospital in Devon. This is my official letter of introduction from the UK Foreign Office signed by the Secretary of State. I'm here to attend the exhumation of Peter Urbawicz tomorrow. I'm due to meet the island coroner in the morning. I wish to visit the site now and get my bearings. These are Detective Sergeant Vidêt and Detective Inspector Lancaster, also from the UK. They're here to accompany me everywhere and make sure I don't upset anybody. Can you tell me if the tenting has gone up over the grave yet?"

The constable looked at the official letter, on headed paper. Then looked at both warrant cards, then looked at his list. All three names were there, but he'd envisaged an old man in a white coat, not a tattooed hulk of a man wearing 'Rasta-dreadlocks'. He made a decision; he wasn't paid enough to argue or question an official document. He gave them directions to a large marquee, erected over a space hidden from view. In front of which stood yet another constable. The officer had them sign in before he'd let them enter the tent. It was good to see procedures being adhered to.

Inside the tent, sheets of plywood had been laid over the grass throughout the entirety of the space. Here and there the strange appearance of gravestones were jutting through the plywood floor, belonging to others who'd bear silent witness to tomorrow's events. At one end of the canvased enclosure stood a newly formed pile of deep brown soil, next to an equally impressive, perfectly formed rectangular hole. Rover cursed softly and approached the pit before apologising for his cursing. He'd thought at first the grave had already been exposed. This would have begun a degradation of both the coffin and its contents. Closer inspection revealed the gravediggers had excavated about half of the pit to give them a head-start in the morning. They'd left enough soil in place to prevent air from getting to the lower levels. To the side of the mound stood the gravestone, resting against a wooden framework, held in place by canvas strapping. Engraved across it the simple text, 'Peter Urbawicz, Beloved Husband, Father, Grandfather and Freedom Fighter, Born 1926, Died August 2008'. Rover was content with the preparations, happy to leave, get back to Pamela's house and grab a shower before dinner. He was starving. They signed out, politely thanking both officers on duty for their assistance and wishing them a good evening.

Despite the actions planned for the following morning, dinner was an enjoyable, sociable event. Pamela, forewarned with regards Rover's unorthodox appearance, took to the man straight away for the same reasons Lancaster and Vidêt did. Like them, Rover was on the fringe of his branch of society. He knew he caused a stir and turned heads when he turned up at seminars or walked around the hospital wearing his name tag around his neck. But it didn't bother him one bit. Landy knew that, as a pathologist, he was good at his job. With a busy time envisaged for the following day, everybody decided on an early night. Lancaster indicated he wanted a word with Pamela before going up. Pamela poured them both after-dinner brandies which they took through to the lounge.

"I don't know what your plans were for the morning, Pamela," Lancaster asked. "But I'd be very grateful if you didn't attend the exhumation. I've been to these things before.

It doesn't matter how much wooden flooring, carpets or artificial grass the cemetery lays down, it'll never take away the grubbiness of the occasion. At the end of the day, the casket never comes out of the ground in pristine condition. It will never be the relative laid to rest previously in a gleaming coffin, and it always comes as a shock to those family members who attend. And on a selfish note, I feel we've become friends, and I really don't want to see you upset. I also don't want pressure put on Rover, who's now sharing your home and becoming part of this story. To do justice, for you and your father, I need Rover to remain impartial and unattached. That casket needs to be just like any other, because when the body becomes friend or family, it makes the task personal, and that's hard. Very hard."

Pamela sat sipping her brandy, thinking. Lancaster gave her time. It had been a lot to ask of her and she needed to think it over.

"You're right of course. To be honest, I was uncertain in my own mind whether to attend or not. It would have been pointless to have started all this, yet not take your advice. But I want your assurance that you will ensure the local police do not cock this up. Is that a promise?"

"That goes without saying, Pamela, and thank you." With that he got up, downed the last of his drink and, leaning forward, gave Pamela a spontaneous yet brief kiss on her cheek. "Rover and I will make sure that Peter's treated with compassion and dignity."

The following morning Lancaster, Vidêt and Rover drove to the cemetery for 7:30. Rover had arranged a meeting with the island coroner to be on-site at 8.00. By the time they got to the main entrance, a uniformed officer standing in front of the gates was ready to turn the public away from the whole site. They announced their names, showed warrant cards, got ticked off the list and parked inside. The ball was now rolling. Before they exited the vehicle, Lancaster had a quick word with the other two.

"There may be hostility from some of the parties on site today, but what I want us to do, and I'm sure I don't really need to say this... But I will anyway, is not show a cocky face. Be business-like and professional at all times. I want you, Marie, to stick by Rover's side. Make sure nobody attempts to get in the way or restrict access at any time. Be firm but polite. I'll leave you to your own devices, Rover. You know your job better than anybody else who'll be in that tent; just make sure that whatever you need, gets done. Don't stand for any nonsense. We've been sent to do a job and nobody must distract us from it. I may disappear for a little while but I won't have gone far. I am hoping to have a word in the ear of whoever the senior officer is and diffuse this situation before anybody gets their backs up. It's worth the try. Rover, have you got any idea where they're planning for you to carry out the autopsy?"

"They plan to move the casket to Jersey General. I suggest we all 'follow the van, and don't dilly-dally on the way'."

"What is 'dilly-dally'?" was Vidêt's next question.

"We'll tell you later," Lancaster replied.

As they approached the marquee there was a huddle of people gathered outside. Three cemetery workers in green overalls, the giveaway were the long-handled spades they were leaning on. Two uniformed constables, one with an obligatory clipboard, were taking names prior to anyone entering the tent. Lancaster figured the other three people wearing civvies were probably the ones they needed to be marking as their opposite numbers. Lancaster took the lead and stepped straight up to the oche.

"Good morning, gentlemen," he said holding out his warrant card. "Detective Inspector David Lancaster, Plymouth CID, my sergeant, Detective Sergeant Vidêt, this other gentleman is Doctor Benjamin Landy, Forensic Pathologist, also from Plymouth. I understand you're expecting us. May I ask who the senior officer is assigned to this case?"

"That'll be me," a tall man, probably in his forties, and by his stance and tone of voice, not quite sure how this was supposed to be handled, said, "Detective Chief Inspector Wardly. This is my second in command, Detective Inspector Beard, both from Jersey CID. This gentleman is Mr Christopher Huxley, the island's coroner. He's here to oversee the exhumation."

"Then if that's the formalities completed, shall we let the coroner and Doctor Landy crack on? They're forecasting rain later this morning, so it would be good to get this done before we make any mess." Lancaster had sized up his opponent and decided it was time to make a strategic move. "Chief Inspector Wardley, may we have a quick chat whilst they make a start?"

Without waiting for an answer, he gave a nod to Vidêt to carry on, then turned his back and stepped to one side of the path away from the group. As Wardley moved across to join him, the pair started walking away from the scene and up the tree-lined avenue. As Wardley was about to speak, Lancaster beat him to it.

"Listen, sir," Lancaster started, acknowledging and bowing to the other man's rank, "I don't know if you've been in this situation before, but I have, having some smart-ass come into my patch and tell me about a crime I had no knowledge of up until then. We have a situation here that neither of us can turn a blind eye to. Lady Stottard is a friend not only of our state-appointed High Sheriff of Devon but also a personal friend of my Chief Constable and my Chief Inspector. She's also in line to be the next Devon & Cornwall Police Commissioner, so my thoughts are that the quicker we carry out this autopsy and go home, the better for all of us, don't you agree?" Lancaster waited two seconds then cut in again.

"What I'd like to do, with your permission, is to get this body over to your general hospital ASAP and get Dr Landy working on it straight away. Hopefully, we can be on our way off the island before anybody knows any difference. The body can be re-interred and the case closed. How does that sound to you?"

"So, you don't think a murder *has* been committed then?" Wardley asked, sounding surprised.

Lancaster smiled at the man. "It would be presumptuous and inadvisable of me to supersede an autopsy, sir, wouldn't it? Especially as so many top people have asked for it. But you can rest assured that should we discover anything untoward; you'd be the first to know. As far as I'm concerned, should this appear to be the case, then the enquiry would then be yours. If there's any glory to be had, then you're welcome to all of it. To be honest, obviously in complete confidence, we just want to get back home. Not meaning any offence to your glorious island."

Wardley stopped and looked at Lancaster. "I was under the impression that you'd already made up your mind on this investigation. Is this not the case?"

"Obviously, Chief Inspector, my sergeant and I haven't been idle; we've done the legwork. Please, don't get me wrong, we're still police officers and being paid to do a job. Yes, we've found irregularities that need some explanation, but with respect, sir, you've been in this business longer than I. Can you imagine any historical case from the past which, when looked at afresh with new eyes and new techniques, wouldn't turn up something new or something missed? It may not change the original diagnoses, but it would be there nevertheless. It's a process we have to go through and we all do it as professionally as we can."

Wardley looked at Lancaster a moment, then held out his hand and they shook to bond this new relationship. "Very good then, Detective Inspector Lancaster, let's get this done, shall we?"

The pair walked to the tented area, stepping through the covers into the brightly-lit confines of the marquee. The excavation team had finished their work. The dark, fresh soil, a testament to their labours, was stacked beside the pit. Standing in the pit, upper body protruding from the hole stood one of the diggers, presumably in his socks, as his rubber wellies were standing side by side on the boards beside the pit. He was attaching straps to the handles of the coffin in readiness for the extraction. Standing next to the wellies, watching, was

Rover, closely guarded by Vidêt, in turn being watched over by Wardley's detective inspector and the coroner, who was keeping a photographic record of events.

The straps were attached and draped up and over a scaffold-tube framework straddling the pit. The three guys hauled the coffin out of the hole, with Rover adding a fourth set of hands. Vidêt slid planks under the casket and it was lowered until it sat supported by them. The coroner and Rover took photos of the coffin, recording the fact that it was still sealed with no visible signs of damage. Lancaster was surprised, after being in the ground for years, though muddy, the coffin carried a shine to the woodwork. He hoped the preservation would be as good with the contents. Wardley made a call on his radio and a van reversed down the avenue. The rear doors opened, the tent flaps folded back and the casket was enclosed within the van, the doors closed tight behind it. Wardley shook Rover and Lancaster's hands. He ignored Vidêt; she was, of course, only a sergeant. He wished them well, saying he'd drop by later to see how things were going and to call him if they needed anything. He handed Lancaster his card. The coroner said he'd follow behind to the Path. Lab and there, sign them all in and sign the body over to Rover. The journey to the hospital was quick and easy, made faster by the blue flashing light on the police car in front of the little convoy. They drove to the back of the main hospital building, reversed to a set of double doors and were signed in. The coffin sat upon a trolley, which in turn stood beside a steel-topped table ready for the body to be placed upon. Lancaster had been in several of these rooms. They all looked and smelt the same. He hated hospitals.

The paperwork complete, the coroner introduced three medical students who'd be giving Rover assistance. As with Rover's lab in Plymouth, the room was rigged with cameras to record the event and take live commentary as the operation proceeded. Rover stated that the first thing he wanted access to was a full-body X-Ray or a CT scan. Huxley said he'd make some calls and see what the schedules were like. Clearly, there'd be members of the public queued up waiting for exactly the same process. Rover reminded the man that in fact he was wrong. The difference was that those people outside were all still alive or they wouldn't be in a queue, whereas Peter Urbawicz had been dead for over ten years. Already, within the confines of the casket, his body would have begun to decompose and the moment they opened the casket and laid him on a trolley to take to the scanner, that process would be speeded up considerably. Time was of the essence.

Huxley conceded his point and went to make the call. Ten minutes later they were on their way to the scanning suite using a staff elevator to keep the casket under wraps and out of sight. Rover waited until the last moment before removing the casket lid and placing Peter's body on the scanner table. He asked for a full-body scan, top-to-toe.

Lancaster asked Rover what he was looking for, to which Rover replied, "Can I give explanations later, Bomb'? I'm in a bit of a rush here. Just trust me; I have my reasons."

Within an hour the process was complete. They'd managed a scan with the body flat on its back and another, with the body on its side. Lancaster wasn't fazed by the process. He'd attended mortuaries before, even watched post-mortems.

But the person lying in front of them was Peter Urbawicz. A Spitfire pilot. He'd survived the war. He'd loved and been loved, raised children, built a new life, a new home. Yet still, the one thing he had in common with billions of other people was he was dead. But he felt sad for this body. He was Pamela's father and he felt he knew the man.

Back in the path. lab., the body on the mortuary table, the coffin waiting next door and being cleaned ready for reuse, Rover had been given a twenty-four-hour timescale for the scan results, but a quiet word in his right ear by Huxley had that altered to two hours. Rover began a physical examination. Talking with a clear voice for the microphone, he started at the feet and worked up the torso. He noted considerable scar tissue formed on either side of the left leg above the knee at or about the connection between the femur and patella. Looking at the old scar, Rover stated he'd expect there to be damage to either or both of these bones and viewing the scan images would give them the detail they needed. He noted that around this scarring there was considerable swelling that continued into the vicinity of the kneecap but would be conducive to the injury sustained and a history of having to limp when walking.

Moving up the body, Rover noted the damage and simple restitching of the stomach wound, originally given as the cause of 'massive blood loss' being the mode of death. Rover refrained from opening the body to inspect the detail until he'd viewed the scan. This was no attempt at cosmetic surgery. This was a simple case of finding what edges and corners they could from the ripped flesh of the belly wound and the pulling together to make good a torso ready for the undertaker. He found no other signs of damage; the man hadn't been shot or stabbed as far as he could tell. He set about inspecting the fingers. He could see that none of them was damaged in any way and both hands were well-manicured. No splitting or cracking and no rust or dirt beneath them. It was unlikely the undertaker's team would provide a manicure prior to burial. He worked his way higher up the body and instantly found one thing that troubled him. Despite the effects of decomposition that had set in, the sunken skin and the protruding teeth as facial muscles lost the ability to hold anything together, the skull moved in its location far too easily. He wasn't sure at this moment if it was part of decomposition or damage done by the undertaker's team, but it was disconcerting to be able to move the dead man's head from left to right with such ease at what was in fact, still early times for decomposition.

Rover called a halt to proceedings until the scan results had materialised and he announced it was time for coffee. They sheeted the body and headed for the cafeteria, leaving the two assistants 'on guard'. Once sat, coffees in hand, Lancaster took the opportunity to ask his question again.

"So what do you want from the CT scan then, Rover?"

"Well, in the notes you sent me, your theory was that the man could have been dead before he hit the spike, correct?"

"It's my theory, yes."

"Well, if that's the case, he had to die from something else. I had a thought about that. Some years ago I did an autopsy on a farmer. He'd apparently fallen from a hay loft and spiked himself on a bale spike on the front of a tractor. Now, there was some evidence of family rifts and financial problems with the farm, so the investigating officer flagged this up to me. Prior to the autopsy, I had a scan done, and lo and behold, lodged within the wound I found two shotgun pellets. Whoever shot him had carefully picked out the pellets and then wedged the body onto the spikes. They then made the whole thing into a film set by arranging bales in the hay loft, bringing in the tractor and pointing the spike upward, as if he'd lifted the bales up into the loft door. Then they cleared up the blood, covering the stains with straw and dust. He almost got away with it but for leaving two pellets behind."

"With Peter, the fact you found nothing under the fingernails is helping to point toward my train of thought," Lancaster continued.

"I agree. From what you've told me, the way the body was originally found I think you're quite right. If I were impaled on a spike and still alive, I'd be scrabbling until my bloody hands fell off. I would've expected the nails to be broken by contact with rocks or the stake, but they're perfect, immaculate even."

"Now that so much of the body tissue has begun to degrade," Vidêt chipped in. "How true a story do you think the scan will tell?"

"I won't truly know that until I see the results."

One of the assistants came to find them. The results had arrived. They returned to the lab. Rover viewed the screen. He studied the damage done to the left knee. When looked at in detail, you could see that something had penetrated the leg, right at the junction of the femur and patella. It had come in clean on the left side, taken a chip out of the kneecap and clipped the bottom end of the femur. There was a lot of callous built around the meeting points of both bones, a sign they'd both had to regrow as best as they could to allow the man to walk again. There would've been muscle and tissue damage at the same time, which would probably have led to almost permanent pain or rheumatic spasms during the man's lifetime. Rover was concerned, however, that the injury was not conducive to the effects of the story he'd been told, that of damage caused by the in-blast of a chunk of shrapnel. Rover had the belief that maybe over the years, the story may have been embellished somewhat because what he was looking at, now enlarged on the screen, looked more like the clean damage created by a bullet.

Moving up the leg, you could see markings on the upper part of the right femur, where the muscles had been attached, now just a sagging mass of fleshy material. The markings on the bones showed the right leg muscles had grown considerably larger than the left, as Peter compensated for the semi-inactive, painful left knee. Rover double-checked the scan to see if any splinters of stone or rust had pierced the skin under the nails but all he could see were clean lines, that even after all this time, showed a man who'd looked after his appearance. Continuing up the body, as Rover had predicted from his exterior inspection, he could find no other intrusions into the flesh or deflated body organs that would indicate any other form of an attack by any weapon. The man had been fit for an elderly gentleman.

When he reached the injury to the stomach he paused and swiped wide across the screen to enlarge the section he was viewing. Even to the untrained eye, Lancaster could see there was serious damage here. Even given the state of decomposition, degradation of the body and shrinkage of the internal body parts, it was easy to see that certain organs were damaged or completely out of place.

Rover stated for the recording, "Looking at the scan, it could be seen that the right-hand side of the pancreas had virtually disappeared along with a sizable chunk of the right kidney."

Also noticeable was that what remained of the deflated, now shrunken intestines, which were in a complete jumble. They'd obviously suffered severe damage by the intrusion caused by the angle iron and, in some places, had been severed completely. The rest had probably just been stuffed back into the cavity, or at least what had been left behind after the body had been pulled off the stake. This told Rover something. He was pretty certain the body had been in a vertical position when it fell on the spike. It had penetrated up through the lower intestines from the left-hand side, ripping through them as the weight of the body forced itself onto the ironwork. It continued upwards, destroying the right-hand side of the pancreas before destroying the right-hand kidney on its way through the body and out the other side to exit through the man's back. No wonder there'd been a lot of blood. Taking out that many organs would have created quite a spill, magnified by immersion in the seawater.

"What does that tell you about the way the man died?" Lancaster asked.

"Well, unless the man stood on the edge of the cliff, spread his arms out, then jumped straight up in the air, dropping down onto the spike, I would struggle to see how these injuries, in this order of damage, could've happened. It'd be more likely that somebody picked the man up and dropped him over the edge, feet first. But that's not a given, it's just my thoughts. Which of those two scenarios is correct, is down to you guys."

Rover turned his attention to the head and neck. He looked closely at the scan on the screen, then back to the body on the slab. He moved the head from one side to another. Then enlarged the screenshot. Lancaster knew not to speak; he went through this process himself. He needed to separate the information in his head, draw it on an internal wall inside the brain, make sense of it and be certain before speaking. He could see Rover going through the same process. Rover turned to Lancaster and Vidêt.

"Well, I'm pretty certain I have found the cause of death."

Lancaster and Vidêt moved to the screen. They could see nothing other than a ghost image of the internal parts of the body that lay on the table. They both looked at the screen and then to Rover for an explanation.

"If you look closely, you can see the vertebral column, the spine in common terms. If you look at the gaps between the vertebrae, most of them, even with the degradation the muscles have gone through, most of them are an equal distance apart. But up here at the top," he said, scrolling the picture down. "Between C3 and C4 vertebra, the gap's much wider, in fact, it's quite easy to see, they're no longer in line with each other, they're even at a cross angle at one point."

Lancaster had to ask. "What does that tell us?"

"Well, I'd say that somebody grabbed Peter from behind,

wrenched the man's head up, sideways and around. Put simply, somebody broke his neck, broke it big time. Rambo style. It's what's known as a forcible hyperextension. A broken neck's not always fatal, but this was violent and catastrophic. It would've broken the neck, caused a complete cervical fracture and almost certainly have severed the spinal cord, the brain stem. It's a bit like having a radio mast on top of a hill. All the cables carrying the messages travel up the tower and the signals are sent out from the antennae on the top. Somebody rips the top off the tower. The cables may still be attached and the tower may still be standing, but nobody is getting the message. In this case, once you sever the spinal cord and disconnect all access to the brain, all the instructions cease and everything stops working. It would have certainly killed him. Almost instantly. He was then picked up, probably with the attacker's hands under his armpits, then dropped, straight over the edge of the cliff. There's something else I just need to check."

Rover called up the scan taken with the body on its side. He pulled down the picture until he could see the jawline full screen. Turning the image on the screen, he found what he was looking for. The left hand, lower mandible or jawbone had been dislocated right at its joint with the rest of the skull. He pointed it out to Lancaster.

"Whoever did it was quick and forceful. He grabbed the head and ripped it up and sideways. Job done."

Lancaster stood looking at the screen. This was what he'd been thinking all along. Not in such detail, but very much in line with his original theories. He'd thought all along it was no accident. Now, confirmed by Rover, he felt no pride or enjoyment in the facts. It was sad, after everything Peter had gone through to forge a new life for himself and his family, that somebody chose to end the man's life so brutally and so late in his life. For some reason, this just seemed to make it all the more pointless.

"I know I don't really need to ask this, Rover," Lancaster said. "But you're sure of this? Because it's the difference between going home tomorrow or staying here and seeing this thing through, whilst truly pissing off the locals, big time."

"Bomber, you know the answer to that. Isn't that why you asked me to come here? And when's it ever worried you... Pissing somebody off? I'm as sure as you were; this wasn't accidental. This man did not accidentally twist his head off and then fall upright onto that spike. The only other thing I will check is to see if he was poisoned. That could have caused him to go rigid or even have a seizure and fall. It's going to be a long shot after all this time, but it is worth giving it a try."

"Hold fire on that Rover, just for the moment. If you're confident this appears to be murder, then let's see what the locals have to say first before we begin cutting the man up."

"So you have your murder, Detective Lancaster, what now?" Vidêt asked.

"Do you know how to download images from the smart screen?"

"It shouldn't be too difficult. What do you need?"

"I want close-up images of the jaw break, neck injury and the wound to the abdomen. Get me full-frontal and side-on views to make sure we get all visibility. Get them printed as A4 images, but also stick them onto your memory stick so we can upload them onto the pad. These are our key areas of evidence."

Lancaster put in a call to Craven. He should be the first to know it was now an active murder enquiry, with all the problems that could cause. He'd been expecting the call.

"When you first said you had doubts, Bomber, I knew where this was going to end up. Your gut instincts haven't let us down so far. So are you going to be OK out there or do you want me to join you? I don't want them giving you any grief."

"Well, sir, if you can't get out here, I'm happy to give it a go. If I need senior backup, you're on the end of the phone. I think I can handle the opposite numbers here and, interestingly, I think Lady Stottard and her deceased father still carry weight, so in answer to your question, yes, I reckon I can handle the enquiry, if I get the chance."

Their conversation finished, Lancaster went back into the room, finding Vidêt already printing off copies of the screenshots and one of the students rushing off with a tooth to get it tested. Lancaster called Rover away from the table and asked once more if Rover was confident. He received a definite yes. The next thing was to call Huxley and show him what they'd found. He wasn't only the coroner; he was an islander. They needed him on board before they announced their findings to Wardly.

The coroner returned immediately. They went through their evidence, using the screen to illustrate. It wasn't difficult to prove, and the man was qualified to make his own call. He could see straight away that there was a case for the death to be re-examined, and once Lancaster told him of the other items he'd found that had never been picked up the first time round, the hire car, the weight stone not in the pot, the wrong location for the pot and the way the body had been found on the iron post, he could see there was enough there to warrant re-opening this as a murder enquiry. He gave permission for it to be registered as such. Lancaster took the liberty of asking if the man would wait around and give his verdict to Wardly, who was next on his list of telephone calls. The coroner agreed.

Wardly was surprised to hear from Lancaster so soon, but as with Huxley, Lancaster gave little away, just told the man they had things to show him. Wardly made it to the hospital in ten minutes. Lancaster decided to make a political move, to undermine any grievance that may be caused by an outsider calling the shots.

"Mr Huxley," Lancaster began, instantly pulling the man into the middle of any conflict. "As the island coroner and senior medical practitioner here, would you please guide Chief Inspector Wardly through the detail of what's turned up following the CAT scan. I'm sure you'll explain it far better than I."

Rover stepped away from the screen, inwardly bowing to Lancaster's side-step manoeuvre. Huxley then pointed out all the points he'd been shown as if he'd discovered them, even to the point of explaining how the body may have been lifted by the armpits and dumped over the cliff, only to fall upright onto the angle iron, thereby causing the damage to the internal organs, as one could plainly witness from the results of the scan. Wardly nodded his way through the explanation, all the while stroking his chin, studying the scans in detail.

"So, you've no doubt then that this was murder?" Wardly asked the coroner. "This damage couldn't have been caused as a result of an accident?"

"Oh, it's most certainly murder, Chief Inspector, there's no doubt about it. I've already filed it as such. I intend to issue the paperwork to re-open the case and reclassify it as 'murder by person or persons unknown'. It will be your job to find out who the person was though, and good luck with that."

Chief Inspector Wardly stood looking at the screen and the close-up of the broken neck. Even he could see that it had been a violent end to another man's life and he was frustrated. Angered that the man had been buried for over ten years in the belief that the death had been an accident. Somebody in the past had made a cock-up. That annoyed him. The only thing that gave any light relief was the fact that it was all before his time. He hoped it wouldn't have been the case if it had happened today. Somewhere in the back of his mind, however, was the thought that Lancaster had known this all along. Had he been taking the piss or was he just being a good detective? He'd need to know that before this case could be moved forward.

"What else have you got planned, Dr Landy?" Wardly asked. "Are you done, or do you need anything else?"

Rover looked to Lancaster first, not certain where authority lay, but Lancaster gave him a nod to carry on.

"Well, Chief Inspector, it's a long shot but there are a few poisons that can cause seizures or even epileptic symptoms that may have caused an accidental fall. I am not optimistic, but it's still to be ruled out; the only place where they may show up would be internally. But I have to say, poison or no poison, I concur with everything that Mr Huxley has said as regards the cause of death, so really that poison analysis is just belt and braces but it needs to be ticked off the list."

"Very thorough, Dr Landy, I can see why they sent for you," Lancaster felt a hint of sarcasm tucked in there, but before he could say anything, Wardly continued, "When do you intend to start the search for possible poisons?"

"With respect, sir, Lady Stottard asked for an exhumation, but before we start to open up her father's remains, I feel we should seek her permission."

"Very well, let's leave a full autopsy for now. I'd like us to regroup in my office at police headquarters, 9.00 in the morning. I ask that you both, I repeat both, bring everything you have on this case to date. Do we all understand each other?"

"Yes, sir," Lancaster responded for both of them.

CHAPTER SEVEN

Returning to the house, it was incumbent on Lancaster to tell Pamela everything they'd found. He did this in private on the terrace, whilst Vidêt and Rover were, as pre-agreed, drinking tea in the kitchen. Pamela took it well; there was no drama, and she was very matter-of-fact. Lancaster thought this was probably a temporary front. She said she'd been expecting this all along. It was the result she'd wanted to hear. Now it was a case of finding out who'd done it and why. Lancaster explained that, to date, they'd only carried out an external investigation of her father's body and it may be necessary to carry out a more in-depth surgical investigation, but he wouldn't do this without her consent. Pamela said that it would be pointless to have come this far and then not do the job properly, so she gave permission to do whatever was needed.

Lancaster told her that the Chief Inspector wanted them in his office first thing in the morning with everything they had on the case. As he was the senior officer, albeit a senior officer on what was to Lancaster and Vidêt, foreign soil, he was still senior. Lancaster was obliged to bow to the man's seniority. 'Do we indeed' was Pamela's only comment. Then, pushing herself up from her chair, she stood, as did Lancaster.

She then gave him a hug, pulled away and just said, "Thank

you, David." They walked into the kitchen, where Lancaster joined the other two in the habitual tea drinking. Pamela left them saying she'd return and thanked them for all the work they'd done. Lancaster was going to say, 'It was nothing' or some other trite saying but had no time as she closed the door behind her, leaving them in the kitchen dunking biscuits, back to the old routine of having missed lunch again.

"Can I ask?" Rover said, followed by a quiet curse, as the end of his tea-soaked biscuit dropped off, splashing back into his mug. "What'll happen now?"

"Well, I'd suggest you get a bloody spoon and fish it out before it sinks," Lancaster replied.

Rover was already on it, but gave up as the soggy mess disintegrated, becoming soup in a cup.

Lancaster continued. "My thoughts are that Wardly will take over the enquiry. Unless somebody on the mainland says anything different, I suspect we'll be on a flight out of here before the end of the week. I'll call Craven and tell him everything we've found, then see what he has to say. Unless he can intervene, my gut feeling is Wardly, as the senior detective, will just gather our info and then run it himself. The problem is that everything Pamela and her mother wanted has happened. We've looked at the case and found it lacking, tick. We've found new items of evidence and persons of interest, tick. We've carried out an exhumation and an autopsy, tick. With the result being that the island coroner has reclassified the death as murder. A very big tick. So if they don't want to make a fuss over here, the powers-that-be back in the UK may just say, 'There you go, Lady Stottard, we've done what you asked, now it's up to your local police force to find out who did it'. To be honest, now they have an actual murder on their hands, I imagine they're quite capable of finishing what we started."

"Would you be happy with that, David?" a voice in the doorway said. Lancaster turned to find Pamela had walked in.

"You already know the answer to that, Pamela... No... I think I speak for both Marie and myself. We've done all the leg work in this. I have to say I think, between us all, you included, Pamela, that we've pulled this one out of the bag in a pretty quick time. I hate to walk away from any case, especially as the locals have had most of the hard graft done for them, but I'm just being honest. Although we were tasked with coming here and doing what we've done, at the end of the day, from a political point of view, the island Chief Inspector beats my Detective Inspector hands down. If he decides to dig his heels in and claim the enquiry for his own, then I have no say in that. I'm sorry; that's just the way it is."

"That might be the way you see it," Pamela continued. "But I don't give in without a fight. I've just come off the telephone following a chat with Chief Inspector Wardly. He'll be joining us for dinner this evening. I thought I knew the name; I went to school with his mother, Jennifer. What a naughty girl she was, I can tell you, very advanced for a sixteen-year-old. Anyway, I've invited him to join us for dinner at eight, followed by a presentation of what you consider to be the case so far. I suggested it would make far more sense for him to see the big picture, away from the confines of the police station, and that it would give him a chance to get his head around the facts as we see them. So, between the three of you, one hopes you've everything you need to regale him with your prowess as a team to be reckoned with. The man may want to run the show, but I am damn sure, if you're on the inside you can ensure he misses nothing and doesn't make a mess of it. I don't think the man is stupid or gullible, so you'll have to use all your guile and persuasive powers to sneak in items he may miss, but something tells me it will not be beyond you to do that."

"Pamela, you're a bloody marvel," Lancaster replied. "Why didn't you become the Police Commissioner?"

"Aah, David. There are some people I was not, metaphorically speaking, prepared to get into bed with, for any job. Is the tea still hot?"

Lancaster and Vidêt borrowed Pamela's office and downloaded the A4 scan pictures from the memory stick. Vidêt set about printing off several sets of each. Lancaster gave her a list of information he wanted copies of, so he could present Wardly with a complete fact file to peruse as he presented his case. Meanwhile, Pamela and Rover went back to the path lab where Rover used his charm to borrow an active whiteboard. It would give them a more professional presentation. Lancaster got Google Maps up and found the Earth images of the car park on the point, the cliff path to the beach, the rocks extending out into the sea and the platform Peter used for fishing. He downloaded the images, dropped them into his fact file on the hard drive and printed them as A4 screenshots. Lancaster took the decision to hold back the images from the CCTV at the bank; he wanted to keep some things in reserve, and anyway, they may be of more use to Interpol than to this case, so there was no point creating unnecessary fog. *I may want them as a bargaining chip later in the game.*

He laughed when he thought of those CCTV shots from the bank. He had a photo of a man he wasn't allowed to mention. He had a photo of the same man being somebody his boss appeared not to have heard of, so he could mention him. He had a photo of somebody who wasn't the person they all thought he was supposed to be, and meanwhile, the person everybody thought he was, was now in custody in Brest. If there wasn't some mileage to be made from hanging onto those images, then he didn't know what was.

By the time Pamela and Rover returned carrying the whiteboard, he had virtually everything he needed for a presentation. Within forty-five minutes, he had a screen presentation ready, with a folder of matching photos and facts. Lancaster had a run-through, roping in Rover for a full explanation of the injuries that had caused the death of their victim. They were going to have one shot at this; Lancaster was keen to get it right. Prior to dinner, it was time to freshen up. He shaved, hit the power button and stepped into the shower, hot droplets smashing against his scalp as he stood with his hands resting upon the wall of the walk-in cubicle. He never heard the connecting door open and close. The first he knew of Vidêt's entrance was when her arms wrapped around his chest as she held his body close, the warmth of her skin felt even through the full force of the shower.

"Are you ready for this?" she asked.

"That depends on what you're offering," he replied, to which he received a slap across the right buttock.

"Wardly, I mean! You know you can do this. You can run rings around him. He may be senior in title but you are better than him, you know this."

Lancaster turned and kissed her. "Thank you for that, you're right. I know I can do this, but it doesn't stop me from getting nervous. It just annoys me that when I phoned Craven and told him what we'd found during the autopsy, he should either have phoned through to Jersey and given us free right of way to finish this case or got on the next plane out here, instead of asking me to run it. It's obvious to me they'd want a senior officer."

"If we lose it to Jersey police then at least we've given them the best start in solving it," she replied. "Pamela cannot blame us if that happens; she will just have to keep the pressure on to make sure they don't make a mess of it." She kissed him, turned his body back to the wall and began giving his back and shoulders a deep massage. "This is the best you get till later on, Detective Lancaster; make the most of it."

Wardly arrived at 7:45 p.m. for 8:00. Smartly though casually dressed for dinner. The meal went well. During dinner, there was casual, non-hierarchal conversation. Topics ranged from summer season tourists, to what it was like growing up on a small island; both Pamela and Wardly had similar stories to tell. It appeared Wardly had also done some homework. He'd been informed of the British team's previous major case, that of Abdul Mehemet, and congratulated them on it. Eventually, the meal could last no longer and coffee was poured. They retired to the lounge where the rearranged furniture gave everyone a comfortable chance to view the presentation.

Vidêt handed Pamela and Wardly files containing everything they'd compiled. Lancaster couldn't help but think, *Wardly now holds the whole case in his hands and could walk out now, should he wish,* but he carried on as planned.

Lancaster worked his way through everything as he saw it. He made no mention of anything to do with the original enquiry; no point rubbing salt in old wounds. He began with a brief overview of Pamela's discovery of her father's body, the fact that he was impaled on a metal stake, attached to a chunk of concrete. He mentioned that Pamela had a distinct, clear memory of the day, and how her father's arms were stretched out in front of him, as though floating. Rover reported that despite the body being impaled, he'd found no signs of damage to the fingernails or hands that would show signs of a struggle. This led to the conclusion that the body was already dead when dropped off the cliff. To this end, he'd carried out the autopsy and discovered the man had died from 'catastrophic forcible hyperextension' which, in plain English, is a severe and fatal neck break. Also, given a look at the damage done to internal organs and the order of damage, the man was undoubtedly picked up by his armpits and dropped off the cliff.

At this point, Pamela excused herself and left the room. At a nod from Lancaster, Marie followed. He continued. To support his view of murder, Lancaster pointed out where Peter placed the stone for the pot, which is still there to this day. He indicated where the pot was actually found, a space Peter would never have placed it, with or without the all-important stone. He mentioned that there'd been a hire car parked in the cliff-top car park, now traced, and all drivers of the car during that week identified. Several were now persons of interest and should be interviewed. In connection with these characters, Lancaster also mentioned those who'd had dealings with Peter and the bank, who may have had an axe to grind.

The presentation took no more than thirty-five minutes, during which Wardly never spoke. Eventually, Lancaster stopped, thanked the man for his time and asked if he had any questions. Wardly sat for a moment looking at him. Lancaster wasn't sure what the man was thinking but thought he'd make a bloody good poker player.

"How long have you and your team spent on this?" Wardly asked.

"Seven days in total, sir," he replied candidly.

"What did you know of the case before you arrived on the island?"

"Nothing, sir."

Wardly thumbed through the photos in his folder. The images of the coast and the cliff top. The body scan downloads, the close detail shots, then casts a cursory glance at the A4 sheets of written text detailing all he'd just been told.

"Do you have a favourite in the frame for it?"

"Not as yet, sir. We've isolated people of interest, but they may not have actually carried out the murder. Two of them are long-term criminals, both out of pocket due to actions taken by Peter. I suspect that if either chose to take revenge against our victim, it's unlikely they'd carry it out themselves; more likely they'd use a 'hitman' for want of a better term. Both characters spent considerable time as individuals, attempting to keep out of sight and off radar; I find it hard to imagine they'd come out of cover and commit murder, thereby threatening their hidden identities. No, I suspect a hired killer was used by one of them, especially since Rover has discovered that the neck-break was swift and critical."

"Rover? Who's Rover?" Wardly asked, looking perplexed.

"That'll be me, sir," Rover said. "Surname, Landy... Landy... Land Rover... hence Rover."

Wardly stared back at him in complete silence. He turned back to Lancaster.

"So in one week, you've reopened an old case without pissing anyone off or even letting them know you were here, discovered significant new evidence missed in the original enquiry, found the cause of death, a possible motive and several possible persons of interest. Would that be correct, Detective Lancaster?"

"Yes, sir, I think that just about sums it up," he replied. The man had asked so Lancaster could see no reason to be modest now. It was an 'all-or-bust' situation.

Vidêt returned quietly and retook her seat, aware that something crucial was happening.

"Well, thank you very much for your presentation, Detective Inspector, and for your time, Dr Landy," Wardly said, shuffling his paperwork into order and sliding them into his folder. "It's been a very enlightening and enjoyable evening, so if you could stick to our original appointment for the morning, I would be very grateful. Is Lady Stottard OK?" he asked, turning to Vidêt.

"She sends her thanks for your time, Chief Inspector, and hopes you enjoyed your meal, but she's retired to bed. The presentation was just a bit too much for her, though she was determined for it to go ahead. I'm sure you understand?"

"Please give her my thanks for a lovely evening," Wardly replied. "I'm just sorry it was about such tragic events. Right then. I'll see you all in the morning and please, tell Lady Stottard she's very welcome to attend."

Vidêt saw him to the door and wished him goodnight.

They regrouped in the lounge.

"So, what do you think now then?" Rover asked.

"I think if we get to the office and he asks us to play poker, we say no," Lancaster replied.

"Seriously though," Rover continued.

"Seriously, Rover, I haven't got a bloody clue, but I do know I'm knackered and ready for bed. Let's call it a night and just see what the morning brings."

Upstairs, Lancaster could see Pamela's bedroom light still on; he gave a light tap on the door and heard her say, 'Come in'. He apologised for being so graphic with his presentation; he often blundered on without thinking. She assured him it was her fault for staying in the first place. Hearing the detail of her father's death was something she'd have to get used to if this whole mess continued the way she and her mother wanted. Lancaster extended Wardly's invite for the meeting; she was adamant she'd be up and ready in the morning. If they were to have the case taken away, she wanted to be there to kick heads. In his room, he found Vidêt curled up in his bed fast asleep. He cleaned his teeth, climbed in beside her and she sleepily wrapped her arm around him. Within minutes they were both sound asleep.

The next morning, they arrived at police headquarters in plenty of time and were led to the inner sanctum by DI Beard. He was matter-of-fact in his greeting. Lancaster sensed no animosity but couldn't feel any warmth either. He led them up a stairwell and along a corridor, on one side was a glass-windowed viewing wall, through which could be seen a group of plain and uniformed officers being given a briefing by a man at the front of the room. A few glanced in their direction for a moment before turning their attention back to the front. They stopped outside a door marked 'DCI Wardly'. Beard knocked twice, then entered and they followed.

"Thanks for that, Sam," Wardly said. "Would you keep your ear in at the briefing? I'll give you a shout when I need you, OK?"

The other man left, closing the door behind him. Wardly offered them all seats. He thanked Pamela for a lovely meal the previous night and hoped she felt better this morning, acknowledging how traumatic these facts can be to the uninitiated. Pamela offered her thanks for his concern.

"I was late to bed myself," Wardly added. "I spent a while going through your case file, Detective Lancaster. I've also done a bit of research on your characters of interest. This morning, I found out that you and Sergeant Vidêt were involved in the apprehension of one of them, Jean-Luc Batise, at present being questioned by operatives from Interpol on drug trafficking charges. You failed to mention that during your presentation last night."

"It wasn't relevant, sir," Lancaster added. "Yes, he's a person of interest. But we stumbled on him purely by chance whilst looking at another possible, Henri Tanguyé. We've now eliminated him from this enquiry. We spotted Batise and, unfortunately, having raised the local police and made them aware of his presence, whilst we were awaiting their arrival, the man made a run for it and I operated a citizen's arrest. We know where he is if he needs further questioning. I've asked both the Brest Drugs Squad and Interpol to grant us access, to which they've agreed, so as you can see, I didn't mention it as it wasn't relevant to last night's presentation, sir."

Wardly looked at Lancaster. "DCI Craven said you were a touchy sod; I didn't raise the Batise issue as a criticism, it was more in some slight awe. Seven days and you two have put all this together," he said waving the folder in the air. "Plus, you've managed to fit in a quick trip into France and find and arrest a known criminal who Interpol have been searching for, well, for the past two years. I'm impressed, that's all, Lancaster, just impressed. You've been having your praises sung by the Lady Stottard here and Craven tells me, and I hasten to say these are his words, not mine, but Craven says, 'you're a nutter and a bit weird but you get results every time'. Would you say that's a reasonable account of your abilities, DI Lancaster?"

"It's not for me to say, sir."

Wardly sat flicking through the folder, scanning the pages.

"I have a dilemma, Lancaster. Next door there's a major briefing going on. I rely on professional confidence here. We have a missing woman on the island. The trouble is she's almost identical in height, size, build, hair colour, etc. to another woman who was reported missing three weeks ago. We're fearful we have a murderer at work. So you can imagine, we've a lot on our plate and not meaning any offence to Lady Stottard, but without a doubt, looking at your report I've absolutely no doubt that Peter Urbawicz's death was murder. My problem is that this is a cold case, whilst next door there are two missing women who may still be alive or they may be dead. At the moment we hope the former. What I've not got time for at the moment, is to open up a cold-case enquiry and pour resources into it, I just don't have the manpower."

Pamela went to speak. Wardly had anticipated this and raised a hand as a sign that he hadn't finished.

"What I'm prepared to do is speak with DCI Craven and have the pair of you placed on temporary secondment to us, and for you both to continue with this investigation. That means your warrant cards will give you access to the station and its resources, but no additional personnel, unless authorised by me. If you find something that's going to need extra muscle or a search team, you run it by me. I decide if it warrants it or not. Agreed."

"Yes, sir," Lancaster replied. He knew this was going to be the best they would get.

"Also, if you need to leave the island, you speak to me first. Is that understood?"

"Yes, sir." Lancaster realised he'd have to put this into action almost immediately; he needed to interview Batise before he got moved deeper into Interpol territory.

"Finally, I want an update and a complete state of play every afternoon by 5. That way, if I have to make a judgment call, I have the evening to mull it over before I sanction it or not, is that also understood?"

"Yes, sir."

"Do you have any questions for me?" Wardly asked.

"Only one, sir. Do you have a spare whiteboard? An active one if possible? As your office is going to be flat out working on the missing persons situation, we could, in fact, keep right out of your hair and continue to work from Lady Stottard's home. You know where we are if you want us and vice-versa. We've put that file together so far, just working from there, so if you've no objections...?"

By 10:30 a.m., they were walking back out of the station with a large active whiteboard carried between them. The four of them got back into the car in silence and waited until they'd passed out through the gates and en route for home, before erupting in whoops of joy and cries of, 'Brilliant. Bloody, bloody brilliant'.

They regrouped back at the house. Rover was the first to speak on the subject once the coffee had been poured.

"Well done, guys, a great result from some good work. I hope Craven appreciates it?"

"Don't downplay your contribution, Rover," Lancaster replied. "If you hadn't nailed the cause of death so quickly, it might have been a different story, and by the way, you can't go home until we have the results of that poison test analysis and anything else you think may help us out here."

"Listen, all of you," came the voice of Lady Stottard. Not loud, but unmistakable. "Before this day moves on another minute, I wanted to say how proud I am of all of you. You've given my father a chance for his death to be recognised, not just as that of an old man falling off a cliff; you've raised the possibility of being able to find who the culprit was and why they chose to commit this crime. My mother and I are going to be eternally grateful to you."

"Thank you, Pamela, it means a lot to all of us," Lancaster replied. "We'll do our best to see this thing through."

"So what now?" she asked.

"Well, Wardly's going to have a lot on his plate this morning. I plan to leave him alone for a few hours. I want to get everything we have transferred onto the board. Are you OK with that, Marie?"

Marie finished her coffee, grabbed the whiteboard and headed for the lounge.

"Rover, as soon as Marie's transferred everything onto the board, would you and Pamela return the one to the path lab please? Then we can cross them off our list. I plan to put a call through to Ferec in Brest and see if they still have Batise in custody. If so, I want to get over there and interview him tomorrow if Wardly gives the OK. Pamela, could you call Max at the bank? Find out if the bank has heard anything from Shawbuck? He was planning to arrive this week; it would be good to know when. When you've spoken to Max, if you don't get any joy, give your man Basil a call and check that Shawbuck hasn't pre-booked a car. Then, if it's not asking too much, telephone the airport, and see if we can book two return tickets for tomorrow to Brest?"

"That's fine. But shouldn't I come along as well?" Pamela replied.

"It's now official police business, Pamela, I intend to go in, ask questions and fly back. You'd be spending the day sitting in the foyer of a police station in Brest, so it just needs to be Marie and me."

"Have you got anything specific for me, Bomber, or shall I book a flight back home tomorrow?" Rover asked.

"In fact, Rover, yes I have. Will you contact Huxley? If he doesn't mind, when Pamela drops you and the whiteboard back to the lab, take another full look at the body. Double-check everything, every millimetre. Make sure we haven't missed anything; I want a 'full and proper autopsy'. Then get a cab back here."

Vidêt popped her head around the door to say the download was complete. She'd wiped the hard-drive of the lab's board and it was ready to go. Rover called Huxley and got the go-ahead for an in-depth autopsy and then he and Pamela headed off. Lancaster called Ferec. It went to answer phone and Lancaster left a simple message. As soon as he'd rung off, Ferec rang back.

"Bonjour, mon ami, what can I do for you?" the Frenchman asked.

"Bonjour, Detective Ferec. Thanks for returning my call, do you still have Batise?"

"Yes, we do, there's been some delay. The two detectives from Interpol were called away, but they'll return in a couple of days to continue questioning. Why do you ask?"

"Are you the holding officer?

"As arresting officer, yes I am."

"Then I have a favour to ask." Lancaster went on to explain they had a cold-case murder enquiry active on the Island of Jersey and Batise was a person of interest; they'd like to question him if possible. Ferec laughed, saying that as Lancaster and his colleagues had been responsible for getting the man into custody in the first place, he'd find it hard to disallow such a request, but he suspected once Interpol returned, they may claim seniority. He asked when Lancaster planned to come over. When he replied he'd arrive the next day, he laughed again.

"You are, as they say, Detective, 'hot' for this man, are you not?"

"It's part of a process, Detective Ferec, you know how it works. I find the suspects, line them up and take them out one by one until I get the right one. At the moment Batise is the nearest to me and I want to talk with him. Either pin this on him or cross him off my list. Will you let me do this?"

"Please, Detective Lancaster, call me Christophe, and yes, if you get here tomorrow, of course I will let you question him."

They agreed Lancaster would keep him in the loop about arrival times, with a promise from Ferec that Batise would know nothing of their mission until they arrived. Lancaster wanted to catch the man on the hop. He'd just come off the phone with Ferec when Craven called. It appeared Craven had been on the phone with Wardly. He was up to date with Wardly's request for Lancaster and Vidêt to be on temporary assignment with the Jersey force. The powers-that-be back home had given their permission and paperwork was being e-mailed. Lancaster informed Craven of his forthcoming visit to France and in reply, Craven said something that surprised Lancaster.

"If you're taking Vidêt back into Brest, my son, you'd better keep a close eye on her and watch her back. There are people in there who attempted to stitch her up good and proper. Give her the option of not going. You could use Ferec as support. It's just a thought, Bomber, that's all I'm saying."

They finished their call. Lancaster thought of what the man had said. Inwardly he kicked himself. In his haste to run up a list and plan a campaign, he'd completely forgotten she had a bad history with the police in Brest. That was the reason she'd been co-opted into the British force in the first place. *I must try and learn to remember things about others, not just think of myself.* He was mulling this over when Vidêt joined him. Everything was OK with the whiteboard, all info was compatible and ready to go. She'd also scanned in all the photographs they had so they could be called up on the screen whenever they wanted. In those few seconds of exchange, Lancaster had come up with a plan to keep her out of harm's way.

"Tomorrow, I plan to fly to Brest to question Batise. Ferec's given me permission. At the moment the guys from Interpol aren't there, so I have a brief window to get in there."

"Do you want me to book tickets for us?"

"Actually no, Marie. Pamela will do it when she gets back. Anyway, I plan to go on my own and come back the same day. I've something else for you to do if you wouldn't mind. Rover will be conducting a full internal investigation of Peter's body tomorrow; I don't want Pamela wandering around at a loose end, blundering into anything she might find upsetting. So I'd like you to use her local knowledge and go around the island boatyards and marinas. Flash the pictures we have of both Batistes. I've a theory that if he was banking here, he may have actually used the island as a staging post for some of his yacht dealings. It's research that needs doing and it'll keep Pamela out of the way. It'll be official business now we're co-opted onto the island force so our warrant cards are valid. Is that OK with you?"

Vidêt was happy to oblige. She hadn't wanted to tell Lancaster, but she really didn't want to go back to Brest. If he'd asked, she'd have gone, but this was another task he'd given her under her own role as supporting sergeant. She liked it when he gave her responsibility and trust. She had the chance to show she wasn't just his driver and note-taker, and anyway he was right, it would keep Pamela in the investigation. It was a good plan and a good use of resources. She might even turn something up that could be a bonus.

"That's fine by me. Can I suggest you get a flight one way? That way, if anything crops up over there, you can stay over and get a flight back when you need. Have you cleared it with Wardly?"

Lancaster smiled. "He's next on my list, but I plan to book a flight anyway."

Lancaster caught Wardley in a coffee break and relayed his plan to fly the next morning. The man was happy for Lancaster to be on the move so quickly. Lancaster said he'd telephone as agreed at 4:30 p.m., with a complete plan of campaign for the next couple of days; the man seemed happy with that. Next, he texted Craven and told him he'd be travelling to France alone, thanking him for his advice.

Pamela returned from the hospital. Lancaster got her straight on the phone to book his ticket. She queried the single but he told her he planned to get in, do the business and get back again, and anyway, he'd a more important job in store for Vidêt and herself. To that end, Vidêt was already drawing up a list of boatyards and marinas snuggled in around the coast. She was planning to tackle them clockwise, starting from the top of the island with the little port of Bonne Nuit. Lancaster reminded Pamela to phone Max at the bank and Basil at Your-Hire. Keen to keep her busy and too busy to dwell on what Rover might be doing in the path lab. Josette appeared on the terrace with a tray full of sandwiches. Lancaster felt it had been a productive morning; everybody is involved in some task or other for the common good.

Pamela rejoined them, asking Lancaster how quickly he could pack. She'd made an executive decision with regard to the ticket. There was a flight to Brest leaving at 4:30 that afternoon. Pamela thought that if he intended to 'get in and get out', it would be better for him to 'get in' tonight. This gave the chance of a night's sleep and early arrival at the police station the following morning. At this time of the year, flights were seldom fully booked, so she'd negotiated an open return; he could come back on any flight he wanted to. She'd also booked him into the Hôtel L'Amirauté, which was central to the city, not far from the police station, and it had a good restaurant. Again, Lancaster was in her debt, financially and organisationally. Following lunch, Lancaster went upstairs to pack.

He returned to the terrace where Vidêt taught him the intricacies of using his phone to record, something he'd never had to do before. Lancaster then called Rover and was told

253

that despite the length of time Peter's body had been in the ground, there was still some structure to the internal organs. Lungs and stomach held mucus remnants, mainly caused by slow decomposition and the dissolving of tissue. None of it had salt content, lending itself to the conclusion that death occurred prior to immersion. Rover figured he'd be done and dusted by evening. Lancaster told him of his plan to fly out that afternoon and asked him to hang around and make himself useful until he returned, hopefully, by tomorrow evening.

Next, Lancaster telephoned DI Ferec and informed him of his arrival that evening, asking if he could set up an interview for the following morning, as early as possible. He also told him he'd be staying at Hôtel L'Amirauté and invited him to join him for dinner that evening at the hotel. Lancaster said he'd be paying. If that was the case, Ferec replied, he'd be coming by taxi. Pamela joined him to tell him that both phone calls, one to Basil and one to Max, proved fruitless. Neither of them had heard from Shawbuck; they had no idea when the man was due to arrive. This suited Lancaster. He was keen to be around when the Irish/American arrived. He hoped to catch him unawares and question the man. If he wasn't arriving anytime soon, then leaving for Brest wouldn't pose a problem.

By 3:30, Vidêt was driving him to the airport. Before heading for the main doors, he gave Vidêt one last pep-talk. 'Don't take chances going around the boatyards, never go alone. Always keep Rover or Pamela near to hand.' There was still a chance that if Batise had been using boats around the island for smuggling, he may have accomplices here. They hugged, kissed and hugged again. It was the first time they'd been going in opposite directions for months, but that was the nature of their profession. The flight itself, apart from being noisy and uncomfortable, was short and uneventful, touching down on the runway outside Brest in under forty-five minutes. Within another twenty, he was out of the airport, heading for the hotel.

Thank you, Pamela, thought Lancaster, stretched out on the bed in his room. The hotel was medium-sized, clean and comfortable. He checked his watch and decided he had time to grab some shut-eye before dinner. He texted Ferec to tell him he'd arrived, then forwarded the message to Vidêt. *My god,* he thought, *we're actually 'an item'*, as social media would put it. He awoke in plenty of time, showered, changed and went down to the restaurant. He'd started sipping at his beer when the concierge brought Ferec to the table.

"Bonjour, Christophe," Lancaster said.

"Bonsoir, David. It is evening now, but well done for trying," the other man said with a smile.

They ordered a beer for Ferec and perused the menus. Both chose from the set list, ordering wine to accompany their meals.

"So, David, do you want to tell me about the case you wish to interview Batise about? Or is this, like your visit the other day, all hush-hush?"

"Seriously, Christophe, there was nothing hush-hush about that visit; what I told you was the honest truth. We came over to speak to Henri Tanguyé about possible involvement in our case. We didn't make it official because we weren't even certain he was involved, but I needed to tick him off my list. We spotted Batise purely by chance. Honestly, there's no secret plan or investigation going on here."

"What is this case?"

Lancaster regaled him with a brief version of the murder hunt. He told him he had a short list of possible candidates; Tanguyé had been one but was now crossed off. Next, mainly because he was accessible, was Jean-Luc Batise. The first course arrived and they began slurping their way into the soup. When finished, Ferec leaned back in his seat, dabbing his mouth with his serviette.

"This sounds like the script for one of your movies. Spitfire pilot shot down fighting the Nazis. Rescued by the daughter of a local resistance hero, Danielo, who, by the way, even I have heard of. He manages to magic them both away to Jersey, where they fall in love, get married and have children, one of whom becomes an English Lady. *'Incroyable'*. Now, you suspect this pilot got murdered by an international drug smuggler. Are you serious? So what connects them?"

Lancaster gave an explanation of Peter's life as a banker and how he closed down the Batise bank account, cutting off the cash until Batise located another bank prepared to manage his financial affairs. As the second course arrived, Lancaster asked if Interpol had had any luck with the yacht Batise had bought at the auction. Ferec stopped eating.

"What yacht?"

"I told Interpol! Batise purchased a blue yacht from Tanguyé. He put in a huge, fixed bid before the auction. Well, Batise, used racing yachts to bring in cocaine and heroin from the Caribbean. Looking at the one he bid for, it looked like it'd been around a while. Batise used to hide drugs in keels or mould fibreglass streamlined sections onto hulls, they'd take them off once they knew the boat wasn't being looked at. I just wondered whether it was one of his yachts he'd been letting sit until the coast was clear?"

"Merde!" Ferec's only reply. He put down his knife and fork and flipped out his phone. He put in a call, a string of verbal French Lancaster understood nothing of, so he carried on eating as the fish was superb. Ferec finished on the phone and raised a glass to Lancaster, they touched glasses and drank the chilled white wine. Ferec had alerted the dive team to get to Morgat first thing the following morning to carry out an inspection of the hull. If there was anything there, they'd find it. After the fish, they had a light, tangy fruit sorbet to cleanse the palate before the cheese selection, the arrival of which had been preceded by the aroma emanating from the trolley. Ferec ordered an appropriate half-bottle of red to accompany the cheese. A Côtes du Rhône, so full-bodied it hung in the bottle and had to be encouraged into the glass.

The two detectives enjoyed their food, the wine and each other's company. They spoke of life in the force. Cases they'd worked and plans for the future. Ferec spoke about his wife and young son and Lancaster told Ferec about the loss of his wife, to which Ferec raised a glass in sympathy and memory. Lancaster asked Ferec if he'd sit in at the interview the following morning as his second. They both knew that Batise spoke English, but should he decide to be awkward and speak French, Ferec could act as an interpreter. The man agreed. They closed their evening with a handshake and a promise that Ferec would pick him up in the morning at 8:00. Lancaster was ready for bed. Within minutes of getting under the duvet, he was sound asleep.

The next morning, he was picked up by Ferec, who drove them to the station and led them upstairs to a suite of offices, one of which was his. They entered, and he asked a junior officer to go and get coffee.

"So, David. How do you want to play this?" he asked.

"I thought I'd start by asking how long he had been dealing with Tanguyé? Why'd he pay such a high price for the yacht? I want him to think we're only interested in the dealings in Morgat. Once he's relaxed into avoiding questions about the yacht, I'll ask him outright about the murder on Jersey and watch his reaction."

"Very well. Once you get to that point, I will come in with other questions, try and keep him, as you would say, 'on the hops', yes!".

The interview had been set for 9:30. They finished coffee and headed to the interview suite. Ferec agreed to furnish Lancaster with a copy of the voice tape from the interview. They were outside the room, with Ferec taking a call on his mobile, when Batise was led along the corridor in handcuffs. As the man walked past, there was a look of recognition as he saw Lancaster, but before he had time to speak, he was dragged into the room. Ferec said they'd have to wait; the solicitor was still on his way up. While they waited, Ferec informed Lancaster that the call he'd taken was from the dive team at the marina and they'd text if they found anything.

The solicitor duly arrived, requesting a few moments alone with his client. Ferec agreed. The uniformed 'door watch' led the man inside. Lancaster thought that he'd love to be a fly on the wall. He couldn't think what the solicitor and Batise would have to say to each other, as at that moment they'd no idea what Lancaster wanted to talk to the man about. After a few minutes, Ferec decided enough was enough; he and Lancaster walked in without knocking and sat down opposite the two men. Ferec turned on the tape and announced himself, then Lancaster introduced himself, staring at Batise all the time. A look of query flashed across Batise's face when he revealed himself to be from Devon and Cornwall Police. Batise and the solicitor looked at each other, then back to him. The solicitor was about to speak when Ferec cut him off, saying they wished to question Batise with regards to an ongoing investigation and the purchase of a yacht in Morgat. Lancaster saw the look of query disappear from the other man's face as he presumed, rightly, that what Ferec had cleverly said made the two things sound linked. Batise now thought this was all about the yacht and that investigation, though he was obviously unsure why it involved a detective from England.

Lancaster was keen to keep the speed up and not allow the man time to think.

"How long have you been dealing with Henri Tanguyé?" Lancaster asked in English.

Batise said something to his solicitor, most of which Lancaster understood.

"My client does not speak English," the solicitor said. "You will need to speak..."

"Don't let's waste time," Lancaster butted in, shutting the man up and maintaining control, continuing to stare at Batise.

"I've listened to phone-taps and recorded conversations with your client; we all know he speaks perfect English. Now, we can sit here for hours having everything I want to say translated into French just for you and your client, or he can stop acting like some kind of teenage bag thief and crack on with this interview. Then I can go home and he can go back to pissing in a bucket in his cell. It's up to you really, Batise."

"No comment," Batise replied. Now the man was engaged. Staring back at Lancaster with unhidden hate in his eyes. He hadn't liked the jibe about being a teenage bag thief; it had riled him. *Good*, Lancaster thought.

"Now, let's start again. You've purchased several yachts from Tanguyé; how long have you been dealing with him?"

"No comment." The man continued to stare at Lancaster, who stared back.

"How's your nose? Looks a bit swollen still. Does it still hurt?"

There was a moment's sullen silence; the man replied, "No comment."

"I was surprised that an international, drug trafficking big player like yourself, couldn't hire some better muscle and drivers. One gets stopped by an old lady in a Volkswagen and the other sticks his hands up to a woman holding a piece of copper pipe. Do you know what my dad's old saying was? 'You can get the staff; you just can't train 'em'. You should never skimp on the money when you're paying good staff, Batise."

"Why do you not just piss off back to England?" Batise snapped.

Lancaster laughed. "You sound like one of the narrow-minded racists we get in the home counties, anyway, Batise, you can talk. From what I know of your record, you've been all over the world. It must be hard to remember which is your country. So, Tanguyé... How long?"

"I hardly know the man," Batise replied, staring darkly at Lancaster. Lancaster knew if he kept the man angry, he was likely to make a mistake.

"Hardly know the man! You struck up a deal and bid high on at least two yachts I know of. Sounds like a business partnership to me, Batise. Don't you think so, Inspector Ferec?"

"Sounds like some kind of fiddle going on to me."

"Let me go back to my cell, you two give me earache," Batise retorted, still staring at Lancaster.

There was something ticking inside the man's eyes that Lancaster didn't like, but he didn't intend to turn away now. *I have to keep the man annoyed.*

"You've got years left to sit in your cell, Batise, sniffing the smell of your own shit day in, day out. I should make the most of my time outside of it while you can. What about the yacht you picked up from Concarneau four years ago, did you buy that from Tanguyé?"

In reality, Lancaster knew full well that Tanguyé had no involvement at all in this man's activities. But it could be a trigger, keep him guessing. As for the Concarneau connection, that was something, remembered from conversations with Vidêt, about the original case and her involvement with the Breton side of the investigation.

Batise smiled. "No comment."

"Come on, you remember, the racing yacht. The one where we almost caught you when you sailed it round to Falmouth. You managed to desert your mates, leaving them to rot in prison in the UK. Like I said, you've got to learn to look after your staff."

"Piss off, English, they knew what they were getting into."

"So you admit they worked for you then?"

"My client admits nothing," the solicitor said quickly. "He just means..."

"Oh, shut up, we know he admits nothing. He may look stupid, but we know he isn't," Ferec said, shutting the other man up. Before he had a chance to speak again, Lancaster was back in.

"It all comes back to who you employ, Jean-Luc. You probably don't know this, but at least three of your abandoned crew have named you as 'the man at the top'. I won't call you 'Mr Big'; none of your crew thought you were. In fact, according to them, you spent most of the trip across the Channel throwing up in the toilet, so you should be used to using a bucket in a cell by now. At least your crew have begun their sentences, so they might be out just as you're settling in."

Batise snapped. In a flash he was out of his seat, lunging toward Lancaster. Lancaster sat perfectly still; he knew what Batise had forgotten. The chain between the handcuffs the man wore had been unfastened, then refastened; the chain running through a metal loop attached to the desk. The desk was bolted to the floor. The chair shot backwards, but by the time Batis's face was within biting distance of Lancaster's, he came to an abrupt halt. Lancaster's heart was racing, filled with adrenaline. He was braced. He knew he had the man where he wanted him. Raging, angry, but completely unable to do a damned thing about it.

"Sit down," Ferec barked. The officer beside the door came forward. Ferec waved him off. Lancaster and Batise faced off over the desk. Lancaster held his nerve, smiling at the other man, though inside his heart pounded so hard he thought Batise could hear it.

"Shall I ask your solicitor to put your chair back for you, Jean-Luc? I don't think you're going to reach it with those cuffs on."

The solicitor picked the chair up, tucking it behind the still-standing Batise.

"I won't tell you again, Batise, sit down," Ferec said again.

"Shall I continue?" Lancaster was enjoying himself now. "So, having established that you're not a good sailor, I must presume you flew to Jersey then? Would that be correct?"

Lancaster watched the man's face change. He'd been hit with a broadside. He was now going in another direction and didn't know where it was heading. Before he had a chance to answer, Lancaster kept up the pressure.

"What about when you threatened the man trading your foreign currency for you? Had you flown over to do your banking or did you risk the big ferry? They have bigger toilets to throw up in. Come on, you must remember that. When you thought you were hiding all your ill-gotten gains in currency exchanges."

"He was a weasel," barked Batise.

"He was smart enough to know you were laundering dirty

money, Batise, and put a stop to it."

"Small change; he could keep it," Batise replied, staring at Lancaster.

"But what I don't understand is, why a man, even as stupid as you, would risk it all and murder Peter Urbawicz just because he stopped your bank account?"

The colour left the face of Batise. If Lancaster had been looking at the solicitor, he'd have noticed it drained from his face at the same time. Neither of them had seen that one coming. Lancaster pushed further.

"I mean, it really takes a complete idiot to not think we'd have a photograph, not just of you, but the other Jean-Luc Batise, you know, the one you sent to deal with the money in Jersey. So did he kill Ubawicz? Or did you pluck up some balls and do the deed yourself? No, come to think of it, I don't reckon you've got the guts for it really."

"Who the fuck is Peter Urbawish?" Batise said, looking genuinely shocked.

"My client has no idea who you are talking about, Detective Lancaster. He has..."

"Shut up," Ferec said. "Your client is capable of speaking for himself."

"So does this mean the other Jean-Luc did the deed?" Lancaster continued.

"Who the fuck is Urbawish? I swear, I've never heard of him. What the fuck is this, some kind of stitch-up, you can piss off, English! The weasel was called... Barren... or Dylan... or something. I've never heard of Urbawish. I remember... it was Warren, somebody Warren, he was the shit who closed my account. Urbawish... I've no fucking idea who he is. I never killed anyone, you bastards."

"We have people who saw you on Jersey in 2008, the same week as Urbawiscz was murdered, a year after your account was closed. God, he must have really pissed you off to make you want to kill him."

Batise now looked seriously riled. "Look... I've no idea who the fuck you're talking about. I swear, I never met anyone called Urbawish. You can't stitch me up with this. I am saying nothing else, nothing. Sanguye, tell them. Enough. I want to go back to my cell, this is done."

The solicitor confirmed the interview was closed. His client had no intention of continuing. He would be advising him not to speak again until they'd produced evidence and wished to press charges. The officer by the door uncuffed Batise from the desk and started to walk him out of the room, when suddenly the man lunged toward Lancaster, who braced himself ready for contact.

"You and I are not finished, English. Watch your back. I will be coming for you."

"Piss off, Batise, it would mean you crossing the channel. I'd hate to see you arrive with sick all down your shirt."

Batise lunged at Lancaster but the door-watch and Ferec had him under control.

"Take him to his cell," Ferec said.

Ferec came back in and leaned against the wall. "You were 'cool-hand Luke' there, detective."

"You think so?" said Lancaster, holding both of his hands out to show how much he was shaking. "I knew he couldn't get me the first time; I just thought it was funny, but that! I thought he was on me. It was a close call."

"We need coffee," Ferec switched off the tape.

In the canteen Lancaster could feel the sweat inside his shirt begin to chill. The whole episode had been intense, now he felt drained. It had however produced results. Without a doubt, Batise had incriminated himself. The man had started making mistakes. Lancaster thought the man had reached his 'Ronnie Biggs' moment when you got tired looking over your shoulder, you just wanted to relax and breathe.

Ferec arrived with two black coffees and a bowl of huge chunks of brown, rugged-looking sugar. They both dropped in chunks and stirred.

"What did you mean, two Batises?" Ferec asked.

Lancaster explained about the separate photos in their possession. How a different Batise was doing the banking, whilst another Batise was out on the front line. He was the man now locked up downstairs. Only time and Interpol would unlock which was top dog; maybe they were equals. Maybe both top dogs. But at least one of them was confined to a cell and talking.

"So what are you thinking about his involvement in your man's murder?" Ferec asked.

Lancaster sipped his bowl of coffee, still thinking.

"Can I reserve judgment until I've heard the tape back again? My first thought is that the Batise downstairs didn't do it. I'd have expected a 'no comment' when I mentioned Peter, but he genuinely looked like he'd no idea what I was springing on him. I think he thought we were fitting him up. There was no recognition of the name at all. Every other question we asked you could see that smug look that said, 'What blue yacht'! But he knew that we knew that he knew exactly what we were talking about but was just playing dumb. Keeping it in his control. It was the same when I mentioned Henri Tanguyé. We know he's just a boat trader. Batise still said 'no comment', just to make us think Tanguyé might be involved. He wants to act like the big man and make us think he knows everybody and is 'the main man'. But the moment we started asking about Peter, he panicked. Suddenly it was out of his control. I'm sure he'd heard nothing about it."

Ferec's phone jangled. He answered and responded.

"We are about to have a visitor. Sanguye wants to speak, off the record. I've told him to come up here."

A minute later they were joined by the solicitor.

"My client wants to make it quite clear; he did visit Jersey a few times but never personally did any banking. He went there to buy or sell boats. He had heard of the man Warren. He cannot remember what the man actually did, just remembers the name. He may even have spoken on the telephone to this man, but he swears he has never heard of anybody called Urbawish, and certainly never committed murder on the island. He knows nothing at all of this man's death, nothing whatsoever."

"Is that it?" Ferec said in reply.

"Yes."

"Then piss off. You're spoiling my coffee break."

The man picked up his briefcase and walked away.

"Batise is being clever," Lancaster said. "He's not certain

what I know about his Jersey account. He's not certain what photos I have of him on the island or what recordings of phone calls. He's rattled by not knowing and he's hedging his bets. The truth is, we've no evidence he was ever on the island; I lied. But we do have pictures of the other Batise. So, in fact, he's given himself away. I knew nothing, now I know more. At some stage he was on that island, probably trading boats for smuggling. Now he's trying to cover his tracks and not get implicated in a murder. I think the other Batise set up the bank account, so he would've met Peter. He may not have discussed names with your Batise, that way they could both keep secrets. Your Batise may be sitting in his cell wondering if the other Batise had committed murder without him knowing. Now he's worried, and I love it."

Ferec took another call, a smile spreading across his face. He rang off.

"Do you want good news?"

Lancaster nodded.

"The dive team have found compartments bonded to the hull. Hard to see at first; the boat's been in the water so long the hull was covered in weed and shellfish, so they lifted it onto the jig and scraped the bottom. There were two bulges, made to look like part of the twin keels. They have cut one of them off and it appears to be carrying four bundles of cocaine. It will need to be confirmed, but it's hard to think what other white powder you would wrap in waterproof plastic and strap inside a container."

"Well done. All you have to do is prove Batise knew about the attachments. If I were you, I'd tell the two accomplices what you've found and put some pressure on them before you tell Batise. You never know, they may just decide to spill the dirt on him."

Ferec laughed. "Well, thank you for that, Detective Lancaster, I would never have thought of doing that," the man said sarcastically.

Lancaster held his hands up. "Sorry, Christophe, old habits. I'll leave you to it. I think I'm done here; he's all yours. I'll keep you updated if we find more about his movements on Jersey."

Ferec made arrangements to get Lancaster back to his hotel. He packed, paid, got a taxi to the airport and texted Marie a time of arrival.

On Jersey, Vidêt was walking around the little harbour at Rozel Bay. The first on her list. The boats, bobbing on the incoming tide, were not much to look at. Not one looked like it could sail around the bay, let alone across from France. She couldn't see anything looking like it would've been used for trafficking drugs. She drove on to the next on her list. Le Graveur, picturesque, but still nothing. No signs of anything ocean-worthy. She strolled to the end of the pier for the exercise, aware that recently, she'd eaten too well, drunk too much and hadn't exercised enough. In any form.

It felt wrong at Pamela's, though she and Lancaster had shared a bed over a few nights, the house was just too quiet. She must get back into a gym soon. When Lancaster's text came in, she laughed at herself, being excited because she'd received a text. *Pathetic.* But she didn't delete it; she may read it again later. She returned to the car and moved on to her next location.

Vidêt took one look around the small marina at Orguil and realised this was proving to be a fruitless exercise. Yes, there were some nice boats moored in the harbour. But unlike Brittany, where almost every harbour that housed moorings, also housed a chandlers, boat-yard, mechanic and shipwright, these harbours were for weekenders. They were just places to tie up your craft until you needed it again. No work was ever carried out here. She felt she may be wasting her time on this task. At least she was fulfilling a Lancaster list, ticking places off, proving they'd been there, done that. She drove along the coast until she reached Saint Helier. This was a better bet.

The whole place was a collection of individual harbours, tie-ups, marinas and floating pontoons. To service this mass of sailing equipment, there were innumerable boatyards and engineering workshops and boat lifts. Yards full of yachts and motorboats were lined up on jigs and trailers, awaiting work or holed up for the winter. Vidêt started in La Collette Yacht Basin. Although she could see several ocean-going yachts moored up, most were luxury boats. She hunted around until she found the harbour master's office and took in her photos of the two Batises. Nobody recognised them. She tried the neighbouring boatyard. None of the workmen in the yard claimed to have seen either man.

The next stop was French Harbour, a more promising possibility. This was luxury and expense. A lot of fine-looking racing yachts, luxury motor cruisers and casual sailing yachts, but at the top end, there was serious money. Interestingly, Vidêt spotted another racing yacht in the same blue as the one in Morgat. She realised that just looking wasn't going to get her anywhere. She had to scout the yards and get a feel for the people working there, sniff out any low life. She walked around the Old Harbour to the warehouses and boat sheds scattered along the quayside, eventually finding a yard where there were people working. She made her way to the main office and poked her head around the door, where a grey-haired lady sat behind a desk looking busy.

"Good morning. I wonder if you can help me," she asked. The old lady looked at her.

"Well, that depends on what you want to buy?"

Vidêt explained that she was searching for anybody who may be able to look at some photos she had of people who may have been using the marinas and moorings around the island. The lady asked who she was. Vidêt showed her warrant card, keeping it back far enough that she couldn't see the Devon & Cornwall logo. The lady accepted the card for what it was. Official. A mark of authority. Vidêt laid the photos on her desk and watched as she put on glasses, then studied them both.

She pointed at the original Batise and said, "Him."

"What do you mean by 'him'?"

"My dear... You asked if I'd seen either of these people and I said, 'Him'. I would think that says it all, don't you?"

"You're sure, you've actually seen this man?"

"Yes, about three, four weeks ago. He came in to book a workspace. We rent yard and jig space. If people want to pressure wash or do some kind of refit, we rent them space. They do the work themselves or bring people in. Often, the DIY people aren't as clever as they think. They end up needing us to fit something or they start a job they can't finish. So it works for everybody, anyway, a yard that looks busy, stays busy, you know what I mean."

"And you're sure this man wanted some work doing?"

"As sure as I know you're not Island Police," the lady said smiling.

"It's a long story, madame, but if you want proof that I am working with your police just..."

"I don't need any proof, young lady. So what's this man done?"

"I cannot tell you that. What else can you tell me about this man?"

"He and his workers have used us before. Always pays cash for space, polite, they bring a boat in, they work on it, they put it back into the water. I tell you this, they're a good team, they turn boats around in a matter of hours, change keels, racing fins. I think that's what their job is, updating or upgrading racing yachts. They work fast, have the boat in the water and floating before the tide changes. They're good."

"So when have they booked the yard for this time?"

"A week next Friday, nine days' time. We have a week of high tides then," the lady said, flipping the page of the diary. "They're coming in on the middle tide and want the yard open for 5:30 in the morning. They plan to get out again before the full tide turns, so a couple of hours work I'd imagine. These yachts are wet versions of the Grand Prix, they like to keep improvements secret. They pay extra to keep the whole yard private. They get it all to themselves."

"Any idea what they have booked in?"

"It's a blue racer, 'Le Moselle'. An eight metre, they've

booked a double workspace."

Having thanked her, Vidêt returned to her car. She hadn't liked to tell the lady, but she didn't think anybody would be bringing a yacht in any time soon; she was pretty certain, 'Le Moselle' was the boat sat in Morgat. The man delivering it was sitting in a cell in Brest. But it was good to know another link in the smuggling process.

Another text came in from Lancaster. 'In the air, on way home'.

She decided to head straight for the airport, meet the man off the plane, and she'd have news for him. She felt she'd done her job.

As she drove away, she failed to notice the two men in the grey BMW parked beside the quay. The BMW pulled from its parking space, smoothly slotted into the traffic, placing itself five cars back where it could see, but not be observed. Unless you were expecting it.

CHAPTER EIGHT

Lancaster was walking out of arrivals when his phone rang. Ferec. He was hitting the accept button when he saw Vidêt approaching; he blew her a kiss and answered the phone.

"Christophe, do you miss me already?" he asked.

Ferec laughed, then replied, "I thought I should warn you that Batise had a mobile in his cell. We think solicitor Sanguye delivered it, but we've no proof. We caught him purely by chance. He was making calls at night when we thought he was curled up asleep; today a standard drug sweep through the cells found his phone wrapped in his blanket. He tried to stamp on it when it dropped, but the guard got to it first. We've checked through it; amongst the calls he's made are several to the same mobile in the last four or five hours. We don't know who it is, but it's unlikely it was a social call. There was a brief call into his number from a landline, but Batise cut it off quickly. I think one of his contacts called him from a hotel room, he didn't know Batise was locked up, anyway, we've traced that one. It is a guest house, 'Ocean View'. It's in a place called Le Hocq. That, my friend, is on Jersey."

"Bugger. We may have stirred the hornet's nest too much, Christophe. I can only think of one reason he'd be contacting anybody over here, to get back at us, and that's interesting.

There was I thinking he had nothing to do with Peter's death, but if he's willing to send somebody after me because I broke his nose and pissed him off, then what would he have done if somebody took away access to money. Bugger, Christophe. I may have to think this through again. Thanks for the warning, I'll alert the local police and see what they want to do about it. Thanks again, Christophe, I'll be in touch."

"Stay safe, David. Keep in touch."

Lancaster ended the call as Vidêt reached him.

"I missed you. Did it go well?"

"Too well. I'll tell you when we get in the car."

En route, Lancaster told her about his interview with Batise. He told her he was now confused. Had almost written the man out of the murder, putting him down just as a drug smuggler. Now, since his call from Christophe, the man may have set the dogs on them. Vidêt explained that there may be another explanation for the calls. She told him how she'd come across the 'rent-a-space' in Saint Helier, and the woman who looked after the books recognised the old Batise. It looked like the purchase of the yacht in Morgat was a planned affair right from the start. They may never know how long Batise had known the yacht or how long it had sat in the Morgat marina, but it would account for why Batise was willing to pay over the odds. So the plan was to get the boat, sail it from Brittany to Jersey and then in one quick move, detach the modules and stash or sell the drugs. They hadn't bargained for Batise to get arrested and banged up in Brest without his phone. The plan was being put into motion until Sanguye got a phone in to the man. It could be that the calls were Batise telling the team to hold off. Disperse. Lancaster thought about this, deciding what he needed was food; he thought better on a full stomach. They drove on toward Pamela's house. If he'd not been thinking about a shower and meal, he may have seen the grey BMW pull into the side of the road, just after Vidêt swung down the drive. But they missed it.

That evening around the table, talk of the case was temporarily banished. The food was good, the wine a joy and the company, as usual, was humorous and enjoyable. Eventually they retired to the lounge with coffee and brandy to go over the day. Lancaster ran over the interview with Batise but left out the violent outburst. He told them how initially his thoughts were that the man had no idea who Peter was, which was quite possible, bearing in mind that the Batise who managed the banking was a different person to the man now sitting in a cell. He also told them of Ferec's phone call and how they'd found the mobile. Vidêt explained her conversations with the booking clerk at the boatyard. Lancaster didn't like to mention that he wasn't sure Batise contacting somebody on the island was as simple as cancelling the team.

Rover said he'd found nothing that would change his opinion on the cause of Peter's death. All his work was finished unless anything else cropped up needing forensic exploration. Lancaster checked his watch: gone 9:00 p.m., still worth giving Wardly a call. Lancaster had texted the previous afternoon to inform the man he'd arrived in Brest and that the interview had been scheduled for the following day. He'd also texted to say he'd be in the air and unable to phone to give the latest update. He was keen to stick to Wardly's schedule and keep on the right side of the man. He retired to his room to make the call. He texted first to ensure it was OK, not yet sure of the protocol with this man. Wardly rang straight back.

"Lancaster. How did your trip go?"

"OK on one level, sir, but may have caused us a problem on another."

"How so?"

He gave a brief outline of how the interview had gone and how initially he'd felt the man could be ruled out of the enquiry. Now actions taken by the man since had him thinking otherwise. He told Wardly of the phone discovery and Vidêt's conversation in the boatyard. This proved Batise had been using the island for a while for more than just banking. He then told him of the cut-off call from the guest house at Le Hocq, the 'Ocean View', and a reply call, possibly to alert the crew of his arrest, but potentially to engage somebody there to seek revenge on the British detectives. Wardly doubted the latter, thinking this was a case of 'the boys from the mainland' wanting to 'big up' the situation further than it warranted. But it could link whoever was at the B&B to Batise, which in itself was enough cause to instigate a raid and see what they could net in the way of evidence. He committed a team for first thing in the morning, inviting Lancaster and Vidêt to join them, with a meeting time of 5:30, to catch whoever was there still in bed.

Lancaster returned to the lounge and told them what had been said. He told Vidêt it would be an early start. Rover asked if there was anything Lancaster wanted him to do. Lancaster said there may well be something that would crop up soon;

there was no point him disappearing off to the UK just yet. 5:00 the next morning, with stomachs craving missed croissants and coffee, the two detectives were parked in a pub car park a mile from the guest house as agreed. The local team arrived in a riot van accompanied by Wardly and Beard in an unmarked car. Lancaster got out and walked to Wardly's car.

"'Morning, Lancaster. You two ready for this?"

"You tell us want you want us to do, sir, and we're all yours."

Lancaster was disappointed when Wardly said he wanted them to follow up the rear and observe. This was a Jersey Police shout. Once they'd managed to apprehend whoever was in the B&B, there'd be a chance to ask questions later. For the moment this raid would form part of a drug enquiry and as such, had nothing to do with the case Vidêt and Lancaster were working; only a circumstantial link between the two. Lancaster agreed with a smile, aware of the smug-looking smirk he saw on the face of DI Beard. *I bloody hate politics,* thought Lancaster as he walked away.

The two detectives fell into line behind Wardly, he in turn fell into line behind the van. The convoy drove to Le Hocq, parking just short of the hotel. The street was quiet, as six black-garbed, helmeted officers piled out of the van. They trotted down the street and right up to the front door of the hotel, whilst two went down a service road beside the building, to cover rear exits. Once all were in place, Beard casually stepped up to the front door and rang the bell.

Lancaster couldn't help but think this looked a little odd: a team of black boiler-suited, helmeted policemen gathered at the front steps, one carrying a door ram, whilst another plain-clothed officer rang the bell. There was, though, a method to this perceived madness. Wardly had made the decision that there could be legitimate holidaymakers in residence and going home complaining they'd been rudely awoken from their beds by a police 'crash team' was not a good idea. So, getting somebody to just open the door could make for a far gentler awakening.

The plan worked. A woman opened the door and the team pushed past her into the small foyer like a boiler-suited tsunami. Lancaster and Vidêt saw no reason to get involved and stayed leaning on the bonnet of their car, just in case they were called upon. For a minute or two, there was silence and then Lancaster saw the 'back-door guards' coming back up the side street having obviously been waved away by Wardly. As these two officers reached the front steps, Lancaster heard the unmistakable sound of screeching tyres. His head whipped around to see a grey BMW saloon stop in the middle of the street a few hundred yards back. Almost as soon as Lancaster saw it, the driver stuck the car in reverse, going backwards up the road.

Lancaster shouted at the officers standing at the bottom of the steps, who'd also seen the car come to a halt.

"Tell Wardly, he's missed them. Grey BMW saloon. Lancaster's giving chase."

He jumped into the driving seat and at the same time, Vidêt landed passenger side. Lancaster had the car started as Vidêt buckled her seat belt. He swung the car around in the street, the pinging noise alerting him to the fact he wasn't wearing his belt. It was too late now; he couldn't take his hands off the wheel. He'd shifted into third before he got to the end of the road, in time to see the BMW swinging around in a controlled handbrake turn, with smoke streaming off its wheels, which told him it was being floored and this was no mistaken turn. Whoever was at the wheel was keen to get away. Before Lancaster hit fourth, he allowed the engine to scream long enough to get his hand into his jacket pocket and extract his phone. He threw it to Vidêt who caught it in mid-air.

"Get Wardly and give him running commentary. Watch for street signs."

Wardly picked up straight away and understood what was happening in an instant. He and Beard were attempting to follow but had come late to the chase. They were pleased to have a direct line to the route the BMW was taking.

"Just keep talking, Vidêt, we're en route, I can listen."

"Still on A4. West toward Saint Helier."

Lancaster was into fourth, keeping out of fifth. He needed to keep the revs up, now the turbo kicked in and he could feel the burst. He recognised the back end of the BMW. A Mk3. He could see a slim, blue, motif sticker on the boot lid, showing it to be a custom. He also knew he'd struggle to keep up if they hit an open road. He was envious; he'd looked at one similar the previous year. He knew the straight-six engine gave it a huge power-to-weight ratio, whereas Lancaster's Golf had serious poke, pumped in by the turbo when the engine was pushed, but the car pulling away from him had the advantage of twin-turbos and a six-speed gearbox; if used properly, it could leave him in the dust.

"Sharp turn onto Rue Samares. North through built-up

area," Vidêt relayed. In the background she could hear Beard shouting the change to other vehicles.

Lancaster was grateful for the early morning; the roads were almost empty. On the other hand, it would be nice if the other car got held up by a tractor or bus. Both cars were now speeding along a road, with houses and farms on both sides. Lancaster glanced down for a second, eighty miles an hour, in a built-up area, he couldn't keep this up for long, someone was going to get hurt.

"Straight over crossroads. North on Samares."

Lancaster caught a glimpse in his rear-view mirror, headlights, flashing blues, then rounding a slight curve they were lost from sight. The BMW would lose him on this straight stretch. He shifted into fifth, risked flooring it to make up ground, then spotted brake lights and smoke from rear tyres as the 'beemer' swung hard right at another crossroads. Lancaster dropped down through the box, braking hard at the same time. He swung the Golf round the corner, using forward momentum, whacked the box into third, hit the throttle hard, then into fourth. The tyres screeched, fighting for grip, spitting gravel as they did. The back end swung around the bend after them, like a counterbalance, attempting to overtake them on the left-hand side, then the front end was flying after the BMW and the distance for the moment narrowed.

"Right. Hard right at crossroads. Grande Route Saint Clement. Heading due east."

Lancaster spotted a sign, school coming up. A glance at the dash told him the big hand was only at 6:00. *Should be clear of children*, he hoped. Should he back off or stay on the chase; he kept his foot down. Two puffs of smoke from the rear wheels of the Mk3, and he automatically changed down as he closed with the other car. Approaching a hard left, both cars slewed around the bend, smoke pouring off wheels from braking and then instantly from wheel spin, as both drivers hit the throttle once more. A car about to turn across their path into the school car park stopped dead in the middle of the road. The BMW went round the front of it on the wrong side of the road and the Golf flew past on the left, with Lancaster catching a look of fear and shock on the face of the woman driving.

"Slight curve right. Saint Clement, heading east."

Lancaster cursed the difference between the two cars. On a long section of straight, the Mk3 pulled away with ease. By the time they reached another built-up section, with houses on one side and a church on the other, Lancaster could see the taillights in the distance.

"Past church, Saint Clements. Still on Saint Clement heading east. BMW losing us."

Lancaster glanced down; 'speedo' ninety-five mph. *This is bloody crazy.* They rounded a curve. Vidêt screamed, "David!" He looked up. In an instant, he saw the BMW pulled up on a driveway, a man in black beside the car, standing, with his body braced against the side of the car, the driver's door open, arms outstretched in front of him and clasping a gun in both hands. There was nowhere for Lancaster to go. There were walls to both sides. Lancaster made an instant choice: *go for the man.*

"Head down!" he screamed, as a hole was punched through the screen by the first bullet.

"Shots fired, shots fired!" Vidêt shouted into the phone,

the first shot followed by a second, then a third. The last of which Lancaster felt hit his left shoulder. Finally, the screen disintegrated in a shower of small chunks of glass, as a fourth shot went past his head, close enough for him to feel the draft of its passing. Lancaster dropped his profile low, still able to see where he was going. He saw the man jumping back to the driving seat as the Golf took the door clean off. Lancaster pulled hard on the handbrake in an attempt to slew the car and block the road. Too fast. The manoeuvre failed. The car spun full circle and, with a crunch of metal, collided with a gateway on the other side of the road and continued up and over the pile of rubble and stone it had created. As both airbags went off, Lancaster's unbelted body flipped up, curved over the top of the bag, somersaulting him through the non-existent screen and pitching him into a huge bush on the outside. The last thing he remembered was looking up through the greenery at a sign hanging on a post beside the disintegrated gateway, reading 'Pilates' in large, gothic script. He remembered thinking, *what a strange choice of script for such a peaceful pastime.* Then he gave up thinking and drifted into unconsciousness.

In his state of semi-consciousness, Lancaster heard sirens and voices calling his name; he chose to ignore them. People were always calling him, wanting him to do things. He was tired and wanted to sleep. What he really wanted was the pain in his back and groin to go away. He wanted a holiday. It was time he and Marie took time off and travelled through France, just the two of them. No Pamela, no Rover, no Craven, no Wardly. But first they'd have to see Basil and apologise for another broken car. He tried to sit up and see how much damage he'd done, but that was when the pain in his back hit him hard. His eyes shot open, in a sea of pain, with flashing lights and noise surrounding him.

"Don't try to move," a woman said somewhere near his head.

Lancaster realised there was something wrong with his perspective. The face attached to the voice was upside down, looking straight at him. Behind the head was blue sky, her face disappearing in a hazy blur of cold bright sunshine.

"You'll be OK; we need to untangle you from this bush and see how injured you are. We don't want to lift you straight out in case you've broken anything. My colleague's gone for some loppers and cutters. Does anything hurt?"

He told the voice he had severe pain in his lower back and he thought somebody may also have castrated him, as the pain in his groin was excruciating. For some reason, this thought triggered another.

"Marie. Is Marie OK?"

"We're still extracting her from the vehicle, sir, but she's talking. I don't know if she's referring to you or not, but she does keep saying, 'the bastard, the bastard', then swearing a lot in French."

This upset him more than anything. He'd put her in danger; the thought she was hurt and angry affected him more than he expected. Between that and the pain in his back, he began to cry. He wanted to sleep but the tears wouldn't let him; he closed his eyes.

"Stay with me, sir, stay with me," the voice said. He ignored her, tired of being told what to do. He just wanted sleep.

The next time he opened his eyes there were faces all around. He remembered the face of the paramedic; she was still there. *Nice smile.* He was on some kind of board and when he tried to move, he realised his neck was clamped in a collar and there were straps across his arms and chest. This frightened him.

"What's happened? How bad is it? Where's Marie?"

"In reverse order, Lancaster," a familiar voice replied. "DS Vidêt has some facial cuts but she's fine. You're buggered. The car's trashed. There's a lady here who wants to know what we're going to do to repair her gate and we've a baddy in custody who appears to have lost a hand, so he's pissed off as well. Apart from that, the day's going quite well really."

Lancaster looked up at Wardly and couldn't help but smile at his black humour. It reminded him of Craven.

"Tell the lady whose gate I trashed to book me in for Pilates. I suppose if we have the driver's hand, we won't have to ask permission to take prints."

Wardly laughed. "Seriously. Good bit of driving, Lancaster. Cocked it up a bit at the end, but we got the man. We were almost up with you when the shooting started, sorry about that. Never thought shooting was on the agenda. I haven't said that OK."

Lancaster had a sudden vision. "Just as I hit the 'beemer', I swear there was another man in the passenger seat, dark-skinned, black jacket."

"Shit," Wardly said. He instantly pulled out his phone and walked away. Lancaster heard something about dogs and a chopper. He turned his face enough to see the paramedic and engaged with her eyes.

"Seriously, what damage have I done to myself?"

"Well, we have you boarded as a precaution; we still don't know if you've spinal injuries. You have an open wound up your lower back, which will need cleaning and a better dressing. It was caused by you breaking a branch, which has caused a deep laceration but luckily hasn't penetrated anything major, but it'll need stitches. We've taped it and dressed it for now; it has splinters still in it. Also, you may have suffered a rupture of the groin, your valuables got hooked on the steering column when you flipped through the screen. I won't bother to bollock you for not wearing a seatbelt, your boss may charge you with that later. The left shoulder of your jacket took a bullet, but the double stitching deflected it. It grazed the skin. Basically, you appear to have gotten away with it, but a proper scan will tell for certain."

Wardly's face came into view. "Chopper and dogs are on the way."

"If you've found the guy's phone," Lancaster said. "Check it for any contact to 07889244345. That's the number of the phone Ferec found on Batise. That'll give you a direct link from here to there."

"Will you shut up and look in pain, your sergeant's on her way over and you should milk it for all it's worth."

Vidêt's face came into view. Lancaster was so pleased to see her but sorry to see the spots of blood across her face, caused by chunks of glass showering her at seventy miles an hour.

"So sorry, Marie; cocked up big time..."

Vidêt leaned down and kissed him, tears dripping from her eyes onto his upturned face. She pulled away and the medics took him to the ambulance. She went with him, holding his hand all the way. Lancaster was annoyed. If he was seriously injured, this case would come to a standstill and it had come so far. He didn't want to let Pamela or Craven down. *I should've backed off and left it to the locals.* It was too late now; the job was done. The next few hours would tell how bad it was going to be.

Those next few hours were a glare of lights, trolleys, noise and machines. Lancaster hated it, but saw it as penance; it had been his fault, his alone. He'd been an idiot giving chase like that. They were on an island; they could've closed the place down, hunted for them. He'd put the case and himself at risk, worse still, he could've caused Marie's death. To lose another woman he loved would've been unforgivable, too much to live with. Although Vidêt stuck with him in the ambulance and stayed by his side in A&E, she'd been very quiet. He was sure she was angry, blaming him. He couldn't fault that logic. He blamed himself as well, but he didn't know what to say to get her back. They weren't in A&E long before they trolleyed him for a body scan, still strapped to the board. They wouldn't let Vidêt accompany him, so she stayed in the red plastic seat in the cubicle to await his return and gave a full statement to DI Beard who'd followed them up.

When he returned to the bay, he was no longer attached to the board. The scan showed no spinal injury. Apart from bruising to his groin and one swollen testicle, he'd survived being launched through the screen. In fact, the shooter had done him a favour, removing the glass prior to Lancaster's exit. The staff turned him on his side and cleaned and stitched the wound to his back, which even with anaesthetic was a painful, uncomfortable process. They finished with a wide stick-on dressing. He was told it would need changing every day. As the team was finishing the dressing, they were joined by Pamela and Rover, whom Vidêt had called to come and pick them up. (The Golf was another non-runner.) Rover picked up a pack of dressings and said he could make the changes, saving Lancaster from having to return to the hospital. In a few weeks, the stitches should disintegrate on their own.

The crew made their way to Pamela's car and for Lancaster, the painful journey back to the house. Once there, Lancaster said he wanted no food or coffee, just sleep. Rover and Vidêt helped him up the stairs to his room. Rover left them alone and Vidêt helped Lancaster off with his clothes, then helped him roll into bed. As she did so, Lancaster grabbed hold of her hand.

"I'm so sorry, Marie, I could've got you killed."

Vidêt wrapped her arms around his neck and began to shake, then burst into tears. Part of this was the 'come down' from the adrenaline rush they'd just endured. It had been bottled up, 'stoppered', by the sudden climax to the episode, then the worry and noise at the hospital. Now in the warm light coming through the bedroom windows and the lush furnishings within the room, the 'stopper' had been released. They were alive, safe, warm, comfortable and, what's more, they were together and alone. The other part of her distress was caused by the fact that she now realised how much she truly felt for this man. She'd realised she was in love. What made this worse was that she'd realised she'd nearly lost him before she'd had the chance to tell him.

When she'd seen that man standing in the road, gun held out, she knew it wasn't just for show. Sat in the hospital awaiting Lancaster's return from theatre, she'd had time to think. The man had deliberately drawn them away from the other officers, chosen the right moment to gain ground on them. Yes, Lancaster was a brilliant, fast-car driver, but the other car had a six-speed box, a sport BMW built for speed. Vidêt thought there were times when the other car could've lost them but didn't. It was a ploy to keep them coming, waiting for the right moment. It could be that Lancaster was quicker in the Golf than the other men were expecting. If the BMW had gained a little more distance before choosing to stop, he might have had time to brace himself properly, breathe and fire steadily at the approaching Golf. But when she'd first spotted him, he'd only just got out of the car, pulling the gun up into shooting position when she'd shouted.

The shooter may have expected Lancaster to slam on the brakes when he saw the gun but the Golf speeding up and heading straight for him, may have unnerved him, which forced his hand, making him shoot too fast. If he'd kept his nerve and let off a fifth shot, he may well have got his man; it had been a close-run thing. Too close for Vidêt's comfort. When Lancaster yanked on the handbrake it nearly worked. But the camber on that corner had taken the car full circle. When they hit the gatepost and went right over it, she knew they were in trouble. The shock of an abrupt halt and the explosion of the airbags was nothing compared to seeing Lancaster flying through the open screen. That had been horrifying. One second, they were together in a shared drama, then she was alone, cocooned in the safety of the airbag, unable to reach her seatbelt release.

After that, it had been hard to bring anything into focus, her vision and mind became fogged and everything took on a dream-like quality. She'd felt something running down her face but could only get one hand up to touch; it came away covered in blood. She was in a situation she'd never been in before. Now here they were, alone and back where they'd started hours earlier, with the realisation that during those last few hours, her life could've changed, could've become empty again and she could've been alone once more.

Eventually, her sobs and tears subsided, she raised her head from Lancaster's neck and looked at him, could see he'd been crying too.

"You don't need to apologise for anything, we are police, this is what we do and we trust each other. We both knew what we were doing when we started that chase. I cry because I nearly lost you. I love you, David, I can't be without you. I don't want to be alone again."

Lancaster wrapped her in his arms, then cried out in pain as he stretched the wound on his lower back. Vidêt touched her fingers to his lips and 'shushed' him.

"Let's just sleep. We need to sleep this day off just laying here in the sunshine."

She curled up next to him, removed his arm from around her neck and held his hand until they both slept, shivering now and then despite the warmth of the duvet and the sun, as thoughts and images of the chase came to mind. When they awoke it was dark outside. Lancaster tried to move but found it hard, like dragging his body through treacle, accompanied by fingers of pain. Pain from everywhere.

"Just move slowly," Vidêt said.

"But I need a wee."

"All the more reason to go slowly, I'm going first." She slid out of bed and disappeared into the bathroom.

Lancaster did as she'd asked. He managed to turn himself onto his side, get his legs from under the duvet and hang over the edge of the bed, but he didn't have the nerve to push his body upright. The feelings of pain from the wound on his back unnerved him, he didn't want to push any further. Vidêt came back from the bathroom sobbing gently again.

"What is it?" he asked.

"Have you seen my face?" she cried. "I look like I've got acne."

Lancaster laughed unsympathetically, grabbed hold of her hair and pulled her to him.

"You look beautiful to me, Marie Vidêt, and I love you too, even with acne."

She slapped him first, then helped pull him upright and onto his feet, then as far as the bathroom door. She declined to help further with his needs, other than putting the light on for him. When he returned, Vidêt suggested he stay where he was for the rest of the night. She'd go and fetch food and find out what had been happening. Lancaster was reluctant at first. He felt he needed to keep moving or he'd stiffen up completely. He did however agree that one night would be OK. Vidêt helped him back into bed, propped him on a pile of pillows and set off to find a snack.

She returned ten minutes later with a tray of cups, coffee and sugar, accompanied by Josette carrying another tray with toast and a pot of apricot jam. She was, in turn, followed by Rover and Pamela, both carrying their own cups of coffee. The room filled up quickly, but they all found places to sit; Josette chose not to stay. Once she'd seen Lancaster was OK, puffed up the duvet, plumped up his pillows and settled his tray in front of him, she said she'd see him again tomorrow.

"So how is it?" Rover asked. "I'm in charge of meds; I can give you more pain relief if you need it?"

Lancaster jumped at the chance. He wasn't sure how long he'd been asleep, but he was sure the last of the painkillers had worn off. Rover went to get what he needed and Lancaster started into the tray of toast with Vidêt applying the jam. Meanwhile, Pamela filled him in on the other events of the day. Craven had been informed of the state of play by Wardly, who'd then attempted to phone Lancaster's mobile but got Pamela, playing 'guard the phone'. She'd given the man a blow-by-blow account of all that had happened and the various injuries sustained. Craven was all for flying out, but Pamela had asked him to wait until morning, then ring again because by then they'd know more about how quickly Lancaster would be up and about. She'd had another call from Ferec in Brittany. Apparently, Wardly had telephoned him to double-check the number Lancaster had given him and had told him the way the morning had gone. They'd confirmed the man with the gun had indeed been in touch with Batise, so this gave a direct link between the two men.

Ferec had called to see how Lancaster was doing, so Pamela

had given him a report of his and Vidêt's injuries. She suggested Ferec may like to inform Jean-Luc Batise that not only had he now lost his 'right-hand man' in Jersey, but his 'right-hand man' had now lost his right hand. Pamela also received a call from Max at the bank. Shawbuck was planning to visit in two days' time. She'd telephoned Basil and enquired if the man had booked a hire car. It appeared not. Maybe he wasn't planning to stick around, but rather travel by taxi whilst on the island. She'd also broken the news to him about the damage to the car but had cheered the man up by offering to pay for a replacement. She'd booked another Golf to be delivered to the house in the morning. Rover returned with what Lancaster thought looked very much like a 'hypo', Rover confirmed this. He assured Lancaster he'd not feel a thing, prior to that, he wanted the room cleared. His patient had had enough chat and it was time for him to rest.

Once Vidêt removed all the cups and trays from the room, giving Rover time to do what he had to do, she returned, settled Lancaster down, undressed, slipped under the duvet and curled up for the night. She had no intention of leaving his side for a while. Part of it was a selfish desire not to be alone, as there were too many images flashing through her brain to want to be alone with.

After a better night's sleep than either of them deserved after their previous day, they awoke to another bright, crisp day of blue sky and sunshine. Lancaster was determined to get mobile and active, but he'd settle with mobile for today. He didn't want to risk getting the dressing wet so skipped the shower. Vidêt insisted he at least wash his hair so, to that end, she had him leaning into the shower enough to wash his hair for him. Little diamonds of screen glass ended up on the floor of the cubicle; it looked like a jewellery raid gone wrong. Vidêt washed the man's face, then left him to clean his teeth whilst she got dressed. It took them a while, but eventually he was up, washed, dressed and managing to walk down the stairs unaided, albeit slowly. He still felt as though somebody had, as he put it, 'kicked him in the nuts and left a shoe behind'.

His first question of the day was levelled at Rover.

"How long before I start to move more freely and become more flexible. I'm not much use like this?"

Rover explained that a lot of that would be down to Lancaster. By rights, the injuries he'd received were mainly superficial, apart from the stitches on his back. What he needed now was exercise, to start to flex himself and get the muscles working again. At present, it was as if he'd fallen down the stairs. He hadn't broken anything, but the joints and muscles had gone into spasms to protect themselves. Lancaster had to tell them it was OK; they could all go back to normal. Rover asked Pamela if there was a gym nearby. She said there was one out in the garage her father used to use. Vidêt, Rover and Lancaster all looked at each other, gulped their tea and made their way to the garage.

Lancaster already felt more mobile having managed to get down the stairs. The prospect of getting into the gym and getting exercise stimulated him further. Vidêt popped back upstairs whilst Pamela was unlocking the garage side door. Pamela flicked a switch and the place was illuminated. It wasn't huge. The end wall was mirrored from top to bottom. The equipment wasn't modern. There was a good-sized punch bag, a running, or in Lancaster's case, a walking machine, benches for step-ups and against one wall, a weights bench.

Vidêt rejoined them in joggers, trainers and a loose sweatshirt. Rover worked out on a regular basis. He surfed when he could and worked out when he couldn't. He wasn't obsessive but liked to be fit. Between him and Vidêt, they came up with the first exercises for the day. Moving a bench to the walking road gave Lancaster access to the handrails for the machine. They got him using the bench as a step-up, step-down. The plan for today was to get his legs moving freely and give him something else to think about.

There were cupboards on the wall. Pamela opened them, revealing towels and several pairs of boxing gloves. After removing her trainers, Vidêt tried several pairs of gloves before finding a pair that almost fitted her. With Pamela's help, she put an ordinary pair of gloves on first to take up the slack. Pamela laced them and watched as Vidêt stepped up to the punch bag, attacking it using boxing techniques and feet. She was agile. Her fists connected with the bag in a classic one-two routine, then after a fist count of six, she engaged the bag using the sides of her feet, kickboxing. She was dancing around the bag, connecting every time. She continued for about five minutes before backing off for a breather, turning to find the other three staring at her.

"What?" she said, staring back.

"You make me feel like an old man," Lancaster said, smiling. "An envious old man."

"A dirty old man," Rover added laughing. "Get back on

your plank."

They all laughed and Vidêt went back to her punch bag, a smile on her face.

They didn't work for long; Rover was keen that Lancaster didn't push too much on day one and undo the work he was doing. Rover and Lancaster went upstairs for privacy so Rover could administer another injection of pain relief into Lancaster's backside, check his dressing and change it. They returned downstairs, joining the others in the lounge.

"You've just missed a call from Craven. I said you'd call," said Pamela.

Lancaster took the phone onto the terrace. Craven picked up immediately.

"Bomber, what the bloody hell have you gone and done now? I can't leave you alone for five minutes before you get yourself into more trouble. One minute you're jumping in the bloody harbour arresting drug runners, then you're doing the old rapid response race car thing and taking the hands off a hitman, what are you like? Will you please calm down over there? What are you after, a bloody medal or something?"

"Good morning, sir. Yes, I'm very well, thank you for asking."

"Seriously, Bomber, go careful, my son. I try and keep you low profile because I know you don't like being the centre of attention, but you make it bloody hard to keep the lid on this thing. Are you OK or do you want to come home to recuperate? It'll be easy to arrange; we can get the two of you on a flight out of there by tomorrow if you want."

"No. Honestly, sir, I'm fine. A few cuts and bruises, but I'm up and about, in fact, I've been out in the gym just to limber up. We can't pull the plug on this; we've come too far. We need to put this to bed."

"You're sure this latest business is down to Batise?"

"Positive. Absolutely no doubt. I had a call from Wardly and he confirmed the phone found on the shooter had the Batise mobile number in it, records show they were in contact. We also know for a fact the shooter or his friend made a call direct to the phone in his cell; there's absolutely no doubting the connection."

"What about his role in your enquiry?"

"Well, I've thought about it a lot and my latest thinking is that he wasn't involved. I keep thinking back to the look on his face when I was asking questions back in Brest; he didn't have the slightest idea who or what I was talking about. No, I think this attempt on Vidêt and myself was anger at the fact that he was banged up and it had been down to us. He had to gain some face amongst the other prisoners and had to be able to show he was still in charge of what was happening. That's what this was about."

"So you're happy to stick with it for a bit longer then?"

"Yes, sir."

Lancaster returned to the lounge, lowering himself gently into a chair.

"How soon before we get back to the gym, Rover, I've got to get my body moving again as quickly as possible?"

"Give it a couple of hours. After lunch, we can go again. Honestly, your muscles and joints won't like it, but they'll get the idea pretty quickly. It'd be different if you'd broken bones, but all you really did was chuck yourself into a bush at seventy miles an hour. I don't know what you're moaning about."

"Cheers for the sympathy, Doctor, I won't forget it," Lancaster replied with a smile. He knew the man was right, that a lot of this was in the head. It was more about the fear of pain than actual pain; he just had to push through it.

Like a military operations room, Lancaster sat while Vidêt rearranged the board. Batise 1 now joined Tanguyé in the margin. Not removed, despite ruling them out. Lancaster liked to keep players visible; although on the fringe or not, they were still part of the enquiry until it was solved. The active 'Persons of Interest' had now become a short list of four.

1. Levon Shawbuck (Sean Devlin)
2. Paul Steiner
3. Batise 2
4. Persons Unknown

Number four frightened Lancaster. So far everything was going the way he always planned it. Work up a list, whittle your way through them and reach a conclusion. The problem with his list as it stood was that Shawbuck had a huge time-lapse between Peter closing the man's account and his death, a gap of almost twenty years. It was true that Devlin disappeared from view almost immediately after the account was closed, reappearing later as Shawbuck, but what happened? Had the man gone to ground? Had he been moved by Counter Terrorism or MI5 and relocated with a new name? Maybe he'd been in prison? That might fit, but he'd struggle to find out anything about Devlin without alerting Craven to Shawbuck. Either way, he had a couple of days to get fit enough to question this man when he appeared to meet with the bank.

As for Steiner. He knew details about the man but nothing that connected him in any way to Peter or the bank. The idea he may have been operating as a hitman for one of the other subjects had dwindled for all the same reasons. Why would Devlin hire a hitman for the job almost twenty years after the offence? Likewise, if Batise had hired him, the timescale would fit. Peter pisses the man off by closing the account and later he dies, which would work. It would take a little time to get the hit organised. Then the man would come to the island, research his hit and choose the right moment to complete the contract. If it was a hit, it had been the right place to execute it and hide the crime. He'd nearly gotten away with it. The problem with this prognosis was that Lancaster had virtually convinced himself that Batise (at least the one they had in custody), knew nothing at all about Peter or his murder. If this was the case, that only left Batise 2 and 'Persons Unknown'. And that meant starting all over again.

"Would someone enlighten me?" Pamela asked. "I thought you'd discounted Batise."

"Well, we thought of Batise because he'd have been pissed off losing access to his cash. When we found the original Batise in Morgat, we latched onto him. But we already know there are two Batises. The main man, and I reckon the one we have in custody in Brest, is that man and a second Batise, seen on the bank CCTV setting up the accounts and visiting the bank on various occasions. Now, if this man was the banker and Peter stopped the accounts, it would've been him that had to tell the boss he'd lost access to the cash, so maybe it was him that either killed or had Peter killed in revenge or to show he could take care of business. It may well be that Batise 1 only knew there was a problem with the bank and that Batise 2 had taken care of it. Hence his completely blank looks when I raised the murder with him. What we need to do is track the whereabouts of Batise 2, then work out how or if he's involved; that's your next job, Marie. Craven, Interpol or anyone you can think of that may have access to this man's whereabouts, use the photo we have. It may be this will be all news to them, in which case we've scored 'brownie' points."

"What about this German chap, Steiner?" Pamela asked.

"Well, we know a bit about him and his history. I'll need to contact the Bundespolizei in Berlin and see what we can pick up. I can do that from the comfort of a chair, but I feel it's time for medicine, maybe in the form of coffee."

Lancaster was settling into his coffee when his mobile (now back under his control) rang. Wardly. He'd phoned to check how Lancaster and Vidêt were. Lancaster reported that both were on the mend and back to work as they spoke. Wardly replied that they'd caught the guy who'd escaped. In the B&B in Le Hocq. Attempting to retrieve items left behind. The man was saying nothing but they had his name from his passport. The man's mobile had Batise's mobile in his call list so he couldn't deny contact with him. Lancaster wished him well and said he'd telephone every afternoon to update him on progress. Lancaster thought progress could be a struggle. He put a call through to Craven, but there was no pick-up.

He left a message for the man to call. He got the pad fired up and researched the German police network to get a feel for the hierarchy of the system. Craven called back.

"Bomber." Straight and simple.

"'Morning, sir. A favour if I may? You had a contact in the German police who found stuff out about Paul Steiner. Any chance you can pass his name on? I want to make some serious enquiries about him."

"He next on your list then?"

"It's time to check him out."

"I'll text it to you in a minute; mention my name, we go back a long way."

Lancaster went back to his research. There were two parts to the German police network. The network was divided into sections looking after different aspects of policing. The Bundespolizei, or Federal Police, similar to the UK, provided uniformed officers, detectives and drug squads. It was here Lancaster was going to have to start, but having a way in via Craven's contact might make things easier.

Craven texted. The man he needed was Chief Inspector Jurgen Klissman, Bundespolizei Berlin, and now he had his mobile number. He phoned straight away. It rang, then went to voicemail. Lancaster knew his number would have come up unknown and been ignored, so he left a message dropping Craven's name, leaving his own name and rank. A few minutes later his phone rang. He didn't recognise the number or the first digits and presumed it was coming in from Germany, so answered.

"DI Lancaster, Devon & Cornwall Constabulary."

"'Morning, Lancaster," a familiar voice said. "Steven Ainscough, CTD, how are you recovering from your recent drama? I hear you and your partner had a close shave."

"Steven, good to hear from you again," Lancaster lied. "Thanks for your concern, we're fine, what can I do for you?"

"We need to have a meeting, I think."

"Why do we need to do that, Steven?"

"Because, David, we asked very nicely if you would please, I do remember saying please, we said please would you leave Sean Devlin alone; he's nothing to do with your murder enquiry, but you just can't leave things alone?"

"You asked me to leave him alone, I have."

"You know very well you haven't. You've been pissing about with his bank, getting them to bugger about with access numbers for his account. I have to say, I don't think the Financial Services Ombudsman would look kindly on a bank sharing information with an individual, but I could soon ask them."

"Steven, I said I'd leave Devlin out of this enquiry and I have. The bank may have accessed somebody else's account, but as the island banking system is a completely separate entity from the UK, then I think you'll find they'll not give a shit about a bank sharing information about a criminal or a terrorist's bank accounts with a representative of the police force, especially if the newspapers got hold of the fact that this terrorist also had links to a government department, so you can stop with the blackmailing techniques. So, I say again, why should we meet?"

"OK, let's stop pissing about, you know I'm talking about

Shawbuck. You and I both know we're talking about the same man. I've inherited the role as his UK minder. He's a valuable asset to the Counter Terrorism Department. I won't ask again, we need a meeting. It's in your interests; I can answer some questions for you about your murder. Let's not play this silly game anymore, neither of us has the time or the patience."

Lancaster thought for a moment. He knew the man was right. If he had information, he'd be a fool to miss this opportunity. He just needed to gain time, time to get better; he wanted to be on the ball.

"OK, let's make it for a couple of days' time..."

"No can do, it needs to be tomorrow. We'll be off the island the day after that."

Damn, thought Lancaster. That was too soon for comfort.

"OK. But we've a busy day tomorrow; it'll have to be at 15:30. How about on the point, in the car park, you remember? Our favourite place."

"15:30 it is then." The line went dead.

"Rover," Lancaster called up the stairs.

Ten minutes later they were back in the garage to work on the step-up bench followed by treadmill. After an hour Rover called a halt. The pair went into the house as Vidêt came down the stairs. She'd had success. She'd uploaded the photo of Batise 2 onto the Europol criminal database and found a match. Europol had him listed as Jean Monbiot, a suspected financier of smuggling gangs, now thought to be linked to people trafficking. Vidêt flagged up online the fact he was listed on Jersey as Jean-Luc Batise. Several contacts from law enforcement had requested details. His banking interests had come as news to them all, though no one had a present location for the man.

Lancaster thought it was typical of international law enforcement. He'd specifically mentioned this double use of the name to the detectives from Interpol, yet no one had asked for the photo or details. They'd obviously not flagged it up on the international database. He then laughed at himself, that was exactly what he'd done. It was a valuable piece of information; he'd kept it to himself until he wanted to share it and waited until he thought it might be useful to him. This made him just as bad as all the rest. Lancaster called Pamela and updated her on the situation so far, suggesting she might call Max at the bank and warn him that one of the men calling themselves Batise was currently in a cell in France and that this flagged up the fact that there was another Jean-Luc Batise; the one they had on file and running the bank accounts on Jersey. Max should be made aware the authorities may well be in touch sometime soon to ask questions. Hopefully, Max wouldn't blame them for this leak. He also warned everyone that they may soon have to drop enquiries with regards to Shawbuck. He told them about tomorrow's planned meeting.

"This time I should be with you as backup and witness. Last time they came two-up; I think it's fair we return the favour," said Vidêt.

"I won't argue, Marie. At this rate, I may need you to carry me."

"Why don't we drive up and wait for them to arrive?"

"I wondered when you'd think of that."

The team had just finished lunch when Lancaster's mobile

leapt into action once more. Lancaster took the phone through to the lounge before picking up the call.

"DI Lancaster, Devon & Cornwall Constabulary."

"Guten mittag, DI Lancaster. This is Chief Inspector Jurgen Klissman of the Berlin Bundespolizei, you left a message for me. What can I do for you, Detective? You say DCI Craven passed on my number, how is he? Well, I hope?"

"He is well, thank you, Chief Inspector, and he sends his best wishes. Thanks for making the time to call me back."

"Please give him my regards next time you speak with him. So, what can I do for you, Detective?"

"Chief Inspector Craven was recently in contact with you asking for information regarding a Paul Steiner, formally a member of the United German Police Force. I understand this role didn't last too long and he's since left your force. I wondered if you still kept tabs on him or knew his whereabouts."

There was a subtle laugh. "Yes, Inspector, we do indeed keep an eye on Steiner. He lives in the same home given to him by the Stasi years ago. Of course, he is an old man now but still manages to upset people, ranting on about the 'good old days' under the Communists. He still feels badly done by but the truth is, he was from a different era. He was too quick to hit people. He was just a violent man, not nice to be around. What do you want of him?"

Lancaster outlined the case, indicating he had an interest in interviewing Steiner to find out why he'd been on Jersey at the time of the murder he was investigating. Lancaster gave the impression that the man was in the vicinity and needed to be ruled out before the investigation could move on. Klissman suggested he leave it with him for a couple of days. First, he'd ensure the man was indeed still where he was thought to be. He'd then set up paperwork so the man could be pulled for questioning regarding this visit to Jersey. Once all this was in place, he'd get back in touch so that Lancaster could visit Berlin and question the man at the Bundespolizei offices. Lancaster said that'd be fine and he was grateful for any assistance.

Lancaster stood looking across the garden. The sun was out, it looked like a nice autumnal day. He had a sudden thought: *it's time for more exercise.* He returned to the kitchen; Vidêt had retired to her bedroom, researching Batise 2. Rover had apparently gone to set up new exercises. Pamela sat doing a crossword.

"I fancy a stroll, Pamela. Would you care to join me?"

They donned jackets. Lancaster decided that he did genuinely feel better than when he first got up; he knew he had to keep moving if he wanted it to improve. They strolled up the path toward the bluff and the car park with Pamela's arm tucked in his, supportively.

"Seriously, David, how are you feeling?"

"Better than I should, to be honest. I felt bloody awful first thing, but I have to hand it to Rover, his massage and exercise regime have made a world of difference, well, that and the drugs. I feel better by the minute, but I don't want to bugger myself up. We've stuff to get on with."

"But we've come a long way in such a short space of time. You know I'm so grateful for all that you, Marie and Rover have managed to achieve. I've every faith you'll finish this. We may not catch the person, but I've no doubt you'll find out who it was."

They walked to the cliff top, looking out at the changing colours of the ocean, the whirling seagulls speeding across the sky. After a few minutes, they strolled back to the house and straight into Rover, keen to get Lancaster into the gym. By the time Rover finished with him, he needed to shower. Before he dressed for the evening Lancaster lay propped on his pillows, contemplating the actions of the last few days. It had been hectic, but it wasn't over. It wasn't the climax, just another side street. Admittedly, action-packed, but it had wasted time and energy and ended by slowing him down, which annoyed him. He had to appear on-the-ball tomorrow when he met with Ainscough. If truth be told, Lancaster had doubts about any involvement Devlin actually had in the murder of Peter. Even with so many doors closed to him, it was easy to find that the man had spent most of his time financing or laundering money for the IRA. It also looked like he'd come into his role against his will, blackmailed into the job under the threat of violence, but once in, he did his job well, if the accounts at the bank were true.

Although the bank closed the account when they smelt a rat, they'd never actually stolen the money. Devlin had been told to make alternative arrangements for housing it. It was after that, that the British Government took a hand in the affair and closed the account fully, transferring the cash under some kind of corporate name to a handling account and then into a new account for Shawbuck. Since then, it'd had a monthly top-up from what Lancaster could see, in the form of a pension. It looked like Devlin was now being paid by the UK.

If the money trail was right, Devlin would've had no reason to kill Peter. Yes, he would've been bloody mad that his funding pot had been frozen, as this would certainly have upset his masters in the 'Provos', but Lancaster had a theory Devlin may have been working for the UK all along. If that was true, he would've been stupid to endanger his cover by killing a bank manager on Jersey. Worryingly, if this was the case, Lancaster was drawing ever closer to 'Persons Unknown', but now was not the time to lose heart. They may yet find a location for Batise 2, which would put him back into the frame. Ainscough may have other light to shine on the case. Steiner may yet prove to be involved in some way. There was still lots to be played for. The game wasn't over.

The next day turned out unusually warm for Autumn. Lancaster could move freely today; a surprise after the previous day's exertions. The day started with him going straight to the garage for treadmill, step-ups and weight training. He was then allowed breakfast and coffee, followed by a regroup as to where they were at with various updates.

Vidêt had e-mails from her online postings of Batise 2. She was going to a great deal of trouble, explaining where the photo had come from and that it was indeed identified as one of the men known and purporting to be Jean-Luc Batise. Pamela had been in touch with Max, warning him there may be interest soon in the Batise saga. He was grateful to have been warned and was preparing copies of all their dealings with the man in readiness for the expected arrival of officialdom any day now.

Rover on the other hand was getting itchy feet. His conscience was getting the better of him. He'd enjoyed the work he'd done on the autopsy, glad to have been of assistance, but now feeling guilty that he was on the island having a bit of a holiday, meanwhile back home, work would be stacking up; he should be taking his share. Lancaster asked if he'd stay at least until the morning; he had a job for him that afternoon. Rover agreed. Pamela went to arrange a flight to Exeter for the following day.

The rest of the day went too quickly for Lancaster's liking. All too soon it was 15.00. Lancaster's plan went into action. Lancaster, Vidêt and Rover took Pamela's car up onto the headland, parked in the car park, with the car facing the exit. Lancaster genuinely didn't think there'd be any trouble, but then he'd thought that when he took off after a BMW, look where that nearly got them. Dead. They didn't have long to wait. Lancaster had braced himself, leaning against the front wing, when he saw a black BMW coming along the headland towards him. As planned, Vidêt was positioned beside the driver's open door, whilst Rover, wearing customary black combat trousers and black, short-sleeved T-shirt showing off his tattoos to perfection, was leaning with his back against the windscreen, arms folded. Rover had pretended to be angry, chosen to represent some sort of 'hard man'. Secretly he relished the opportunity.

The BMW stopped outside the entrance. Lancaster saw the passenger seat was occupied by Chris Cross. He watched the head movement of the driver, Ainscough, turning around and talking to a shadow in the back seat. There was discussion going on. Lancaster knew it would be about the other people in the car park; too many witnesses came to mind. He stood up straight, putting his hands in his pockets, looking casual, trying to convey the image of somebody who didn't care if the car entered the car park or turned around and left. The driver's door opened. Ainscough got out and started to walk into the car park. In the background, Lancaster saw Cross exit the car, walk around and slide into the driver's seat. The car didn't move. Ainscough walked toward Lancaster until they were within speaking distance, then stopped.

"I thought we were meeting alone. I presume these people are with you, not just inquisitive tourists?" Ainscough said, nodding in the direction of the other two. "It may mean I have to call this meeting off. I've somebody in the car I want you to talk with, but he won't want any witnesses."

"That's fine, Steven, let's all just piss off home again. I've had a busy couple of days and could do with some sleep; let's do this another day."

"I did say on the phone that this has to be done today. We leave the island first thing in the morning. Why don't you just send your friends away?"

"Listen... Steve. You will have already heard from somebody that Vidêt and I went to a simple house search two days ago and ended with somebody firing four shots into my car. They weren't random; they were designed to kill. They failed, but I won't take that chance again. I honestly don't trust you people from Counter Terrorism, seriously. I'm one of those people who believe the fake news. Your sort of people arrange death for their own interest or, worse still, for politics. In your eyes, what you do is for the good of the state, in my eyes, it's death by another hand, so if your boss or whoever you have sitting in the back seat wants a chat, I'm happy to talk through the window if he is too afraid to get out of the car, but this time I keep my people over there in full view as back-up, end of. OK?... Steve."

Ainscough looked at Lancaster, then waved the BMW forward. It stopped next to Lancaster and Cross stepped out.

"Stay in the car, Chris, keep the engine ticking; we won't be long," Ainscough said.

Ainscough leaned across and opened the rear door. The passenger climbed out. Lancaster recognised him even before Ainscough introduced him.

"DI Lancaster, may I introduce Sean Devlin a.k.a. Mr. Levon Shawbuck."

The man held out his hand. Lancaster ignored it. He'd no wish to even touch this man's hand. This man, in Lancaster's eyes, was as low down the food chain as anyone could get.

"I can see we're not going to be friends, Detective, so let's not waste anymore 'feckin' time out here. You want to talk to me about murder? Ask away before I show you my arse," the man said in a strange, Belfast/American accent.

Lancaster stared at the man. In truth, he wanted to punch the man's lights out. He had his reason for hating anything to do with the IRA, but this enquiry was too important to seek personal pleasure from head-butting the man clean into next week.

"It's a simple set of questions, Mr Devlin. They should be simple enough for even you to understand. Number one, did you know a man here on Jersey named Peter Urbawicz."

"Urbawicz. Of course I knew Peter Urbawicz. He worked

311

at the bank where I had my accounts. Next question?"

"When he closed your accounts in December 1987, did you murder or arrange to have murdered the said, Peter Urbawicz?"

"Are you 'feckin' serious, Detective? Do you seriously think I'd bother to murder the man just because he closed my accounts? What the 'feck' do you take me for, an 'eejit'? If I went around killing every bank manager who closed my account, they'd be dropping like flies on a dog turd all over the 'feckin' place, Jesus, Ainscough, is this all you brought me out here for?"

"So the simple answer that's eluding you then, Mr Devlin, is no."

Devlin looked at Lancaster. Lancaster could see the anger rising in the man.

"Listen to me, ya smart arse," Devlin said, moving closer until he could smell the whiskey on his breath. "Ainscough here said I should talk to you and answer your questions. I have. Now I am only going to say this the once. I didn't kill anyone and I didn't have anyone killed, is that plenty good enough for you?"

"So when Peter closed your account, you weren't pissed off?"

"Jesus, you really are stupid, of course I was pissed off. He caused me grief. There were people depending on that money; they had to go without until I got myself sorted. There were other people who doubted if the bank had actually closed the account. Some people back home thought I had my hand in the till and that was just an excuse. Sure, the man caused me grief, but what would I have gained from killing him? People like you would have been all over my arse. No, Detective, you're looking in the wrong direction; I didn't even know the man was dead until Steve here told me about it. But I say this for the last time, it wasn't me. Now, are we done here?"

"Not quite. Do you know a man by the name of Paul Steiner? Maybe in connection with your smuggling, sorry, I mean gun-sales business."

Devlin looked like he may just flip into the dark side. Lancaster braced himself.

"I've never heard the name before, am I supposed to have killed him as well?"

"No, Devlin, I think he's above your league."

Devlin took one step forward and stood toe-to-toe with Lancaster. The latter gave no ground. The pair stared into each other's eyes, both could see the hatred they had for one another, almost tasting it.

"What the 'feck' have I ever done to you, Detective?"

"You will never know, Devlin. But to be honest, just being alive and spending my taxes is enough for me to hate you."

Devlin stood for another minute face-to-face with Lancaster.

"We're done here, Steven, time for a drink." He turned and slid back into the BMW, closing the door behind him.

"Well, you've heard it from the horse's mouth, I can second what he said. He's not involved in your murder. I'm sorry, that's all there is to it."

"How can you do this job, Ainscough? That man's a terrorist. He's a complete bastard. He's responsible for hundreds of deaths. He funded the deaths of hundreds more through his arms deals and now you look after him and pay him a bloody salary."

"He's also given us inside information on IRA movements and policies; there's a chance we wouldn't have reached the Northern Ireland Agreement without his help. It was with his help that we managed to intercept the 'Eksund' in the 1980s. If that had got through, the IRA would've had better firepower than our troops. As for the money he gets paid, a lot of that was from his own legitimate business with plant hire and construction. By fiddling the books and running a selection of accounts, only two of which were here on the Island of Jersey by the way, we, the UK government managed to syphon off a huge chunk of IRA cash, and that went straight into the UK coffers, then to us at Counter Terrorism. So we were using their money to fight them. All you've got is one murder to solve; we've been stopping hundreds. Now, since we signed the Peace Accord, it's over, it's done, they think he's dead, end of story, Lancaster. Now please, let it go. Don't bring this up again or your feet won't touch the floor. While we're at it, your boss Craven and your sergeant over there will all be looking for security jobs in supermarkets. Do I make myself clear?"

Lancaster was too angry to speak. At that moment he thought he could probably kill them all. It was always about politics. Not just criminals. As far as Lancaster could see, there wasn't a lot of difference between politicians and criminals, except of course that most criminals never pretended to be anything other than that. Criminals.

"I repeat, DI Lancaster, do I make myself clear on this? Devlin and Shawbuck are no longer part of your enquiry."

Lancaster knew he had to agree but couldn't bring himself to do so; he just stared back at Ainscough. Finally, Ainscough turned his back, got into the passenger seat and Cross drove them away.

Rover and Vidêt walked to where Lancaster stood, watching the BMW disappearing down the road, a ghost-like dust haze in its wake.

"Was that who I thought it was that got out of the back seat?" Vidêt asked.

"Yes, indeed it was."

"And who was it?" Rover asked.

"Sadly, Rover... I'm afraid from now on, I'm not allowed to tell you."

CHAPTER NINE

Lancaster asked Rover and Vidêt to drive back to the house. He was ready for the stroll back. He spent a few minutes standing on the bluff looking out to sea. Not far out, there were two small fishing boats, the fishermen pulled pots and emptied the contents into buckets on the deck. Peter did that from his rocky outcrop. Somebody denied him that simple pleasure. He was a well-paid bank official, he didn't need to farm the sea to supplement his meal table, he did it for fun, enjoyment and fresh air after a day in the office. Yes, he enjoyed the crab or lobster he occasionally brought home, but somebody had taken away the man's right to live a long life, fish when he chose. The family had lived with the consequences of that death, knowing it was murder, but being told it wasn't.

He, Vidêt and Rover had proved the man had definitely been murdered. This wasn't good enough; if anything, it made it worse. He had to find the person responsible and, as the cliché went, bring them to justice. So far, the team had 'done good'. Despite Pamela saying she was happy to have been proved right, he couldn't leave it at that, the culprit had to be identified. Part of his anger though was the festering realisation that Devlin was getting away with other murders. Lancaster had no doubt the man had blood on his hands, so what if he'd fed crumbs to the British Secret Service or Counter Terrorism; it was for his own survival, now that he had a new life and a pension.

Lancaster remembered his father coming home on leave, remembered the smell of starch and washing powder that permeated the fatigues he wore to travel home in and the green beret rolled and tucked tightly into the epaulette atop his shoulder. He could remember the giant kitbag dumped in the hallway. Once, he'd asked his father if he could try it on his back. His father had said, 'If you can pick it up, you can wear it'. Lancaster had tried to get it to leave the floor but to no avail, it was as if it had been glued down, yet later his father would pick it up and swing it onto his shoulder as if it were a paper bag. His father opened the bag on one return, pulling out a floppy-legged, stuffed toy Leprechaun, wearing green knee britches, with a big red beard and scruffy red hair sticking out from under a green tartan beret stitched onto its head. His father had called it 'Murphy' and told the young Lancaster, 'You can give it a hug, you can keep it on your bed, but whatever you do, don't tell it any secrets, 'cos it'll tell everyone'.

He remembered coming home from school, aged six, holding his mother's hand, talking incessantly about what he'd been doing that day and what they'd done at playtime. He remembered his mother stopping, halfway down their street, holding his hand so hard he almost cried, then looking down the street to where two smartly dressed soldiers stood on the pavement outside their garden gate, beside a shiny car, awaiting his mother's return. The day they'd come to tell them his father wouldn't be coming home again with his kit bag.

He'd been blown to smithereens in a small market town in Northern Ireland. He wasn't even meant to be there. He and a friend had gone to a market to buy gifts for Christmas. The bomb had been planted to kill RUC men returning to their border post. His father and his friend were passing in the opposite direction at the same time. 'Wrong place, wrong time,' the smartly dressed soldier had said. 'Wrong bloody country,' his mother replied. But that wouldn't bring him back. For many years, right up until secondary school, his mother, teachers, their GP and finally the local police had all put his behaviour, his anger, his inability to make friends, his clumsiness and almost every other issue Lancaster had spat out along the way, down to losing his father at such an impressionable age. When all along it had been an inbuilt brain-to-motor malfunction, dyspraxia. Diagnosed far too late to do anything about it, all hidden from view by the label 'grief', well, that and his mother's drinking problem.

Since that time, anger and hatred had built a wall inside Lancaster's brain, built as far as Lancaster believed, on very firm foundations. He now had an irrational hatred for anything Irish, north or south. They were all as bad as one another; the more he learned the more he hated. He hated the glorification of the men who formed the membership of the Irish Republican Army, who in Lancaster's eyes were never an army. An army stood up and fought, was visible, fighting face to face, the best man would win. They didn't hide behind walls, amassing huge amounts of weapons, then sneak out to blow up and kneecap civilians. He hated their failure to govern the country that had been handed back to them on a plate, despite being given all the tools they needed following the Northern Ireland Peace Accord. He hated the fact that the UK government had given amnesty to whole prison wings full of gunmen, bombers and murderers, as appeasement to end 'the troubles', yet allowed the hunting down and prosecution of British soldiers, accused of killing innocent civilians in running battles during 'The Troubles'. If anyone was guilty, it was the politicians who sent them there in the first place. In fairness, he also hated the Loyalists for perpetuating their anger. Now, most of all, he hated Sean Devlin and the politics that paid him a pension.

Lancaster watched the two boats below turn for home, he breathed deep, held and exhaled and he too turned for home. It was turning grey and chilly, he felt the need for warmth, the company of friends. Before he reached the garden gate, he was met by Vidêt who had come to check he was OK. She stopped him in the middle of the pathway and gave him a big hug and a small kiss.

"How are you doing?" she asked.

"I'll survive, Marie, but I'm in need of tea." Vidêt tucked her arm through his and they walked together back to the house.

Inside, the smell of an evening meal being prepared, it was time for the daily round of telephone calls. First Craven. He updated him on where the enquiry was at, call-backs they were waiting on, people to trace, etc., but left out mention of Ainscough and the meeting with Devlin. Lancaster warned him there was a chance they'd have to travel to Berlin to interview Steiner once the local police had located him. He was unsure if he should be seeking permission from him or Wardly. Craven was adamant that the go-ahead would have to be from Wardly.

His next call was to Wardly. He gave him the same update, still neglecting to inform the man with regards to the Counter Terrorism visit. It would only confuse matters. Lancaster mentioned he and Vidêt may need to travel to Germany to interview a suspect. Much to Lancaster's surprise, the man had no problem whatsoever, 'if it gets the job done', just keep him in the loop. Finally, a call to Berlin and Klissman. Lancaster had grown tired of waiting for the man to call; he needed to get this job done. Klissman answered straight away.

"Good evening, Detective Lancaster. You're working late, yes? What can I do for you?"

Lancaster checked his watch, realising that with the time difference with Berlin, Klissman was probably at dinner.

"Sorry, Chief Inspector, spur of the moment thought to give you a call. I forgot what the time was with you over there, would you like me to call again in the morning?"

"No, no, what can I do for you?"

"I was following up on our previous call, see if you've located Steiner yet?"

"You are in a hurry, are you not, Detective? The answer is yes, we have located him. He was away when we first went to his home; he has since returned. He does not know you wish to interview him, but now we know he is home, we can get him any time. We have rules for the process of non-German police, questioning a German resident, even those we do not particularly like the company of, but once we have the relevant paperwork together, we will give you a call. You will be able to come, sign them off and then we bring him into the station. I will be present right through the interview; he has the right to have a solicitor present should he feel he needs one. Do you think he may need one, Detective?"

"To be honest, Chief Inspector, we think he was present during a murder here on the island, in fact, if I'm to be completely honest, there's a possibility he may actually have carried out the murder, but we genuinely don't know for certain. There's no doubt he was in the right place at the time, and at present, we've no reason for why he was on the island."

"That sounds to me like more than just a chat, Detective."

"Well again, to be honest, during the last day, we've had a major 'person of interest' taken out of the frame, so Steiner has risen to the top of our list. Maybe you can help me though; if Steiner is involved, then we can find no direct link with our victim, but the sort of people around the fringe of this enquiry are likely to have used a contract killer. Is there any chance Steiner could be involved in that aspect?"

There was a pause before the man replied.

"If you had not suggested it, Detective, it would not have been in my thoughts, but that is not to say it is not so. The man has money, we know that much, it could be from savings or, as you say, from another lucrative source of income, so the answer is... It is possible."

"Thank you, Chief Inspector. So you see, we need to eliminate this man if we can."

"Eliminate or charge him, Detective," Klissman replied. "I should have the paperwork arranged within the next day or so, but leave it with me, I will get it sorted as soon as I can."

The following morning, after fried eggs, toast and coffee, Rover gathered his things and they took him to the airport. Pamela thanked him for all his work, saying they should all meet up again when they were back in Devon. Vidêt gave him a goodbye hug and a double kiss. Lancaster shook hands, then opted to include a hug, promising he'd keep him updated on events. They waved him into departure, then returned to the house.

Back at base, Lancaster told Pamela where they were with the enquiry. The ball was in the hands of Klissman and anyone from Interpol who had a location for Batise 2. She was happy with the progress; she'd get on to the airport and find out about flights to Berlin. She was visiting her mother that afternoon and would give her an update. Lancaster didn't mention his meeting with Devlin.

When they'd begun this enquiry, everything had followed a series of progressive steps. Steps that proved murder over an accident, located potential suspects and identified locations. To date, none had produced a credible culprit. Lancaster was becoming disheartened. The normal course of events was to identify prospects and interview them. During this process, he'd develop a gut feeling about one of them, then follow through doggedly until the case was proven or they moved on. But during this enquiry, they'd proven murder and isolated possible culprits, but Lancaster hadn't felt that gut feeling. Yes, he'd thought, this person's guilty of something, but at no stage had he thought, you're lying and I know why. To make matters worse, his back and shoulders ached and he actually felt physically tired.

He and Vidêt were back on the phones, recontacting everyone they'd already spoken to with regards to Batise 2: Europol and Interpol detectives, the European Drug Enforcement Agency, the CIA and the FBI. So far there'd been sightings and whispers, but nothing concrete. The only mistake the man appeared to have ever made was not noticing the hidden bell-push camera at Les Banque des Isles. If it hadn't been for that one slip-up, they'd never have known of the man's existence. Lancaster realised what else was niggling him. The number of mistakes he'd been making. It wasn't unusual to have a 'hiccup' here and there, but when he thought about it, he'd 'hiccupped' quite enough in this case. He should never have involved Pamela in that ridiculous rough-and-tumble in Morgat; he should've left it to the locals. If he'd not called the bluff with Batise in the interview room, mentioning he knew about the other Batise, maybe Batise 2 wouldn't have gone to ground. Now they knew that Batise 1 had had a mobile, it was obvious he'd have alerted '2' to the fact he was 'blown'. Also, he should have stayed sitting on the bonnet of their car when that BMW screeched to a halt. Then his back and shoulders wouldn't hurt so much. Not only that, he'd endangered Marie. There must be no more mistakes.

This trawling through his thoughts threw up one little ray of hope. He put in a call to Ferec.

"Bonjour, Detective, comment ça va?"

"I'm well, Christophe, and you?" Lancaster replied.

"Aa, so-so, what can I do for you, David?"

"It's a simple request really. Could you e-mail me all the numbers contacted from Batise's phone, from the day before we collared him in Morgat to when you found the phone? I have a hunch and want to test it out."

"Not a problem, I'll get my sergeant to do it during the next hour or so, OK?"

"That would be brilliant, Christophe, many thanks. Will speak again soon."

"What do you hope to find?" said Vidêt.

"Well, we send the numbers to our tech guys in Plymouth and see which ones they can put a name to. At least one of those numbers is our one-handed hitman and we have his phone. We also have numbers for his accomplices at the boat auction in Morgat and we have the numbers for both Henri Tanguyé's landline and his mobile, and the boatyard here on Jersey. So if we identify as many as possible and eliminate them, somewhere amongst the numbers left, there should be a contact for Batise 2. I wouldn't mind betting that it won't appear until I was stupid enough to have told him we knew of Batise 2 in the first place."

The e-mail with the numbers arrived within the hour. There weren't many. Once they'd cross-referenced and underlined the ones they already knew, it left five unknown numbers. Of those five, only two had been contacted after Lancaster's interview, this meant they were calls made whilst the man was in his cell. It was still too soon, but Lancaster had a feeling one of them was Batise 2. Vidêt forwarded the list to the tech team at Plymouth with an explanatory note.

They joined Pamela for lunch and she told them of flights into Germany. It wasn't possible to fly Jersey to Berlin. You could fly Jersey to Munich, then an internal flight to Berlin-

Tegel Airport. Then it was a taxi ride to the Berlin Police Central Service Unit. Pamela had run up a list of hotels; they wouldn't get in and out in one day. Lancaster felt there was little that could be done until he'd got the call back from Klissman. What he needed now was more time in the gym; keeping moving was the way to go. After an hour of this, Lancaster decided enough was enough. They went back into the house and showered. Vidêt changed the dressing on Lancaster's back, a task she performed with genuine care, the wound already starting to heal. They were getting dressed when Lancaster's mobile went. Klissman. Lancaster picked up.

"Chief Inspector, good to hear from you so soon. No problems I hope?"

"Quite the opposite, Detective Lancaster. Your man Steiner has been picked up for drunk driving. He hit another car. We have him in a cell sobering up before we charge him, but for you, it is good news. As we will be charging him for the driving offence, he loses some of his civil liberties protection; we no longer have to give him the same courtesy we would provide for a German civilian. As a person under charge, he can be questioned regarding other crimes. We cannot charge him until we consider him sober enough to understand the charges, but once we've charged him, we can then hold him for further investigation for another forty-eight hours. I do not think we will be charging him until tomorrow morning. How soon could you get here?"

"We've been looking at flights, we'll have to make a connection in Munich, but can probably be with you by early afternoon, say 2:00, if that's OK?"

"That's fine. We can delay the whole process. He needs to cool off overnight before we speak to him. He'll have to wait until we think he is sober. We can leave him in his cell till late morning before we start our charging procedure and then we'll hold him until your arrival. We will see you tomorrow then, Detective Lancaster."

Vidêt phoned to book tickets. Pamela booked them a double room at a hotel in Karl-Liebnecht Street, a short stroll from the police station. The following morning, straight after breakfast, Pamela dropped them outside departures. They said their goodbyes and the pair disappeared inside. This time, despite the fact that yet again the plane was a 'prop job', Lancaster enjoyed the flight. Vidêt slept, her head resting on his shoulder, the smell of apple shampoo awash in his airways. The stop-over in Munich took less than an hour. The internal flight to Berlin was a jet, which amused Lancaster; it was due to cover half the distance they'd just travelled from the Channel Islands. In under an hour from lift-off, they touched down outside Berlin. They hailed a taxi as they exited the main doors. Lancaster texted Klissman and told him they were on their way ahead of schedule and would be with him by 13.00, according to the driver. True to the man's word, they pulled up outside the police station at 12:25 p.m., grabbed their bags and strolled up to reception. Klissman came to meet them and 'badged them up'. The whole station was a hive of activity, uniformed and plain clothes people everywhere. At one point, as they walked along a corridor, Lancaster thought they'd been beamed onto the 'Death Star' from *Star Wars*. They had to step aside to make way for a column of black-clad, machine pistol-toting, black-helmeted storm-troopers coming from the other direction, an ominous air about them that Lancaster thought they probably enjoyed.

They waited until they were inside Klissman's office before they talked more freely.

"We are about to bring your man up from the cells," Klissman said. "We had to wait for him to sober up, then we gave him breakfast. Since then, we've been stalling. We actually have a lot going on today as you may have heard on the news."

"No," Lancaster replied. "We were on the plane early and haven't heard anything. What's going on?"

"We've had a terrorist shooting a couple of hours ago in the east of the city outside a synagogue. Luckily, he was useless and crashed his car into a wall before he started shooting. Nobody has been injured, but he got away, so areas of the city have gone into lockdown whilst our teams are trying to find the man before he tries again."

"Then we apologise if this is an inconvenience, Chief Inspector."

"It's not a problem, Detective. It will not involve us here unless he goes to ground, then they will want a CID presence. At the moment, it's a job for the Anti-Terrorist Department; we'll let them go and wave their guns around for a while before we get involved. It keeps them happy, you know."

"So how do you want to play this out with Steiner, sir?" Lancaster asked.

"We get him up here and let another detective charge him with driving under the influence. He'll take a statement, do paperwork, get it signed, then we go in. I'll introduce both of you. The man speaks perfect English, so we'll not need an interpreter, but ask what you need too. I have to warn you though, if I think your questions are not in order, I will ask for them to be removed, unless of course, I think the man is guilty of anything, then I may turn 'a blind eye' as you would say. If that is in order, shall we have coffee while we wait for our turn?"

Over coffee, Lancaster gave Klissman a run-down on the case so far. There was no point in keeping anything back. There was nothing to be gained by doing that; he needed the man's co-operation. Lancaster was aware he was in another foreign land with different rules and a different attitude to policing. But he also knew he needed to get this done before he could move on again. Klissman was intrigued by where the two detectives fitted in. Lancaster explained their connection with Lady Stottard, that the murder victim was her father and originally his death had been listed as 'Accidental' by Jersey police.

"So you two arrived as outsiders and proved the case as otherwise?"

"Quite simply, sir, yes."

Klissman's radio bleeped; they were ready in the interview room. Though Lancaster had seen a photo of Steiner, he was still taken aback when he entered the room. He was six foot tall, broad-shouldered and upright. He had a full head of silver and black hair, well cut, and considering the man had spent the night in a cell, was not dishevelled in any way. Steiner was well over seventy years old but looked to be in his early sixties. He looked fit, able and capable of causing harm if he chose.

Lancaster was impressed and slightly disappointed; he'd hoped the man would be aged, worse for wear, keen to talk and go home, but this man looked like he would not suffer fools.

Lancaster and Vidêt sat to one side of the room just behind Klissman. Klissman welcomed the other man in German and waved him to take a seat on the other side of the table. The two men continued to talk for a while; Klissman was quite animated. Steiner, accepting, monosyllabic. Lancaster heard the word '*Englander*' and 'English' used in the conversation and Klissman aimed his hand in their general direction and the other man peered over Klissman's shoulder to where he and Vidêt were sitting. Lancaster nodded back. Then Klissman turned to them.

"Mr Steiner is willing to talk with you in my presence. I have not told him what you wish to discuss other than you have an ongoing enquiry and need his co-operation."

With that the man got up and Lancaster and Vidêt slid into the seats on that side of the table. Klissman pulled a chair up as an observer or referee, Lancaster wasn't sure which.

"Guten mittag, Mr Steiner. Are you OK with us speaking English?" Lancaster asked with a friendly smile.

"Of course, but who am I speaking with?" the other man replied.

Lancaster introduced himself and Vidêt, giving the fact that they were from the Devon & Cornwall Police in the United Kingdom. He was casual over this, hoping to set the man at ease. Lancaster told Steiner they were conducting an enquiry with regards to the death of a man and hoped he may be able to help them in some small way. Lancaster thought he noticed a quiver of knowledge ripple through the man's face, only for a second, but something was there.

"How can I be of help, detectives, though I have never been to England?" he answered, also with a smile.

"That's OK, Paul, is it OK to call you Paul? I am never quite sure of the formalities in Germany."

The other man confirmed first names were OK.

"Well, the thing is, Paul, the death we're looking into happened on the Island of Jersey in 2008. We know you went there, even if not to the UK mainland."

There was a definite look of recognition and a slight loss of colour to the man's face. Lancaster could see behind the staring eyes; the man was now wondering how much the detectives knew of his travels. He was trying to think quickly, plan ahead. Lancaster went in fast to keep him guessing.

"You hired a car from Your-Hire, based at the airport, a new Ford Fiesta, a red one."

Again, Lancaster could see the man was thinking fast, looking for a way out.

"I..." was as far as the man got before Lancaster went in again.

"You had it on hire from the 18th of August 2008. You took it back on the 24th, just before your flight back to Germany. That was you, wasn't it, Paul? I mean the CCTV picture we have of you looks different to you today, but then my passport photo looks nothing like me now." Lancaster was bluffing about the CCTV, but Steiner wasn't to know.

"So what of it? I hired a car. I know laws are different in the UK, but hiring a car is not illegal surely?"

Lancaster forced himself to laugh at this little joke, Vidêt, on cue, smiled and giggled along before Lancaster replied,

"So may I ask what the purpose was for your visit to Jersey?"

Steiner turned to Klissman. "Do I have to answer these questions?"

"Either you answer them, or I ask the same questions. Then if you don't reply to me, I charge you with non-compliance in an investigation, it's up to you," Klissman replied, displaying no emotion. Lancaster was still unsure what the man thought of them, but to be honest, it was irrelevant.

"Shall I ask the question again, Paul?"

"I went there for a holiday. I was a tourist. Again, it's not a crime."

"No, of course not," Lancaster replied with a broad, friendly smile. "We were just asking. So did you enjoy your stay? Did you like the island?"

"The truth! It was OK. Very small, too many tourists and the food was not good. I will not be rushing back I can tell you that."

"That's a shame, Paul, we're sorry to hear that, aren't we, Detective Vidêt?"

"Yes, we are; we like people to enjoy our islands," Vidêt said, noticing the look in Lancaster's eyes and picking up a telepathic instinct for what he wanted her to do. She continued. "I'm surprised it took you so many visits to decide you didn't like Jersey. We have you hiring cars from the same company during early June of '08 and again at the end of July. Surely, you must have made up your mind you didn't like the place when you first visited in June. The island didn't change

331

that much during the year, did it? Maybe you disliked the place so much on your first two visits, that you came back again to make sure." She laughed at this and so did Lancaster.

Steiner went to speak but Lancaster cut him off. "So, what were you doing on top of the cliffs and parked in the car park above Le Portelet on the 20th of August?"

Steiner looked taken aback and went to speak again, but this time Vidêt cut him off.

"Your car was seen during the afternoon, early evening of the 20th. What were you doing there, Paul?"

"Did you go there to kill Peter Urbawicz, Paul?" Lancaster saw the look on Steiner's face. They'd triggered something.

"A man answering your description was seen on the cliffs; was it you, Paul?" Vidêt asked.

"Of course, it was you. Did you go there to kill Peter Urbawicz?" Lancaster asked again.

"Or was it an accident? Is that it? Is that why you finished your visit to Jersey, packed up and went home?" Vidêt asked quickly.

"Or had you fulfilled your contract? Went home to collect your fee, job done, is that the case?" Lancaster came in quickly. Not wanting to leave space for the man to think.

"You were hired to carry out the murder, is that the case, Paul? Did you get lots of cash for it? Maybe you banked it on Jersey?" Lancaster continued. "Did you seriously think you'd got away with it? Well, clearly, you did. Now finally, out of the blue, we turn up. Must be a shock, I mean, there you were, a man of your age, happy in retirement, spending your money wisely."

Steiner sat bolt upright. Lancaster saw a change in the other man's demeanour. There was colour in his face and red veins now criss-crossed the man's cheeks. It annoyed Lancaster. He could read the body language; he knew they'd just lost him. It had been so close, but the Stasi officer was back. Lancaster knew Steiner had been on the ropes, but the bell had rung, end of the round. Steiner had space to breathe. Breathe and think. Steiner spoke calmly and slowly, in German, directly to Klissman, then sat back in his chair and folded his arms. Klissman replied to the man, again in German. Steiner repeated the same words. Lancaster didn't understand German but he had a pretty good idea of what the man had said from his mannerisms and general smugness. There was a look that Lancaster had seen so many times during interviews, the look that said, 'I'm saying nothing until my solicitor arrives'. This was confirmed seconds later by Klissman, speaking in English.

"Mr Steiner will say no more until his legal representative is here, as he has a right to do. Sadly, detectives, this interview is finished for the time being."

Lancaster watched as Steiner was taken away to await the arrival of his solicitor. It was mid-afternoon, though it was a job to tell in the artificially lit room. Klissman invited them to take coffee with him and they retired again to the 'Officers Mess'.

"How high is Steiner on your list of suspects, Detective Lancaster?" Klissman asked.

"Honestly?" Lancaster thought for a moment. "Honestly, Chief Inspector, he was somewhere near the bottom when we started this enquiry. But we've eliminated virtually all other candidates. That's brought Steiner level pegging at the top. Our point of reference for all this is a set of hire cars rented out by a specific hire company. One of those cars was parked in the car park close to where our victim was murdered. We've identified every person who had one of those cars on hire during the period of the murder. We've eliminated most of them, now we're down to Steiner. We have other options, but until we remove the hire car from the equation, Paul is our only visible and accessible contender."

"Your line of questioning leads me to think you've already made your mind up, Inspector. It was at times quite forceful if I may say so; not a complaint merely an observation."

"Oh, please, don't be fooled, Chief Inspector, I would've treated every suspect in exactly the same manner. I just wanted to provoke the man."

"I think you succeeded. I'm interested though, how do you feel about the man now, has your opinion changed in any way?"

"I'm more certain now than when I flew in this morning. I've no evidence other than he was near the scene at the time of the murder, by that I mean a hire car was seen parked there at the time of death. The man didn't deny it or come up with some explanation such as he broke down or went for a walk, which leads me to believe he was either involved, carried out the crime or he drove somebody else there to do the deed. So, yes, I'm more certain now than when I arrived."

"You mentioned CCTV images, were these at the car park?"

"Actually, I lied. We don't have any pictures, if he'd just

said, 'I wasn't there, I've no idea what you're talking about', I would've been buggered, if you excuse my turn of phrase, but then, he didn't know that did he. He's now admitted he was on Jersey and he's admitted hiring the car. Now we can place him on the island at the time of the murder and we've reason to believe that car was on the headland. As yet he's not come up with any alibi that would rule him out, so yes, he's high on our list."

Klissman sat looking at them. Lancaster was unsure what the man thought of them. He couldn't work out if he was on their side or Steiner's.

"Well, I was watching the man. I think you're right. There was a definite flicker as you drip-fed information. He was taken by surprise by what he thought you knew, there was a look of panic. As you say, I don't know if he is your murderer or not, but he definitely knows something, but what that is, only time will tell."

Klissman ordered up sandwiches as again they'd missed lunch. He left them in the canteen eating, promising to come and fetch them once Steiner's legal counsel arrived. Lancaster and Vidêt sat contemplating where they were with the enquiry so far.

"One day, Marie, we'll start an investigation, walk into a room, see the person who committed the crime and make an arrest. He or she will be charged, found guilty, sent to prison and everyone will go off to the pub and have a drink, you know, like they do on the telly."

"But where would be the fun in that? I know that sometimes it would be nice if it was a little easier, but be honest, you know you love the challenge when things get tough or do not go to plan, is that not so?"

"Yes, of course, I was only joking. But sometimes it would be nice to have a little going our way."

They were finishing lunch when Klissman arrived. Steiner's lawyer had arrived. They made their way back to the room with the dismal lighting. Steiner, wearing cuffs and escorted by a uniformed officer, came into view, accompanied by a bespectacled gentleman in a shabby suit. The lawyer. They let Steiner and his man enter, then followed. Formal introductions were made. Klissman restarted the tape, stated the day, time and date and introduced those present.

The lawyer, Jacob Schleeman, appeared to be in his late sixties, maybe even seventies with yellowing skin and sunken eyes which gave the impression of a man who didn't have many cases left to work. Schleemen talked to Klissman in German but the latter cut him off.

"I'm sorry, Herr Schleeman, but this interview must be conducted in English for the benefit of my colleagues from the UK. It is their enquiry. Your client was quite happy to speak in English at the start of this interview, so for the sake of continuity and common courtesy I must insist we continue in English."

Schleeman looked at his client. Steiner looked back and shrugged, resigned to the fact that was how it was going to be.

"My client wishes for me to read a statement on his behalf. He hopes it may help clear up misunderstandings the detectives have with regards to his trips to Jersey in 2008. I should also tell you that my client is a diabetic and may have to eat sweets or chocolate should this interview go on for long. He needs to keep his sugar levels up…"

"Herr Schleeman," Klissman interrupted. "Herr Steiner speaks perfectly good English, so why does he not just tell us himself? If he says something incriminating, you may intervene, but I'd rather that if he has something to say, we hear it from the man himself. Is that not a better idea, Paul?"

Schleeman conferred with his client, who shrugged again, leant forward, placed his arms on the table and told his story.

Steiner was born in 1944. The son of German officer, Heinrich Steiner. Paul never met his father; he'd died during the last days of war. Paul's mother raised him alone, like many mothers after the war. They were left behind in eastern Berlin overrun by the Russian army. To begin with, mother and baby kept their heads down, hiding in cellars of derelict buildings in East Berlin, hearing screams and sounds that told them what would happen to any woman found by the Russians. Nobody thought the Russians would stay; they were making a point. They were a force to be reckoned with and wanted that fact acknowledged before they went home.

Eventually, Paul's mother made a choice. She'd realised that Russian troop movements appeared to be concentrated in an unclassified 'front line'. They were piling debris, barbed wire and masonry into informal barricades across plazas and street junctions, ostensibly to control vehicle and pedestrian movements, but the Russians were marking territory and laying down boundaries. Before long they'd clear the ruins; there'd be no more hiding. She made the decision to move.

She thought the danger lay in crossing from where they

were hiding into the American sector; she didn't know if they'd treat her any better. She made the choice to head east into the countryside, find some sympathetic Germans who might take her and her son in long enough to sleep, be safe and get some food inside them, then she'd think what to do next. Paul's mother crawled, hid, crawled again, with young Paul wrapped in blankets, gagged and strapped to her back. It took her two days to break out into fields and woodlands to the east.

Lancaster, although interested in this tale of survival, was aware that none of this had any bearing whatsoever on his enquiry and interrupted Steiner in full flow.

"I'm sorry, Paul, but all we really want to know is, what was your reason for being in Jersey during August 2008?"

Steiner, Schleeman and Klissman all looked at him with a look that said he'd spoken out of turn. He'd seen the look before during briefings when they didn't get to the bits that interested him and he spoke up. He was always wrong, but never learnt from experience.

"With due respect, Detective," Schleeman said. "You've accused my client of being involved in a serious crime. At least have the courtesy to allow my client to put his case as to why he would not have carried out such a crime. Is that really too much to ask?"

"I apologise, Herr Schleeman. Paul, please continue," Lancaster replied, surprised he was capable of uttering such words.

Steiner continued.

Eventually, they found a farm that would take them in. Paul was looked after by his mother and the farmer's wife, whilst

Paul's mother helped work the farm. The pair became part of the family, a family who'd lost both sons during the war and had to work the farm by themselves, carrying the yoke of grief around their shoulders. Having a youngster around helped make up for it in some small way, and Paul's mother worked hard and shared the load. Communism now draped its cloak over the entire country. The Russians were here to stay.

By the time Paul reached his tenth birthday, he was a member of the Communist Youth Movement, the farm being part of a cooperative producing crops and animals for the state. Paul's mother always spoke of his father. She'd kept two photographs throughout their journey. One was of his father in an officer's uniform, standing in the sunshine, proud and happy. The other was of him sitting in long grass with his arm around Paul's mother as a young woman. Happy and in love, With neither knowing what the future held. Paul's mother hoped that one day she'd find where her husband had died. She'd some strange belief that his spirit would be waiting for her, wherever that place was. It kept her going through the years, the thought that one day she'd leave the East and find the grave in the dirt of some foreign land. During childhood, Paul had gone to school, done well, was told he was bright and would go far in this utopian land.

By the early 1960s, Paul left the community farm with his mother's blessing, joining the East German Police Force on a sponsored cadetship. The reward for meeting good grades, his name was submitted by local leaders of the Communist Youth Movement. He flourished and passed his exams, impressing his superiors in college. He was soon a qualified police officer, living in police accommodation and visiting his mother when he could. When Paul passed his sergeant's exams, he did so with such a high pass rate that the local party committee sponsored a holiday for him and his mother to a purpose-built development on the Baltic coast. It was the first time Paul had ever seen the sea, but the water was freezing, the hotel was in worse condition than their farm and the food was terrible. They made no complaints, but during that holiday, Paul's mother made him promise that if he got away from the East, he'd find his father's grave and lay flowers for her. Paul told her that one day they'd do it together, but in truth, she knew better. Paul's mother died in 1974, aged 52. Years of suffering, farm work and worry had taken their toll. Before her final curtain, she'd made Paul promise that he'd find his father's resting place, lay flowers and tell him she was searching for him.

Paul was then recruited into the Stasi, becoming a senior officer in East Berlin. He lived a comfortable life, doing his job and living in his government home; he was happy. During the late '70s into the 1980s unrest rippled across the bloc countries. The Stasi had a busy time attempting to keep a lid on people's urge to break free of chains that had bound them for the past 45 years. Then the damn broke. The freedom tsunami roared through Poland, rippled through Hungary and Czechoslovakia and flowed across the East German countryside until it crashed against the Berlin wall, which cracked and fell apart. During 1989 and into 1990, a flood of Germans rushed into the world beyond. For a short while anarchy reigned in East Berlin. There were reprisals. Paul survived this. Then as part of a German people's repatriation process, in 1992, he applied for a position in the newly restructured, Unified German Police Force. Once he'd settled into this role, he used his position to research his father's war. With access to West Berlin archives, he had a wealth of information to wade through. One thing to be said for the German army was that it had been efficient in record keeping. Despite efforts to destroy incriminating evidence, details of what troops were in which regiment and where they were stationed had been deemed irrelevant for destruction. Eventually, he put together the story of his father's war.

But the crucial information had been harder to find as at the time of his father's death, during the last weeks of the Second World War, there was so much confusion, death and destruction, that fewer records had been kept. Eventually, a chance conversation with another German also searching for relatives, led him to the British War Graves Commission in the UK. From this, Paul found where German Military Cemeteries were and from there he cross-referenced where his father's regiment had been based at the end of the war. His father had died on Jersey, the victim of an RAF raid. And it was here records showed he was buried.

It wasn't until 2006 that Paul found the location of his father. In 2008 he made his first visit to Jersey to fulfil his mother's wish. His initial visit had been early summer to find his way around the island and get a feel for the place. He'd had little time to fit in a full holiday but returned at the end of July and located his father's burial site in the German Military Cemetery on the island. During August, the anniversary of his mother's death, he returned to visit the graveside, lay flowers and say his piece to the father he'd never seen. On that visit, he'd gone to the headland, walked the cliff tops to the place his father had been, during a morning in 1945, gunned down by a lone RAF plane crossing the channel. He'd been in the wrong place at the wrong time, dying only months before the war ended.

Steiner finished by saying that it must have been during his walk on the clifftops that his hire car was seen in the car park. He was willing to accept the date Lancaster said he was there, but whilst walking couldn't remember seeing anyone. Since then, he hasn't returned. He hoped he'd now cleared this matter up. If there were more questions, he'd be happy to assist as he was, after all, only a retired policeman on the island, fulfilling his mother's dying wish.

Lancaster looked at the man. Somewhere, behind those cloudy grey eyes, he felt the man was laughing. The face may have the air of someone sorry he'd caused a misunderstanding and who'd have cleared it up quicker had he understood what was needed of him. But Lancaster sensed a smugness, that they were being fobbed off. But he couldn't gauge how.

"Thank you, Herr Steiner," Klissman said. "I'm sure the detectives are grateful for your assistance. There were tragic losses on all sides during the conflict, but again, many thanks for your explanation. Do you have further questions, Detective Lancaster?"

Lancaster could think of nothing. He felt deflated, at a loss for words. He could find no reason to keep the man, but that feeling of smugness galled him; if he could arrest the man for being smug, he would.

"No, Chief Inspector, I don't think I've anything else to ask of Herr Steiner, at the moment."

It was late afternoon as they watched them walking away. Lancaster looked on, quietly seething. He couldn't put a finger on it; something didn't feel right. He was certain they'd meet again. Klissman offered them tea in the canteen, but they declined, not because Lancaster felt the man had taken sides, but because he and Vidêt had reached that point of an unproductive day, when all they wanted was to be in their room, licking wounds and rethinking the plan. Klissman called a car to drop them at their hotel and Lancaster thanked him for his assistance, telling him they'd let him know how the case developed. Klissman sensed their dejection and offered one piece of advice.

"At least, according to what you've told me, you've investigated everyone on your list, now you can concentrate on other options. Your process of elimination has worked well; you should be pleased with the results so far?"

Lancaster wasn't but thanked the man anyway. The car dropped them at the hotel, where they checked in and went straight to their room. It was modern, plush and large, with treble-glazed windows keeping out city noise. They dropped their bags and then dropped themselves into the armchairs. Vidêt kicked off her shoes and rested her feet on the coffee table.

"So," she said closing her eyes, flexing her toes on the table. "Was I the only one in that room that thought that bastard Steiner told a good story, but it was all bullshit?"

"The man got under my skin, Marie, but I don't know what it was. I'm interested though; what makes you think his whole story was bullshit?"

"If he and his mother were close enough to the demarcation line to claim they saw Americans, there would have been nowhere to hide. Anyway, why did she stay? Every other Berliner who could walk escaped before the Russians arrived. They all knew which army would treat them better; it wouldn't be the Russians, not after what the Germans had done to them. If she was stupid enough to stay, then there would have been nowhere to hide. The boundaries in Berlin between occupying forces had been fought over so much that there was nothing but rubble left, rubble and dead bodies. The Russians were skilled in slipping in amongst the ruins, so it would've been impossible to find a safe space for a mother and baby to hide, and a baby that didn't cry must have been dead. Then they escaped into the countryside. Well, the place was crawling with Russians. They poured into the space. Stalin didn't want the Allies moving across Berlin and shifting the borders so he flooded the land around his front lines with troops as a deterrent and destroyed as much of Germany as he could as they went. Do you know that they reckoned that by the end of the war, something like seventy percent of all German housing had been destroyed? It was even worse in the east. The Russians dismantled entire factories and shipped it all back into Russia, sometimes they never even used them, it was just out of spite. Then came the reprisals."

"What sort of reprisals?" Lancaster asked, fascinated by his partner's apparent knowledge of the war in Germany.

"Well, before 1945 was finished, countries like Poland and Yugoslavia started evicting anyone that was ethnic German, sending them back into Germany. People were starving. Europe went into one of the worst winters in 30 years. Everyone but the Russians was tired of fighting. The Allies didn't want to contest the Russian boundaries. They thought, like many Germans, that it was just a ploy to get compensation for the war. Once they'd gotten paid off, they'd have gone home, leaving the rest of the world to police the German nation or what was left of it. If Steiner's mother survived without getting raped by the Russians, then she must have been really ugly. They reckon Russian troops raped all the German female population and many of the men and most of the animals, yet according to Steiner, he and his mother quite luckily found a farm that had not been burnt down, where a farmer and his wife, who must also have been bloody ugly, let them come and starve with them. She then looked after what would appear to be some of the only livestock left in Germany. I do not believe any of it. And, if he made all that up, why should we believe that story about his reasons for being on Jersey?"

"Marie, you're a bloody marvel. Where did you get all this knowledge from?"

"We were taught it at school. We were taught that if the world had not been so harsh on the German people after the First World War, the Second may not have happened. Lessons were not learnt from the first war, but then who could have predicted what the Russians had in mind? I think it was lucky we met them in Berlin; what would have happened if they'd got as far as Paris?"

Lancaster was hungry, so he called down to the restaurant and reserved a table, then headed for the shower. When he came

345

out, Vidêt was asleep in the armchair. He let her sleep whilst he dressed. He emptied his pockets, then noticed he still had his mobile turned off. He'd switched it off when he'd interviewed Steiner. Once it was fired up, his screen told him he'd missed calls and had a message waiting. The calls were both from Pamela. He checked the message; it was from Pamela.

"David, I hope you get this message. When you speak with Steiner, you might like to ask him why he came to the house the day before my father died! Josette decided she'd do a bit of cleaning through the lounge and spotted the photo of Steiner in his police uniform pinned next to the whiteboard, pinned into the wallpaper I might add; she was less than amused. Anyway, she asked me who it was, so I told her. She said she recognised the man as coming to the house the day before Peter died, to speak with Peter. She presumed it had to do with the bank. Apparently, the two of them spoke and then the man left, anyway, I don't know if it's important but I thought I should tell you. 'Bye for now."

Lancaster sat in a state of shock. How had this escaped the whole enquiry? Why had Josette never said anything before? He woke Marie and played her the message. She said exactly the same thing. Lancaster forgot the meal and went into overdrive, punched in Pamela's number. She picked up.

"Hi David, did you get my message?"

"Pamela, why did Josette never say anything about this man before? Has she never spoken to you about the visit?"

"Why should she? My father often had visitors. He was a private banker, we had all sorts of clients coming to the house, but it was nothing out of the ordinary."

"But a day later her employer was found dead, surely that must have raised a query?"

"I remind you, David, that as far as everyone but me was concerned, my father's death was an accident. Nobody came to interview the staff, why would they? Josette had never seen the man before and never saw him again afterwards, so why should she have thought anything of it? The police didn't. It wasn't until she saw the picture that she saw a likeness and when she looked closer, she was positive it was the same man. Josette has nothing to blame herself for, David, nothing at all. Now what about this man Steiner, how did the interview go? Did you ask him about the visit to the house?"

Lancaster explained that he had not picked up the message until a few moments ago and Steiner never mentioned knowing Peter, let alone visiting him. The man had been released and was probably sitting at home, laughing at them. Marie was waving at him; she had her pad fired up and had been looking something up whilst he'd been on the phone. Marie asked to speak to her. He handed over the phone.

"Pamela, we need you to do some research. There are cemeteries on the island that hold German soldiers; can you track down the list of gravestones? They're not all listed online; some of the dead were repatriated after the war but their names will still be listed as buried on the island first. We need to find a dead officer reputed to have been killed in 1945 during an RAF airstrike. His name was Heinrich Steiner, he was supposed to be buried on the island. Can you do that for us?"

"Of course, there's still time for me to phone Civil Records before they close."

"Any problems, telephone Wardly; this is a murder enquiry, and this is important and very urgent. Steiner must know we're going to check these details so he may run before we can get him."

Lancaster telephoned Klissman and told him new evidence had come to light. Klissman's problem was that he couldn't rearrest the man on the say-so of one individual. Lancaster recognised this; he would've done the same, but after putting on some pressure, telling him they were checking the man's story on the island and waiting for callbacks, Klissman agreed to make sure the man didn't disappear overnight. Lancaster's next call was to Wardly. He told him the situation and the records they needed tracking. Wardly said he'd call Pamela and take over this task, as he knew the person in charge of Military Records and would have a better chance of getting them to work late. He'd call back later. Lancaster and Vidêt sat for a moment in silence. The chase was on again. The room telephone rang. Lancaster answered. The man on reception asked if they still wanted the table in the restaurant or if should they let it go. Lancaster told them to hold it, as they were on their way. He was suddenly starving again.

CHAPTER TEN

Having ploughed through a filling, if not exciting, meal, the pair were tucking into some kind of warm strudel, when Lancaster's mobile rang. Klissman.

"Chief Inspector."

"Detective Lancaster. We have a problem."

Lancaster's strudel lost its flavour.

"Hopefully not unsurmountable, Chief Inspector?"

"I cannot answer that at the moment. My people have been parked outside Steiner's home. Since darkness fell, they've realised there don't appear to be any lights in the house. At the moment I don't know what this means. My feeling is that Herr Steiner is not at home. I will leave it for a while before we go in. You must realise that we've no reason for any interest in the man. Have you heard anything from your people yet?"

Lancaster was annoyed, but now wasn't the time to put the man offside.

"Not yet, but as soon as I have something, I'll call you."

Klissman said he'd keep them informed.

"It would appear, Marie, that your gut feeling that Steiner was lying may have been right. He's taken the opportunity of us not being able to charge him and 'legged it' as we would say."

"But he can't have gone far though?"

"This is the beating heart of the European Union, Marie. The moment he walked out of that office, he could have gone as far as Greece, Spain, Italy or West into France. About the only place in Europe where you'd have to show a passport is the UK, and he's unlikely to go there. No, if he's made a run for it, he could be anywhere. But... I don't think he has. Why would he? The man is in his seventies, lived his entire life in Germany. The wall came down in '89. Did he rush off into the world? No. The best he could do was Jersey. According to Klissman's research, it doesn't appear that his travel documents, passport or anything else, has been outside of Germany but for those occasions. If the man is a professional hitman, then he's got another identity, passport, maybe even several; it could be that he's been all over the world. But even if that was the case, Germany's been his home, it's all he knows. I have this feeling he's still here."

Lancaster's mobile rang. Wardly.

"Yes, sir," Lancaster said.

"We've checked the German military death roll on all the islands. There's no Steiner listed. Not in cemetery records or the repatriated body list. In fact, we managed better than that. The Germans left entire records of troop movements on the islands; not one mention of any soldier called Steiner, on any list, at any time. He was never here. I hope that helps?"

"Thank you, sir. I'll get back to you in the morning."

Lancaster phoned Klissman and told him the news. If Steiner showed his face, then he should be brought in. Klissman told him they'd get on it straight away. Now it was a case of waiting. They turned in for the night and slept right through until woken by Lancaster's mobile. Klissman. It was 7:30 already.

"Good morning, Chief Inspector. Any news?" Lancaster asked.

"Steiner's arrived home. I've asked my men to get him back to the station. I can keep him in the cells until his solicitor arrives, so you have about an hour for breakfast, then join us here."

The pair were in Klissman's office by 8:45 a.m.

"It would appear Herr Steiner had been expecting us," Klissman said. "When my men arrived, he had an overnight bag packed, with washbag, a change of clothes and his pyjamas; at a guess I'd say he's expecting to spend the night in our cells. It may be that he knew all along you'd be back. He's downstairs waiting for Schleeman."

"Any idea where he went all night?"

"We haven't asked; we thought it would wait until he was formally cautioned."

The front desk rang. Schleeman had arrived. In the interview room, they settled into the same seats as before. Klissman switched on the tape, cautioning Steiner he was being formally questioned with regards to possible involvement in a murder enquiry. Steiner and Schleeman voiced their agreement. Klissman explained the interview would be held in English, with Lancaster and Vidêt asking the questions. Again, both men agreed.

"May I still call you Paul?" Lancaster asked. The other man nodded.

"Yesterday, Paul, you told us you were on Jersey to visit the location of your father's death and visit his grave. We've carried out research overnight; I have to tell you there is no record of any German soldier named Steiner serving on any of the Channel Islands during the war. So I'll ask again, why were you on Jersey during the summer of 2008?"

Steiner looked sideways to Schleeman. The pair smiled slightly to each other, then Schleeman reached forward and patted Steiner's hands as they lay folded and resting on the tabletop in front of him.

"Let us stop with these tales, Inspector; I killed Peter Urbawicz," Steiner said, in a slow, calm, but deliberate voice. "But I want you to know that it was not meant to be like that; I did not go there to kill him."

Even though Lancaster had thought this, hearing it spill from his lips so readily was a shock. He'd never thought it was going to be this easy.

"Would you care to expand on that, Paul?" Lancaster said.

"At the risk of boring you, Inspector Lancaster, would you allow me to explain how this all came about? You were not in a hurry, were you? I promise that what I tell you now will be, as you would say, the truth, the whole truth and nothing but, etc., etc."

Lancaster nodded, realising there was little point in doing anything else at this moment. He folded his arms and made himself comfortable.

Steiner unwrapped a sweet, popped it into his mouth and then went on to tell his story. Most of his descriptions of his early years and about him and his mother hiding in the rubble were true. But that life began in Gdynia in Poland. His mother was Rebeka Urbawicz, older sister of Peter Urbawicz. Prior to the outbreak of war, Peter was living outside Poland, studying in Denmark, when the German army invaded his country. He wanted to return and join the fight, but his parents forbade it; they told him to get as far away as possible and make for England. Peter joined other refugees, made it to England, was admitted into the RAF and began training. The last time the family had contact was a letter via the Red Cross in Gdynia saying he was well and training to be a pilot.

Being Jewish in Poland became the end of the world as humans knew it. Rats in sewers were treated better and even ate better. Paul's mother, Peter's sister, survived because she'd been working in the City Hall when the Germans arrived. They were impressed by her knowledge of the city archives and very impressed with her establishing a city-wide census of the population, its businesses and its residents. The Germans, with their impeccable reputation for efficiency, appreciated her work, allowing her to remain in her post within the City Hall provided she wore the star attached to her clothes and kept her eyes down on the floor at all times. They set about using her data to identify Jewish members of the city population, isolating them and eventually removing them altogether. Most were taken to the concentration camp at Treblinka to be exterminated.

Within months of the occupation, Paul's mother was spotted by a young German officer who took a shine to her. Heinrich Steiner was no fascist but knew how to survive in an army where many were. He played the role to the full but had no hatred of the Jewish race, though he didn't hesitate to sign papers to round up another trainload of Jews. Paul's mother always believed the German man genuinely loved her and chose to hide the fact that she was Jewish. He arranged for them to be married, using a sympathetic chaplain. With a new surname and documents, they moved into a house, where she remained hidden from the public gaze in case she should be recognised and informed on.

As the catastrophic decision to invade Russia backfired and the Red Army began pushing the invading forces ever backwards, Heinrich Steiner performed a selfless act. He furnished his wife with travel documents, gave her the keys to his old home in Berlin and packed her off, saying he'd return as soon as his paymasters decided it was time, not knowing of course that they'd all be sacrificed in the name of their great leader's pride. From that period onwards, the story of Paul Steiner paralleled the one he told previously. Paul was born shortly after his mother arrived in Germany. His father never returned from Gdynia. He died there.

Their story was much the same as the first, but Paul's mother, Rebeka, had continually spoken of her younger brother, Peter. She told him of his bravery in going to England, flying Spitfires and fighting the Luftwaffe, and made him promise that if he escaped East Germany, he should make for England and find her brother. Tell him, she and Paul, were the only members of the Urbawicz family to have survived, but they'd all been so proud of him. Sadly, his mother didn't live to see the collapse of the Communist regime. It was left to Paul to fulfil her request. When Paul became a member of the

German Police Force, he began putting his research skills to good use, eventually finding the Military Records Department at the Imperial War Museum. There, he tracked his uncle's development through the ranks until he became a Flight Officer with a squadron flying reconnaissance missions.

Paul discovered discrepancies or conflicting reports of his father's last mission over occupied France. One report had him recorded as MIA whilst flying over Brest, while another appeared to show he'd survived his crash landing and eventually repatriated, but no further record had been found in any archive or census in England. Once Paul realised he'd reached a brick wall, he'd travelled into France to visit the location of his uncle's last mission, the Brest area of Brittany. After researching in Brest, he'd discovered a book about the local resistance and he pieced together the whole story of survival, love and escape to the Island of Jersey for his uncle and his young French wife. The following year, he made two visits to Jersey, eventually locating the home of his uncle. Paul was so happy to find his only true family member left still alive. Better still, he and his wife were living a comfortable life on the island and had children, his cousins. Now he had a family.

When he visited the island in August of 2008, he was excited. It had taken a while to pluck up the courage and to visit the house and introduce himself. A housekeeper answered the door and showed him to a room. When his uncle entered, Paul introduced himself as the son of Rebeka, Peter's sister, and gave him the sad news that she was no longer alive but that he, Paul, was Peter's nephew and had travelled from Berlin to find him. Imagine his shock that the man his mother had been so proud of despite not seeing him for over fifty years and the man she was adamant he should seek out and find whenever he could, that this man told him that he didn't have the slightest idea what he was talking about. He even said he had no family, which had hurt more than anything. He'd been shocked into silence. When Peter Urbawicz showed him out, wished him well on his travels and then closed the door behind him, he walked away with a heavy heart.

The following day, Paul made the decision that there must have been some misunderstanding. He should have shown Peter the photographs to see if he recognised his own sister. He'd try once more for his mother's sake if nothing else. He'd driven toward the house but lost his nerve at the last minute. What if he was rejected a second time? He drove past the house and continued on to the car park. Paul had sat in his car looking at the sea when he'd noticed a figure coming up the path. At first, he took no notice of the man in scruffy clothes, carrying a basket and a rope over one shoulder. The man passed across Paul's line of vision. He realised it was Peter Urbawicz.

Paul watched the man head across the cliff top and disappear over the edge. He realised there'd be some path or steps so decided to see where the man had gone. He saw Peter crossing the beach and climbing a rocky outcrop jutting into the sea. Paul decided that this location may give them the privacy they needed to discuss the matter further; maybe he didn't want his family to know his Polish history, some simple explanation for this misunderstanding.

When Paul climbed onto the rocks beside Peter, he said he wanted no trouble, just wanted to talk. He explained that his mother made him promise to seek out her brother. He told Peter he had photos of Rebeka and Peter as children; he should look at them. Peter's reaction was that Paul was mistaken and that he'd found the wrong man. He had no family in Germany or Poland. He'd never heard of Rebeka and asked that Paul leave him and his family alone. That final comment had been the tipping point. He and his mother had been alone for years, waiting to escape the confinement of communism and search for their only surviving family; now they were being rejected. Worse still, Peter turned his back on Paul and continued preparing his fishing pot. This had been the final insult. He'd spent nearly eight years tracking this man down, to have him turn his back! He reached around the man's head and grabbed his chin to force him to look at him, but in that moment of rage, he forgot his own strength. He pulled the man's head sharply. He was shocked when the man's body didn't follow suit but slumped in his arms and slipped to the floor. Paul realised he'd killed the man.

Paul recognised the severity of his actions. He was, in part, devastated but also angry. Angry that this man had forced him to commit murder, killing the last living member of his family. He made the choice; he wouldn't stand there and be caught for this crime. He picked up the body, lifted it as high as he could and dropped his uncle over the rock face into the sea. He tossed the basket in, keeping the rope wrapped around the rock where he'd found it. At this point, dizziness arrived, almost overwhelming, and he realised his sugar levels were reduced. He leant against the rock face, pulled a chocolate bar from his pocket and quickly devoured it. Before his dizziness passed, it was time to leave. He retraced his steps to the car park.

He'd reached his car when he was aware of another figure, a woman, coming up the same path Peter had. Paul ducked down inside his car but when he next looked, she'd also disappeared. He was intrigued; he slipped out of the car and across to the cliff edge. From his vantage point, he saw the woman climb to where he and Peter had been. She jumped down to where the body must surely be, floating between the rocks. He returned to his car, closing the door just as the woman came over the cliff top. Again, he ducked out of sight, but when he peered over the dashboard, she'd gone.

Paul left. Driving to his hotel, he packed, signed out, returned the car to the airport and caught the first flight home that morning. He'd waited for somebody to find him ever since. He knew as a former Stasi officer; he'd left too many clues. He knew somebody would remember him visiting the house and had seen the hire car visiting the house or the car park on the cliff. It was the only car there; he knew it could be traced. It was only a matter of time before they found his hotel and tracked his flights in and out. But after a year there was no sign of anyone so, as time passed, he actually thought he'd gotten away with it. So, when Lancaster arrived, he knew the game was up. He'd told his mother's grave as much the previous evening and was awaiting the second knock.

"Why didn't you just tell us all this yesterday, Paul? Why all the lies?" Lancaster asked.

"I had to buy a little time, Detective. I needed to visit my mother and tell her I wouldn't be able to see her for a while, then get my life in order, make arrangements, revisit the hospital. Now, I have everything in order and telling you all you need to know; is that not enough?"

Lancaster sat looking at the elderly man opposite.

"Chief Inspector," Lancaster said. "Would you be willing, having heard the evidence and testimony from Herr Steiner, to charge him with murder on our behalf? Then we can begin looking at extradition to Jersey, where he'll stand trial for the murder of Peter Urbawicz?"

Just as Klissman was about to speak, Schleeman spoke up.

"I need to inform you, gentleman, that on behalf of Herr Steiner, I shall be fighting extradition to any country. My client has advanced lung and liver cancer; it is incurable. At best he has six months left to live. In that time, he will be in and out of hospital and once he's sold his house, will be residing in a nursing home for his final days, so I wish you all the best, detectives, but I find it hard to imagine any judge granting extradition under those circumstances, whatever crime he has committed."

Klissman and Lancaster looked at each other. Lancaster nodded in Steiner's direction. Klissman turned to face the man square on.

"Paul Steiner, I formally charge you with the murder of Peter Urbawicz on the Island of Jersey on the 20th of August 2008..."

As Klissman continued the scripted process for the tape, Lancaster sat and listened, relieved it was all over. He turned to Marie. He knew they were thinking the same thing. Their job was to investigate and prove the murder was not an accident, then find who and why was at an end. The conclusion wasn't the best they could've hoped for. It was going to be down to the legal teams to get the best result they could. Lancaster wasn't sure how Pamela would react. It would be unlikely Steiner would be standing trial. He'd speak with her soon but he had a chain of command to go through first. Back in his office, Klissman sent for coffee.

"Are you happy with the result, Detective Lancaster?" Klissman said. "You do not look like a man who had, as they say, 'got their man'."

"Chief Inspector, you must be aware that there's more to this process than 'getting your man'. It's also about bringing justice and seeing a result that'll give the family of the victim some closure. This job is only half finished. For Sergeant Vidêt and myself, sadly, this is the second murder in the last eighteen months where we've found the murderer, but the culprit is unlikely to be incarcerated for that crime."

"My god, Detective Lancaster, two murder enquiries in eighteen months and you have managed to solve them both is not a bad result; you should be grateful for that."

"I apologise, Chief Inspector. I didn't mean to sound arrogant. We were just lucky that was all."

"Ah, you do yourselves a disservice, for both of you. I've done my homework; I know it was more than luck."

"May I ask, what happens now, Chief Inspector?" Vidêt asked.

"Now Steiner has been formally charged, we'll be keeping him in the cells until his first appearance before a local judge. It will be up to him to decide if Steiner can be released under bail restrictions but, I have to say, it's almost certain he will be.

I think murder or no murder, a judge can see that Steiner is going to die. We can only wait and see that if the man makes it to trial, the judge may decide that as Steiner pleaded guilty on tape before witnesses that, yes, he is guilty and can be tried in Berlin. Again, that will be out of the hands of mere policemen like ourselves."

Lancaster and Vidêt left Klissman's office with a copy of the interview tape to verify the confession. Lancaster hoped it would alleviate the frustration he expected Pamela and her mother would feel when he returned with no prisoner, just a confession on a memory stick. Back at the hotel, the pair had a sandwich in the bar, Vidêt booked flights for the following morning and Lancaster telephoned Craven. DCI Craven was matter of fact about the result, but as for not being able to bring their man home to Jersey he was less bothered. 'That's life, my son, don't sweat it.' They'd done the job they'd been sent to do. 'Well done. End of.' It was now up to 'other bods' to 'faff about with the paperwork'. Lancaster was happy the man hadn't asked when they'd be coming back to the UK. As far as Lancaster was concerned, there were still t's to be crossed and i's to be dotted before he'd consider this case over.

Lancaster's next call was to Wardly; it went to answer phone. He left a message asking for a call-back. He pulled up the Berlin website and looked for a French restaurant but couldn't find one. He did however find a Greek taverna with good reviews, so he made an early evening booking for 19.00. Tonight, they'd celebrate their success, even though it felt a little hollow. They retired to their room to call Pamela, but by the time they'd got there Lancaster's phone was going.

Wardly. Lancaster told him they'd found their murderer and had a taped confession; a signed version would follow. Wardly sounded surprised. He asked the obvious question, 'Would they be bringing the man home with them?' Lancaster had to tell him about the man's illness and age and confessed there was a very good chance Steiner might not live long enough to stand trial. Wardly reiterated Craven's words that they'd done their job, But it was up to others to attempt the paperwork. Lancaster informed Wardly they'd return to Jersey the following afternoon and, with his permission, he'd like to tell Lady Stottard the news. On return to the island, they'd draw up the whole enquiry ready to present to himself at his office within a couple of days. Wardly agreed.

Lancaster, about to call Pamela, had a sudden thought. He threw his phone to Vidêt and suggested she make the call, aware of how fond Marie was of the lady.

"Tell her I'm in the bathroom or something," he said, then laid his head back against the support of the wing-back armchair and closed his eyes.

"Hello, Pamela, I have news. You may want to be sitting down." Vidêt went on to tell her what had happened but not in detail. She explained that there was more to the story of Paul Steiner but they'd tell her on their return to the island. Pamela decided she'd wait before she told her mother. Vidêt rang off. She turned to hand the phone back, to find Lancaster fast asleep. She pulled the fancy 'throw' off the bed and placed it gently over her boss, tucking it in at the sides, then curled up on the bed and slept. Later that afternoon, when she awoke it was to the soothing sensation of Lancaster stroking her hair, so she opened her eyes, smiled and said 'hello'.

"We need to get ready to eat; I've booked us a table at a Greek taverna. I couldn't find a French restaurant; hope that's OK?"

She propped herself up onto her elbow, kissed him then said, "Lovely."

Their taxi deposited them at the restaurant just before 7.00 p.m.

The meal was good, full of flavour and textures, and accompanied quite literally by an elderly man sitting in the corner of the room playing Greek music on a bouzouki. There were only two other tables occupied when they'd arrived, but as the evening went on an entire Greek family arrived and took over the long central table. They were lively and celebrating, with regular breaks for toasts and raised glasses. The two detectives reached the dessert stage, tucking into portions of baklava, a sweet, nut-filled pastry covered in honey when the musician was joined by a member of the family group with another bouzouki-style instrument. The two men struck up a tune and the dancing began. A waiter arrived at the detectives' table with a tray of shot glasses, a gift from the family. He duly visited the other customers in turn doling out rich-coloured Greek brandy. The 'main man' at the head of the central table raised his glass to all and insisted they drank.

It only took a couple of glasses of 'Metaxa' before Lancaster and Vidêt were persuaded to join the dancing; Lancaster more reluctantly than Vidêt. This Greek dancing looked complicated; you had a specific set of footwork, arm-over-shoulder holds and a forward and back motion, that continued in a circle, between the tables... How had he managed to become embroiled in this madness? Then he remembered the 'Metaxa'. To be honest, it hadn't really taken that much and besides, he appeared to be enjoying himself.

Within the language barriers created by the use of German, Greek, English and brandy, they'd found out the family were originally immigrants, arriving in Germany some fifty years before. Successive generations had either been born here or come up from Greece to join them. The family owned a travel agency, arranging holidays in Greece for rich Germans. For some reason the Germans had developed a love for Greece and the eastern Mediterranean. The family catered for it and looked as if they'd done well. Eventually, the 'head man' stepped out of the line and began dancing alone in the centre of the circle, somebody handed him a pair of linen serviettes which he flourished, one in each hand, using them to extend and accentuate wrist and arm movements. Several dancers dropped on one knee, slow hand clapping the man, now performing just for them, his moves more accentuated, definite, individually chosen. The dance became an art form; those on their knees showed admiration for his skill and depth of emotion.

When the final chords were strummed, the dance finished to a round of applause. Several of the audience were in tears. The single dancer was completely drained by his total commitment to the dance. Lancaster, moved by the whole event, felt he'd been witness to something very special. Two members of the family, a husband and wife, came and thanked them for joining in and offered more brandy. It turned out the dance was a Greek story dance. Loosely, it told a story of migration, love and loss and although the origins of the dance were over a hundred years old, it still applies today. All who knew its story recognised an individual's pain and loss of homeland, by watching the emotional transcript in the telling by the individual performing, in this case, their grandfather. Lancaster asked where his pain had come from. Pouring them both another shot of Metaxa, the man just said, 'The night sadly is not long enough to tell you his story, but thank you for asking and thank you both for joining in'. They gave Lancaster a business card and offered them the best deal should they ever want to visit Greece for a holiday.

Lancaster thanked them but told them neither of them earned a luxury holiday salary. The couple smiled saying, 'Don't worry, we will tailor you a special Greek experience at a special price'. Lancaster and Vidêt thanked them again and declined the chance to make a long night of it, explaining they had a flight to catch and both needed sleep. They said their goodbyes, paid their bill and had a taxi called for. When they left the taverna, the party was heading into top gear. Both of them felt they'd just gotten away in time but couldn't help thinking they were missing out on a great night's entertainment.

The next morning, they headed for the airport. The flight was through a cloudless sky. Blue from horizon to horizon. Despite the hour-long wait at Munich for the connecting flight, they managed to land in Jersey for 16.00. Having phoned before they landed, Pamela was outside when they walked out. She hugged them and said, 'Thank you, both'. Lancaster didn't think it was over until somebody paid for the crime, but Pamela appeared happy.

Back at the house, Josette was at her usual place, pouring tea in readiness for their arrival. Lancaster walked around the bar, gave Josette a hug and kissed her cheek before thanking her for her help in solving the case. Josette was overwhelmed by the gesture and tissues were needed. Pamela picked up her tea and led the way through to the lounge. She wanted to know the full story of Steiner and where he fit into the family history. With a nod from Lancaster, Vidêt filled her in, attempting to fill all the colour Steiner had imbibed his story with. She felt it important that Pamela knew why the man made the journey to Jersey and invested so much in tracking down his uncle. None of it would ever excuse what the man had done. There could never be an excuse for murder, but being Breton, she understood the strength and power of emotions. For Paul Steiner she had some understanding; being trapped behind the communist walls most of his life and told the story of this hero uncle living somewhere on the other side, who never knew he still had a sister who'd survived and had borne a son.

Vidêt had a modicum of sympathy for Steiner, who must have been in complete shock. But she struggled to reconcile the actions of Peter with the stories Pamela and bank officials had told. He'd appeared a caring, thoughtful guy who'd fought to make for himself and his wife a new life, away from death and destruction. The thought that he'd turn away a family member who'd struggled to find him for so many years was an anathema to her. They'd never know what went through Peter's mind that day, why he claimed not to know his old family. Whatever his reasoning, the rejection of Paul Steiner as being family had catastrophic consequences for them all.

When Vidêt finished telling her version of Steiner's story, Pamela sat looking tearful.

"When I was a child, my mother and father never, never, ever talked about the war. Once when I was at school, we had a project about the war. I asked them if they'd tell me what they remembered from that time. They said neither of them could remember anything of any interest. Most of what we found out, my brother and I, was from my grandparents when they'd come and stay. They loved the island and would take John and me swimming at the beach or walking along the cliffs. It was they who told us about our parents' escape from France and that Father had been a Spitfire pilot. When John and I went to Brittany to stay with our grandparents, they'd tell us more stories; for them, it was obviously still very fresh in their minds. I'm pretty certain we went at least once to visit my great-grandparents' farm, where we all went the other week. But Mama and Pa were always too busy to go; they never came with us. It was as if they just couldn't face visiting that starting place of their love together. Of course, when we were growing up, we asked why we had the name Urbawicz. Our parents were happy to tell us we were originally Polish but they never ever mentioned any Polish family. As I grew up, I remember people from the bank patting me on the head and congratulating me on having a 'war hero' for a father, so they obviously knew. It was obviously a secret shared with a chosen few."

"Has your mother never said anything about your father since his death, Pamela?" Lancaster asked.

"She's probably said more in the past few years than at any

time in my entire life, but still very little; she was obviously distraught when he died. When I broke it to her that I didn't think his death had been an accident, she'd been adamant I find who was responsible. It'll be good to tell her of Steiner, though I don't imagine she'll be happy when I tell her he was a Polish/German relative and it was he who'd murdered Pa."

Pamela asked Lancaster and Vidêt to join her when she visited her mother; she'd love to meet them and it made sense that it be tomorrow. Lancaster called DCI Craven and told him they were back on Jersey. Craven congratulated Lancaster, then followed by asking when they were coming back to Plymouth. Lancaster stalled for time; he was in no hurry to return to his view of the shopping mall. He told him Wardly wanted a complete fact file put together for the Crown Prosecution Service. After an evening meal, they all had an early night. Reconciling sleep was needed.

The following morning, both detectives went with Pamela to the rest home where her mother, Brigitte Urbawicz, was in her private apartment, with a stunning view out over the bay. The room, well furnished, reminded Lancaster of a very expensive hotel suite he'd once searched during an enquiry. Plush and luxurious. Brigitte was settled into a large armchair, looking for all the world like royalty preparing to give an audience. Pamela introduced the detectives. Lancaster was struck by just how beautiful the woman was, who was now in her early nineties but could easily pass for late sixties. She had a strong, Nordic-style facial bone structure, long, thick, silver hair and bright blue eyes which still held the sparkle of youth within their depths. She had a broad smile and appeared genuinely pleased to finally meet them. She waved them into various chairs and sofas around her and the audience began.

"My daughter tells me you have news; I can only hope it is good news or why would she have brought you here?" she said with a deep, accented voice. *Hint of a Breton twang*, Vidêt thought, recognising the lilt in the lady's speech. "Pamela has been keeping me informed of your work. But what is this latest news?"

Lancaster explained that they'd just returned from Berlin where they'd identified, interviewed and charged a man with her husband's death. The man had admitted murder, and they believed he was definitely the right man and had acted alone.

Brigitte asked the obvious question, "Why?"

"With your permission, madame," Lancaster said. "I'd like Marie to tell the story as he told it. It will not excuse the final act, but it may give you some understanding of why he did it."

Lancaster knew Vidêt told a good story. He'd never match her ability to colour the picture and, in this case, he felt it important for Brigitte to understand the man responsible for her husband's death. Vidêt then told the tale of Paul Steiner as she'd told it to Pamela the previous night, leaving out no detail. How Steiner's mother, Rebeka Urbawicz, Peter's sister, survived the extermination of the Polish Jewish population by marrying German officer, Heinrich Steiner, who'd kept her religion a secret. How Paul's German father had died fighting the Russians. How he and his mother ended up trapped behind the Iron Curtain. How Rebeka had made Paul promise that if he ever escaped the wall, he should search for Peter, and if alive, tell him his sister had always loved and remembered him and that all the rest of their family had died in the concentration camp.

Vidêt told how after Communism had crumbled, he'd travelled to Brittany to find the location of his uncle's death, only to find that Peter had been spirited away by the resistance, ending up on Jersey. He'd found where Peter was living and came to Jersey to seek him out, just as he'd promised his mother he would. He'd come to the house expecting a family reunion but received complete rejection and denial at the hands of Peter. Paul had gone away shocked, despondent, feeling that he and Peter had let his mother down. Marie told how Paul tracked Peter to his fishing spot and attempted to get himself recognised one last time, but in the heat of the moment of one last rejection, Steiner reacted angrily to Peter's complete lack of recognition of his mother and killed the man in a sudden violent act of rage.

Brigitte was sobbing gently into a handful of tissues, glistening tears ran slowly down each cheek. Pamela sat on the arm of her mother's chair, her arm wrapped around her shoulders supportively. Vidêt knelt in front of Brigitte and reached out to hold her hands, a move Lancaster thought very touching.

"I am sorry I had to tell you all of that, madame, but I thought it necessary for you to know that it was not just some pointless random murder."

"But that's the saddest part, Detective Vidêt," Brigitte replied. "It was completely pointless. I feel so sorry for that sad man Paul. He spent all those years wanting to find the only relative left alive from his entire family, but in fact, he found the wrong man."

"What do you mean, Mama?" Pamela said looking worried. "He killed Pa! He killed your husband."

"Exactly. He killed your father, believing him to be his long-lost Uncle Peter. But he killed the wrong man. He wasn't to know, of course, but he killed the wrong man. How pointless."

"Mama! I don't understand! How did he kill the wrong man?"

Brigitte took a long, shuddering breath, blew her nose into the tissues in her hand, turned sideways and gave a long look at Pamela, before raising her hand and stroking her daughter's face.

"I had hoped to die soon and take this story with me to the grave. There would never have been any reason for you to ever know anything other than the life you have known. All you ever needed to know was that your father and I loved you and your brother very much and showed you that love as often and in as many ways as we could. All we ever wanted was to be together and raise our family. We wanted nothing more from the world. I'm sure you realised that, my darling, we just wanted to be together in peace. This island gave us that for so many years until Paul Steiner arrived."

"I still don't understand. What do you mean he killed the wrong man?"

"Your father was not Peter Urbawicz. Peter Urbawicz died in the wreckage of his plane in 1945."

Pamela knelt on the floor next to Marie and stared at her mother's face.

"You're frightening me, Mama, what do you mean?"

Brigitte reached out her hand and stroked her daughter's face again.

"When I was sixteen," Brigitte said. "My parents sent me away from Crozon. It was too dangerous. I knew Mother and Father were involved in the resistance; we often had people hiding in the loft at the schoolhouse. I don't know if they thought that one day I might say something wrong or just felt it was wrong for me to have to keep secrets, but they decided I would be safer with my grandparents. It was fine with me; I loved it up there. I fed the chickens and cows, cleaned out the stables and brushed the big horse they used for the wagon; it was wonderful, and I always loved my grandparents. They looked after me well. We often saw soldiers driving up onto the 'point'. Grandmother and I delivered to the camp, using the handcart, eggs, water, milk. They paid us; it was just business. Then the Gestapo decided we should not be allowed onto the headland. They didn't want us to see what the defences looked like; they put up fences and gates so our cattle did not wander there, and we were told to stay away. We'd take supplies as far as the gate they'd erected, at times they sent a young soldier down, two or three days a week, to get supplies from us. His name was Gunter. Gunter Heisman, he was only nineteen, just a boy really."

"Gunter was funny," Brigitte continued. "He wasn't a Nazi, just a boy soldier, drafted in to fill gaps made by troops moved onto the Russian front. Yes, he played the part, but he was no fascist; he hated war. Quietly, he'd told me his country should never have started it in the first place; there were Germans at home who thought like him but were too frightened to ever say anything. Gunter thought Russia would push the German troops all the way back into Germany, then they'd all have to go home and defend the homeland. Many Germans were tired; they were spread too thin. They'd rather be with their families than in countries where the people hated them."

Brigitte drank a little water, licked her lips, smiled at Pamela and continued.

"I am so sorry to have deceived you all these years. We always hoped we'd never have to tell you this story. I suppose it's better you hear it from me now than find out some other way. Anyway... Gunter and I... Fell in love. We were both tired of war. Both loved the same things, the walks, flowers, the sea birds. We just loved being with each other. The trouble was it was so dangerous. My grandparents took me to one side and told me it would have to stop. I argued that we were just in love, but they told me if the resistance saw us or found out, I would be tarred and feathered, my grandparents' farm would probably be burnt down, and if the resistance ever caught Gunter and me together he'd almost certainly be shot. I knew what they said was true, but we couldn't stop, we just became much more careful, always looking as if we were just normal youngsters, but when we got into those gorse bushes, we had our own little hiding place, we'd lie there and watch the clouds go by."

Brigitte drifted into a world of remembrance, taking another sip of her water before continuing. Gunter, she said, was most frightened of his sergeant, a brute of a man called Steif, a bully and a bastard. Steif knew Gunter came from a wealthy family; he hated that. He also knew Gunter had been protected from call-up until things were very bad. At every opportunity, he picked on Gunter. So the few hours spent together watching the clouds go by were a godsend to them both. Brigitte asked her grandparents if there was any way they could help Gunter escape from the army. Her grandparents were adamant that, if this happened, the German army would turn the countryside upside down until they found him. Lives would be lost along the way. Brigitte's grandparents tried desperately to get her to give Gunter up but to no avail, she was having none of it. She was in love.

Then one day, on her way up to the gate, excited and going to see Gunter again, she'd heard the roar of the airplane heading up the estuary. She was too far down the trackway to see it, but she could tell it was travelling fast. When she got to the gate, she sat on the verge, waiting for Gunter to pick up the produce, but instead, she heard the sound of gunfire further up the estuary, then the sound of the airplane, the noise of the engine bouncing off the hillsides. She couldn't resist the temptation; she climbed the gate and ran across the grass toward the cliff top. Brigitte remembered as if it was yesterday, the Spitfire hurtling down the estuary toward the sea. It was crazy, almost daring the Germans to do something. All around it, puffs of smoke bore witness to the gunfire being thrown at it and she saw with her own eyes the tragic moment when the puffs of smoke and the shape of the plane overlapped in one brief moment. She'd felt so sad when she saw the plane shudder and watched as smoke curled from the engine. He'd so nearly made it. Brigitte remembered feeling deep sadness as the plane climbed up into low cloud and disappeared from view. Moments later, she heard Gunter shouting and waving her back toward the gate as he ran towards her.

"You must not be here, Brigitte, get behind the gate before you are seen," he'd said in a panic.

No sooner had she climbed over the gate, than she heard noises and shouts coming from over the brow of the hill. Gunter made her get down; he thought they may be under attack. Then they heard explosions, saw the glow of fire over the gorse and heard the sounds of ripping, tearing metal and the sound of people screaming. Terrible, terrible screams. Gunter started to run back up the track, shouting at her to stay where she was. She lay hidden, but the sounds of explosions and men screaming were too much to bear. Brigitte couldn't let Gunter be there alone; she needed to be with him if this was how life was going to end. She climbed back over the gate and ran toward the camp. She'd got to the point where the ground levelled onto the bluff and she could see in the distance great flames around the gun emplacements, explosions and hear the whizzing of bullets everywhere. She was terrified, sure the camp must be under attack and she knew she must get Gunter away before he got killed. It was then she realised that she'd run past the wreckage of the Spitfire with its nose buried amongst the bracken and gorse bushes, and there standing on the wing was Gunter, trying to help get the pilot out. Then she saw Steif standing on the grass to the rear of the plane holding a gun and shouting at Gunter.

Later, Gunter told her the man was calling him a coward because instead of helping his comrades he was helping the pilot. There was a shot from Steif. Gunter dropped onto the wing holding his knee, and the pilot dropped back into his seat. Gunter was swearing at Steif, but he was just laughing. He cocked his pistol once again and started to walk toward the plane. It had been an instant decision by Brigitte. She looked around and found a length of twisted iron, part of the fence the plane had skidded through on its way to this last resting place. She calmly walked up behind Steif and smashed him over the head with it, hard. The man went down. Brigitte hit him several times to make sure he wouldn't be getting up again, then went to help Gunter. Steif's first shot had gone right through Gunter's knee and straight out the other side. There was a lot of blood but Gunter said they had to get the pilot out before the plane went up. Between them, they hauled the man out onto the wing, out of sight of anybody in the camp.

As they'd lain the man down on the wing and tried to wake him, they'd realised he was already dead. He'd lost masses of blood from a bad leg wound and had shrapnel wounds through his chest. Gunter peered over the cockpit to make sure nobody was coming, then decided this was a gift from the gods. All the troops at the base knew the Allies had invaded, so it was only a matter of time before they were recalled to the homeland or abandoned to their fate. Gunter decided this opportunity was not to be missed. Between the two of them, they stripped the pilot of his uniform and flying boots, grabbed the leather folder from the cockpit with the man's paperwork inside, and Gunter was dressing himself when they heard the 'whoof'-like noise of flame breaking out. Gunter peered over the cockpit, horrified to see the flame trail racing along the skid line of the fallen plane; there was no time to lose. They pulled Steif's body to the wreckage, so it looked as if the plane had hit him. Then they dropped the body of the pilot back into the cockpit in his 'long johns' and socks, jumped into the bracken and crawled through the gorse bushes. In a matter of seconds, they heard the unmistakable rush of flame as the fire reached the flammable remains of the Spitfire, it went up with a roar.

Brigitte and Gunter dragged their way down the hillside, keeping under the gorse as much as they could. It was painful for them both; Gunter with his injured leg and Brigitte in front, using her bare hands to clear a way through. They were covered in blood by the time they emerged on the lower part of the track, well out of sight of anybody at the camp. Gunter, now dressed in the pilot's uniform, hid his own clothes underneath the tunnel they'd forged through the bushes. Brigitte ran up the track, retrieved her hand cart, then ran back down. They both knew troops from Crozon would arrive to see what the explosions were, so they had to move fast. Brigitte helped Gunter onto the cart, hiding the milk and water churns under the bushes for retrieval later, then pushed the cart back down the hill towards the farm. They hadn't gone far before they met her grandparents running toward them. They recognised Gunter immediately, but Brigitte quickly said,

"This is the English pilot from the Spitfire. We have to help him."

Her grandparents made the choice to help with the subterfuge. They hid Gunter in the loft with the chickens. Brigitte tended to his needs day and night. They'd gone through the uniform's pockets and found the pilot wasn't British but was, in fact, Polish, Peter Urbawicz. They realised this could work in their favour. Gunter spoke reasonable English, thanks to a private education in Germany, so hearing him speak English with a course, guttural, German accent, they hoped he'd pass for Polish. Brigitte's grandparents realised that it was time to call in Brigitte's father. Brigitte's grandfather made the journey to Crozon. He returned with him and another resistance fighter pushing a sturdy two-wheeled hand cart.

"You already know the rest of this story," Brigitte said to her daughter. "There was an uncle, Jean-Claude, a doctor, who lived in St Brieuc."

Brigitte and her 'Peter' stayed with Jean-Claude for several weeks. By January of 1945, 'Peter' was free of infection and undergoing physio. In May, the war was finally over. 'Peter' realised that the end of the war could mean he'd have to return to his homeland; something he didn't want to do. It was either that or play out this game and hope nobody ever found out anything different. He knew he didn't want to travel to England or be repatriated to Poland, a land he didn't know, or his actual homeland, Germany. He wanted to hide away and start a new life. Brigitte and 'Peter' were in love and wished to be married. Brigitte was now 18 years old. They were married the following week. Jean-Claude had family, Marie, who lived on Jersey with her husband, Clement, a bank manager.

The following week, the pair set off for Jersey and the start of a new life. Brigitte and 'Peter' always expected some officer to turn up looking for him or, at least, the real 'Peter', but it never happened. Either the Airforce believed he'd died in action or they thought that being 'Polish', he'd decided to just go home. It wasn't as if he put in for back pay and never applied for any pension; they just began a new life on Jersey. Like so many displaced persons after the war, he had new papers drawn up and became Peter Urbawicz, a Polish refugee, who worked in the bank. Brigitte and 'Peter' never returned to Brittany for fear that somebody may still recognise Gunter. They'd hoped that if they just stayed away, they'd be forgotten. Bit by bit the story of 'the Spitfire pilot who got away' filtered out, but was never enough of a story to warrant investigating.

"So you see, detectives, when Paul Steiner arrived saying he was Peter's long-lost nephew, it must have caught Peter completely by surprise, frightened him maybe. Of course, my husband would have said he had no idea what the man was talking about. Because he didn't. He had no idea who Rebeka was. No idea at all who Paul was. So your Paul Steiner killed the wrong man. His Uncle Peter... Sadly... Was already long dead."

EPILOGUE

It was a glorious summer day on the Crozon peninsula. Lancaster and Vidêt drove toward Roscanvel. *Is there ever a month when gorse isn't in flower?* Lancaster thought. The scrub and woodland edged with the golden flowers and prickly points of the bushes thronged any unmanaged sections of rough farmland here on the windswept coast. It had been almost a year since the detectives had last been driving these roads, this was their first week's holiday they'd managed to book together since then, so the pair felt relaxed and definitely 'off duty'. Once through the little village of Roscanvel, they followed signs up toward the Pointe des Espagnols.

Vidêt spotted the sign, 'LA FERME DANIELO'. It marked a newly cut, hard-core trackway through a section of scrub. Vidêt turned onto the track and drove slowly along it. The last time they'd come this way it had been almost completely overgrown. Vidêt pulled into a parking bay in the yard, narrowly avoiding a forklift truck coming in the opposite direction. They walked down the track onto a full-on building site. The overgrown, derelict farm buildings encased in brambles and young trees were all but gone, with only base outlines and one section of the gable end remaining. Across the yard was a stack of huge old timbers and another stack of neatly organised piles of rocks, stones and bricks. Now you could make out the ghostly footprints of the old farm and outbuildings clearly. They covered a sizable area.

As they walked across the yard, Pamela came out of a blue portacabin. She greeted them with hugs and kisses, pleased to see them both.

"So what do you think of my farm?" she asked. "Huge, isn't it? We didn't really know just how much space we had until we started to cut back and dig out all the scrub and trees, isn't it brilliant?"

She walked them around the site, explaining the proposed layout she and the architect had designed: a main house covering the footprint of the original farmhouse and its attached barn. A glass and steel, box-like corridor linking that building to another section of the house would sit upon the footprint of the old winter cow barn and would house a large kitchen-diner. Upstairs in this section, the main kitchen ceiling would continue right to the eaves of the old barn roof on the gable end, lit by huge 'skylights', giving a view straight up to the clouds or the stars. At the other end of this space was a mezzanine area for quiet reading and a glass wall, revealing the original enclosed space where both Gunter, Brigitte and the chickens had spent time in hiding.

The previous year, after dropping the bombshell that Pamela's father was not Peter Urbawicz, a Polish Spitfire pilot and hero, but was really Gunter Heisman. A young German soldier, tired of war, who fell in love with Pamela's mother, Brigitte. She, in the depths of guilt, decided it was time to sign over everything she owned to her daughter, and for Pamela to manage her finances from then on. It meant that Brigitte could continue living in the rest home and could hand over responsibility for her final years without worries. It was whilst going through the various paperwork that came with this responsibility, that Pamela came across the deeds to her great grandparent's farm. It appeared that on their death, they'd left their farm and the land that came with it to Brigitte. She and Peter hadn't wanted to do anything about it, though she'd never have given it up for sale. When Pamela had reminded her mother of the deeds, her mother had smiled and told her they were hers to do with as she wished. Pamela had revisited the site almost straight after Lancaster and Vidêt had returned to England the previous year, partly to see what actually lay under the brambles and partly to cry. She'd cried a lot in those first few days, cried because her parents had lied to her, or at least withheld the truth and she'd trusted them. She'd cried because her father had been murdered and she'd not been able to say goodbye. She'd cried because her mother had been given a farmhouse and a piece of Breton coastland by people who loved her, had endangered their lives for, and she'd allowed it to completely fall apart and become overgrown. She'd listened to her mother's apologies and realised that whatever her father's name had been, it was irrelevant. The one thing she'd been sure of when she was growing up was that both her parents loved her very much and, surely, that was worth more than any name!

Pamela had decided she'd do nothing about the information she now held. If it all came out, then so be it. If it stayed a secret, so be it. Life had moved on. It genuinely was history. Nobody cared. Returning to the old farmstead, she'd been determined it would no longer be a wasteland, she was going to do something with it. Her plan had been accepted by the local council and, more importantly, the local mayor. He was just pleased to see the old farm being taken in hand, and the thought that it would come back to life and have people visiting again was a joy.

Pamela asked Lancaster and Vidêt to follow her along a roughly-cut pathway, the remains of the original track that wound its way onto the headland. At the top, standing proud of the grassy hummocks that surrounded them, stood two, rust-stained, pre-formed, concrete gateposts, where the Germans had erected their gate, with the gate itself long gone. They continued toward the headland beyond. Pamela turned toward what appeared to be the remains of twisted fence posts protruding from the recently cutback gorse. What they were looking at was the final remains of a burnt-out Spitfire, a melted lump of aluminium, struts and engine block. The only piece recognisable was a wheel. It had no tyre but was still recognisable as a wheel. There was also one, partially burnt, wooden blade of a propeller.

"I intend to have a plaque made; the builders will make a plinth to place it on," Pamela said. "I haven't worked out exactly what the sign will say, maybe, 'In memory of Peter Urbawicz who died here. One of the few'."

"You could get an artist to gather all these pieces of metal and molten lumps together and make a work of art as a monument," Vidêt suggested.

"I like that idea," replied Pamela.

"I'm sorry we never got Steiner into court, Pamela,"

Lancaster said.

In December of the previous year, Lancaster and Vidêt had returned to Berlin to oversee the extradition paperwork. They'd little hope it would be granted, but the UK government were determined. It was whilst they were there that somebody, they suspected the solicitor, Schleeman, leaked the story to the Berlin press, in an attempt to win sympathy for his dying client amongst the German people. It failed. The story made the Berlin papers but wasn't picked up by the nationals; probably not deemed appropriate to print a story of an 'ex-Stasi officer in murder investigation'. Most Germans already knew enough of those stories to last a lifetime. But to Lancaster's annoyance, the paper mentioned their names and snapped at least one photo of himself that he felt was not at all flattering and, worse still, placed on the front page. Shortly after this debacle, Paul Steiner cheated them all, well, everyone other than the Grim Reaper by succumbing to the onslaught of cancer in the prison hospital.

"To be honest, it really doesn't matter," Pamela said. "We know who killed my father and why. You did what was asked of you; you proved it was murder and found the person responsible so, to me, it's the end of the story. Steiner dying was quite a clean end. It meant we didn't have to discuss my father's history; his story can rest in peace. My mother was more than happy with that as well. Have you managed to find your illusive Jean-Luc Batise 2 yet?"

"Not a whisper, Pamela. He must show his head at some stage; he'll need to access one of the accounts at some point. The moment he does, somebody will spot him. I can't see him being on the loose for much longer."

"And what happened to that Irish chap? Sean Devlin? The chap Craven warned you away from. What happened there?"

Lancaster smiled. "Ah, Mr Devlin. Well, he turned out not to be involved in Peter's death in the slightest, Pamela. A complete 'Red Herring'. We had to turn our backs on that one I'm afraid. You know how it is; you win some you lose some. Now then, what's the chances of that cup of tea?"

As they walked towards the bustle of the building site, Lancaster found he couldn't lose the smile from his face, thinking about the advert that had been placed in the Belfast Gazette a couple of months before. It had read:

Sean Devlin
Formally MD Devlin Ground Works & Construction.
Wishes it to be known that his new name is,
Mr Levon Shawbuck
His new address is:
The Shawbuck Gunsmith
Philadelphia, Pennsylvania, USA

The advert, posted and paid for anonymously, had been in the paper for three nights before it disappeared. Lancaster had always thought that there should be no amnesty for bombers and murderers, whatever the politicians thought or agreed.

WITH THANKS TO...

'Ludlow' Jane & Nigel, Lin, Paul, Greg, Matt & Julian, who gave me encouragement, constructive criticism and lots of support. And many thanks to the team at Cranthorpe Millner, for giving me the chance to get this story between the covers and out onto the shelves.